For Katherine, Jake, and Julia

PETE

HE STOOD POISED on the edge of a sheet of glass. Barefoot. Perfectly balanced. One foot in front of the other. Arms at his side. That was the game now.

The sheet of glass went down and down and down forever. Like a shimmering, translucent curtain.

The top edge of the glass was thin, so thin it might cut him if he slipped or fell or took a too-hasty step. That top edge was a thin ribbon of rainbow reflecting bright reds and greens and yellows.

On one side of the glass, darkness. On the other, jarring, disturbing colours.

He could see things down there on the right side, down below his right hand, beyond the reach of his fingers. Down there were his mom and his dad and his sister. Down there were jagged edges and harsh noises that made him want to clap his hands over his ears. When he looked at those things, those people, the wobbly, insubstantial houses, the sharp-edged

1

furniture, the claw hands and hooked noses and staring, staring, staring eyes and yelling mouths, he wanted to close his eyes.

But it didn't work. Even through his closed eyes he saw them. And he heard them. But he did not understand their wild, pulsating colours. Sometimes their words weren't words at all but brilliant parrot-coloured spears shooting from their mouths.

Mother father sister teacher other. Lately only sister and others. Saying things. Some words he got. Pete. Petey. Little Pete. He knew those words. And sometimes there were soft words, soft like kittens or pillows and they would float from his sister and he would feel peace for a while until the next jangling, shrieking noise, the next assault of stabbing color.

On his left, down, down below the endless sheet of glass, a very different world. Quiet, ghostly things drifted silently, shades of grey. No hard edges, no loud sounds. No horrible colours to make him start screaming. It was dark and so very, very quiet.

Down there was a softly glowing orb, like a faint green sun. It would reach out to him sometimes. A tendril. A mist. It would touch him as he stood balanced, one foot in front of the other, hands at his side.

Peace. Quiet. Nothingness. It would whisper these thoughts to him.

Sometimes it would play. A game.

Pete liked games. Only the left side would play his games his way; games had to be his way, the same way, always and unchanging. But the last game Pete had played with the Darkness had turned harsh and overbright. It had suddenly stabbed Pete with arrows in his brain. It had broken the game.

The sheet of glass had shattered. But now it was whole again, and he balanced on top and as if it was sorry the soft green sun said, *Come down here and play,* in its whispery voice.

On the other side – the agitated, jangly, hard side – his sister, her face a stretched mask beneath yellow hair, a mouth of pink and glittery white, loud, was pushing at him with hands like hammers.

'Roll over. I have to get this sheet out from under you. It's soaked.'

Pete understood some of the words. He felt the hardness of them.

But Pete felt something else even more. A strangeness. An alienness. Something wrong, a deep, throbbing musical note, a bow drawn over strings, that pulled his focus away from the left and the right, away even from the sheet of glass on which he balanced.

It came from the place he never looked: inside him.

Now Pete looked down at himself, like he was floating outside himself. He looked down at his body, puzzled by it. Yes: that was the new voice, the insistent note, the demanding voice more compelling even than the soft murmur of the Darkness or the jangly words of his sister. His body was demanding his attention, distracting him from his game of balancing on the sheet of glass.

'You're sweating,' his sister said. 'You're burning up. I'm going to take your temperature.'

ONE

SAM TEMPLE WAS drunk.

It was a new experience for him. He was fifteen and had once or twice snuck a sip of his mother's wine. He'd drunk half a beer when he was thirteen. Just to see. He hadn't liked it much, it was bitter.

He'd taken a single hit off a joint back before the FAYZ. He'd practically hacked up a lung and then spent an hour feeling bleary and strange and finally sleepy.

It had never been his thing. He'd never been part of the partying crowd.

But this night he'd gone to check on the caged monster that was both Brittney and Drake and had heard Drake's vile, obscene threats and howling, murderous rage. And then, far worse, he'd heard Brittney's pleas for death.

'Sam, I know you're listening,' she'd said through the barricaded door. 'I know you're out there, I heard your voice. I can't take it, Sam. Sam, end it. Please, I'm begging you,

5

let me go, let me go to Heaven.'

Sam had been to see Astrid earlier in the evening. That hadn't gone too well. Astrid had tried, and he had tried, but there was too much wrong between them. Too much history now.

He had kissed her. For a while she had kissed him back. And then he'd pushed it. His hands went where he wanted them to go. And she'd shoved him away.

'You know I'm going to say no, Sam,' she said.

'Yeah, I've kind of gotten that message,' he said, angry and frustrated but trying to maintain some semblance of cool.

'If we start, how long do you think it will take before everyone knows?'

'That's not why you won't sleep with me,' Sam said. 'You won't do it because you think it would mean giving up control. And you are all about control, Astrid.'

It was the truth. Sam believed it, anyway.

But if he were being honest instead of just angry, he'd have admitted that Astrid had her own problems. That she was filled with guilt and didn't need one more thing to feel guilty about.

Little Pete was in a coma. Astrid blamed herself, although it was stupid to do so and she was the furthest thing from stupid.

But Little Pete was her brother. Her responsibility.

Her burden.

After that rebuff Sam had stood awkwardly while Astrid

spooned artichoke and fish soup into Little Pete's nerveless lips. Little Pete could swallow. He could walk if she guided him. He could use the slit trench in the backyard but Astrid had to wipe him.

That was Astrid's life now. She was a nurse to an autistic boy with all the power in their world locked inside him. Beyond autistic now: Little Pete was gone. No way to know where he was in his strange, strange mind.

Astrid hadn't hugged Sam when he said he was leaving. Hadn't touched him.

So that had been Sam's evening. Astrid and Little Pete. And the twinned undead creature Orc and Howard kept watch over.

If Drake somehow escaped, there were probably only two people who could take him on: Sam himself, and Orc. Sam needed Orc to act as Drake's jailer. So he had ignored the bottles beside Orc's couch and 'confiscated' only the six-pack in plain view on a kitchen counter.

'I'll dump this,' Sam had told Howard. 'You know it's illegal.'

Howard shrugged and smirked a little. Like he'd known. Like he'd seen some gleam of greed and need in Sam's eye. But Sam himself hadn't known. He had intended to dump the cans out on the street.

Instead he had carried them with him. Through the dark streets. Past burned-out houses and their ghosts.

Past the graveyard.

Down to the beach. He'd cracked the seal, ready to pour one out on the sand. Instead he'd taken a sip.

It burned like fire.

He took another sip. It burned less this time.

He headed up the beach. He knew in his heart where he was going now. He knew his feet were taking him to the cliff.

Now, many sips later, he stood swaying at the top of the cliff. The effect of the booze was undeniable. He knew he was drunk.

He looked down at the small arc of beach at the base of the cliff. The slight surge painted luminescent curves on the dark sand.

Right here, right where he was standing, Mary had led the preschoolers in a suicide leap. All that kept those kids alive was Dekka's heroic effort.

Now Mary was gone.

'Here's to you, Mary,' Sam said. He upended the bottle and drank deep.

He had failed Mary. From the start she'd taken charge of the littles and run the day care. She'd carried that load almost alone.

Sam had seen the effects of her anorexia and bulimia. But he hadn't realised what was happening to her, or hadn't wanted to.

He'd heard nervous gossip that Mary was grabbing whatever meds she could find, anything she thought would ease her depression.

He hadn't wanted to know about that, either.

Most of all he should have seen what Nerezza was up to, should have questioned, should have pushed.

Should have.

Should have.

Should have . . .

Another deep swallow of liquid fire. The burning made him laugh. He laughed down at the beach where Orsay, the false prophet, had died.

'Goodbye, Mary,' he slurred, raising his bottle in a mock toast. 'Least you got outta here.'

For a split second on the day that Mary poofed, the barrier had been clear. They had seen the world outside: the observation platform, the TV satellite truck, the construction underway on fast food places and cheap hotels.

It had seemed very, very real.

But had it been? Astrid said no: just another illusion. But Astrid was not exactly addicted to the truth.

Sam swayed at the edge of the cliff. He ached for Astrid, the booze had not dulled that. He ached for the sound of her voice, the warmth of her breath on his neck, her lips. She was all that had kept him from going crazy. But now she was the source of the crazy because his body was demanding what she wouldn't give. Now being with her was just pain and hollowness and need.

The barrier was there, just a few feet away. Impenetrable.

Opaque. Painful to touch. The faintly shimmering grey dome that enclosed twenty miles of Southern California coastline in a giant terrarium. Or zoo. Or universe.

Or prison.

Sam tried to focus on it, but his eyes weren't working very well.

With the exaggerated care of a drunk he set his bottle down.

He straightened up. He looked at the palms of his hands. Then he stretched out his arms, palms facing the barrier.

'I really hate you,' he said to the barrier.

Twin beams of searing green light shot from his palms. A torrent of focused light.

'Aaaaahhhh!' Sam shouted as he aimed and fired.

The light hit the barrier and did nothing. Nothing burned. Nothing smoked or charred.

'Burn!' Sam howled. 'Burn!'

He played the beams upward, tracing the curve of the barrier. He raged and howled and blazed.

To no effect.

Sam sat down suddenly. The bright fire went out. He fumbled clumsily for the bottle.

'I have it,' a voice said.

Sam twisted sideways, looking for the source. He couldn't find her. It was a her, he was pretty sure of that, a female voice.

She stepped around to where he could see her. Taylor.

Taylor was a pretty Asian girl who had never made a secret of her attraction to Sam. She was also a freak, a three bar with the power of teleportation. She could instantly go any place she'd ever seen or been before. She called it 'bouncing'.

She wore a T-shirt and shorts. Sneakers. Unlaced, no socks. No one dressed well, not any more. People wore whatever was halfway clean.

And no one travelled unarmed. Taylor had a large knife in a nice leather sheath.

She was not beautiful like Astrid. But not cold and remote and looking at him with defensive, accusing eyes, either. Looking at Taylor did not fill his brain to overflowing with memories of love and rage.

She was not the girl who had been the centre of his life for all these months. Not the girl who had left him frustrated, humiliated, feeling like a fool. Feeling more alone than ever.

'Hey, Taylor. Bouncy bouncy Taylor. T'sup?'

'I saw the light,' Taylor said.

'Yeah. I am all about light,' Sam slurred.

She held out the bottle tentatively, not sure what she should do with it.

'Nah.' He waved it off. 'I think I've had quite enough. Don't you?' He spoke with extreme care, trying not to slur. Failing.

'Come sit with me, Taylor, Taylor, bouncy Taylor.'

She hesitated.

'Come on. I won't bite. Good to talk with someone . . . normal.'

Taylor rewarded him with a brief smile. 'I don't know how normal I am.'

'More normal than some. I was just checking on Brittney,' Sam said. 'You have a monster inside of you, Taylor? Do you have to be locked in a basement because inside you is some psycho with a whip arm? No? See? You are so normal, Taylor.'

He glared at the barrier, the untouched, unfazed barrier. 'Do you ever beg to be burned into ashes so you can be free to go to Jesus, Taylor? Nah. See, that's what Brittney does. No, you're pretty normal, bouncy Taylor.'

Taylor sat beside him. Not too close. Friend close, conversation close.

Sam said nothing. Two different urges were battling in his head.

His body was saying go for it. And his mind. . . well, it was confused and not exactly in control.

He reached over and took Taylor's hand. She did not pull her hand away.

He moved his hand up her arm. She stiffened a little and glanced around, making sure they weren't seen. Or, maybe, hoping they were.

His hand reached her neck. He leaned toward her and pulled her to him.

He kissed her.

She kissed him back.

He kissed her harder. And she slid her hand under his shirt, fingers stroking his bare flesh.

Then he pulled away, fast.

'Sorry, I . . .' He hesitated, his wallowing brain arguing against a body that was suddenly aflame.

Sam stood up very suddenly and walked away.

Taylor laughed gaily at his back. 'Come see me when you get tired of mooning over the ice princess, Sam.'

He walked into a sudden, stiff breeze. And any other time, in any other condition, he might have noticed that the wind never blew in the FAYZ.

TWO

IT WAS AMAZING what decent food could do for a starving girl's looks.

Diana looked at herself in the big mirror. She was wearing clean panties and a clean bra. Skinny, very skinny. Her legs were knobby, with knees and feet looking weirdly big. She could count every rib. Her belly was concave. Her periods had stopped and her breasts were smaller than they'd been since she was twelve. Her collarbones looked like clothes hangers. Her face was almost unrecognisable. She looked like a heroin addict.

But her hair was starting to look better, darker. The rusty colour and the brittleness that came from starvation, they were disappearing.

Her eyes were no longer dead, empty shadows sunk into her skull.

Now her eyes sparkled in the soft lamplight. She looked alive.

Her gums weren't bleeding as much. They were pink, not red, not so swollen. Maybe her teeth wouldn't fall out after all.

Starvation. It had driven her to eat human flesh. She was a cannibal.

Starvation had deprived her of her humanity.

'Not quite,' Diana said to her reflection. 'Not quite.'

When she had seen that Caine would destroy the helicopter with Sanjit and his brothers and sisters she had sacrificed her own life. She had toppled from the cliff to force Caine to make the choice: save Diana or kill the children.

Surely that act of self-sacrifice balanced out the fact that she had bitten and chewed and swallowed a cooked chunk of Panda's chest.

Surely she was redeemed? At least a little?

Please? Please, if there is a God watching, please see that I have redeemed myself.

But it wasn't enough. It would never be enough. She had to do more. For as long as she lived she would have to do more.

Starting with Caine.

He had shown just a glimmer of humanity, saving her and letting his intended victims go free. It wasn't much. But it was something. And if she could find a way to change him . . .

A sound. Very slight. Just a scrape of foot on rug.

'I know you're there, Bug,' Diana said calmly, not looking back. Not giving the little creep the satisfaction. 'What do you think Caine would do to you if I told him you were spying on me in my underwear?'

No answer from Bug.

'Aren't you a little young to be a pervert?'

'Caine won't kill me,' a disembodied voice said. 'He needs me.'

Diana crossed to the California king-sized bed. She slipped on the robe she'd chosen from among the many in the closet. They belonged to the woman whose bedroom this had been. A famous actress with very expensive taste who was only one size bigger than Diana.

And her shoes fit almost perfectly. Close to seventy pairs of designer shoes. Diana slipped her feet into a pair of fleece-lined slippers.

'All I have to do to get rid of you, Bug, is to tell Caine your powers are increasing. I'll tell him you're becoming a four bar. How do you think he'll react to having a four bar sharing this island with him?'

Bug faded slowly into view. He was a snotty little brat of a kid. He'd just turned ten.

For a moment Diana felt something like compassion for him: Bug was a damaged, messed-up little creep. Like all of them, he was scared and lonely and maybe even haunted by some of the things he'd done.

Or not. Bug had never shown any evidence of a conscience.

'If you want to see naked girls, Bug, why don't you creep up on Penny?'

'She's not pretty,' Bug said. 'Her legs are all . . .' He twisted his fingers around to demonstrate. 'And she smells bad.'

Penny was eating better, like Diana. But she was getting worse. She had fallen from one hundred feet on to water and rocks. Caine had levitated her back up the cliff. But her legs were broken in a dozen places.

Diana had done what she could to set the breaks, made splints out of duct tape and boards, but Penny was in constant agony. She would never walk again. Her legs would never heal.

She lived now in one of the bathrooms so that she could drag herself to the toilet when she needed to. Diana brought her food twice a day. Books. A TV with a DVD player.

There was still electricity in the house on San Francisco de Sales Island. The generator supplied a weak and faltering current. When Sanjit had lived here, he'd been worried that fuel for the generator was running out. But Caine could do things Sanjit couldn't. Like levitate barrels of fuel from the wrecked yacht rusting at the bottom of the cliff.

Life here was very good for Diana and Caine and Bug. But life would never be good for Penny. Her power – the ability to make others see terrifying visions of monsters and flesh-eating insects and death – was of no help to her now.

'She scares you, doesn't she, Bug?' Diana asked.

She laughed. 'You tried, didn't you? You snuck in on her and she caught you.'

She saw the answer on Bug's face. The shadow of a terrifying memory.

'Best not to make Penny mad,' she said. She pulled on slacks. Then she patted Bug on his freckled cheek. 'Best not to make me mad, either, Bug. I can't make you see monsters. But if I catch you spying on me again, I'll tell Caine it's either me or you. And you know who he'll choose.'

Diana left the room.

She'd resolved to be a better person. And she would be. Unless Bug kept bothering her.

The three Jennifers. That's what they called themselves. Jennifer B was a redhead, Jennifer H was blonde, and Jennifer L had her hair in black dreadlocks. They hadn't even known one another before the FAYZ.

Jennifer B had been a Coates kid. Jennifer H was home-schooled. Jennifer L was the only one who'd attended the regular school.

They were twelve, twelve, and thirteen, respectively. And for the last couple of months they had shared a house on a cul-de-sac away from the centre of town.

It was a good choice: the big fire had come nowhere near the development.

Now, though, it seemed like a bad choice. The so-called hospital was blocks away and the three of them could all have used a Tylenol or something because they all had the same headache, the same sore muscles, and the same hacking cough.

It had started twenty-four hours ago, and they had just figured it was the flu coming back around. There'd been a mini-epidemic of flu that had left a lot of kids feeling bad. But it hadn't been very dangerous except that it kept some kids immobilised who could have been working.

Jennifer B – Jennifer Boyles – had been asleep for no more than an hour when she was awakened by a loud, percussive sound close by, not from outside, from the room next to hers.

She sat up in bed and fought down the woozy, head-swimming feeling. She felt her forehead. Yeah, still hot. Definitely hot.

Whatever the noise was, forget it, she told herself. Too sick to get up. If something was breaking into the house to kill her, so much the better: she felt rotten.

Kkkrrraaafff!

This time the walls seemed to shake. Jennifer B was up and out of her bed before she could think about it. She coughed, paused, then veered toward the door, eyes not quite focused, head pounding.

In the hallway she found Jennifer L. Jennifer L was coughing, too, and looking as scared as Jennifer B. They were both in sweatpants and T-shirts, both miserable.

'It's in Jennifer's room,' Jennifer L said. She had her weapon, a lead pipe with a grip bound with black electrical tape.

Jennifer B was annoyed with herself for having forgotten her own weapon. You didn't jump out of bed at night in the FAYZ without going armed. She staggered back to her bed and fished out the machete. It was stuck into a canvas scabbard between her mattress and box spring, handle protruding.

It wasn't all that sharp, but it looked crazy dangerous and it was. A two-foot-long blade with a cracked wooden grip.

'Jennifer?' Jennifer B called at Jennifer H's room.

Kkkrrraaafff!

The door rattled on its hinges. Jennifer B opened the door and stood with her machete at the ready. Jennifer L was right behind her, pipe clenched in nervous hand.

Jennifer H had always had a fear of the dark so she had a very small Sammy sun in one corner of the room, hovering beneath what had once been a hanging light fixture. The light was green and eerie, more creepy than illuminating. It showed Jennifer H. She wore a flower-print nightgown.

She was standing up in her bed. She clutched her throat with one hand and held her stomach with the other.

She looked like she'd seen death.

'Jen, you OK?' Jennifer L asked.

Jennifer H's eyes bulged. She stared at her two roommates.

Her stomach convulsed. Her chest heaved. She squeezed her own throat like she was trying to choke herself. Her long, blonde hair was wet, sweat-matted, plastered to her face and neck.

The cough was shockingly loud.

Kkkrrraaafff!

Jennifer B felt the explosion of air. And something wet slapped her face.

She reached her free hand and peeled a small shred of something wet from her cheek. She looked at it, unable to make sense of it. It looked like a piece of raw meat. It felt like chicken skin.

Kkkrrraaafff!

The power of the cough threw Jennifer back against the wall. 'Oh, God!' she moaned. 'Oh . . .'

Kkkrrraaafff!

And this time Jennifer B saw it. Pieces of something wet and raw had flown from Jennifer H's mouth. She was coughing up parts of her insides.

KKKRRRAAAAFFF!

Jennifer H's entire body convulsed, twisted backward into a crazy C. She crashed into the windowpane. It shattered.

KKKRRRAAAAFFF!

The next spasm threw Jennifer H into the wall headfirst. There was a sickening crunch.

The other two stared at her in horror. She wasn't moving.

'Jen?' Jennifer B called timidly.

'Jen? Jen? Are you OK?' Jennifer L asked.

They crept closer, now holding hands, weapons still at the ready.

Jennifer H did not answer. Her neck was twisted at a comic angle. Her eyes were open and staring. Seeing nothing. Liquid, black in the eerie light, ran from her mouth and ears.

The two Jennifers fell back. Jennifer B sank to her knees. Her strength was gone. She let the machete fall from her hand.

'I . . .' she said, but had no second word. She tried to stand but couldn't.

'We have to get help,' Jennifer L said. But she too had sunk to her knees.

Jennifer L tried to stand but sat down again. Jennifer B crawled back to her room. She wanted to help Jennifer L, she did. But she couldn't even help herself.

Jennifer B struggled to push herself up and into her bed. *Need help*, she thought. *Hospital. Lana.*

Some still-functioning part of her delirious mind understood that the best she could hope to accomplish for now was to reach the sanctuary of her bed.

But finally even that was too much. She lay on the cold wood floor staring up at her bed, at the motionless ceiling fan. With the last of her strength she pulled the mess of dirty sheets and blankets down on top of herself.

She coughed into the once-soft quilt she'd taken from her mother's room long ago.

The thing on Hunter's shoulder didn't hurt. But it did distract him. And he couldn't be distracted when he was hunting Old Lion.

The mountain lion never bothered Hunter. The mountain lion didn't want to eat Hunter. Or maybe it did, but it had never tried.

But Hunter had to kill Old Lion because he had stolen too many of Hunter's own kills. Old Lion crept around behind Hunter after he had taken a deer. Hunter was off chasing other prey and Old Lion had snuck around and dragged off Hunter's deer.

Old Lion was just doing what he had to do. It wasn't personal. Hunter didn't hate Old Lion. But just the same he couldn't have the mountain lion running off with the food for the kids.

Hunter hunted for the kids. That's what he did. That's who he was. He was Hunter the hunter. For the kids.

Old Lion was out of the woods now, over the hill, over where the dry lands started and the rocks grew big. Old Lion was heading home for the night. He had eaten well. Now he was heading back to his lair. He would spend the day lying out on the sun-baked rocks and toasting his bones.

Hunter walked carefully, weight balanced, light on his feet, quick but not rushing. Dangerous to rush about with nothing but moonlight to show the way.

He had learned a lot about hunting. The killing power from his hands didn't reach very far. He had to get close to make it work. That meant he had to really concentrate, which was hard ever since his brain had gotten hurt. He couldn't concentrate enough to read or remember lots of words. And words still came out of his mouth all messed up. But he could concentrate on this: on swift and quiet walking, on weaving through the red rocks while keeping his eyes peeled for the cat's faint star-silvered tracks in the little deposits of sand.

And he had to look out for Old Lion changing his mind and deciding he would like him a tasty boy after all. Old Lion didn't just steal food, he killed it, too. Hunter had seen him once, his tail flicking, his whiskered jaw juddering, quivering with anticipation as Old Lion watched a stray dog.

Old Lion had exploded out of cover and crossed one hundred feet in about one second. Like a bullet out of a gun. His big paws had caught the dog before the dog could even flinch. Long, curved claws, fur, blood, a desperate whine from the dog and then, almost leisurely, taking his time, Old Lion had delivered the killing bite to the back of the dog's neck.

Old Lion was already a hunter back when Hunter was just a regular kid sitting in class, raising his hand to answer questions and reading and understanding and being smart.

Old Lion knew all about hunting. But he didn't know that Hunter was coming after him.

Hunter smelled the cat. He was close. He smelled of dead meat. Dried blood.

Hunter was below a tall boulder. He froze, realising suddenly that Old Lion was right above him. He wanted to run, but he knew that if he backed up, the cat would drop on him. He was safer closer to the rock. Old Lion couldn't drop straight down.

Hunter pressed his back against the rock. He stilled his own breathing and heard the big cat's instead. But Old Lion wasn't fooled. Old Lion could probably hear the heart pounding in Hunter's chest.

The thing on Hunter's shoulder squirmed. It was growing. Moving. Hunter glanced and could see it move beneath the fabric of his shirt. It seemed almost to be trying to chew a hole through Hunter's shirt.

Hunter had no word for the thing. It had grown over the last day. It had started out as a bump, a swelling. But then the skin had split apart and gnashing insect mouthparts had been revealed. Like a spider. Or a bug. Like the bugs that crawled on Hunter as he slept.

But this thing on his shoulder wasn't a regular bug. It was

too big for that. And it had grown right where the flying snake, the greenie, had dropped its goo on him.

Hunter strained to think of the word for the thing. It was a word he used to know. Like worms on a dead animal. What was the word? He leaned forward, hands to his head, so mad at himself for not being able to find the word.

He had lost focus for just a few seconds but it was enough for Old Lion.

The cat dropped like mercury, liquid.

Hunter was knocked to the ground. His head banged against the rock. Old Lion had missed his grip, though, and he had to scramble in the narrow space. The cat spun, bared his yellow teeth and leaped, claws outstretched.

Hunter dodged, but not fast enough. One big paw hit him in the chest and knocked him back against the rock, knocked the wind from him.

Old Lion was on him, claws on his shoulders, snarling face just inches from Hunter's vulnerable neck.

Then, suddenly, the mountain lion hissed and leaped back, like it had landed on a hot stove.

The lion shook its paw and flung droplets of blood. One claw toe had been badly bitten. It hung by a thread.

The thing on Hunter's shoulder had bitten Old Lion.

Hunter didn't hesitate. He raised his hands and aimed.

There was no light. The heat that came from Hunter's hands

was invisible. But instantly the temperature in Old Lion's head doubled, tripled, and Old Lion, his brain cooked in his skull, fell dead.

Hunter pulled his shirt back from the shoulder. The insect mouthparts gnashed, chewing on a bloody chunk of the lion.

THREE

ASTRID HAD FED Little Pete.

She read a little, perched beside the window, book held at an uncomfortable angle to try and take advantage of the faint moonlight.

It was slow going.

It wasn't a book she'd ever have read back in the old days. She wouldn't have been caught dead reading some silly teen romance. Back then she'd have read a classic, or some work of great literary merit. Or history.

Now she needed escape. Now she needed not to be in this world, this terrible world of the FAYZ. Books were the only way out.

After just a few minutes Astrid set the book aside. Her hands were trembling. Attempt to escape into the book: failed. Attempt to forget her fear: failed. It was all right there, still, right there in front of every other thought.

Outside, a breeze caused tree branches to scrape the side of the house. A corner of Astrid's mind noticed, and wondered, but set it aside for more pressing concerns.

She wondered where Sam was. What he was doing. Whether he was longing for her as she longed for him.

Yes, yes, she wanted him. She wanted to be in his arms. She wanted to kiss him. And maybe more. Maybe a lot more.

All of it, all the things he wanted she wanted, too.

Stupid jerk, didn't he get that? Was he so clueless he didn't know that she wanted it all, too?

But she wasn't Sam. Astrid didn't act on impulse. Astrid thought things through. Astrid the Genius, always so irritatingly in control. That was the word he'd thrown at her: control.

How could Sam not realize that if they crossed that line it would be one more sin? One more abandonment of her faith. One more surrender to weakness.

There had been too many of those. It was like little pieces of Astrid's soul were flaking off, falling away. Some pieces not so small.

Her self-control had crumbled so swiftly it was almost comic. After all the temptations and provocations, the calm, civilised, rational girl had evaporated like a bead of water on a hot skillet, sizzle, sizzle, all gone. And what had emerged then had been pure violence.

She had tried to kill Nerezza. In screaming, out-of-control rage. The memory of it made her sick.

And that wasn't all of it. She had wanted Sam to burn Drake to ashes even if it meant murdering Brittney as well.

Astrid couldn't be that person. She had to put herself back together. She had to take time to rebuild herself. She was afraid she would shatter. Like a glass sculpture, chip chip chip away and all at once it would shatter into a thousand pieces.

And yet, a cool, calculating part of her knew she could not alienate Sam too much. Because it was only a matter of time before everyone else figured out that there was a way out of the FAYZ.

The exit door was right in front of them. Lying just a few feet from Astrid.

A simple act of murder . . .

Others had seen what Astrid had seen on that cliff, when Little Pete's mind had blanked out, overwhelmed by the loss of his stupid toy game.

A simple act of murder . . .

She sat beside her motionless brother. She ought to brush his teeth. Ought to change his pyjamas. Ought to . . .

His forehead was damp.

Astrid put her hand to his head. He'd been hot all night, but this was worse. She pushed the button on the thermometer by the bed, waited for it to zero out, and stuck it under Little Pete's tongue.

She felt a cool breeze in the room. Her eyes went instantly to the window. It was open wide. Pushed all the way up.

There was no question: it had been closed. She'd been sitting beside it. It had been locked. And now it was open.

And for the first time since the coming of the FAYZ, a cool breeze blew into the room and wafted over the damp forehead of the most powerful person in this little universe.

Drake felt the Darkness touch his mind. He shivered with pleasure.

It was still out there, Drake was sure of it. Still calling to him, to Drake, the faithful one, the one who would never turn against the Darkness.

Drake cracked his whip hand just to hear the sonic-boom snap of it. And to let Orc hear it, too.

'Hey, Orc! Come down here so I can whip that little patch of skin off you!' Drake demanded.

Drake Merwin could see a little by the light of the tiny, dim Sammy sun. He hated that light – he knew where it had come from, and what it represented: Sam's power, that dangerous light of his.

Drake remembered the pain of that light. He'd been on his back, helpless. And Sam, his face a mask of rage, glorying in his moment of revenge, had burned off Drake's legs and was working his way methodically up Drake's torso.

Then that stupid little pig Brittney had emerged.

31

Drake didn't know what happened next, he couldn't see or hear when Brittney was in control. All he knew was that Sam hadn't vaporised him. And here he was, trapped. Locked in this basement listening to Orc's heavy tread upstairs.

Drake didn't know what had happened to make him this way, to cause him to share a body with Brittney. Much of recent life was a mystery. He remembered Caine turning on him. He remembered the massive uranium rod flying straight towards him.

And the next thing he knew, he was in a nightmare that went on and on and on forever. There was a girl in the nightmare, the little piggy, the stupid little metal-mouth moron, Brittney.

Hadn't they killed her? Long ago? He remembered a crumpled, bleeding form on a polished floor.

Brittney had died. Drake had died. And then, neither of them was dead, and both somehow were connected in a nightmare world where dirt filled their mouths and ears and held them pinned.

Digging like worms. That was the nightmare reality. Drake and the piggy digging in a nightmare, digging dirt, pushing it aside, compressing it to buy half an inch of clearance.

Dark, that dream. Utterly dark. No Sammy sun. No light.

He remembered thinking in the nightmare, thinking, 'There's no air.'

Buried alive, there couldn't be any air. No light and no air, no water, no food, forever and forever.

It had taken a long time before his mind had cleared enough for him to realise the wonderful truth: he was dead . . . but alive.

Unkillable. Buried in the damp earth and yet somehow alive.

And then, hard-won freedom of a sort. The nightmare was no longer one of being buried in the earth but of walking the earth. He would be in one place, and then quite suddenly, in another. It took him a while to realise what had happened. The piggy was a part of him. They were joined, connected. Melded into one creature with two minds and two bodies.

Sometimes Drake and sometimes Brittney Pig.

Sometimes himself, and other times that little idiot with her lunatic visions of her dead brother.

Then the fight with Sam, the burning, and yet he had survived. Unkillable.

'You're a monster, Orc! You know that, right?' Drake shouted the taunt. 'People look at you and they throw up. You make them all sick.'

Trapped. For now. In this dank, gloomy basement. Nothing down here but a wooden work table. They had cleaned the place out, Sam and Edilio and the rest. Barely a nail left behind on the concrete floor.

A roomier grave than the one he'd shared with Brittney Pig before. Here there was air. But Drake no longer needed air.

They shoved food in, and Drake ate it but he didn't need it. Unkillable.

What could not be killed could not be imprisoned forever. Just a matter of time. Orc was a stupid drunk. Howard was a clown. Drake would have already dug his way out – he had loosened a section of cinderblock wall, working at the mortar with a piece of broken glass.

But he had to be careful not to leave any clues for Brittney to find when she emerged.

That meant working slowly. Putting the piece of glass back in the sweepings right where she would expect to see it.

In the meantime as he worked and waited he howled threats up at Orc. There were two ways out of this trap: working on the wall, and working on Orc's mind.

'Hey!' Drake shouted. 'Orc! If I whip that last bit of skin off you, what do you think will happen? Might as well get rid of it and be all gravel. Why pretend you're still human?'

Orc stomped the floor, which was Drake's ceiling. But he did not come down to do battle.

Not yet. But he would eventually. Orc would snap. Then Drake would have his chance.

Through the wall or through Orc: one way or the other, Drake would escape.

He would go then to the Darkness. The gaiaphage would know how to kill the Brittney Pig and let Drake live free.

'I'm going to kill you!' Drake screamed.

He whipped at the walls, whipped at the ceiling, screamed and kicked and whipped in a lunatic frenzy.

Until at last, exhausted, his whip hand bleeding, he fell to his knees and became Brittney.

'Brittney Pig,' Drake slurred as his cruel mouth melted and twisted and became the braces-toothed mouth of his most intimate enemy.

Lana, too, felt the dark distant mind of the gaiaphage reach out for her.

She woke, eyes open quite suddenly. Patrick was beside the bed, panting, worried, wagging his tail uncertainly. He could tell, somehow.

'It's OK, boy, go back to sleep,' Lana said.

Patrick whimpered, but then went back to his bed, turning around a couple of times before settling himself in.

The gaiaphage could no longer trick her into believing it had a voice. Those days were gone. But it could still touch her with a tendril of consciousness. It could still remind her of its presence, and of her connection to it.

This must be what it was like to be a victim of some awful crime, and to know that the person who did it to you was still alive, still looking for a way to do it again.

The gaiaphage lusted after Lana's power. Using her power it

could do miraculous things. Like replace an amputated arm with a snake-like whip.

But she was no longer quite so weak.

'Anxious, are you?' she asked the cool night air. 'Down under the ground nibbling on your uranium snack?'

The Darkness did not answer. But Lana felt her instinct was right: the creature was anxious.

But not afraid.

Lana frowned, thinking about the distinction. Anxious but not afraid. Anticipating? Waiting for something?

She was torn between getting up and smoking a cigarette – she was hooked, she accepted that now – and lying there with her eyes closed and failing to fall asleep. Sleep, even if it came, would now be invaded by nightmares.

So she sat up, fumbled for and found the pack of Lucky Strikes and her lighter. The lighter sparked, the cigarette glowed, and the smell of smoke filled her nostrils.

'What are you up to?' she asked. 'What do you want?'

But of course there was no answer. And she could sense the Darkness turning its attention away.

Lana got up and padded over to her balcony. The moon was high overhead. It was either very late or very early.

The barrier was so close, she felt as if she could almost touch it.

Was it true that the world was just on the other side of that barrier? Was it really so close that she'd have been able to smell the French fries at the Carl's Jr they built for gawkers who came to see the dome?

Or was that just another lie in this small universe of deceptions?

What if it came down? Right now, just pop: no more barrier? Or what if it cracked, like a gigantic egg?

Her mom and dad . . .

She closed her eyes and bit her lip. The pain of memory had snuck up on her, hit her when she wasn't ready.

Tears filled her eyes. She wiped them away impatiently.

Suddenly, just down on the cliff above the beach, an eruption of blazing green-white light. Sam stood silhouetted by his own light show. She heard him yelling, roaring in frustration.

He was trying to burn his way out of the FAYZ.

It went on for a while and then stopped. Darkness returned. Sam was invisible to her now.

Lana turned away.

So, she was not the only one fantasising about cracking the shell and emerging like a newborn chick.

Strange, Lana thought as she stubbed out the end of her cigarette, *I've never thought of it as an egg before.*

A gust of breeze blew her smoke before her.

FOUR

SAM WOKE UP in the last place he'd have expected: his bedroom.

He hadn't been to his former house in ages.

He'd hated it when he lived here with his mother. Connie Temple. Nurse Temple.

He barely remembered her. She was from another world.

He sat up on the bed and smelled the sick. He'd thrown up on the bed. 'Nice,' he said with thick tongue.

His head exploded in supernovas of pain.

He wiped his mouth on the blanket. This was one house no one had raided or vandalised or moved into. It was still his, he supposed. There might still be drugs in the bathroom.

He staggered there. Leaned against the sink and threw up again. Not much came up.

In the medicine cabinet nothing but a small bottle of generic ibuprofen.

'Oh,' Sam moaned. 'Why do people drink?'

Then he remembered. Taylor.

'Oh, no. Oh, no.'

No, no, he hadn't made a grab for Taylor, had he? He hadn't kissed her, surely? The memory was so hazy it could almost have been a dream. But pieces of it were too immediate and real. Especially the memory of her fingertips on his chest.

'Oh, no,' he moaned.

He swallowed two ibuprofen dry. They didn't go down easily.

Holding his head, he went to the kitchen. Sat down at the little table. He'd had meals here with his mom. Not a lot of days, because she'd be up at Coates, working.

And keeping a worried eye on her other son.

Caine.

Caine Soren, not Temple. She had given him up for adoption. They had been born just a few minutes apart, fraternal twins, him and Caine. And their mother had given Caine away and kept Sam.

No explanation. She'd never told either of them. That truth hadn't come out until after the coming of the FAYZ.

And no real explanation for what had become of their father. He was out of the picture before Sam and Caine were born.

Had it just been too much for their mother? Had she decided she could handle one fatherless boy but not two? Eeny meeny miny moe?

He had a new family now. Astrid and Little Pete. Only now

he didn't have them, either. And now he had to ask himself what he had done to deserve it, his father's disappearance, his mother's lies, Astrid's rejection.

'Yeah,' he muttered. 'Time for self-pity. Poor me. Poor Sam.'

He meant it to sound ironic, but it came out bitter.

Caine probably had a pretty good case of resentment, too. He'd been rejected by both birth parents: two for two.

And yet, Caine still had Diana, didn't he?

How was it fair? Caine was a liar, a manipulator, a murderer. And Caine was probably lying in satin sheets with Diana eating actual food and watching a DVD. Clean sheets, candy bars, and a beautiful, willing girl.

Caine who had never done a single good or decent thing was living in luxury.

Sam, who had tried and tried and done everything he could, was sitting in his house with a raging headache, smelling vomit with a pair of ibuprofen burning a hole in his stomach lining.

Alone.

Hunter brought his kills to the gas station any day he had some. Today, bright and early, with the sun just warming the hills behind him, he had walked down from his hillside camp carrying four birds and a badger and two raccoons and a bag of squirrels. He forgot how many squirrels. The bag felt heavy, though.

It was a lot to carry. If you added it up it was probably about as heavy as carrying a kid. Not as heavy as a deer though – those he had to butcher and carry down in pieces.

No deer today. And he had not yet butchered Old Lion. That was a big job. He wanted to keep the skin in one piece, so he had to take his time.

He would wear the lion's skin over him when he had dried it out. It would be warm and remind him of Old Lion.

Hunter carried the squirrel bag slung over one shoulder. He roped the other animals together and draped the rope over his other shoulder. He had to be careful about that, though, because of the thing on his shoulder.

That kid named Roscoe was coming. He was pushing a wheelbarrow. He didn't look very happy. Every day Hunter came it was either Roscoe or this girl named Marcie. Marcie was nice. But Hunter knew she was scared of him. Probably because he couldn't talk well.

'Hey, Hunter,' Roscoe said. 'Dude, are you okay?'

'Yes.'

'You're all clawed up, man. I mean, jeez, that has to hurt.'

Hunter followed the direction of Roscoe's gaze. His shirt was ripped exposing his stomach. Two claw marks, deep, bloody, just beginning to scab a little, were plowed right across his stomach.

He touched the wound gingerly. But it didn't hurt. In fact he couldn't feel it at all.

'You're a tough dude, Hunter,' Roscoe said. 'Anyway, looks like you have a good haul today.'

'I do, Roscoe,' Hunter said. He spoke as carefully as he could. But still the words didn't sound like how he made words back before. He sounded as if his tongue was covered with glue.

Hunter carefully lifted the rope off his shoulder. He was careful not to scrape the thing on his shoulder. He set the animals in the wheelbarrow. Then he upended the squirrel bag and dumped the squirrels on top. They all looked the same. Grey and bushy-tailed. Each cooked inside a little. Enough. Sometimes he cooked their heads and sometimes their body. It wasn't that easy to aim the invisible stuff that radiated out of his hands.

He forgot what it was called. Astrid had some name for it. But it was a long word.

'You doing OK, Hunter?' Roscoe asked again.

'Yes. I have food. And my sleeping bag is dry after I cleaned it in a stream.'

'You got fresh water to wash in, huh?' Roscoe asked. 'I'm jealous. Feel this shirt.' He invited Hunter to feel the stiff saltwater-washed cotton.

'It feels OK,' Hunter said warily.

Roscoe made a rude noise. 'Yeah, right. Salt water. Feel your shirt.' And Roscoe reached out to touch Hunter's shirt. He touched the shoulder of Hunter's shirt.

The wrong shoulder.

'Aaahh!' Roscoe cried in shock and pain. 'What the –'

'I didn't mean to!' Hunter yelled.

'Something bit me!' He held out his finger for Hunter to examine. There were teeth marks. Blood.

Roscoe stared hard at him. And at his shoulder. 'What's on your shoulder, man? What is that? What's under there? Is that some kind of animal?'

Hunter swallowed. No one had seen his shoulder. He didn't know what would happen if anyone did.

'Yes, Roscoe, it's an animal,' Hunter said, seizing gratefully on the explanation.

'Well, it bit me!'

'Sorry,' Hunter said.

Roscoe grabbed the wheelbarrow handles and hefted it. 'I'm not doing this job any more. Marcie can do it every day, I'm not dealing with this.'

'OK,' Hunter said. 'Bye.'

Jennifer B set out sometime around dawn.

If she stayed in the house she was sure she would die. She'd slept for an unknown period of time – hours? days? – on the floor, with her blankets gathered around her.

The chills came in waves. She would be too hot and would kick off her blankets. Then the fever would start to spike again and she would feel cold, cold all the way down to her bones.

Jennifer H was dead. Jennifer L didn't answer when Jennifer B moaned to her to join her.

'Jen . . . I'm going to . . . hospital.'

No answer.

'Are you alive?'

Jennifer L coughed, she wasn't dead, and she coughed normally, not the crazy spasms that had killed Jennifer H. But she didn't answer.

So Jennifer Boyles set off, on her own. She slid on her butt down the stairs, blankets gathered around her. Shivering, teeth chattering.

She managed to stand long enough to reach the front door and open it. But she sat down again very unexpectedly on the porch. Hard on her butt. She sat there shaking until the chills passed.

She tripped walking down the porch stairs. The fall bruised her left knee badly. This destroyed the last of her will to stand up. But not the last of her will to live.

Jennifer began to crawl. Hands and knees. Down the sidewalk. Impeded by her blankets. Delayed by coughing fits. Pausing whenever the chills rattled her so hard she could only moan and hack and roll on to her side.

'Keep going,' she muttered. 'Gotta keep going.'

PLAGUE

It took her two hours to crawl as far as Brace Road.

She lay there, facedown. Coughing wracked her chest. But it was not yet the superhuman coughs that had killed Jennifer H.

Not yet.

FIVE

62 HOURS 18 MINUTES

'**LESLIE-ANN,** TRY TO do a little better on cleaning my night pot, OK?' Albert told the cleaning girl. 'I know it's not a fun job, but I like it clean.'

Leslie-Ann nodded and kept her eyes down. She was a little afraid of him, Albert knew. But at least she didn't seem to hate him.

'There's not much water,' Leslie-Ann mumbled.

'Use sand,' Albert said patiently – he'd already told her this. 'Use sand to scrub it clean.'

She nodded and fled the room.

Not everyone liked Albert. Not everyone was happy that he had become the most important person around. Lots of people were jealous that Albert had a girl to clean his house and the porcelain basin where he did his business at night when he didn't want to go outside to the only actual outhouse in Perdido Beach. And that he could afford to send his clothes to be washed in the fresh water of the ironically named Lake Evian.

46

And there were definitely people who didn't like working for Albert, having to do what he said or go hungry.

Albert travelled with a bodyguard now. The bodyguard's name was Jamal. Jamal carried an automatic rifle over his shoulder. He had a massive hunting knife in his belt. And a club that was an oak chair leg with spikes driven through it to make a sort of mace.

Unlike everyone else Albert carried no weapon himself. Jamal was weapon enough.

'Let's go, Jamal.'

Albert led the way towards the beach. Jamal as usual kept a few paces back, head swivelling left and right, glowering, ready for trouble.

Albert bypassed the plaza – there were always kids there and they always wanted something from Albert: a job, a different job, credit, something.

It didn't work. Two littles, Harley and Janice, moved right in front of him as he walked briskly.

'Mr Albert? Mr Albert?' Harley said.

'Just Albert's fine,' Albert said tersely.

'Me and Janice are thirsty.'

'I'm sorry, but I don't have any water on me.' He managed a tight smile and moved on. But now Janice was crying and Harley was pleading.

'We used to live with Mary and she gave us water. But now

we have to live with Summer and BeeBee and they said we have to have money.'

'Then I guess you'd better earn some money,' Albert said. He tried to soften it, tried not to sound harsh, but he had a lot on his mind and it came out sounding mean. Now Harley started to cry, too.

'If you're thirsty, stop crying,' Albert snapped. 'What do you think tears are made of?'

Reaching the beach Albert scanned the work site. It looked like a salvage yard. A five-hundred-gallon oval propane tank lay abandoned on the sand. A scorched hole in one side.

A second, slightly smaller tank should have been resting on steel legs right at the water's edge. Instead it was tipped over. A copper pipe stuck out of the top. This pipe was crimped tightly over a slightly smaller pipe that bent back toward the ground. A third, still narrower pipe was duct-taped heavily in place and this pipe reached the wet sand.

In theory at least, this crude, jury-rigged contraption was a still. The principle was simple enough: boil salt water, let the steam rise into a pipe, then cool the steam. What dribbled out of the end would be drinkable water.

Easy in theory. Almost impossible to do practically. Especially now that some fool had knocked it over.

Albert's heart sank. Soon Harley and Janice wouldn't be the only ones begging for water. The gasoline supply was down to a few hundred gallons at the station. No gas: no water truck. No water truck: no water.

Even worse, the tiny Lake Evian in the hills was drying up. There had been no rain since the coming of the FAYZ. Kids knew there was a plan to relocate everyone to Lake Evian when the last of the gas was gone; what they didn't realise was that things were far worse than that.

The first tank, the burned one, had been an earlier effort to create a still. Albert had tried to get Sam to boil the water using his powers. Unfortunately Sam couldn't dial it down enough to heat without destroying.

This new effort would require a fire beneath the tank. Which would mean crews of kids to rip lumber from unused houses. Which might make the whole thing more trouble than it was worth.

The crew was lounging. Tossing pebbles at the surf, trying to get them to skip.

Albert marched over to them, his loafers filling with sand. 'Hey,' he snapped. 'What happened here?'

The four kids – none older than eleven – looked guilty.

'It was like this when we got here. I think the wind knocked it over.'

'There is no wind in the FAYZ, you . . .' He stopped himself from saying 'moron'. Albert had a certain reputation for being in control of himself. He was the closest thing they had to an adult.

'I hired you to dig a hole, not play around,' Albert said.

'It's hard,' one said. 'It keeps filling up.'

'I know it's hard. It won't get any easier. And if you want to eat, you work.'

'We were just taking a break.'

'Break's over. Get on those shovels.'

Albert turned and walked away with Jamal in his wake.

'Those kids are flipping you off, boss,' Jamal reported.

'Are they digging?'

Jamal glanced back and reported that they were.

'As long as they do their work they can flip me off all they like,' Albert said.

It was then that Roscoe came up to report his haul from Hunter. And to tell Albert a crazy story about Hunter's shoulder biting him.

'Look,' Roscoe said and held out his hand for Albert's inspection.

Albert sighed. 'Save the crazy stories, Roscoe,' he said.

'It's like, like, green, kind of,' Roscoe said.

'I'm not the Healer or Dahra,' Albert said.

But as he walked away something nagged at the edges of Albert's thoughts: the wound really had looked a bit green.

Someone else's problem. He had plenty of his own.

It was then that he spotted someone lying on the sand, just lying there like he might be dead. Far down the beach.

He felt in his pocket for the map.

Was it time? He glanced back at the still. The hopeless still.

His insides squirmed a little at what he was about to do. Panic would not be good. Everyone was on edge, weird, freaked since Mary's dramatic suicide and attempted mass murder.

The people could not take another disaster. But disaster was coming. And when it hit, if there was panic, then Sam would be needed here in town.

But there was no one else Albert could trust with the mission he had in mind. Sam would have to go. And Albert would have to hope that no new disaster arose while he was gone.

Sam felt a shadow.

He squinted one eye open. Someone was standing over him, face blanked by the sun behind him.

'Is that you, Albert?' Sam asked.

'It's me.'

'I recognise the shoes. I don't feel good,' Sam said.

'Would you mind sitting up? I have something important to talk to you about.'

'If it's important, go talk to Edilio. He's in charge.'

Albert waited, refusing to speak. Finally, with a sigh that became a groan, Sam rolled over and sat up.

'This is just between us, Sam,' Albert said.

'Yeah, that always works out so well when I keep secrets

from the council,' Sam said sarcastically. He rubbed his hair vigorously to knock some of the sand out.

'You're not on the council any more,' Albert said reasonably. 'And this is about a job. I want to hire you.'

Sam rolled his eyes. 'Everyone already works for you, Albert. What's the problem? Does it bother you that I don't?'

'You liked it better when no one was working and everyone was starving?'

Sam stared up at him. Then he made an ironic two-finger salute. 'Sorry. I'm in a lousy mood. Bad night followed by bad morning. What's up, Albert?'

'There's a big problem with the water supply.'

Sam nodded. 'I know. As soon as the gas runs out we're going to have to relocate the whole town up to Evian.'

Albert tugged at his pants, then sat down carefully on the sand. 'No. First of all, the water level in Lake Evian is dropping faster than ever. There's no rain here. And it's a small lake. You can see where it's dropped from, like, ten feet deep to half that.'

Albert pulled a folded map from his pocket and opened it. Sam scooted closer to see.

'This isn't a very good map. It's too big to show much detail. But see this?' He pointed. 'Lake Tramonto. It's like a hundred times bigger than Evian.'

'Is it inside the FAYZ?'

'I drew this circle with a compass. I think at least part of Lake Tramonto is inside the barrier.'

Sam nodded thoughtfully. 'Dude, it's, like, what, ten miles from here?'

'More like fifteen.'

'Even if it's there and even if the water is drinkable, how are we going to bring it down to Perdido Beach? I mean, look.' Sam traced lines with his finger. 'Going or coming back it's right through coyote country. And that would take a lot more gas, that drive. I mean, a lot more.'

'I don't think my saltwater still is going to work,' Albert admitted. He gazed moodily down the beach towards his work crew. 'Even if it does, it may not produce enough.'

Sam took the map from him and studied it intently. 'You know, it's weird. I kind of forgot there were such things as paper maps. I always used to use Google maps. Maps dot Google dot com. Remember those days? What's this?'

Albert peered over the edge of the map. 'Oh, that's the air force base. But look, it's pretty much all on the other side. The runway, the buildings and all. Why? Were you hoping to find a jet fighter?'

Sam smiled. 'That might be useful if it came with a pilot. It's one thing for Sanjit to crash-land a helicopter. It's a whole different thing flying a Mach two jet around inside a twenty-mile-wide fishbowl. No. I don't know what I was hoping for. Maybe a magic ray gun that could blow holes through the barrier.'

'You know,' Albert said, trying to sound casual, but sounding instead like he was delivering a well-rehearsed speech. 'I read in a book where in the old days – I mean, really old days – business-men would hire explorers to go search out new territory. You know, to find gold or oil or spices. Of course these explorers would have to be tough and be able to deal with all kinds of problems.'

Sam had no trouble grasping Albert's meaning. 'You want to hire me to explore this lake.'

'Yes.'

Sam looked around at the sand. 'Well, as you can see, I'm very busy.'

Albert said nothing. Just waited and watched Sam like a lizard watching a fly.

'You don't want the council to know about this. Why?'

Albert shrugged. 'Anything the council hears about, the whole town knows ten seconds later. You want panic? Anyway, it's not about them. It's me doing it. Me and you. And a couple of other kids to back you up.'

'Why not just send Brianna? She'd get there fast.'

'I don't trust her. Not for something like this. I mean, Sam, we could be in trouble on water really soon. I mean, soon. I've got a truck going later, after that, maybe half a dozen more runs.'

Sam fell silent. He drew little abstract shapes in the sand, thinking.

'I'll do it,' Sam said. 'I'm not happy about keeping it secret from Edilio.'

Albert pressed his lips into a line. Like he was thinking. But Sam could see Albert had an answer ready. 'Look, secrets don't last long in this place. For example, Taylor's been telling an interesting story all over town.'

Sam groaned. Had to be Taylor, he reproached himself. What was he going to tell Astrid? Not that it was really her business. They'd never said he couldn't see anyone else, make out with anyone else. In fact once, in a flash of anger, Astrid had told him to do just that. Only she hadn't said 'make out'. She'd used a phrase he'd been a little shocked to hear coming from Astrid.

'Sam, Edilio's a good guy,' Albert said, breaking in on Sam's gloomy thoughts. 'But like I said, he'll tell the rest of them. Once the council knows, everyone knows. If everyone knows how desperate things are, what do you think will happen?'

Sam smiled without humour. 'About half the people will be great. The other half will freak.'

'And people will end up getting killed,' Albert said. He cocked his head sideways, trying his best to look like the idea had just occurred to him. 'And who is going to end up kicking butts? Who will end up playing daddy and then be resented and blamed and finally told to go away?'

'You've gained new skills,' Sam said bitterly. 'You used to just be about working harder than anyone else and being ambitious. You're learning how to manipulate people.'

Albert's mouth twitched and his eyes flashed angrily. 'You're not the only one walking around with a big load of responsibility on your shoulders, Sam. You play the big mean daddy who won't let anyone have any fun, and I play the greedy businessman who is just looking out for himself. But don't be stupid: maybe I am greedy, but without me no one eats. Or drinks. We need water. You see anyone else in this town that's going to make that happen?'

Sam laughed softly. 'Yeah, you've gotten good at using people, Albert. I mean you offer me a chance to go off and save everyone's butt, right? Be important and necessary again. You have me all figured out.'

'We need water, Sam,' Albert said simply. 'If you find water up at this Lake Tramonto and come back and tell people they have to move up there, they'll do it. You tell them it's going to be OK and they'll believe you.'

'Because I'm so widely loved and admired,' Sam said sarcastically.

'It's not a popularity contest, Sam. People love you when they need you, and then ten minutes later they're tired of you.

In a very short while they're going to realise we're very close to all dying of thirst. And there you'll be with the solution.'

'And they'll love me. For ten minutes, until they've had enough to drink.'

'Exactly,' Albert said. He stood up. 'We have a deal?' He extended his hand down for Sam to shake.

Sam stood up. 'And the lake? I mean, if it's there?'

'If it's there, it's my lake,' Albert said coolly. 'I'll sell the water and control access. Maybe then we won't end up in the same bind all over again.'

Sam shook his hand and laughed out loud. 'You are less full of crap than anyone around, Albert. If it's there, I'll find it. I'll leave tonight.'

He took the map.

'You want someone to go with you?'

'Dekka.' Sam thought a moment longer. 'And Jack.'

'You want Computer Jack? Why?'

'It's a good idea to have someone around who's smarter than you are.'

'I suppose so,' Albert said. 'You need someone to communicate, too. Take Taylor.'

'Not Taylor. I'll take Brianna.'

Albert shook his head. 'You kissed her, get past it. We need someone in this town who can fight if necessary. I mean at the freak level, no diss on Edilio. Taylor's useless in a battle of any kind, while Brianna can take on just about anyone.'

Sam nodded. It made sense. If he wanted Dekka along he'd have to leave Brianna behind. But Taylor?

Suddenly the trip, which he had started to anticipate just a little, seemed much less like fun.

Lana disliked going into town. In town people asked her for things. But she needed a gallon of water to take back up to Clifftop anyway, so she figured she might as well stop by the so-called hospital and clear up the usual backlog of kids with broken arms, burned hands, and a rumoured cut wrist.

She wasn't that sure she should be fixing anyone dumb enough to try and slit his wrist. After all, the FAYZ would kill you soon enough, why be in a hurry? And if you wanted a quick trip out of the FAYZ there was always Mary's way: the cliff.

Dahra Baidoo was reading her medical book and telling some kid with a sore tooth to be quiet. 'It's just loose, it will come out when it wants to come out,' she said irritably.

She looked up with a weary smile when she noticed Lana.

'Hey, Lana.'

'Hey, DB,' Lana said. 'How's medical school?'

It was an old joke between them. They had worked together closely in times of crisis. The flu that had gone around a couple of weeks ago, the various battles and fires and fights and poisonings and accidents.

Dahra would hold the injured kids' hands and feed them Tylenol while waiting for Lana to come around. The fire had been the worst. The two of them had been down here together for days, barely seeing the sun.

Bad, bad days.

Dahra laughed and tapped the book. 'I'm ready to perform heart transplants.'

'What do we have?' Lana asked. 'I heard you had an uncommitted suicide.'

'No suicides. Broken ribs. And a burn. Not too bad, and I should probably let her suffer since she got it from trying to light a bag of poop and throw it.'

Lana heard a hacking cough from a very sick-looking girl. 'What's that?'

Dahra gave her a significant look. 'I think our flu is back. Or never went away.' She pulled Lana off to the side, to where the patients couldn't hear. 'I think this may be worse, though. This girl is hallucinating. Her name is Jennifer. She came crawling in here this morning. She keeps talking about some other girl named Jennifer who coughed so hard there were pieces of her lungs coming up. And then she supposedly coughed so hard she broke her own neck.'

'Fever brings on the crazy sometimes,' Lana said.

'Yeah. Still, I wish I had someone to go check on her house. See if there's anything going on.'

'Where's Elwood?'

Dahra sighed. 'That's over.'

Lana had never liked Elwood much and she kind of wanted to know what had happened – Dahra and Elwood had been going out for a long time. But Dahra didn't look like she was interested in spilling her guts.

Lana healed the broken ribs, then checked out the girl with burned fingers. 'Don't do stupid things like this,' Lana snapped at the girl. 'I don't want to be wasting my time on stupidity. Next time I'll let you suffer.'

But she healed the burn as well and did a quick touch-and-go with the coughing girl.

'Can I fill a jug before I head out?' Lana asked.

Dahra winced. She had an old water cooler in one corner with a clear glass five-gallon jug on top. But there was nowhere near five gallons in there.

'How about half a gallon?' Dahra said.

'Deal,' Lana said. 'Albert needs to keep you better supplied. Me, too, while we're at it. He's supposed to send one of his people up with a gallon a day. It's been two days. It's not smart for a hypochondriac like Albert to grind my nerves.'

Then, with a nod to Dahra, Lana headed off again, back towards her lonely eyrie.

She took a shortcut that took her up the hill to Clifftop. It was a bare trail through the brush, a place where a hungry coyote might be. But Patrick would warn her long before she walked into a coyote. And in any case Lana carried an automatic pistol she had no compunction about using.

Suddenly Patrick growled and Lana had the automatic out and aimed with both hands in a split second.

'Step out where I can see you,' she said.

There was no coyote. Instead there was Hunter. Lurking. Looking ashamed to be here. He had been banished from town, although he was allowed to come see her anytime. Still he preferred to stay out of sight.

Lana liked Hunter. First because he often saved her some tasty morsel, a rabbit or a couple of plump frogs. And he brought stomachs and intestines for Patrick to eat.

Second because even though he was brain damaged he at least had the sense not to waste her time. If he was looking for her there was a reason.

'T'sup, Hunter?' she asked. She stuck the gun back in her waistband. 'Whoa. I see: bad scratches there.'

'No,' he said. 'It's something else.'

He pulled on his T-shirt neck.

Lana didn't breathe for a few seconds. 'Yeah,' she said. 'That is something else.'

NO ONE KNEW quite how to deal with Hunter. He wasn't supposed to come into town. So the council had to go to him.

They met on the highway.

No one had ever cleaned up the crashed and abandoned cars on the highway. They were all just where they'd been since the coming of the FAYZ.

The big FedEx truck was still on its side. Kids had long since broken into the back and rifled through the packages. The wrapping, torn paper, plastic packing peanuts, curls of tape, and packing slips had mostly drifted into a section of construction barrier on the side of the road.

Funny, Lana noticed: it looked almost cleaned up today. As if someone had come along with a leaf blower and scooted all the garbage off the road.

The town council was now Dekka, Howard, Albert, Ellen, and Edilio. Sam was entitled to attend but he usually didn't. Astrid had made it clear she wanted no part of it any more, but

Lana had sent Brianna to tell her to be there. She wanted Astrid's eyes on this.

So Astrid was there. Sort of. Lana had seen Astrid in a lot of different situations and moods, but this was a new Astrid: withdrawn, preoccupied. Like she was somewhere else entirely. She was biting her lip, twisting her fingers together, then catching herself and wiping her hands on her jeans.

Lana was sure she saw Astrid start guiltily when she noticed the trash blown against the barrier. But maybe she was just feeling touchy because of the story going around about Sam and Taylor.

Edilio was in charge. Which was fine with Lana. Almost everyone else had shown some weakness, some bit of crazy. Very much including herself, she acknowledged wryly.

Edilio seemed like the last sane, decent person left in the FAYZ. The undocumented kid from Honduras was the single most trusted person around. And yet, if the barrier ever came down, Edilio and his family – if they were still alive out there – would be kicked out of the country.

Of course, Lana thought, if the barrier ever came down, half the kids would be shipped off to juvie and the rest would be sent to mental institutions or rehab. So maybe getting kicked out wasn't so bad.

Hunter looked like he was meeting the president. He stood tall and tried to smooth his hair down – a hopeless effort.

63

Lana hid a smile as he picked a tick off his arm and flicked it away.

'Hi, Hunter,' Edilio said. 'First up, man, thanks for all the good work you do, right? You're helping to keep everyone fed and healthy, so thanks.'

Hunter searched for something to say, eyes shifting left, right, and finally down. 'I am the hunter.'

'Well, you're a good hunter,' Edilio said. 'Lana says you have a little medical problem.'

Hunter nodded. 'Mouths.'

'Yeah. Well, do you mind letting us look? We don't want to embarrass you or anything.'

'Just take off your shirt,' Albert said a bit abruptly. He considered Hunter an employee. But then Albert considered almost everyone an employee.

'He can take it off or not, it's up to him,' Dekka said in her low growl.

Hunter was confused by the back-and-forth. So Lana said, 'Would you mind taking your shirt off, Hunter, so we can see? Might as well take off your jeans, too.'

Hunter pulled his T-shirt over his head. He dropped his jeans to his ankles.

There was a collective gasp.

Lana stepped up beside Hunter. She pointed to the protruding mouthparts on Hunter's shoulder. It looked exactly like a very large ant's head, or maybe a wasp's head, but with oversized, gnashing mouthparts. 'This was the first one. I tried to cure it. You'll notice it didn't work.'

She pointed to a smaller silvery, almost metallic, mouth on his calf. 'Do us a favour and raise your arms up, Hunter.'

He did. Albert looked away.

There was a third mouth gnashing its teeth in Hunter's armpit.

Lana watched Astrid watching Hunter. Her ice blue eyes flickered.

'You have a question, Astrid?' Lana asked.

Astrid pursed her lips like she didn't, but her curiosity got the better of her. 'Hunter, has anything bitten you?'

'Yes. Fleas bite me. And ticks.'

'How about a wasp?' Astrid asked.

'No,' Hunter said.

'Why a wasp?' Edilio asked Astrid.

Astrid shrugged. 'I'm just trying to get information.' She was lying, Lana thought. That scary smart brain of hers was already on to something. Something she didn't want to talk about in front of Hunter.

'Anything else strange happen?' Edilio asked.

'Just the greenie,' Hunter said.

'The what?' Edilio asked.

'They're no good for hunting. I caught one and cooked it

but it shrivelled all up and there wasn't any meat on it.'

'What's a greenie?' Albert demanded.

Hunter frowned, looking for a way to describe it. 'It flies. It's like a snake that flies.'

Howard said, 'Oh, good, I was worried we didn't have enough weirdness to deal with. Flying snakes. That's excellent.'

'They squirt,' Hunter said helpfully. Then his eyes widened. 'It squirted me once. Right here.' He pointed to his shoulder. To the slowly gnashing insect mouth.

'Does anyone have anything sharp?' Astrid asked.

Three knives flashed out.

'I was kind of thinking of a pin,' Astrid said. But she took a knife from Howard. 'Don't worry, Hunter,' she said. She poked very gently with the point of the knife just beside the largest mouth. 'Did you feel that?'

Hunter shook his head.

Astrid poked again, farther from the first spot. And again on Hunter's upper arm.

'I guess I don't feel stuff much.' Hunter seemed baffled.

'Something's anaesthetising him,' Astrid said. A spasm, a look of nausea, quickly suppressed, twisted her lips.

'It doesn't hurt,' Hunter said.

'You can get dressed,' Edilio said kindly. 'Thanks for showing us.'

Hunter obediently pulled his clothes back on.

'Back to work, huh, Hunter?' Edilio said with a wretched, forced smile.

Hunter nodded. 'Yes. I have to get Albert some meat or he gets mad.'

'No I don't,' Albert protested weakly.

Hunter started to walk away. Albert called after him. 'Where did you see this flying snake of yours?'

Hunter, eager to answer Albert's question, smiled because he knew the answer. 'They're all over on the morning side.'

'The what?'

'That's what I call it. On the other side of the hills. There's a cave. By the road.'

'The road to Lake Evian . . . the lake where we get water?' Albert asked in a quiet voice.

Hunter nodded. 'Yes. By the dirt road that goes there.'

'Thanks,' Edilio said, dismissing Hunter, who looked relieved and walked quickly away without looking back. Edilio turned to Astrid. 'Okay, Astrid. What are you thinking?'

'I think the reason Lana couldn't heal him is that it's not a disease.'

'It sure looks like a disease,' Howard said. 'Like a disease I don't want to get.'

'It's a parasite,' Astrid said.

'Like when a dog gets worms?' Edilio asked.

'Yes.'

'But they're coming out through his skin,' Edilio said.

Astrid nodded. 'He should be in excruciating pain. They're probably secreting something that deadens the pain.'

'What's going to happen to him?' Dekka asked.

'There's a type of wasp,' Astrid said. 'That's why I asked him about wasps. It lays its eggs inside a caterpillar. The eggs hatch. The larvae then eat the living caterpillar from the inside out.'

Lana felt sick herself. She had long since learned to protect herself by affecting a certain indifference to the pains and wounds she healed. But this was awful beyond anything she had ever seen. And she had been powerless to help.

'Everyone keep this quiet till we figure out what it is,' Edilio said. 'No one talk to Taylor, that girl can't keep quiet for . . .' He trailed off, noticing a stony glare from Astrid. 'Council meeting tonight,' he finished lamely.

Lana called to Patrick, who was sniffing around in the weeds beside the road, and headed towards home.

Astrid caught up to her.

'Lana.'

'Yeah?' Lana had never been Astrid's biggest fan. She admired Astrid's smarts and looks. But they were very different people.

'It's Little Pete. He . . .'

'He what?' Lana demanded impatiently.

'He has a fever. I think he has flu or something.'

Lana shrugged. 'Yeah, one of the Jennifers has it, too. I don't think it's any big deal. Take him to see Dahra, I'll stop by there later.'

Lana expected Astrid to nod her head and take off. But Astrid glanced down the road to make sure no one was coming toward them. This got Lana's attention.

'I need you to come to my house,' Astrid said firmly.

'Look, I get that you're more important than, you know, normal people,' Lana snarked. 'But I'll take care of him later. OK? Bye.'

Astrid grabbed her shoulder. Lana turned back, angry now. She didn't like being touched, let alone grabbed.

'It's not about me,' Astrid said. 'Lana . . . I have to ask you. The gaiaphage . . .'

Lana's face darkened.

'Can it see what you see?' Astrid asked quietly. 'Can it know what you know?'

Lana felt a chill. 'What is going on, Astrid?'

'Maybe nothing. But come with me. Come see Petey. Help me out, and I will owe you one.'

Lana laughed derisively. She was the Healer: everyone owed her one. But she followed Astrid just the same.

SEVEN

CAINE HAD FOUND a telescope in the house. He carried it out to the cliff on the eastern edge of the island. It was afternoon. The light was pretty good, low, slanting rays that lit up the far shore. Sunlight glinted off windows and car windshields in Perdido Beach. Bright red tile roofs and tall palm trees made it seem so normal. As if it really was just another California beach town.

The nuclear power plant was closer. It, too, looked normal. The hole in the containment tower was on the far side, not visible from here. The hole he'd made.

He was startled by the sound behind him but didn't show it. Much.

'What are you looking at, Napoleon?' Diana asked.

'Napoleon?'

'You know, because he was exiled to an island after he almost took over the world,' Diana said. 'Although he was short. You're much taller.'

Caine wasn't sure he minded Diana tweaking him. It was better than the way she'd been lately, all depressed and giving up on life. Hating herself.

He didn't mind if she hated him. They were never going to be a cute romantic couple like Sam and Astrid. Clean-cut, righteous, all that. The perfect couple. He and Diana were the imperfect couple.

'How did it work out for Napoleon?' he asked her.

He caught the slight hesitation as she searched for a glib answer.

'He lived happily ever after on his island,' Diana said. 'He had a beautiful girlfriend who was far better than he deserved.'

'Stop worrying,' he said harshly. 'I'm not planning on leaving the island. How could I, even if I wanted to?'

'You would find a way,' Diana said bleakly.

'Yeah. But here I am anyway,' Caine said. He aimed the telescope back at the town. He could see the blackened hulks of burned-out homes just to the west of downtown.

'Don't do it,' Diana said.

Caine didn't ask what she meant. He knew.

'Just let it go,' Diana said. She put her hand on his shoulder. She caressed the side of his neck, his cheek.

He lowered the telescope and tossed it on to the overgrown sea grass. He turned, took her in his arms, and kissed her.

It had been a long time since he'd done that.

She felt different in his arms. Thinner. Smaller. More frail. But his body responded to her as it always had.

She did not pull away.

His own response surprised him. It had been a long time for that, too. A long time since he'd felt desire. Starving boys lusted after food, not after girls.

And now that it was happening, it was overwhelming. Like a roar in his ears. A pounding in his chest. He ached all the way through.

At the last second, the second when he would have lost the last of his self-control, Diana gently but firmly pushed him away.

'Not here,' she said.

'Where?' he gasped. He hated the neediness in his voice. He hated needing anyone or anything that badly. Need was weakness.

She detached his hands from her body. She took one step back. She was wearing an actual dress. A dress, with her legs showing and her shoulders bare and it was like she was a visitor from another planet.

He blinked, thinking maybe it was all a dream. She was clean and wearing a yellow summer dress. Her teeth had been brushed. Her hair was brushed, too, still a mess from cutting it all off and having it grow back while too hungry, but a shadow at least of its former dark, tumbling sensuality.

She bent down demurely and picked up the telescope. She handed it to him.

'Your choice, Caine. You can have me. Or you can try to take over the world. Not both. Because I'm not going to be part of that any more. I can't. So it's up to you.'

His jaw dropped. Literally.

'You witch,' he said.

Diana laughed.

'You know I have the power . . .' he threatened.

'Of course. I would be helpless. But that's not what you want.'

Caine spotted a boulder, not far away. Impressively big. He raised one hand, palm out, and with a scraping sound the boulder lifted into the air.

'Sometimes I hate you!' he yelled and with a flick of his wrist sent the boulder flying off the cliff and falling toward the water below.

'Just sometimes?' Diana raised one sceptical brow. 'I hate you almost all the time.'

They glared at each other with a look that was hate but also something else, something so much more helpless than hatred.

'We're damaged people,' Diana said, suddenly sad and serious. 'Horrible, messed-up, evil people. But I want to change. I want us both to change.'

'Change? To what?' Caine asked, mystified.

'To people who no longer have dreams of being Napoleon.'

She was her usual smirking self again as she looked him slowly up and down. Slowly enough that he actually felt embarrassed and had to overcome a modest urge to cover himself. 'Don't decide right now,' she said. 'You're in no condition to think clearly.'

And she turned and walked back towards the house.

Caine threw many more large boulders into the sea.

It didn't help.

Sam stood on the street corner watching Lana and Astrid enter the house he had shared with Astrid. Lana was carrying a water jug. Patrick stopped and stared in Sam's direction, but the girls didn't notice him and Patrick quickly lost interest.

He had come to tell Astrid he was going out of town. Astrid would keep the secret. And he wanted at least one person other than Albert to know where he was and what he was doing.

Anyway, that was what he told himself. Because admitting that he still, even now, even after everything that had happened, and everything that hadn't happened, couldn't just walk away from Astrid . . . that would be too big an admission of weakness.

He couldn't not tell her he was leaving. She had to know that he was still . . . whatever he was. He kicked at a crumpled soda can and sent it skittering down the trash-strewn street.

Why was Lana going over to see Astrid? Little Pete must

not be feeling well. But how could anyone tell what Little Pete was feeling?

Sam frowned. He didn't want to have some scene with Astrid in front of Lana.

The sky was getting dark. He would be leaving soon. Dekka, Taylor and Jack would be meeting him across the highway. Each was supposed to keep the whole thing secret.

In reality, of course, Jack would tell Brianna. Taylor would keep it quiet only because she didn't know what was going on, and by the time she did they'd be out of town. Dekka would tell no one. And Sam? He would tell Astrid.

Sam knocked at Astrid's door.

No answer.

Feeling strange and wrong he opened the door to what had until very recently been his own home and went inside.

Astrid and Lana were upstairs; he could hear the murmur of voices.

He took the stairs two at a time and called out, 'Astrid, it's me.'

They were in Little Pete's room. Astrid and Lana stood a few feet apart with their backs to Sam.

A woman – a grown, adult woman – was sitting on the bed with Little Pete's head in her lap.

'Mom?' Astrid said.

The woman was in her late thirties. She had streaked blonde

hair and Astrid's translucent pale skin, somewhat aged by sun. Her eyes were brown. She smiled sadly and cradled Little Pete's head. She stroked his hair.

'Mom?' Astrid said again, and this time her voice broke.

The woman did not speak. She did not look up at Astrid. She kept all her attention focused on Little Pete.

Sam stood in the doorway, looking from Astrid, to Lana and then to the bed.

What was going on here?

'She's not real,' Astrid said, and took a step back.

Lana glared at Astrid. Then she noticed Sam, standing there.

Lana's eyes narrowed. 'You knew about this, didn't you?' she accused.

'She's not real,' Astrid said again. 'That's not my mother. That's . . . it's an illusion. He's sick. I was out so . . . so he made her appear. To comfort him.'

'He made her appear.' Lana practically spat the words. 'He made her appear. Because that's something just anyone can do, any of us can just make a three-dimensional real-life mommy appear to cuddle us when we feel bad.'

'Stop it, Petey,' Astrid said.

The woman – the illusion of a woman – did not react but kept stroking Little Pete's head.

'Cure him, Lana. Cure him and it will stop.' Astrid was pleading. 'He has a fever. He's coughing.'

As if demonstrating, Little Pete coughed several times.

It was weird. He didn't cover his mouth or change his expression. He just coughed.

'Give it a try, Lana,' Sam urged. 'Please.'

Lana rounded on him. 'Interesting power for an autistic to have, isn't it?' she demanded. 'Especially when you think about all the stories going around about how the dome went clear for a few seconds when Little Pete blacked out.'

'There are a lot of mutants,' Sam said as blandly as he could.

There was a mixture of shock and anger on Lana's face as the truth began to dawn on her. 'Wasn't he at the power plant when the FAYZ came?' she asked.

Astrid and Sam exchanged a glance. Neither spoke.

'He was at the plant,' Lana said. 'The plant is the center of the FAYZ. The very center.'

'Please try to heal him,' Astrid urged.

'He's got a fever and a cough, big deal,' Lana said. 'Why is it so urgent that he be healed?'

Again, Sam had no answer.

Lana moved closer. The woman's hand was still on Pete's forehead. But she didn't react when Lana laid her own hand on Little Pete's chest.

'So, that's your mother,' Lana said more calmly.

'No,' Astrid said.

'Weird seeing an adult, isn't it?'

'It's an illusion,' Astrid said weakly. 'Little Pete has the power to . . . to make his visions seem real.'

'Yeah,' Lana said dryly. 'That's all it is. The blink, when everyone saw the outside, that was just an illusion. And your mom, here, that's an illusion.'

The woman disappeared suddenly. Little Pete's head fell back against his pillow.

'You're helping him,' Sam said. 'He's getting better.'

'You know what's interesting?' Lana said in a mockery of casual chitchat. 'The sun and the moon and the stars here are all illusions, too. So many illusions. So many coincidences. So many secrets.'

Sam didn't look at Astrid. He wished he hadn't come. More, he wished Astrid hadn't brought Lana here, although he understood it.

After a while Lana stepped back from Little Pete. 'I don't know if that fixed him or not.'

'Thanks,' Astrid said.

'I can feel it, you know,' Lana said softly.

'The healing?'

Lana shook her head. 'No. It. I can feel it. It touches him. It watches him. I can feel it. It reaches him.' Her brow creased and she seemed almost to be wincing in pain. 'Just like it reaches me.'

Without looking at either of them, Lana rushed from the room.

They stood silent, neither knowing what to say.

'I'm going to be away for a couple of days,' Sam said finally. 'The water situation . . . I'm going to search out another lake.'

A tear spilled down Astrid's cheek.

'That must have been hard,' Sam said. 'Even knowing it wasn't real.'

Astrid used one finger to brush away the tear. 'Lana's smart. She'll put it all together.' She sighed. 'If things get bad they'll come after him. The kids will come after Petey.'

'Before I go I'll ask Breeze to keep an eye on you,' Sam said.

Astrid stared gloomily at her brother. He coughed twice and then lay quiet. 'The thing is, I don't know what would happen.'

'If he got sick?'

'If he died. I don't know. I do not know.'

PETE

THE DARKNESS WAS watching him, touching him with its wispy tendril, listening for him to speak.

He would not speak. The Darkness could not help him. The Darkness only wanted to play, and it was so jealous when Pete played with anyone else.

Come to me, it said over and over again.

Pete's legs were weak. He stood poised atop the glass but his legs hurt and his feet, too, like the glass sheet was slicing into him.

He had felt better when his mother was there. She was quiet, the way he liked. She had not tried to touch him except to let him lie there against her breast and feel the soft rise and fall of her breathing.

But then the breathing had begun to wear on him, making him distracted. If it didn't stop . . .

But then it did stop when he made her go away. He could remember the good part, before the sound of breathing got to be too much, and not have to hear it any more.

Loud sister was talking and then another. The other touched him with her hand. He looked at her and was puzzled. A faint green tendril spiralled up to touch her. She seemed to be on both sides of the glass at once.

He felt her touch and it made him tense. He endured it, but inside he was feeling worse and worse.

Hot. Like fire was inside him.

He didn't want to hear any more from his body.

The other left. She took her hand away and left. But he could feel an echo of her inside him. She had touched the Darkness, but she refused its pleas to come and play.

He wondered . . . but now his body was drawing his attention again. Hot and cold, hungry and thirsty.

It bothered him.

EIGHT

'**KILL** IT! KILL me!'

It was muffled, but you could still hear it. They'd closed the air-conditioning vents – wasn't like there was air-conditioning any more – but still the desperate wail came up from the basement.

Howard was out at some kind of stupid meeting. Some big deal. Howard always had big deals.

Charles Merriman, who everyone called Orc, rummaged in the mess beside his couch. There had to be something left in one of these bottles. He didn't want to have to go into the back room closet and get another bottle.

'It's the only way. Sam! Sam! Tell Sam to do it!'

Orc wasn't drunk. Not drunk enough to ignore the sound of that stupid girl's voice. That took a pretty good drunk and right now he was only drunk enough that he didn't want to get up off the couch.

His stony fingers lifted a bottle. Wild Turkey. Only about

half an inch of brown liquid left in the bottom. He twisted the cork. The glass neck of the bottle shattered in his grip. That happened fairly often. Orc had a hard time gauging his strength when he was a little drunk.

He blew slivers of glass away. He raised the bottle high, careful to keep the sharp points away from his still-human mouth.

The one part of him that could be cut: his mouth.

Well, his mouth and his eyes.

He drained the fiery liquid into his mouth and swallowed. Oh, yeah. Yeah. But not enough.

Orc levered himself up. He was heavy, like you'd expect of a boy made of wet gravel. Like a walking creature of wet cement. He couldn't fit on a scale although Howard had tried once to weigh him.

He had crushed the scales.

He stomped towards the booze closet where Howard kept his stash. With the exaggerated care of a person not in control of his body, Orc opened the closet door.

A few bottles of clear booze. A few bottles of brown booze. A couple bottles of Cabka, the liquor Howard made by distilling cabbage and rotten oranges. It was nasty stuff. Orc preferred the brown booze.

He snagged a bottle and after a few seconds of clumsy fumbling he gave up and twisted the glass neck off.

'Is that you up there, Orc? I hear you stomping around.' Drake. The girl Brittney was gone now, replaced by Drake.

'You still alive, you stupid, alcoholic pile of rock?' Drake taunted. 'Still following Sam's orders? Doing what you're told, Orc?'

Orc stomped angrily on the floor. 'Shut up or I'll come down there and smash you like a bug!' Orc roared.

Drake laughed. 'Sure you will, Orc. You don't have the stones. Wait, that was a funny! The stone monster who doesn't have any stones.'

Orc stomped again. The entire house shook when he did it.

Drake called him various names, but now Orc had about a quarter of the bottle inside him. The warmth spread throughout his body.

He yelled something equally rude back at Drake. Then he staggered back to his couch and sagged heavily into it.

He didn't mind Drake so much. Drake was a creep.

It was the girl who made Orc want to cry.

She was a monster. Like Orc. Begging for death. Begging for someone to let her go to her Jesus.

Kill me, kill me, kill me, she begged every day and every night.

Orc took a deep swig.

Tears seeped from his human eyes and fell into the rocky crevices of his face.

Someone was knocking at the front door. Normally Howard

would answer. But then Orc heard Jamal's voice yelling, 'Hey, Orc! Open up, man.'

Jamal was one of the very few people besides Howard who ever came to see Orc. Of course it was just so he could get a drink. But still, any company was better than listening to Drake or Brittney. Orc opened the door.

'Want a drink, Jamal?'

'You know it,' Jamal said. 'Albert's busting on me all day.'

'Yeah,' Orc said. He didn't care. He snagged a bottle and handed it to Jamal, who took a deep swig.

Orc flopped on to his mattresses, the floor groaning beneath him. Jamal took a chair and kept the bottle.

'Who is that up there?' Drake's voice floated up. 'Is that Jamal or Turk? Too heavy to be Howard.'

'It's Jamal,' Jamal yelled.

'Don't talk to him,' Orc said, but without much conviction.

'Hey, Jamal, how about letting me out of here?' Drake asked, almost playful.

Orc yelled something obscene back at him.

'Only if you kill Albert first,' Jamal shouted, then laughed and took another drink.

'How come you work for Albert if you hate him?' Orc asked.

Jamal shrugged. 'I'm tough, he needs someone tough.'

'Yeah,' Orc said.

'But he treats me like crap.'

'Yeah?'

'Should see how he's living, man. You think he's living like the rest of us? Get this: at night he doesn't even go out to take a leak. He's got, like, a jar he pees in.'

'I got a jar I pee in.'

'Yeah, well, he's got a maid to take it out and dump it for him.'

Orc's head was buzzing, not really paying attention, but Jamal was getting fired up, listing complaints about Albert, starting with the fact that Albert had meat every day and kids to clean up after him.

'See, man, he loves it like this, right?' Jamal said, already slurring his words. 'Back in the world Albert was just some shrimpy little nothing. In here he's a big man and I'm, like, his, you know . . .'

'Servant,' Orc supplied.

Jamal's eyes flared angrily. 'Yeah. Yeah. Like you, Orc, you're Sam's servant.'

'I ain't anyone's servant.'

'You're babysitting Drake all day and night, man, what is it you think you are? You're doing what the Sam Boss tells you.'

Orc didn't have a ready answer. He wished Howard was home because Howard was smarter at talking.

Jamal pushed it. 'Guys like you and me and Turk and Drake, right? We used to be in charge. Because we were tough and we weren't afraid and didn't take anyone's crap, right?'

Orc shrugged. He was feeling very uncomfortable. 'Where's Howard?' he muttered.

Jamal made a rude noise. 'Howard's not the one stuck being a jailer, you are, Orc. Sam's prison guard. Keeps you busy, right, and trapped here all the time. So it's like Turk said.'

'What'd Turk say?'

'Said Sam got you and Drake locked up at the same time.'

'It's not like that.'

Jamal laughed derisively. 'Man, all you have to do is see who is top dog and who is bottom dog. See, that's where Zil was wrong: it's not about moofs and normals, freaks and non-freaks, it's about top dog, bottom dog. You and me, Orc, we're bottom dogs. Should be top dogs.'

Just then Brittney's voice came up from below. 'Is Sam there? Get Sam! You have to call Sam!'

Orc levered himself up off his bed and yelled, 'Hey, shut up. I already gotta listen to Drake all day and night.'

He swayed, tried to catch himself and couldn't. He slipped and fell back on his rear. Jamal exploded in derisive laughter.

This time Orc leaped to his feet. 'Stop laughing!'

'Orc, get Sam!'

'It was funny, man,' Jamal said through his own braying laughter.

'Orc, Drake is trying –'

Orc cursed loudly. He stomped on the floor. 'Shut up, shut up!'

And suddenly, with a rending, ripping sound, the floor beneath Orc gave way.

He fell through wood and plaster. He landed hard and lay flat on his back, winded. Splinters and dust settled on him.

He blinked, too stunned to make sense of what had just happened. His first thought was that Howard would be pissed. His second thought was that Sam would be even more pissed.

Brittney was standing over him, looking down at him.

Flat on his back. Drunk and foolish. A monster. And from above came Jamal's donkey laughter.

Orc reached to touch the skin that still stretched over a part of his face. He was bleeding. Not bad, not a lot, but bleeding.

In blind rage Orc got to his feet. He punched Brittney with all his strength. The girl went flying into the wall. Her head snapped against cinderblock, a hit that would have killed any real, living girl.

But Brittney couldn't die.

Which was the final straw. Something in Orc's brain snapped. He leaped, trying to grab the floor above and pull himself through, but he slipped and fell again and Jamal was pointing and laughing and Orc ran for the door, the barricaded door that had kept the Drake/Brittney thing locked up. He body-slammed the door. It held, but barely. He reared back and kicked and kicked and splinters flew.

'No! No!' Brittney screamed. 'He'll escape!'

Orc stepped back, raised both his gravel-skinned arms and ran straight at the door.

It didn't fly open, it simply came apart. The frame shattered and splintered. The door itself split. And Orc tore through.

'Want to laugh at me?' he roared as he pounded up the stairs and emerged in the kitchen.

Jamal was still standing next to the hole, laughing.

'You wanna laugh?' Orc roared.

Jamal spun around, realising too late the danger he was in. Orc was over six feet tall and almost as wide as he was tall. His legs were like tree trunks, his arms like bridge cable.

Jamal fumbled for his gun, but Orc wasn't having any of that. He grabbed Jamal by the neck, lifted him off the floor, and threw him down the hole.

Jamal hit hard. The gun flew, scraping across the floor.

Orc was panting, sweating, heart pounding in his chest. Now reality was starting to penetrate the alcohol-fueled rage and he saw what he had done.

Howard. He should . . . Or Sam . . . Someone, he should tell someone, get someone . . .

It was all over now for Charles Merriman. He had redeemed himself; he had been given something important to do. But now all that was gone. And he was just Orc again.

He wanted to cry. He couldn't face it. He couldn't face Howard's disappointment and pity. Sam's cold anger.

Down in the dark basement a long, reddish tentacle reached for the gun.

Orc turned and ran.

Sanjit Brattle-Chance had not enjoyed his first week in Perdido Beach. Virtue Brattle-Chance had enjoyed it even less.

'It's like a giant lunatic asylum,' Virtue said.

'Yeah. It is, kind of,' Sanjit said. They had spent the afternoon inspecting the helicopter. Edilio had assigned them the job of reporting back on whether it was totally broken or just mostly broken.

So far it was looking totally broken. Both skids – the ski-like things it landed on – were crumpled. Part of the glass bubble canopy was shattered, just gone, and the rest of it was starred and cracked.

Night had fallen and that was the end of inspecting anything. Virtue had wanted to go straight home. Sanjit had stalled.

'Let's just hang out and talk, Choo,' Sanjit said. 'I mean, look, we've had all this stress, right? But now Bowie's getting well –'

Virtue made a rude noise. 'If you believe that so-called Healer.'

'I believe her completely,' Sanjit said.

The girl named Lana had come and laid her hand on Bowie. She'd barely spoken, had replied to polite inquiries with single-syllable answers or grunts. Or annoyed silence.

But Sanjit had been fascinated. He'd thought about little else ever since. After all, how could he not be attracted to a girl who could heal with a touch and yet walked around with a massive automatic pistol stuck in her belt?

His kind of girl.

He had learned that she lived up here at Clifftop. In fact, Edilio had carefully and repeatedly warned Sanjit not to irritate her while he was checking out the helicopter.

His exact words had been, 'For God's sake, don't get in Lana's way.'

To which Sanjit had said, 'Is she dangerous?'

Edilio had given him a strange look. 'Well, she shot me once. But it was under the influence of the Darkness. Which she had tried to kill all by herself with a truckload of gas. And then she healed me. So I don't know if that makes her dangerous. But if it was me, I would definitely not make her mad.'

So Sanjit and Virtue sat on the grass and watched the sun go down and the stars appear. And Sanjit secretly watched the hotel.

'Did you hear about the talking coyotes?' Virtue demanded.

Like if there were such a thing, it was Sanjit's fault.

'Yeah. Creepy, huh?'

'And the thing they call the Darkness?' Virtue shook his head dolefully. He'd always been gloomy. The cloud to Sanjit's sunshine, the pessimist to Sanjit's optimist. They were adopted brothers, from Congo and Thailand, respectively. From a desperate refugee camp, and from the tough streets of Bangkok.

'Yeah. I wonder what it is?'

'The gaiaphage. That's the other word they use. "Gaia," as in world. "Phage," as in a worm or something that eats something up. I'm going to go way out on a limb here and say I don't think something that calls itself a "world eater" is a good thing.'

'No?' Sanjit made an innocent face, deliberately provoking his brother.

'Fine.' Virtue pouted. 'But have you seen the graveyard they put in the plaza? There's, like, two dozen graves there.'

Sanjit twisted around to look back at the helicopter. It had saved them. It seemed a shame just to let it lie there, dead. 'I'd need some big wrenches. A ladder. Hammer. And then, you know, someone who actually knew what to do with all of it.'

'Fine, you don't really want to talk.'

They had landed the helicopter – well, crashed it, anyway – behind Clifftop hotel. In some scruffy trees and bushes just past the parking area.

The barrier was close at hand. So even if the helicopter could ever be flown – and Sanjit couldn't imagine what the point would be – it would take a lot of luck not just to fly it straight into the barrier.

The barrier was a trickster. At ground level it was opaque, while suggesting translucence.

Higher up it was sky. But when you were up there it wasn't like you could see beyond the barrier. If you tried, the barrier was just opaque again.

Tricky tricky. Like a street magician's sleight of hand, Sanjit thought.

He realised Virtue was talking again.

'. . . once Bowie's completely better. Maybe Caine isn't totally unreasonable. I mean, he was starving before and that would make anyone unreasonable.'

'Choo,' Sanjit said. 'Caine is pure, distilled essence of evil. What are you even talking about?'

'OK, even if he's evil, maybe we can work out some kind of deal.'

'You don't even believe that,' Sanjit said.

Virtue slumped back, deflated. 'Yeah.'

'We are not going back to the island, my brother. We've been voted off. This is our home now.'

Virtue nodded. He looked like a kid who had just gotten the news that he would be shot at dawn.

'Cheer up, Choo,' Sanjit said. 'There are a lot of good things about this place.'

'You heard about the zombie, right? The one they've got locked in a basement? Half the time it's this nice Christian girl. And the rest of the time it's a psychopath with a whip for an arm?'

Sanjit made a thoughtful face. 'I do believe I heard something about that. But really, Choo, it's not like a basement-dwelling Dr Jekyll and Mr Hyde zombie is all that unusual.'

Despite himself Virtue very nearly smiled. 'Fine. Be that way.'

'You're not looking at the bright side, Choo,' Sanjit said. He had in fact just spotted the bright side.

'Bright side? There's no bright side. What bright side?'

'Girls, Choo,' Sanjit said, smiling hugely. 'You'll understand in a few years.'

Lana had come around the back of the hotel and was throwing a tennis ball to her dog. They were outlined against the faint glow of western horizon, and illuminated by the light of the moon just coming from behind the hills.

'I'm going to refuse to do puberty,' Virtue grumbled. 'It makes you stupid.'

Sanjit barely heard him. He was walking towards Lana.

'Hi.'

'What are you doing here?' Lana snapped. 'No one comes to Clifftop without me saying so.'

Sanjit said, 'You missed a beautiful sunset.'

'It's an illusion,' Lana said. 'It's not the real sun. None of it's real. The moon, the stars, all of it.'

'Still beautiful, though.'

'Fake.'

'But beautiful.'

Lana glared at him. And Sanjit had to admit: the girl could glare. The pistol in her waistband definitely added to the tough-girl look. But more it was that hurt-but-defiant expression.

'So asking you to take a moonlit walk with me, that would totally not work?'

'What?' Again that glare. 'Go away. Stop being an idiot. I don't even know you.'

'You're healing my little brother Bowie.'

'Yeah, that doesn't make us friends, kid.'

'So no moonlight.'

'Are you retarded?'

'Sunrise? I could get up early.'

'Go away.'

'Sunset tomorrow?'

'Just what is your problem, kid? Do you know who I am? No one messes with me.'

'Do you know my name?'

'Which part of "go away" do you not get? I could shoot you and no one would even say anything.'

'It's Sanjit. It's a Hindu name.'

'One word to Orc and he'd play basketball with your head.'

'It means "invincible".'

'That's great,' Lana said.

'Invincible. I can't be vinced.'

'That's not even a word,' Lana said. Then she ground her teeth, obviously annoyed with herself for having been baited.

'Go ahead: try to vince me,' Sanjit said.

Just then Patrick came rushing over. He dropped the ball at Sanjit's feet, grinned his delirious dog grin, and waited.

'Don't play with my dog,' Lana said.

Sanjit snatched up the ball and threw it. Patrick went tearing after it.

'You don't scare me,' Sanjit said. He held up a hand, cutting Lana off before she could answer. 'I'm not saying I shouldn't be scared. I've heard some of the stories about you. About what happened. You went up against this gaiaphage thing all by yourself. Which means you are the second bravest girl I ever met. So I probably should be scared. I'm just not.'

He watched her struggle to resist asking. She lost. 'Second bravest?'

'I'll tell you the story when we go for that walk,' Sanjit said. He jerked a thumb towards the helicopter. 'I better get back to town. Edilio wants a report from me.'

He turned and walked away.

NINE

54 HOURS **9** MINUTES

SAM FOUND HIS little crew where they were supposed to be.

Dekka was almost smiling. Almost smiling was giddy for Dekka.

Taylor was checking her fingernails, being elaborately bored. Sam wondered if he should say something about the kiss. Something like, 'I'm really sorry I groped you.'

Yeah: that would be really helpful.

Better to pretend it all never happened. Unfortunately Taylor was not known for letting things just drop.

Furthermore, she irritated Dekka. Dekka was Sam's friend and his ally. The three people Sam knew he could always count on were Edilio, Brianna and Dekka. Strange, because it wasn't like they hung out together. Sam spent his time alone or with Astrid. He barely saw Edilio lately. He had nothing at all in common with Brianna – she was too young, too crazy, too . . . too Brianna to be someone Sam would hang with.

Quinn had been his best friend back before. But Quinn had

a big job, a job he loved. Quinn's friends were all his fishing crews. They were as tight as a very close family, the fishermen.

The fourth member of the expedition was Jack. Formerly Computer Jack – there were no longer any functioning computers around. Jack was wasting his days reading comic books and pouting.

Jack's superhuman strength might come in handy, but Jack had never been much use. Although, Sam noted thoughtfully, Jack had stepped up during the big fire. Maybe he was growing up a bit. Maybe getting his head out of a computer was actually a good thing.

'You guys up for this?' Sam asked.

'Do I have to go?' Jack whined.

Sam shrugged. 'Albert's paying you, right? It's better than playing strong man for him all day, isn't it?'

Jack's eyes flashed. Albert had started using Jack's physical strength – to carry loads to the market, to move furniture – and Jack resented it. In Jack's mind he was still the tech genius, the supergeek, not the freak strong man.

'Why do we have to do this in the middle of the night?' Taylor asked.

'Because we don't want the whole town knowing why we're going and where we're going.'

'How can I tell anyone if I don't even know myself?' Taylor stuck out her lower lip.

'Water. We're going to look for water,' Sam said.

He could almost hear the wheels in Taylor's head spinning. Then, 'OMG, we're out of water?' She bit her lip, took a couple of dramatic breaths, and wailed, 'Do you mean we're all going to die?'

'That would be a pretty good example of why we're keeping this secret,' Sam said dryly.

'I just need to go –'

'Uh-uh!' Sam said. 'No you don't, Taylor. You don't bounce anywhere or talk to anyone without me agreeing. Are we clear?'

'You know, Sam, you're nice. And very hot,' Taylor said. 'But you're not really much fun.'

'Let's get out of here while we can,' Dekka said. 'I brought a gun, by the way.'

'Are we going to be in danger?' Taylor cried.

'The gun's in case you get on my nerves, Taylor,' Dekka warned.

'Oh, so funny,' Taylor said.

Sam grinned. For the first time in a while he was actually looking forward to something. A mission. And at least a temporary escape from Perdido Beach.

'Dekka's right. Let's get out of here before something happens I have to deal with,' Sam said.

Just at that moment he heard a sound like something large

breaking. It was some distance away. A noise like twigs snapping. Probably some drunk idiot.

Sam chose to ignore it. Edilio's worry, not his.

He headed towards the dark hills above town.

After a while Dekka took Sam's arm and slowed him down. She let Jack and Taylor move out in front.

'Did Edilio or Astrid tell you?'

'I haven't talked to Edilio. I steered clear. He's going to be mightily annoyed with me when he realises I skipped town and didn't even tell him.'

Dekka waited.

'OK,' Sam said with a sigh. 'Tell me what?'

'It's Hunter. He's got some kind of . . . Well, it's like these bugs all inside him. Astrid says they're parasites.'

'Astrid says?' Sam snapped.

'So I guess you did see her before you left. And she didn't tell you?'

'We had other things going on.'

'Oh?'

'No,' Sam said. 'Not like that. Unfortunately. Tell me about Hunter.'

Dekka told him.

Sam's face grew darker as he listened. So much for getting out of town before anything went wrong. This had 'wrong' written all over it.

It sounded as if Hunter wasn't going to be hunting much longer. Which meant the town would be running out of meat as well as water. They could probably survive without Hunter's kills, but it sure would increase the sense of panic.

This mission had just gotten more important, not less.

'He said the greenies are on the morning side? Off the lake road? That's what he said?'

Dekka nodded.

Sam called up to the other two who were arguing over something stupid. 'Taylor! Jack! Veer right up there. We're stopping off to see Hunter.'

Hunter woke suddenly. A noise.

It was a noise unlike anything he'd ever heard before. Close! Very close.

Like it was on him. Like it was . . .

Just in one ear.

He twisted his head. It was full night. Black as black in the woods far from the starlight.

He couldn't see anything.

But with his hands he could feel. The thing on his shoulder.

His ear . . . gone!

A terrible fear wrung a cry of horror from Hunter.

He couldn't feel it, his ear, or his shoulder, couldn't feel with anything but his fingers and he felt, reached beneath

103

his shirt, felt the flesh of his belly pulse and heave.

Like something inside him.

No, no, no, it wasn't fair. It wasn't fair!

He was Hunter. The hunter. He was doing his best.

He cried. Tears rolled down his cheeks.

Who would bring meat for all the kids?

It wasn't fair.

The sound of munching, crunching started again. Just in one ear.

Hunter had only one weapon: the heat-causing power in his hands. He had used it many, many times to take the life of prey.

He had fed the kids with that power. And in a moment of fear and rage he had accidentally taken the life of his friend, Harry.

Maybe he could kill the thing that was eating his ear.

But it was too late for that to help.

Could he kill himself?

He saw Old Lion's head, eyes closed, hanging where he'd hung him for skinning. If Old Lion could die, so could Hunter.

Maybe they would meet again, up in the sky.

Hunter pressed both palms against his head.

Drake was free! Before him the shattered door. Above him a collapsed ceiling. His jail cell had been torn apart by his own jailer.

Now Drake was worried. At any minute the Brittney Pig might emerge. She could call for help, run to Sam, something, anything.

Drake had Jamal's gun. He ran his whip hand over it, loving the feel of it, loving the weight of it in his hand. With this gun and his whip he was unstoppable.

Except that he wasn't just himself, he was Brittney, too.

His mind raced feverishly. What could he do?

Jamal groaned. He started to get up but leaned on an arm that gave way with a sickening crunch.

Jamal shrieked in pain. His left arm hung limp, the shoulder dislocated. There was blood running freely from his nose. Blood seeping out of his ears. Oh yeah, Drake thought, the boy had taken a hard fall.

Drake straddled Jamal. He wrapped his whip arm around Jamal's throat, cutting off his cries of pain. He pressed the gun barrel against Jamal's forehead.

'You have three seconds to make a decision,' Drake said, his voice silky. 'Are you with me or against me?'

It didn't take Jamal three seconds. 'I'll help you, I'll help you!' he blurted as soon as Drake relaxed the pressure on his throat.

'Yeah? Well, listen good, jerkwad, because I don't give second chances. Mess with me, disobey me, even hesitate, and I won't kill you.'

Jamal's brow creased in confusion.

'No, see, death, that's the end of pain,' Drake said. 'No, no killing. But I will whip you.'

With sudden gleeful ferocity Drake reared back and struck with his whip hand. It cut through Jamal's pants and cut a stripe on his thigh.

Jamal bellowed.

Drake struck again, twice more while Jamal writhed and tried to cover himself with his one good arm.

'I wanted you to know what it will feel like,' Drake said. 'Hurts, doesn't it?'

Jamal was crying now, crying and too terrified to answer.

'I said: it hurts, doesn't it?'

'Yes! Yes!' Jamal sobbed.

'No matter what you do, Jamal, no matter how smart or how tough you think you are, if you betray me, if you even look like you might betray me, I'll whip you. And I'll make it last. For hours. And I'll leave you where the Healer can't find you. Do you believe I'll do that, Jamal?'

Jamal nodded frantically. 'Yes! I believe it!'

'I can't be killed, Jamal,' Drake said.

'I know!'

Drake handed him the gun. He watched closely to see whether Jamal truly did understand. He could see the moment when Jamal thought, 'I can shoot him and run away.'

But he also saw the wheels spin in Jamal's head as the boy worked it through to the inevitable conclusion.

He saw Jamal's resistance evaporate.

'Smart boy,' Drake said. 'Now, here's what you do.'

TEN

'**WHY** DID WE have to sneak out of town in the night-time?' Jack grumbled. 'I'm tripping over everything.'

Jack, Sam, Dekka and Taylor were across the highway, past the gas station, and climbing uphill. Moonlight touched the tall, dry grass with silver. But it didn't reveal the smaller rocks that poked up through the dust-dry ground and stubbed toes or tripped you so you landed on your hands and knees and looked like an idiot.

Jack was not interested in going on some long, dangerous walk. Especially at night. Or in the daytime, for that matter. What he wanted to do was just lie in his bed. Just lie in his bed and read.

He had a pile of books. They were the only thing to do. No internet. No computers. Not even electricity.

Of course that was his fault. His fault for being tricked by Caine and especially that witch, Diana.

He had a hard time saying no to girls. Especially Brianna, who seemed to be able to get him to do anything she wanted.

Brianna kind of lived with him. They were kind of going together, he guessed. Although they didn't actually do anything. Like make out or anything. That didn't happen.

Jack had thought seriously about asking Brianna if she would make out with him. She was cute. He liked her. He guessed she liked him. They had taken care of each other when the flu was going around.

But . . . It occurred to Jack that Sam had not answered.

'Why are we sneaking out in the night?' Jack repeated.

'I already explained,' Sam snapped. 'If you don't listen –'

Taylor jumped in to say, 'Because otherwise Astrid would find some way to stop him.' She mimicked Astrid's voice, injecting it with steel and a tense, condescending tone. 'Sam. I am the smartest, hottest girl in the world. So do what I tell you. Good boy. Down, boy. Down!'

Sam remained silent, walking steadily just a few feet ahead.

Taylor continued, 'Oh, Sam, if only you could be as smart plus as totally goody-goody as I am. If only you could realise that you will never be good enough to have me, me, wonderful me, Astrid the Blonde Genius.'

'Sam, can I shoot her now?' Dekka asked. 'Or is it too soon?'

'Wait until we're over the ridge,' Sam said. 'It'll muffle the sound.'

'Sorry, Dekka,' Taylor said. 'I know you don't like talking about boy–girl things.'

'Taylor,' Sam warned.

'Yes, Sam?'

'You might want to think about how hard it would be to walk if someone were to turn off gravity under your feet every now and then.'

'I wonder who would do that?' Dekka said.

Suddenly Taylor fell flat on her face.

'You tripped me!' Taylor said, more shocked than angry.

'Me?' Dekka spread her hands in a completely unconvincing gesture of innocence. 'Hey, I'm all the way over here.'

'I'm just saying: you can see where that could make a long walk just a lot longer,' Sam said.

'You guys are so not fun,' Taylor grumped. She bounced instantaneously to just behind Sam. She grabbed his butt, he yelled, 'Hey!' and she bounced away innocently.

'To answer your question, Jack,' Sam said, 'we are sneaking out at night so that everyone doesn't know we're gone and why. They'll figure it out soon enough, but Edilio will have to have more of his guys on the streets if I'm not there playing the big, bad wolf. More stress for everyone.'

'Oh,' Jack said.

'The big, bad wolf,' Taylor said. She laughed. 'So, when you play that fantasy in your head is Astrid Little Red Riding Hood or one of the Three Little Pigs?'

'Dekka,' Sam said.

'Hah! Too slow!' Taylor said. She was suddenly twenty feet away and behind Dekka.

They had reached the ridge. The trees started in the valley beyond and spread up the next hill. The small valley tended to capture damp breezes off the ocean – back when there were breezes. And a small stream – now almost dry since it was cut off from the high, snow-capped peaks beyond the barrier – ran along the floor of the valley.

'Try not to make too much noise, huh, guys? Hunter may be out hunting. We don't want to stomp around and scare off his prey.'

'So no more falling on your face, Jack,' Taylor teased.

A sound, a wail, rose from the trees downhill.

'What was that?' Jack asked.

It came again. A cry of utter despair.

Jack expected Sam to take off running. Instead he took a deep breath and in a low voice said, 'I don't think you guys need to see this.'

'See what?' Taylor asked.

Sam set off downhill. He didn't ask them to come with him. But he didn't order them not to. So they followed.

Once in the pitch-blackness under the trees Sam used his powers to turn one hand into a sort of dull, glowing green light. It made it easier to see the trees, but it turned everything into a nightmare scene.

'Hunter?' Sam called out.

'Don't come here!' Hunter's voice, wracked with sadness, was closer than Jack expected.

They followed the sound of his voice. Closer, and now they could hear him crying. It wasn't a big kid's cry, it was like a toddler's. Big, heaving sobs.

Again Sam said, 'Guys, stay back. You don't have to see this.'

But again they ignored him. Not Jack at first but Dekka, who went because she was brave and wanted to help, even though she guessed what she would find; Taylor because she was curious and wanted to see; Jack because he didn't want to be left behind alone in total darkness.

Hunter was sitting up. He was in the middle of a neat camp: glowing embers from a dying fire, a small tent, a makeshift shelf of sticks and vines where Hunter had a pan and a pot and a plate. A mountain lion hung from a rope looped over a high branch.

Hunter's entire body writhed and squirmed.

The side of his head was partly gone. A creature, like some monstrous melding of insect and eel, protruded from Hunter's shoulder and as they stood there rooted in horror it took a vicious bite of Hunter's flesh.

Dekka's face was grim, her eyes wet.

'I tried . . .' Hunter said. He held up his hands, mimicked pressing them against his head. 'It didn't work.'

'I can do it,' Sam said softly.

'I'm scared,' Hunter said.

'I know.'

'It's 'cause I killed Harry. God has to punish me. I tried to be good but I'm bad.'

'No, Hunter,' Sam said gently. 'You paid your dues. You fed the kids. You're a good guy.'

'I'm a good hunter.'

'The best.'

'I don't know what's happening. What's happening, Sam?'

'It's just the FAYZ, Hunter,' Sam said.

'Can the angels find me here so I can go to heaven?'

Sam didn't answer. It was Dekka who spoke. 'Do you still remember any prayers, Hunter?'

The insect-like creature was almost completely emerged from Hunter's shoulder. Legs were becoming visible. It had wings folded against its body. It looked like a gigantic ant, or wasp, but silver and brass and covered with a sheen of slime.

It was emerging like a chicken breaking out of an egg. Being born. And as the creature was born, it fed on Hunter's numbed body.

Jerky movements beneath Hunter's shirt testified to more of the larvae emerging.

Taylor whimpered, fear etched on her face.

'Do you remember "now I lay me down to sleep"?' Dekka asked.

'Now I lay me down to sleep,' Hunter said. 'I pray the Lord my soul to keep.'

Sam raised his hands, palms out.

'If I should die –'

Twin beams of light hit Hunter's chest and face. His shirt caught fire. Flesh melted. He was dead before he could feel anything.

Sam played the light up and down Hunter's body. The smell was sickening. Jack wanted to look away, but how could he?

Sudden darkness as Sam terminated the light.

Sam lowered his hands to his side.

They stood there in the darkness. Jack breathed through his mouth, trying not to smell the burned flesh.

Then they heard a sound. Many sounds.

Sam raised his hands and pale light glowed.

Hunter was all but gone.

The things that had been inside him were still there.

His knock at her door was soft. Diana almost didn't hear it.

She took a shaky breath. He had come. She'd figured he would.

'Who is it?' Diana asked.

'Sam,' Caine said.

Diana opened the door. He was leaning against the frame. His body language and expression were not those of someone who was happy.

'Funny,' Diana said.

Caine pushed past her into the room. 'Close the door and lock it,' Caine ordered. 'Bug: if you're in here and I catch you I will kill you. You have till I count to ten to get out.'

Caine and Diana both waited and watched the door. It did not open.

'I don't think he's here,' Diana said. 'I can usually smell him.'

They stood awkwardly apart. Like strangers. Diana noticed that Caine had bathed and combed his hair. He was usually as well put-together as circumstances would allow. But this was a special effort.

Diana had decided against any special outfit. It wasn't about lingerie or whatever. She was dressed in jeans and a blouse. Barefoot. She had avoided make-up.

'You want me to be Sam,' Caine said. 'I'm not Sam. I'm me.'

'I don't want you to be Sam,' Diana said.

'You don't want me to be me,' Caine said.

Diana considered him. Handsome, no question. Cruel. Intelligent.

'There's more than one you, Caine,' Diana said.

He blinked. 'What's that mean?'

'You're not Drake.'

Caine waved off the suggestion and his face registered disgust. 'Drake's a sick creep. I just do what I have to do. I don't get off on it. He's a psycho. I'm . . .' He searched for the right word. '. . . ambitious.'

Diana laughed. Not a derisive laugh, a genuine laugh of astonishment.

'What? I *am* ambitious,' Caine said.

'That's one word for it,' Diana said. 'Power hungry. Domineering. A bully.'

'I'm not good at taking orders,' Caine said.

Diana grinned. 'No. You're not.'

They both fell silent. Diana looked at him. He looked down at the floor.

'But you did take orders. From the Darkness, Caine.'

Caine flushed angrily. He turned away. He walked quickly back to the door. But he stopped before touching the handle.

'The lights are off in Perdido Beach because you took orders,' Diana said.

'Who was it that buried that thing in its mineshaft?' Caine demanded, his voice ragged.

'You.'

'Yeah,' Caine said. 'And saved Sam in the process.'

'Yes. And soon after that we became cannibals.'

'We have food now,' Caine said. 'Lots of food.'

He walked back to Diana, reached to touch her, but this time she walked away. She stood at the window. The false moon was setting. It dabbed the distant hilltops with silver.

'It was too much,' Diana said, almost to herself. 'Everything else I could kind of accept. The violence. The battles. What we did to Andrew and what you did to Chunk. And all the rest. I mean, it all sort of left a bruise on me, you know?'

Caine did not answer.

'Inside. In my heart. In my soul.' She laughed at herself. 'Diana Ladris's soul. Right.'

'It was a low point,' Caine admitted.

'You think?' Diana snapped, looking over her shoulder at him with a trace of her usual mockery. 'Eating human flesh, that was a low point?'

'We had no –'

'Oh, shut up,' Diana said. She turned away from the window. There were tears in her eyes and she hadn't wanted him to see. The last thing she wanted was to seem weak.

But he did see now. The shock on his face almost made her laugh again.

'All my life I've been a tough girl,' Diana said. 'I was cool with that. People would say, *Diana's a bitch. Diana's a slut. Diana's mean.* All that I could deal with because I guess it was basically true. Now they're going to look at me and say, *Diana's a cannibal?* How do I live with that?' She was shouting suddenly.

'Who are these people you're worried about? Penny? Bug?'

'What if we get out? People! People!' She hesitated. 'And

God.' She lowered her voice to a whisper. 'And my kids. Someday.'

'Kids?' Caine's look of confusion and consternation finally did force a laugh from Diana.

'Yes. Someday. Could happen. That's right: the day may come when I have a baby. Maybe even more than one.'

Caine said, 'Um . . .' He made a vague gesture with his hands. He made several attempts to say something. None were successful.

'Do you love me?' Diana asked.

Caine's eyes widened. She could actually see him twitch. Like a startled animal. Like a rabbit who had just heard a fox.

'It's a yes or no question,' Diana said acidly. 'But I'll accept a nod or a shake of the head or an incoherent grunt.'

'I . . . I don't know what you mean by that,' Caine said lamely.

'When I jumped off the cliff, you saved me even though it meant letting Sanjit and the others escape.'

'You didn't give me much choice,' Caine said peevishly.

'You had a choice. You wanted to destroy them.'

'OK.'

'Why did you make that choice?'

Caine swallowed and seemed to find his palms sweaty since he rubbed them on his sides.

Diana walked to the door. She unlocked it and held it

open. 'Go away,' she said. 'Come back when you figure out your answer.'

'But . . .'

'Yeah: not happening. Not tonight.'

Caine escaped into the hallway.

Diana undressed and crawled under the sheets. Then she beat the pillows with her fists until feathers flew.

ELEVEN

50 HOURS 21 MINUTES

'EDILIO. WAKE UP!'

Edilio blinked. Rubbed his eyes. Saw Brianna standing there next to his bed.

'What?' he mumbled.

'Albert told me to get you,' Brianna said.

Brianna always looked determined, pugnacious, and tough. Just sitting around, she looked all of those things. But now she was armed for battle.

She had a small runner's backpack converted to a sort of holster. She'd cut a hole in the bottom so the barrel of a sawed-off shotgun could stick through. The stock was just where she could reach over her shoulder and grab it.

She had a long knife, a bowie knife, in a scabbard hanging from a camouflage belt. The scabbard was tied to her leg so it wouldn't flap when she ran. A dozen red plastic shotgun shells rode snugly in slots on the belt.

A summons in the middle of the night was bad. A

summons in the middle of the night from a heavily armed Brianna was worse.

Much worse.

'What happened?'

'Drake,' Brianna said. Then she grinned. Because that was Brianna.

Edilio sat up. 'OK. You got Sam?'

'Can't find Sam,' Brianna said.

Edilio felt an overpowering desire to go back to sleep. Drake on the loose? And no Sam? 'Where's Albert?'

'He said he'd meet you at town hall,' Brianna said. 'He's rounding up the others. The council.' She said that last word with a sneer.

Edilio stabbed a finger at her. 'You do not go after Drake on your own.'

'Yeah? Who else you got?' Brianna said.

Edilio didn't have a good answer to that. 'Get Dekka. And get Astrid. I don't care if you have to drag her by her hair, you get Astrid to town hall.'

Brianna was way too happy at that prospect. She spun, blurred, and was gone.

Edilio dressed quickly, grabbed his weapons, and ran the few blocks to town hall, hoping he could make it that far without running into Drake. He would fight if he had to, but it was hard to win a fight against someone who couldn't be killed.

He was the first to arrive at town hall. Albert was next, dressed in spotless business casual as always. Howard came in, looking shell-shocked.

'I can't find him. I can't find him.' Howard was weeping. 'I think he fell through the floor, I mean, you know how big Orc is. Then Drake, he busted out and . . . Orc's most likely drunk.'

'Most likely,' Edilio snapped. 'Since you make sure he stays that way, Howard.'

'We didn't ask to be running some prison for zombies,' Howard shot back.

'Where were you when this went down?' Edilio accused.

'I was . . . I had to see a dude.'

Delivering bottles of booze, Edilio knew. When would the alcohol supply run out? Everything else had run out. 'Have either of you seen Sam? Brianna can't find him.'

Albert sighed. 'He's out of town.'

Edilio felt the blood drain out of his face. 'He's what?'

Astrid arrived, coldly furious. 'I'm not on the council any more. You have no right –'

'Shut up, Astrid,' Edilio said.

Astrid, Albert, and Howard all stared. Edilio was as amazed as any of them. He considered apologising – he had never spoken to Astrid that way. He'd never spoken to anyone that way.

The truth was he was scared. Sam was out of town? With Drake running loose?

'What makes you think Sam is out of town?' Edilio asked Albert.

'I sent him,' Albert said. 'Him and Dekka. Taylor and Jack, too. They're looking for water.'

'They're what?'

'Looking for water.'

Edilio shot a glance at Astrid. She looked down. So: she knew it, too.

Edilio swallowed hard. He was finding it hard to breathe. And at the same time he was finding it hard not to scream at Albert and Astrid both. Both of them so smart, so superior. Dumping this on him now.

Howard said, 'Orc must have gone after Drake. Oh, man, I don't know if he can beat Drake, not like Drake is now. Oh, man.'

Edilio hoped Howard was right that Orc was chasing Drake. He hoped it mightily because the alternative was that he had not one but two monsters running around town. Mostly when Orc was drunk he just sat. But sometimes he got himself worked into an angry drunk, and then things got crazy.

Edilio glanced at the door. One or both could come busting in here at any second.

His gun was at his side. For all the good it would do.

'Brianna's looking for Drake,' Edilio said, thinking out loud.

'You sent her out against Drake?' Albert demanded.

'Sent her? Who sends Brianna out to get into a fight? She goes on her own. Anyway, it's not like you've left us with anyone else.'

Albert had the decency not to say anything to that.

'You know, you guys put me in charge. I didn't ask to be in charge. I didn't want to be in charge. Sam was in charge and all you guys ever did was give him grief,' Edilio said. 'You two, especially.' He pointed at Albert and Astrid. 'So, OK, Astrid takes over. And then Astrid finds out it's not so much fun being in charge. So it's like, OK, let's get the dumb wetback to do the job.'

'No one ever –' Astrid protested.

'And me, like a fool, I'm thinking, OK, that must mean people trust me. They asked me to be in charge, be the mayor. Come to find out, I'm not making decisions; Albert's making decisions. Albert's deciding we need to find more water and sending our two best fighters off into the countryside. Now I'm supposed to fix everything? It's like you go, "Fight a war," but you sent my army off on a wild goose chase.'

'The water situation's worse than you realise,' Albert said.

'Listen to yourself, man!' Edilio exploded. 'Why don't I know what the water situation is? Because you run all that and you don't tell me. You don't tell me what's going on and then you send Sam off on a nice walk. You know, Albert, you want so bad to be the big man, the Donald Trump of Perdido Beach, why don't you go deal with Drake? Why are you coming to me?'

He was starting to fantasise about using his gun on Albert when Taylor suddenly appeared in the room. Everyone jumped about six inches.

'Jeez, would you stop that?' Howard yelled. 'Give me a heart attack.'

'Hunter's dead,' Taylor said without preamble. 'It was these . . . these things. They came crawling up out of him and were eating him, oh God, I mean, it was like . . . I mean he was crying and Dekka prayed with him and he tried to fry his own brain just like he did with Harry only I guess it didn't work, I guess he couldn't do it, so Sam . . .' She swallowed. 'Anyone have some water?'

'What about Sam?' Astrid demanded.

'He did it for him. Sam. I mean, he . . . Hunter was, you know . . . so Sam.' She pantomimed raising her hands, like Sam, like he would do when using his power.

Astrid closed her eyes and crossed herself.

'Rest in peace,' Edilio said and crossed himself as well.

'Sam burned the boy?' Howard asked. Then, bitterly sarcastic said, 'Yeah, you all pray to Jesus. Because Jesus is really providing a lot of help here. Sounds to me like Sam was the one doing what had to be done.'

'Look, I need a glass of water or something,' Taylor pleaded. She sat down on the floor, leaned back against the wall, and started crying.

Edilio pulled open a drawer in the big desk. He had a water bottle, but just an inch was left in it. Reluctantly he handed it to Astrid, who passed it to Taylor.

Taylor drained the water. 'That's not all. Sam sent me to give you a message, Edilio. He said, "Tell Edilio I couldn't kill the bugs."'

'The things that came out of Hunter?' Howard asked.

Taylor closed her eyes. Tears squeezed out and rolled down her cheeks. 'Yes. The things that came out of Hunter. Sam shot them, you know, with his light. But they're like, reflective or whatever. Anyway, it didn't kill them.'

'Sam can burn through a brick wall,' Howard said. 'What kind of thing is it he can't kill?' Then he answered his own question. 'Something very nasty.'

'Taylor, bounce back and tell Sam to come back to town,' Albert said.

'I'm not going back there!' Taylor cried.

'Whoa,' Edilio said, holding up both hands. 'Hey, you don't decide this, Albert. You don't give orders. I'm the mayor, and there are four council members here. You, me, Ellen, and Howard.'

Albert looked like he might argue, but Astrid stepped in.

'Taylor, what did Sam say he was going to do next?'

'He said something about going to take out the cave where the greenies live. Where Hunter told them they are. That's why I'm not going back. You didn't see those things crawling out of Hunter, eating him alive.'

Suddenly Albert jerked. Like someone had stuck a pin in him. 'I forgot. I was busy . . . I was . . .' His eyes were fearful. 'Roscoe. Roscoe was bitten by one of those things in Hunter. He told me, I didn't think that . . .' He looked at Astrid. 'When Hunter was delivering his kills. Roscoe said something under Hunter's shirt bit him. I just forgot.'

From outside there came the sound of a bellowing, anguished roar. Then the sound of smashing glass.

'Orc,' Howard said.

'See if you can find him, talk to him,' Edilio said. But Howard was already on his way out the door.

No one spoke for a few minutes. They heard another smash, more like metal this time.

Edilio used the silence to think. Orc drunk and on a rampage. Well, it wasn't the first time, but it was bad. Orc had become an asset lately. If he was back to being a danger again then that was very bad news. More likely it was just temporary and Howard would get him under control.

The Roscoe thing was bad. Very bad. Edilio knew what he should do. And he didn't like it.

As for Drake, well, that was the real problem, that and the water.

Edilio had some help, some soldiers, some pretty good, some pretty useless. He had Brianna.

Could Brianna take on Drake?

'What will Drake do?' Edilio asked.

'He's not just Drake,' Astrid said. 'Remember, he's Brittney, too. That makes it hard for him. If he makes some plan, she can unmake it when she takes over. If he tries to sneak up on anyone, he has to worry that she'll emerge and screw it up.'

'Yeah,' Albert said, brightening. 'Yeah, that's right. It's not Drake, it's Drake slash Brittney.'

'If we get a chance at Brittney, we could tie her up, lock her up,' Edilio said. 'Yeah. If Brianna finds him we have her follow him, watch, and let us know when Brittney comes out.'

'That's a plan,' Albert said, obviously relieved. 'So we let Sam keep going.'

Edilio nodded. 'For now. But Taylor, we may still need –'

Taylor was no longer in the room.

TWELVE

48 HOURS **54** MINUTES

SO VERY, VERY sweet to be out of that basement. To be breathing fresh air.

Drake stuck close to the shadows of burned-out houses so the fresh air smelled of ash and charcoal and melted plastic. But it was better than the mildew and dust in the basement.

Drake had a list in his head. Sam. Caine. Dekka. Brianna. They would die first. As quickly as Drake could kill them.

That had been his big mistake with Sam at the power plant. He had taken his time to enjoy whipping him. Even now the memory of it sent a shudder of sheer pleasure through Drake's body.

But he had taken too long killing Sam and then Brianna had showed up.

Not this time. This time he would start by killing Sam. Then, if he could find him, Caine.

That was the thing with the powerful freaks, you had to kill them quick. You had to strike with speed and surprise.

Sam. Caine. Dekka. Brianna. Orc and Taylor, too.

And then, with them gone, he could take his sweet time with Astrid. And even longer with Diana.

Drake laughed out loud.

Jamal said, 'What's so funny?'

'I'm Santa Claus, Jamal. Making a list, checking it twice.'

Jamal stayed a few steps behind him. Toting his big automatic rifle in his one good arm. The other arm in a makeshift sling. Scared out of his mind, no doubt. Still feeling the burn of Drake's whip. Oh, yes, he would feel that for quite some time.

'Where is Sam staying?' Drake asked Jamal.

'Albert sent him off to look for something out in the woods or whatever. Out there.' Jamal gestured vaguely. 'I wasn't supposed to know, but I heard.'

Drake turned on Jamal. 'What? Sam's not here?' He'd missed out on a lot, being trapped like an animal.

'He'll be back in a couple of days, I guess.'

Drake cursed. 'Where's Caine, then?'

'He's on some island, like, where these rich dudes lived in the old days.'

Worse and worse.

No. No . . . Better and better.

Drake grinned. Neither of the big powers was around to stop him. Change of plans.

'Dekka?'

Jamal shrugged. 'I don't know, man, I don't follow that scary dyke around town.'

'Now, now,' Drake chided mockingly. 'We mustn't diss people because of what they are.' He took Jamal's face in his hand and squeezed. 'I'm going to kill her but not because of what she is, right? I'm going to murder her because she has to be murdered. You good with that, Jamal?'

Jamal was as tense and stiff as a board. He made an affirmative grunt.

'You down with murder?' Drake pressed, sticking his face right in Jamal's. 'I want to hear it from you.'

He watched as a curtain dropped behind Jamal's eyes. Jamal said, 'Yeah. Yeah, Drake.'

'Then let's go murder some people,' Drake said cheerfully and released Jamal's face.

Drake walked half a block and stopped.

'Not now,' he groaned. He cursed extravagantly, but already he was changing. Metal braces formed on his teeth. His lean body grew flabbier.

'Brittney's coming,' Drake snarled. 'But I'll be back, Jamal. Don't for–'

Sam, Dekka and Jack had stopped for a meal a half mile from Hunter's camp. Some cooked fish that smelled none too fresh, boiled artichokes and some pigeon jerky.

They'd thought about just going to sleep, but no one had wanted to. The horror was far too fresh. Sleep would only mean nightmares. And Sam did not want to see Hunter again.

In the dark they could only make slow progress, but everyone wanted some distance and to get the expedition done. The high spirits were gone. Fear and loathing tracked them in the dark.

Jack was trailing well behind when Sam and Dekka had started talking, killing time as they walked slowly, cautiously, through waist-high brush. Talking, talking about anything but Hunter's sad cries.

It had started with Sam admitting that yes, he had made a play for Taylor but noting that he had been very, very drunk. From there it had gone to his relationship with Astrid, which he did not want to talk about. Any thought of Astrid was laced with pain and loneliness. What he had done to Hunter, what he had seen happening to Hunter, filled him with a powerful longing to be with Astrid. They had been through so much already. How many times had he held her and reassured her everything would be all right? How many times had she kissed him and put her arms around him when she knew he was spiralling down into depression?

From the start, from the first day, they had been each other's strength.

Not that they'd never fought. They were both strong willed and they had fought many times over things large and small.

But the fights had always gone somewhere, they'd been worked through and resolved.

But now this cold distance between them. Something inside Astrid had broken after Mary's death. That day had killed some part of Astrid and now it was like she didn't even care enough to fight.

Sam said some of that to Dekka, talking out of sheer loneliness and need. But it made him uncomfortable, like he was betraying Astrid even talking about her.

And the truth was, so much of the problem between him and Astrid wasn't about anything earth-shattering, it was just about sex. And Sam couldn't really talk about that without sounding more like a jerk than he could stand.

So he diverted the conversation to Dekka. Which led to talking about Brianna. And Sam found himself quickly trapped in a conversation that was every bit as uncomfortable as talking about Astrid.

'I know you mean well, Sam,' Dekka was saying.

'The worst that happens is Brianna says, "No way, I'm not gay."' He glanced back at Jack to make sure he was out of earshot.

Dekka sighed. 'You don't understand, Sam. You think that's all there is to it – just be honest. But see, right now I have this little, tiny like, like flower of hope, right? It's not much, but it's what I am holding on to. I just . . . I can't have her look at me

133

and laugh. Or make a face and be grossed out. Because then I have nothing.'

It was the longest speech Sam had ever heard Dekka deliver.

'Yeah,' he said. 'I get that.' He fervently wished he'd never opened his mouth.

There was a noise in the bushes off to one side. 'Is that you, Jack?' Sam called in a loud voice.

'I'm over here,' Jack said, from the completely opposite direction. 'I'm . . . I'm peeing.'

Sam stopped. He made a gesture to Dekka, indicating she should shield her eyes. Then he launched a fireball into the air, a Sammy sun. The bushes immediately became a green-tinged ghost space.

Just off the trail a coyote flinched at the light but did not run away. It snarled, bared its teeth, and crouched for a leap.

Dekka was faster than Sam. The coyote found itself floating a few feet off the ground, unable to kick, unable to leap.

It was a bizarre sight, the mangy, dirt-yellow coyote squirming and yowling in mid-air. But at last it let itself go limp.

'Why are you attacking us?' Sam asked. 'Does Pack Leader know you're trying to kill humans?'

'I Pack Leader,' the coyote said in its strangled, weird voice.

Sam stepped closer. Humans were not the only creatures to have evolved in the lawless universe of the FAYZ. One of the earliest had been the coyotes who served the gaiaphage. Some had mutated to develop the shorter tongues and flattened muzzles that allowed them a mangled sort of speech.

'Look,' Jack said. He was coming closer, pointing. 'He has them, too.'

Sam walked cautiously around Pack Leader to see the other side. There were the insect jaws protruding from the matted fur. Two, maybe three of them.

'I came for hunter kill me,' Pack Leader said.

Sam knew this was not the original Pack Leader. Lana had killed that Pack Leader. But whether this was the second coyote to hold the title or some other coyote, he didn't know. This one had slightly better powers of speech than the first.

'Hunter's dead,' Sam said.

'You kill.'

'Yes.'

'Kill me, Bright Hands.'

Sam had no sympathy for the coyote. The coyotes had participated in the town plaza massacre. There were bodies buried in the cemetery that had been so badly ripped by coyote teeth that they were unrecognisable.

'The flying snakes cause this?' Sam asked, pointing at the awful parasites.

'Yes.'

'Where are they?'

Pack Leader made a purely coyote growl deep in his throat. 'No words.'

'Then show us,' Sam said. 'Take us to them.'

'Then you burn me?'

'Then I'll burn you.'

At first Brittney was confused. She wondered if she was dreaming. Dreaming of fresh, cool air and a sky overhead.

But no, she was not in the basement.

Drake had escaped!

She had to do something. Had to warn someone. Even if it meant being returned to the basement. If Drake was loose in the world, he would do evil.

But to be locked away again . . . Surely she could take just a moment to be free. Just a moment . . .

She realised she was not alone.

'Who are you?'

'Jamal. I . . . I work for Albert, kind of. A bodyguard, like.'

The boy stood stiff, rigid, hand gripping the stock of his rifle too tightly. His other arm had been hurt.

'Why are you here, Jamal? Are you here to catch Drake?' She noticed a few feet of rope coiled and hung from Jamal's belt. 'I don't think you can tie him up. He's very dangerous.'

'I know that,' Jamal said. He was tugging the rope free.

Brittney suddenly understood why Jamal was there. She bolted.

Jamal ran after her.

'Don't run or I have to shoot you,' Jamal cried.

He was faster than she was. Everyone was faster than Brittney. But he was fumbling one-handed with the rope and had to sling the gun over his shoulder. All Brittney had to do was run.

She burst into the town plaza. Not knowing what she was looking for, not consciously. But she found herself running up the stone steps toward the ruined church.

Jamal caught her on the steps, grabbed her hair, and yanked back. Her legs went out from under her and she fell hard on her back, slamming on to sharp-edged granite.

But Brittney no longer felt real pain. She had long since gone beyond pain.

Jamal tried to straddle her, but he tripped on the rope and she pushed away from him.

'Stop it!' Jamal yelled.

Brittney rolled down a couple of steps, climbed to her feet, and ploughed straight back into Jamal. She knocked him aside and dashed past him.

The church roof had collapsed long ago. But a path had been cleared to the inside. The cross had been propped back upright, leaning a bit but still there, silver in the moonlight.

Brittney ran towards the cross, tripped on debris and slammed into a pew.

Jamal was on her in a flash, cursing, fumbling, trying to grab her, swat away her punching hands, trying to get the rope around her.

'No! No! No!' Brittney shouted.

Jamal punched her in the side of the head.

Brittney blinked and punched back. She kicked and flailed and punched as well as she could from her position half beneath a pew. And Jamal kicked her back viciously.

But Jamal could still feel pain. He backed away suddenly, eyes wild and dripping sweat. He levelled the rifle at her.

'I don't want to shoot you,' Jamal pleaded.

'You can't kill me,' Brittney said and got heavily to her feet.

'I know. Drake told me you'd say that. But I can blow up your face and then you won't be better right away. That's what he said. He told me to shoot you right in the face and tie you up.'

'I wish you could kill me,' Brittney said. And then, in a loud voice, trying to shout at heaven, she cried, 'Jesus, I am in your house. I am in the house of the Lord begging you for death!'

'Just let me tie you up,' Jamal pleaded. 'He'll whip me if I don't.' There were tears running down his face and Brittney felt sorry for him. They were both bound to Drake, unable to get away from him.

Jamal aimed the gun at her face.

'Don't,' Brittney said. 'We have to fight Drake, we have to

get help. Sam. He has to burn Drake to ashes and scatter the ashes in the ocean.'

'Please don't make me do this,' Jamal pleaded.

Brittney yelled, 'Help! Some –'

Orc had run until he was tired. That didn't take long. He was drunk and dehydrated. Weaker than he should have been. More easily tired.

But despair drove him on, staggering and weeping and bellowing in rage through the night.

'Never wanted to be no guard,' he yelled at the closed and darkened houses. 'Everybody hear that? I didn't ask to be no prison guard!'

He stood swaying back and forth, big stone-fingered fists clenched.

'No one wants to talk to me, huh?'

He smashed one arm down on the roof of a car. The driver's -side window had long since been beaten in so the door could be opened and the car could be searched. The trunk was open, too, and the recoil from Orc's blow made it bounce.

'Need another bottle,' he muttered. Then louder, yelling at the darkened windows and locked doors, 'I want a bottle. Someone give me a bottle so I won't hurt anyone.'

No answer. The streets were silent.

He started crying again and brushed angrily at the tears.

He started running once more, ran for a block and stopped, wheezing and threatening to topple over.

Then he spotted the boy. A kid. Maybe eight, maybe nine or ten, hard to say. The boy was walking bent over, holding his stomach. Every few feet he would stop and cough and then groan from the pain of coughing.

'Hey-ey!' Orc yelled. 'You! Go get me a bottle.' The word 'bottle' came out 'bah-hull'.

The sick boy blinked and seemed only then to notice the monster in the street ahead of him. He clutched a stop sign to keep himself from collapsing.

'Hey. You, kid. I'm talking to you!'

The boy started to answer, then started coughing. He coughed and groaned and sat down.

Orc stomped over to him. 'You ig, um, ig . . . ignoring me?'

The boy shook his head weakly. He made a gesture towards his throat, tried to speak, couldn't.

'I don't want to . . .' Orc began, but lost the thread of his speech. 'Just go get me a bah-hull.'

The boy coughed in Orc's face.

Orc swatted him with the back of his hand.

The boy hit the signpost so hard it rang. Then fell on to his back on the sidewalk.

Orc stared stupidly, expecting the boy to start crying. But the kid wasn't moving. Wasn't coughing.

Orc felt ice water flood his veins.

'I didn't . . .' Orc started to say.

He looked around, feeling sudden, overwhelming shame. No one had seen him.

He tried to lean down and prod the boy with his finger, but the blood rushed to his head and he almost passed out.

'Whatever,' Orc said sullenly, and headed off again into the night.

But quieter now.

THIRTEEN

BRIANNA TOOK A deep breath of chilly night air. Was that a breeze? Excellent: a breeze for the Breeze.

'Here, Drake-y, Drake-y,' she said.

She was in the middle of the street. As long as Drake hadn't found a gun, she would be safe. Drake was quick with that whip hand of his, but not Breeze quick. No one was Breeze quick.

'Oh, Dra-ake,' she sang in a loud voice. 'Oh, Dra-ake. Come out, come out wherever you are.'

She ran down Pacific Boulevard, turned on to Brace, and shot back up Golding.

She heard Orc bellowing drunkenly in the distance. It would be easy to locate him. But Orc wasn't the problem.

No sign of Drake. She paused at the corner. Either she could just zoom randomly around or she could go methodically, street by street.

Methodical was not Brianna's thing.

Better to taunt him, tease him into showing himself. 'Here, Drake-y, Drake-y.'

She zoomed to Astrid's house. No sign of him there.

She zoomed to the firehouse. To the school. To Clifftop and down the beach, kicking a tail of sand behind her as she ran.

Where would he go? What would he do?

It dawned on her then: Brittney. What was Drake going to do about Brittney?

As far as Brianna knew, Drake had no power to stop Brittney from emerging.

Where would Brittney go if she were free?

Brianna turned her gaze to the ruined church. And just then, she heard the sound of voices from within.

She zoomed up the stairs and into the church as . . .

BLAM!

The explosion, a stab of yellow, blinded her. She stopped as fast as she could, but not fast enough. She slammed into a pew and flew headfirst through the air, unable to see.

Anyone else would have smashed face-first into the marble altar, but Brianna was not anyone else. As she was flying she tucked, spun and landed on her feet on the altar. Like a cat.

The wave of pain from the impact with the pew made her gasp. But she fought down the urge to scream.

Then she saw.

And then she did scream.

The rifle blast had hit Brittney in the face and neck. The entire left side of her face was gone. Her neck was torn open. She should be spouting blood. But although the shattered flesh was red and raw as uncooked hamburger, no arteries sprayed.

And Brittney was still standing.

Jamal made a sound like a tortured animal, a howl of fear.

He levelled the gun at Brittney's chest but in the half second it took him to find the trigger with his finger Brianna was on him.

She hit the barrel and knocked it away just as *BLAM!*

She grabbed Jamal by the neck, yanked him forward so fast his head snapped back. She punched him six times in less than a second and Jamal crumpled, blood gushing from his nose and lips.

'Don't hurt me, it's not my fault!' Jamal wailed as he dropped and curled into a ball protecting both the gun and his face.

Brianna did not want to look at Brittney, really really didn't.

'Are you OK?' she asked over her shoulder. No answer from Brittney. Not surprising since her mouth was smeared all around the back of her head.

Brianna steeled herself and shot a glance at Brittney.

Brittney wasn't there.

The whip hand of Drake was already reaching, yanking Jamal's rifle away.

Brianna pulled her knife free and leaped at him.

She buried the knife in Drake's chest. It was a huge blade, a bowie knife, as big as a chef's knife and a lot thicker. The blade was in all the way, up to the hilt.

Drake grinned. 'This should be fun.'

Brianna expected him to try to turn the gun towards her but instead he tossed it aside. Then, with his real hand, he drew the knife out of his chest, slowly, as if relishing every inch of steel.

Brianna stared, mesmerised. And almost missed the sudden flick of Drake's tentacle arm as it swept behind her.

Almost missed.

Not quite.

Brianna dropped and the whip went over her head. Drake threw Brianna's own knife at her, but it wasn't even close. The knife stuck into the back of a pew.

Brianna pulled her sawed-off shotgun from her runner's pack, levelled, aimed and fired.

The blast caught Drake in the mouth. It turned his thin-lipped smirk into a gaping hole, like a sinkhole.

Drake reached with his tentacle to feel the hole. He stuck the end of his whip hand into his own destroyed mouth. The pink-red tip came out through the back of his head and waved at Brianna.

Drake made a grunting sound that might have been a laugh if he'd had tongue and teeth and lips.

Brianna dropped back a few feet.

Drake's face seemed to melt and re-form. She could see individual teeth, white pearls in the starlight, moving like insects, crawling out of the shredded flesh to find places in newly reshaped gums.

Brianna felt for the wire she hung from her belt. It was an E string from a cello she'd found. She'd wrapped the ends around short pieces of wood to form a four-foot-long garotte.

'This is what you were going to do to me at the power plant, remember, Drake?' Brianna winced as Drake's tongue grew inside the still-gaping hole of his mouth.

'Oh, sorry, you can't really chit-chat, can you?' Brianna taunted. 'Well, the thing is, whether it's me running into a wire at two hundred miles an hour, or the wire running into you at two hundred miles an hour, it works just the same.'

She grabbed the garotte and was behind Drake before he could blink. The wire went around Drake's neck as she was still running. The wire bit and sliced, and she felt a powerful jerk in her hands that tore one handle from her grip as the wire sliced through neck bone.

Drake's head fell. It hit the stone floor hard, and rolled on to its side, rocked a few times, and lay still.

Not enough, Brianna thought, turned, raced back, threw the loose end of the wire around Drake's waist, caught the handle, and gripped with all her strength as she backpedalled at super speed.

The wire cut through Drake's still-standing torso just below his ribs. It stopped at the spine.

Brianna yanked, but the wire would not cut the spine. She yanked and yanked and the meat of Drake's body twisted sideways so she could see the insides, see the organs, the sliced raw flesh like steak, the pale intestine, and all of it clinical, like a drawing, like some hideous display.

And suddenly her frenzied yanking, legs pummelling the slippery marble for purchase, succeeded, and with a grinding, grisly sound the spine parted and Drake fell in two pieces to the floor.

Brianna was aware of screaming. Jamal, hand over his face but eyes staring in horror. Screaming and screaming like he would never stop.

Brianna wanted to scream, too. But not in horror. In sheer, vicious triumph. She wanted to dance and smear herself with the blood of her beaten enemy. She wanted to leap atop the body chunks and kick them in contempt.

Brianna threw back her head and howled at the broken rafters and the sky beyond. 'Yaaaaah! Yaaaaah! The Breeze!'

Jamal stopped screaming. He was gibbering, making word like sounds, like a crazy street person. He was crawling away across the floor.

Brianna laughed. 'What's the matter, tough guy? Did you figure out you picked the wrong side?'

The tentacle was around her legs before she knew what had happened.

She looked down and stared, unable to believe what she was seeing. Drake's whip hand was coiled twice around her ankles, squeezing hard, crushing the bones together.

Brianna tried to kick but couldn't even budge.

Drake's head was four feet away from his upper torso, but now the cruel mouth was back, and grinning. The cold eyes were watching.

Alive!

The upper torso used its good hand to shove itself towards the head while the tentacle held her tight with a python's strength. The lower torso and legs were kicking and flailing, trying to move towards the upper torso.

Drake was putting himself back together.

Brianna fell on her butt. She reached reflexively for her knife, but it was too far away.

Her sawed-off shotgun. She had re-holstered it. Her hand found it, yanked it free. She took aim at the tentacle that held her fast, aimed at the part just beyond her feet, squeezed the trigger.

BLAM!

The blast came from Jamal's gun. He had found it. She saw smoke curling from the muzzle.

Brianna fumbled with her shotgun, but her fingers wouldn't work right and her ears were ringing and somehow there was blood all over her chest.

Drake's head made a silent laugh.

Brianna lay helpless, watching as the legs, the lower third of the creature began to change. Not Drake's legs. A girl's chubby limbs.

Drake's head cried out without sound.

The tentacle was already sliding away.

Jamal walking as if in a dream, his smoking rifle held at his side.

Brianna could see Drake's lips form the words, 'Kill her. Kill her.'

But without lungs, no sound came out.

The body parts moved together. The arms of a girl fumbled for and found what was now Brittney's head and dragged it to its perch on her shoulders.

The legs kicked and scrabbled until the lower third melded back. Brianna watched it all, unable to move, unable to think clearly.

The last thing she saw was Jamal using Brianna's wire to wrap Brittney's hands tightly behind her. He tore a sleeve from his own shirt and made a gag of it and stuffed it in Brittney's mouth.

Then he stepped back to Brianna. She could barely hear his

words through the ringing sound and could barely understand what she did hear.

'I could kill you,' Jamal said. He pointed the automatic rifle down at her, the barrel an inch from her face. 'Most likely Drake comes out on top. But if not, you remember that I coulda killed you.' He shouldered the gun. 'But I didn't.'

It was only a few minutes before Edilio, accompanied by Ellen, both armed with automatic rifles of their own, came rushing in. Jamal and Brittney were long gone.

Edilio knelt beside Brianna. She saw worry and compassion in his dark eyes and in her delirium really liked him for that.

'Ellen, get Lana. Now!' Edilio ordered.

To Brianna, he said, 'Is he gone?'

Brianna found it hard to get her voice to do what she wanted. But she managed after a few tries to say, 'Have to . . . get Sam. Sam. I . . . I can't beat Drake.'

Edilio looked grim. 'Yeah, that's a good idea,' he said as he examined the bloody wounds in her shoulder. 'Unfortunately Taylor took off. And no one exactly knows how to find Sam.'

'Jamal . . .' Brianna whispered. But before she could complete the thought, the marble floor seemed to open wide and drag her swirling down into darkness.

Lance came bursting in the door.

'Drake is out!' he yelled.

Turk – formerly Zil's number one guy, at least he thought so, and boss of what was left of Human Crew – said, 'Yeah, whatever.'

Human Crew had been a group formed to defend the rights of normals against freaks. At least that was the Human Crew line. Most people now saw Human Crew as a straight-up hate group.

Lance grabbed Turk's shoulder and practically yanked him up off the stinking couch where he lay. 'Turk, listen, man, listen to me: don't you see what this means?'

Turk did not see what it meant, or at least not whatever Lance thought he should see. Turk mostly disliked Lance. They were friends, kind of, but only because they'd both been with Zil and riding high. And now they were reduced to doing the worst work Albert could find for them: digging slit trenches for kids to go in, and then covering them up when they were full.

Cesspool diggers. The Crap Crew, kids called them.

And they had to kiss Albert's butt because otherwise they didn't eat. They'd been lucky they weren't exiled. Turk had talked the council out of sending them off to live in the wild. He'd begged, that was the truth of it. He'd convinced them that it was better to find a place for him and the others from Human Crew.

He'd put all the blame for the fire on anyone but themselves. Kept saying, 'It's not our fault, guys, not me and Lance and all, we were forced by Zil and Hank. Hank was scary, man, you know that. You know he was a creep and he would have shot us or messed us up.'

Turk had whined like a baby. And wept. And in the end convinced that smug wetback Edilio, and especially Albert, that they wouldn't make trouble any more, ever again, lessons learned, their lives all turned around now.

The Human Crew became the Crap Crew. And harsher names as well. A laughingstock.

Turk hated Albert with a burning, undying passion. Albert had everything and tossed the worst crumbs to Turk and Lance and the former Human Crew.

Lance wasn't going away. His handsome face was lit up with excitement. 'Dude, don't you get it? If we hit Albert now, everyone will blame Drake.'

That got Turk's attention. 'We tried to pin the fire on Caine and no one believed us.'

'This is different. Look, do you like living like this?' He looked wildly around the room, stabbing his hand finally towards the reeking stew pot they used as an inside toilet. 'Eating the worst food, doing the worst job and being in this dump?'

'Yeah, I love it,' Turk said with savage sarcasm. 'I just love being the biggest loser in town.'

'Then listen to me.' Lance rested his hands on Turk's shoulders. Turk shrugged them off. 'Because I'm telling you:

Drake can't be killed or stopped. So everyone's scared. Maybe we find a way to hook up with Drake, right? Or maybe we just wait until everyone's freaking out over him, and we make our move.'

Turk didn't dismiss it out of hand. Maybe Lance was right. Everyone knew Albert had tons of gold and 'Bertos and all kinds of food – even cans of stuff from before, good food.

'I don't know, man,' Turk said. 'Human Crew is supposed to stand for something. I mean, we're the defenders of humans against freaks, right? We stand up for normal people. We don't just steal stuff. We're not, like, a gang.'

Lance laughed derisively. 'Man, sometimes you are clueless. You don't even see what's happening.' He perched himself on the arm of the couch so he could look down at Turk. 'It's not just about freaks. I mean, you're the guy who thinks of ideas and all, but you're missing it. You don't even notice that the whole council is either black or Mexican. See, that's what's happening: it's all these minorities hooked up with freaks.'

The wheels in Turk's mind began to turn slowly. But they were picking up speed. 'Jamal's with us and he's black.'

'So? We use Jamal. He gets us into Albert's. You do what you gotta do. All I'm saying is, you and me, we're normal people. We're not black or queer or Mexican. And we're the ones digging toilets. How come?'

Turk knew the answer: because they had failed in their attempt to take over. But he'd never thought about this new angle.

'Astrid's a normal white person,' Turk argued halfheartedly. 'So's Sam.'

'Sam's a freak, and I think he might even be a Jew,' Lance said. His eyes were glittering. He was showing his teeth, grinning as he talked. It wasn't a good look for him. 'And Astrid? She's not even on the council any more.'

Turk was buying it. He felt the new ideas settle into the dark places in his aggrieved mind. 'Drake's white. So is Orc, you know, underneath it all. But they're kind of like freaks. Only . . . only not really. Because they didn't like, turn into freaks, they had accidents or whatever that made them what they are now.'

'Exactly,' Lance said.

Yes, Turk thought. *This could be good. This could be very good.* Taking out Albert would cause more problems than burning a bunch of houses. Albert was the one who was really in charge. He had the money and the food. That made him even more important than Sam.

Lisa came in then with cabbages she'd picked from the fields, and a fat rat she'd bought. Turk's mouth watered: dinner was late.

'Let's eat,' he said. 'Then we think about what comes next.'

FOURTEEN

EDILIO WAITED UNTIL the sun was up to go for Roscoe.

It was all very peaceful. Roscoe wasn't the kind of guy to make much trouble.

'We just have to put you somewhere safe,' Edilio explained.

'So I don't give it to anyone else,' Roscoe said.

'Yeah. While we figure out how to cure you.'

'I want to say goodbye to Sinder,' Roscoe said softly. He jerked his head indicating that she was in the house.

'Of course, man. But listen. Don't let her touch you, OK? Just in case.'

Roscoe struggled a little then, not against Edilio but against himself. He fought to stop a quiver in his lip. Fought to keep the tears from filling his eyes.

Edilio took him to town hall. There was an unused office with a cot. Edilio had made sure there were books for Roscoe to read. And a covered pot for Roscoe to do his business. A jug of water was on the shelf next to the window. A cabbage and a cooked rabbit were there, too.

The rabbit was a delicacy.

Roscoe thanked Edilio for being decent.

Edilio closed the door. Then he turned the key in the deadbolt.

Quinn's fishermen had had a good day. The boats were reasonably full of fish, squid, octopi, and the weird things they called blue bats. Those they fed to the zekes – the worms in the fields – to buy safe passage for the vegetable pickers.

The prize of the morning's work was a five-foot-long shark. Quinn's boat was actually cramped because of the thing. He was sitting on the tail as he rowed, which was awkward and would give him a backache later. But no one in the boat was complaining. A shark was a two-for-one: not only was it great eating, it was a competitor for the limited supply of fish.

'Here's what we ought to do,' Cigar was saying as he pulled at his oar. 'We ought to sell the teeth at the mall. I mean, did you see all those teeth? Kids would pay a 'Berto for, like, a necklace of teeth.'

'Or they might, like, glue them on to a stick and make a gnarly weapon,' Elise suggested.

'What do you think it weighs?' Ben wondered.

'Ah, not much,' Quinn said.

That got a laugh. It had taken eight kids just to haul the fish over the side into Quinn's boat, and then they'd practically swamped the boat.

'Weighs more than Cigar,' Ben said.

Cigar plucked at his ragged T-shirt and revealed a hard, almost concave, stomach. 'Everything weighs more than me nowadays. When this all ends and we get out, I'm writing a diet book. The FAYZ diet. First, you eat all the junk food you can. Then you starve. Then you eat artichokes. Then you starve a little more. Then you eat someone's hamster. Then you go on the all-fish diet.'

'You left out the part where you fry up some ants,' Elise said.

'Ants? I ate beetles,' Ben bragged.

They went on like this for a while, rowing their heavy-laden boat and bragging about the awful things they had eaten.

Quinn noticed something he hadn't seen in a long time.

'Hold up,' he said.

'Aw, is Captain Ahab tired of rowing?'

'You've got good eyes, Elise, look over there.' Quinn pointed towards the barrier across a half mile of water.

'What? It's still there.'

'Not the barrier. The water. Look at the water.'

The four of them shielded their eyes from the sun and stared. 'Huh,' Quinn said at last. 'Does that or does that not look like there's a breeze blowing over there? It's a little choppy.'

'Yeah,' Cigar agreed. 'Weird, huh?'

Quinn nodded thoughtfully. It was something new. Something very strange. He would tell Albert about it when they got into town.

'OK, enough with that. Let's get back on those oars.' The other boats were catching up to them. Quinn could see each of them in turn stop and stare at the clear evidence of wind.

'What's it mean?' Ben asked.

Quinn shrugged. 'That's above my pay grade, as my dad used to say. I'll let Albert and Astrid figure that out. Me, I'm just a dumb fisherman,' he said.

'Oh, look,' Elise teased. 'I see an oar with no one pulling it.'

Quinn laughed. He seated himself properly, braced his feet, and grabbed the available oar. His back, like those of all the fishing fleet, was thick with muscle.

He was happy. This life made him happy. The sun, the salt water, the smell of fish. The backbreaking work. It all made him happy.

It was simple. It was important.

Quinn thought about the breeze blowing across the water. There was nothing sinister about a nice breeze. And yet he had the feeling it spelled trouble.

Dahra Baidoo had seven new cases of flu. That made thirteen in all. The so-called hospital rang with the percussion of coughing.

No one had died in the night.

But no one had gotten well yet, either. Lana's touch did not heal this illness. Which meant Dahra was no longer in the business of keeping kids comfortable until Lana came around and made everything better: she was now in the business of trying to understand this sickness.

She took temperatures. She kept more-or-less careful charts showing the progression of the sickness.

She tried not to think about Jennifer's story. Jennifer wasn't backing off her tale: she had seen the other Jennifer cough herself to death.

Dahra also tried not to think about what it meant if illness could develop an immunity to Lana.

A kid named Pookie was her worst case right at the moment. She stared at the thermometer in her hand, not quite believing it – 106 degrees. She had never seen a number that high.

Pookie was shaking like he was freezing. He was no longer able to answer questions sensibly. He had started talking to someone who was not exactly there, talking about how he didn't want to go to school because he hadn't finished his report.

And his cough was getting louder and more violent.

The flu had laughed at the Tylenol she gave Pookie. His fever had burned right through it. Whether or not he developed some kind of killing cough, he would die of fever if it rose much higher. She had to bring it down.

The book suggested an ice bath. The odds of that were precisely zero. No water, let alone ice. If Albert didn't arrange a water delivery soon, kids would be falling out from thirst, not even waiting to die of fever or cough.

Dahra made a decision. Ellen was there helping out, along with one of the new kids from the island, Virtue. She wished she had time to talk to Virtue: Dahra's parents were from Africa. And so was Virtue himself.

'We have to cool him down,' Dahra said. 'Virtue? Hold down the fort here, OK? We're going to the beach.'

Ellen and Dahra manoeuvred Pookie into a wheelbarrow. The three of them made an odd procession down San Pablo Avenue to the beach.

Crossing the sand was the hard part. But finally they made it to the lacy surf and set the sick kid down. Water surged around him.

Not an ice bath, maybe, but close enough. She figured the cold salt water should drain away some of the heat inside Pookie's body.

'There,' Ellen said. 'Hopefully he can walk back on his own.'

Dahra flopped on to the sand beside Ellen. Ellen said, 'You heard about Drake, right?'

'Him escaping? Yeah. Don't worry, Sam will get him.'

Ellen shook her head. 'Sam's out of town. Albert got him to go off for water. Or something like that.'

'Sam's gone?' Dahra looked nervously over her shoulder. No reason Drake would come after her. But Drake didn't need a reason. 'It'll be OK. Dekka and Brianna and –'

Pookie coughed, coughed, doubled over, choked on seawater, and then coughed so powerfully that it made a clear indent in the water.

'Whoa,' Ellen said.

Pookie sat up. His head lolled back and forth like a marionette with a loose string.

He coughed and the force of it threw him backwards into the water with a splash.

Dahra ran to pull him up, but he'd done it on his own. He got to his feet, staggering.

He coughed and it was like an explosion. He flew backwards. Like he'd been hit by a car.

'Oh, my God,' Dahra cried.

Pookie rolled over, on hands and knees, and coughed again so powerfully that sand flew. Something pink and raw was sprayed across the sand crater.

'No, no, no,' Dahra moaned and backed away.

Pookie coughed again and the force of it lifted him up on to his toes, bent him back in a C. Blood sprayed from his mouth and drained out of his ears.

With blank, uncomprehending eyes he stared at Dahra.

And fell dead, facedown in the surf.

No one spoke.

Dahra barely breathed.

For several very long seconds Dahra stood paralysed.

She blinked. 'Ellen, quick, into the water. Get wet all over. Scrub off with your hands!' Dahra followed her own advice. She plunged in and submerged.

When she came up, she yelled, 'Now stay away from Pookie's body. Stay in the sun for a while. Until you're dry. Sunlight is supposed to kill flu virus on your skin.'

'Oh, my God,' Ellen said and her face went pale. 'He coughed his insides out.'

'Just do what I tell you! Face up to the sun, I have to go!'

She ran back across the beach, her insides churning, panic eating at her.

She spotted Quinn and the fishing fleet pulling wearily up to the dock down at the marina. She ran as fast as she could, waving her hands over her head to attract attention.

Quinn and some of the others saw her, they just didn't understand why she was yelling. Dahra was sweating hard by the time she reached the dock.

'No! No! Don't come any closer!' she yelled to Quinn.

'What the –'

'Pookie just died,' Dahra panted. 'Flu. Maybe. But, oh, God. Just don't come any closer. In fact, don't get off the boats.'

'I already had the flu,' Cigar said.

'So did Pookie,' Dahra said. 'Listen to me: it's catching and it's way bad.'

Quinn motioned for his people to stay in their boats. 'What are we supposed to do, Dahra? We can't just float around forever.'

Dahra sighed. 'Let me think.'

'I have to go check on my –' one of the fishermen said.

'Shut up, I'm thinking!' Dahra yelled. She had acquired a fair amount of medical knowledge since stupidly volunteering to run the so-called hospital. But that didn't make her a doctor.

She remembered reading about flu, though. Nothing spread faster. Nothing mutated and adapted faster. Hand washing removed it, alcohol killed it, sunlight killed it a little, anyway. But once it was in your nose and lungs it could go crazy and kill you. Especially some new strain.

'Stay in your boats,' Dahra said. 'We're still going to need food. Throw your fish on to the dock. I'll get Albert to send someone here to collect it. Then go back out, row up the coast a little ways, and camp out.'

'Camp out?' Quinn echoed.

'Yes!'

'You're serious.'

'No, it's my idea of a joke, Quinn,' Dahra snapped. 'Pookie just coughed up a lung and fell over dead. You understand what I'm saying? I mean he coughed his actual lungs out of his mouth. Hah hah hah, it's so funny.'

Quinn took a step back.

Dahra waited for him to make up his mind. She had no right to give orders. Except that she knew what was happening and no one else did.

'OK,' Quinn said. 'We'll take enough for ourselves and then head to a spot up the shore. Tell Albert to send someone right away for the fish. We have a nice big catch here. We got a shark.'

'Yeah, whatever.' Dahra's thoughts were already turning to her next move. The virus was the enemy: she was the general in this battle. But only two thoughts were really clear in her mind: One, Jennifer B had been telling the truth. And two, how could Dahra hope to avoid catching it?

'**NEAR,**' PACK LEADER said.

'Where?' Sam asked wearily. It had been a long night, followed by a long morning of tired feet and bruised shins.

They were over the hills, coming down the long slope towards the road and Lake Evian. It would have been easier to come up the road, this was definitely the long way around, but Sam had needed to see Hunter first.

To kill Hunter.

And now, if he could, he meant to find the nest of greenies and take them out.

Once more he saw the dark, troubled looks of the judges he feared would someday weigh his every action. He heard their questions. *What right did you have to take Hunter's life, Mr Temple? Yes, we understand that he did not wish to be eaten alive, but still, Mr Temple, don't you understand that every life is sacred?*

The road was below them, cut off from view by a large, rocky outcropping. He'd been down that road a few times, back during the early water runs. Enough times to picture the spot in his head.

'The rock is all busted up down there, boulders and crevices,' Sam said. 'It's like a shallow cave, only it doesn't go in very far, I don't think.'

'The snakes that fly are there,' Pack Leader confirmed. 'Now kill me, Bright Hands.'

'How do I know you're not lying?'

'Why lie?' Pack Leader snarled.

'Because you're a murderous creepy animal who obeys the Darkness,' Sam said. He was too tired and sleepy to be diplomatic.

'The Darkness is dead,' Jack said.

'No,' Pack Leader said.

'No,' Sam agreed with a significant look at Jack. This was the first outside confirmation that the gaiaphage still lived. If you could call it living.

A new bug mouth erupted from Pack Leader's flank. The canine looked at it, snapped at it, and bit it. Black liquid gushed from the insect head.

'Is this his doing?' Sam asked. 'Are these things creatures of the Darkness?'

'Pack Leader not know.'

Sam nodded. 'How do we kill it? The Darkness, I mean? How do we kill the gaiaphage?'

'Pack Leader not know.'

Sam sighed. 'Yeah, well that makes two of us.'

Sam could see the creatures writhing within Pack Leader's skin. Like he was a baggie full of worms.

'Ready?'

'I am Pack Leader,' the coyote said. He tilted back his head and howled at the sky.

Sam aimed both his palms at the beast just as his hide split open.

The killing light burned and burned. Pack Leader was dead instantly. His fur stank as it burned. His flesh crisped like bacon.

The creatures, the insects, whatever they were, crawled out of the flames and popping fat. Unfazed. Unharmed. Bright-lit and yet seemingly invulnerable.

Sam had used his power to burn through concrete and solid rock and steel. It was impossible that he couldn't kill these things. It was like they had some magical power to shrug off his deadly light. Like they had developed an immunity to him.

'Jack,' Sam said. 'Get a rock. A big one.'

Jack was frozen until Dekka smacked him on the back of the head. Then he leaped to a rock the size of a Smart Car. It was half-buried in the ground. Jack grunted with the effort, but the rock tore free of the dirt with a little gravity-cancelling help from Dekka.

Jack lifted the rock high over his head. He smashed it down

with all his strength on two of the squirming, escaping bugs.

The rock hit so hard it shook the ground, literally making Sam bounce.

'Now push it back off,' Sam ordered.

Jack did. The rock rolled easily from Jack's shove.

Beneath it were two very crushed bugs. Their carapaces were dully reflective, like smoky mirrors. They had short, crushed wings held tight against their bodies. Their wicked, curved mandibles had not been broken. Their slashing mouthparts still glittered like tiny knives.

'Like cockroaches,' Sam said. 'Hard to kill. Not impossible.'

'Yeah. Roaches. A couple more over there,' Dekka said, and pointed. As she pointed she suspended gravity and the two bugs lifted into the air. They motored helplessly on their legs.

'Your turn, Jack,' Sam said.

Dekka let gravity flow, the boulder rose and fell and scored two more dead bugs.

Others, though, were skittering down the hill.

Sam, Dekka, and Jack pelted after them, high on the discovery that the nasty creatures could in fact be killed.

Half a dozen of the monsters raced over rock and through scrub grass.

Jack snatched up a smaller boulder and threw it one-handed. It hit one of the bugs and missed the others.

'Dekka!'

'Yeah,' she said, and raised her hands. Dirt and litter and gravel floated into the air ahead. Another one of the insects floated with it. Jack grabbed a rock but it wouldn't come free, it was an outcropping of something too big even for Jack's strength.

He scrabbled and found a head-sized rock. He threw it hard and missed the floating bug.

'The others are getting away!' Sam yelled.

'What's that noise?' Dekka cried, and made a shushing gesture.

The three of them froze and listened. A sound like a mountain stream rushing over stones.

No, a beating of wings.

'Greenies!'

The flying snakes came in a cloud, rushing up from their lair below like swarming bats emerging from a cave at sundown.

Like tiny dragons, most just a few inches long, some as much as a foot long. They had leathery wings and whipped their tails back and forth to sustain a very shaky aerodynamic ability.

Sam yelled a curse and fired. Too late to catch them by surprise. A mistake that might prove fatal.

Bright beams of light sliced through the attacking cloud. Greenies burned and fell flaming.

Not enough. Not nearly enough and the greenies were not backing off.

Dekka cancelled gravity beneath the leading edge of the

swarm, but it only had the effect of disorienting some of the snakes, who responded by flying upside down or in wild circles.

They began to squirt greenish-black fluid.

Sam remembered Hunter telling him about being hit by some secretion from a greenie.

'Don't let them hit you!' Sam yelled. 'Run!'

Running uphill would be too slow on the steep slope. They ran at right angles to the swarm, ran all-out, panic speed, tripping and jumping back up, oblivious to bruises and scrapes.

The swarm was slow to react, but react they did, and wheeled after them.

Sam hit the road, staggered, caught himself, and spun around. The swarm was still emerging from its lair in the rock face above. Sam aimed hastily and fired.

Brush on the hillside instantly caught fire. Rocks heated and cracked. He played his light on the cave itself, lighting it up, making it a bright, blazing green mouth.

The swarm was lost now, unsure. It swirled in the air, dropping green-black droplets like an evil rain, but not over Sam and the others, not yet.

Confident he had burned out the cave, Sam swept his light upward into the swarm itself.

A mistake. Attacking their lair confused the greenies, but a direct attack on the swarm gave them a target.

Sam aimed again at the rock wall, hoping to distract them. Too late: the swarm was coming.

'Run! Run!'

Dekka ran backwards, cancelling gravity behind her. A cloud of gravel and dirt rose into the swarm. This slowed them.

Dekka turned and ran full speed after Sam and Jack.

The swarm seemed to be losing interest in following them. But a few of the more persistent greenies were still after them as they ran.

Dekka fell hard. Sam could see she was winded. He ran back to her but the greenies were faster than he was.

Dekka rolled over and looked up just as one of the greenies fired its fluid. The dark drop hit her bare shoulder. A second drop hit her jeans. Other drops fell around her.

Sam fired. The hovering greenies flamed.

Dekka jumped to her feet. 'It got me, it got me!'

'Get your jeans off,' Sam ordered.

She complied. Jack grabbed the garment and carefully inspected the fabric. 'It didn't get through.'

'My shoulder,' Dekka moaned. 'Oh, my God, it got me. It got me. Oh, God.'

'Hold out your arm, Dekka,' Sam ordered. 'This is going to hurt.'

'Do it,' Dekka agreed. 'Do it, do it!'

Sam formed a narrow beam of light. Carefully, carefully he

moved it closer and closer to the dark splotch on Dekka's shoulder.

Dekka gritted her teeth.

The beam of light burned and she cried out in pain but then yelled, 'Don't stop, don't stop!'

But Sam did stop. He quickly grabbed Dekka as she came close to fainting. 'Let me see the arm,' he said.

There was a burned scoop mark in Dekka's skin. Maybe half an inch deep. Twice as wide. The flesh was cauterised, so there was no blood.

'Got it,' Sam said.

'You don't know that,' Dekka said through gritted teeth.

'I got it. It didn't get anywhere else. I burned it off.'

Dekka grabbed the neck of Sam's shirt. 'Don't let it happen, Sam.'

'It's not going to, Dekka.'

'Listen to me: don't let it happen. You understand? You see it happen, you take care of me. Like Hunter.'

'Dekka . . .'

'Swear to me, Sam. Swear it to me by God or by your own soul or whatever you believe, swear to me, Sam.'

Sam gently pried her fingers loose.

'I won't let it happen, Dekka. I swear it.'

'Stay inside unless absolutely necessary,' Edilio shouted into the megaphone. Using up precious batteries. Albert had not wanted to give up the batteries. But he really didn't care what Albert wanted or didn't want.

He walked down San Pablo, shouting through the megaphone. 'We have flu going around and it's dangerous. Stay inside unless absolutely necessary! Work is cancelled today. Mall is closed.'

Flu. Yeah. A flu that makes you cough up your insides.

It was unreal, Edilio thought as he walked halfway down the street and repeated the loudspeaker warning.

Epidemic. The so-called hospital was full. All through the morning, feverish, coughing kids had dragged themselves to the hospital. The disease was spreading like fire and Lana was useless.

No way to know how many it would kill.

Maybe everyone who got it.

Maybe everyone, period.

'Quarantine,' Dahra had said, pounding her fist into her palm. 'You have to shut everything down.'

'Kids have almost no food or water in their homes,' Edilio had protested.

'You think I don't know that?' Dahra had cried in a shrill voice tinged with panic. 'If we don't stop this epidemic, no one will be thirsty, they'll be dead. Like Pookie. Like that Jennifer girl.'

Kids poked their heads out of windows or stepped out on to the darkening streets. Which was kind of the opposite of what he was going for.

'I already had the flu,' kids would yell.

'Yeah, well, no one is immune,' Edilio would shout back.

'How am I supposed to eat?'

'I guess you'll be hungry for a day. Give us time to work things out.'

'Is this the thing with bugs coming out of your body?'

How had that news spread so fast? Everyone knew about Roscoe being locked up. No phones, no texts, no email, nothing, and still kids heard things almost instantly.

'No, no, this is just flu,' Edilio said, stretching the truth almost to the breaking point. 'Coughing and fever. One kid's already died, so just do what I'm asking, OK?'

In fact, three kids had died. Pookie and a girl named Melissa and Jennifer H. Three, not one. And maybe more than that, no way to know what was happening in every house in this ghost town. No point in spreading more panic than was necessary.

One death should be enough to get their attention. Three deaths, on top of the bugs some kids were nicknaming maggots and others were calling gut-roaches, that was enough to create panic.

Edilio had no idea if a quarantine would work. He would get his guys to try and enforce it: the sheriffs at least would still be on the street. But what were they supposed to do if kids decided to ignore it? Shoot them to save them?

He couldn't tell people to wash their hands: no one had washing water in their home. He couldn't tell them to use hand sanitiser: not enough to go around and what they had was just for the so-called hospital.

Nothing they could do but ask kids to stay home.

Probably too late.

Three dead. So far.

Edilio thought of Roscoe locked in his prison. Were the bugs eating him from the inside yet?

He thought of Brianna – Lana's healing touch had fixed her, but the Breeze was shaken up. Scared.

He thought of the monstrous thing that was both Drake and Brittney.

He thought of Orc. No one had seen him. Plenty had heard him, and there were a few smashed cars testifying to his previous presence.

He thought of Howard, out walking the streets looking for Orc, refusing to stop, even when Edilio ordered him to get to some shelter and stay inside.

And he thought of the two people who had held his job before him: Sam and Astrid. Both beaten into despair by trying to hold this group of kids together in the face of one disaster after another. Both of them now happy to let Edilio handle it.

'No wonder,' Edilio muttered.

'Stay inside unless absolutely necessary,' Edilio shouted, and not for the first or last time wished he was still just Sam's faithful sidekick.

BLAZING SUNLIGHT, DIRECTLY overhead, woke Orc.

It took him quite a while to sort out where he was. There were desks. The kind they had in school. He was on the floor, a cold linoleum-tile floor, and the desks were tossed and piled around him. Like someone had tossed them all around in a rage.

Someone had.

There was a chalkboard. Something was written on it, but Orc's eyes wouldn't focus well enough to read it.

The really confusing thing was the hole in the ceiling and part of the wall that allowed sunlight to pour so directly on his face, on his blinking eyes. The wall had been partly torn down, and without support a part of the ceiling had collapsed.

He felt something in his right hand. A hunk of wallboard.

He had done it. He had attacked the desks and the windows and the walls.

The memories were flashes of desaturated colour and wild, jerky motion. He saw, as if standing outside himself, a drunken rock-bodied monster storming and rampaging and finally beating at the walls with great stone fists.

Orc groaned. His head was pounding like someone was using a sledgehammer on it. He was thirsty. His stomach felt as if it had been filled with coals.

Other memories were coming back. Drake. He had let that psycho creep get loose.

Howard would . . . well, actually, Howard wouldn't say much. Howard knew better than to ever really attack Orc.

But what about Sam? And Astrid?

Sudden fear. Astrid. Drake would go after her. Drake hated Astrid.

He should do something. Go and . . . and find Drake. Or guard Astrid. Or something. Astrid had always been good to him. She'd always treated him nice, like he wasn't a monster. Even back in school.

Suddenly Orc recognised the room. It was the room they used for after-school detention. Astrid would sometimes come and tutor him there.

Truth was, he had always liked it better in detention than at home.

Orc squeezed his eyes shut. He needed a bottle. Too many things coming into his head. Too many pictures and feelings.

He noticed an awful smell and knew right away what had

caused it. When he had passed out his muscles had all gone slack. He'd wet himself and worse.

He was lying in a puddle of urine and faeces.

With a sob he rolled over on to hands and knees. The fat-guy sweatpants he wore were stained and reeking.

Now he would have to walk down to the beach to clean off. He'd have to walk down there like this, like this depraved, disgusting, drunken, stinking monster.

Which was what he was. What he'd always been.

And then, one more memory. A sick little boy. A stop sign.

God, no. God . . . no.

Orc stumbled from the room, sick and weeping and hating himself so much more than anyone else could ever hate him.

Drake became conscious and was likewise confused about where he was and why.

His hands were tied behind his back and the wire cut uncomfortably into the pulpy flesh of his whip hand.

'Untie me,' he snapped at Jamal, who was dozing with his back against a palm tree, rifle cuddled to his chest like a stuffed animal. Jamal looked about six years old when he was asleep.

Drake noticed a rope tied from his ankle to Jamal's ankle. He yanked on it and Jamal snapped awake.

'Untie me,' Drake repeated.

Jamal crawled over and fiddled with the knot until Drake was free.

'Where are we?' Drake asked.

'Down the highway. You know, up past Ralph's?'

'What are we doing here?'

'I had to get Brittney out of town,' Jamal said. 'I barely got you out of the church before Edilio came.'

Drake remembered the fight with Brianna. It brought a savage grin. 'Did you finish that skinny little witch?'

Jamal shrugged. 'I shot her.'

'Did you finish her?'

'No, man, I don't think so.'

Drake stared hard at him. 'I told you to do her.'

'Did you?' Jamal licked his lips. 'I saw you saying something, but you were, you know, changing and all. It was hard to understand.'

Drake knew he was lying. Jamal had disobeyed him. But did he really want a Jamal tough enough to shoot a helpless person in the face?

No, he needed Jamal to be a little weak. Just a little. Still . . .

Drake snapped his whip and caught Jamal across the back.

Jamal cried out and backpedalled away.

'Don't disobey me,' Drake said. Then he smiled in what he hoped was a friendly way. 'I didn't cut too deep. Just a little reminder for you.'

'It burns like fire!'

'Yeah, well, man up, Jamal. And get me some water.
I'm thirsty.'

'Don't have any water.'

'Well get some!'

'Where?'

Drake jumped up and looked around. They were near where
the road came down from Coates and met the highway. He
tried to think if there was anything left at the old school. Had to
be some kind of water up there.

Or he could head back into town. Of course they'd be ready
for him now. And by the time he got there he might be Brittney
Pig again.

Drake felt a surge of frustration. If it was just him, he'd go
straight into town and take out anyone who got in his way. He
might not be able to take Orc down, but he could wear the
stupid, fat drunk out. And Brianna? Bring it on.

With Sam and Caine both away there was no one who could
take him on in a fight. But if Brianna was backed by a few of
Edilio's guys with rifles, well, they might be able to get Jamal,
and if they got Jamal, they could grab him when the Brittney
Pig emerged. Lock him up again. And this time when Sam came
back Sam would finish the job.

It had been supernaturally cool putting himself back together
after being sliced in three pieces. But he wasn't sure that would

happen if Sam incinerated him, burned him to ashes.

Threw the ashes in the ocean.

That image made Drake very nervous.

He had to find a way to rid himself of the Brittney Pig. Otherwise he'd be dependent on Jamal. But how was he supposed to do that? It was hopeless. For a moment Drake felt despair. He would be trapped like this forever.

But then, faint hope. Maybe there was someone who could help. He felt its touch on his mind. It had never forgotten him.

'Get up. We're going,' Drake said.

'Where to?' Jamal asked.

'Going to see . . .' He'd been about to say, 'a friend.' But friend wasn't the right term. Not a friend. Much more.

'My master,' Drake said, self-conscious about the word. But when Jamal didn't laugh, Drake repeated it, more confidently. It felt good. 'Going to see my master.'

Sanjit found flowers easily enough. A lot had been picked for eating, but there were still untended gardens behind abandoned houses where it was possible to pick a small rose or a marigold or whatever. He didn't really know what flowers they were. Some were probably just weeds.

When he had a half dozen he stopped to check in on Bowie, who was being watched by Virtue. Bowie was better today.

Maybe a permanent improvement, maybe not. Sanjit never counted his chickens before they'd hatched.

Virtue stared at him and at his flowers. He stared like Sanjit had lost his mind.

'What are those?'

'These?' Sanjit looked in mock surprise at the bouquet. 'I think these may be flowers.'

'I know they're flowers,' Virtue said. 'Why are you carrying flowers?'

'I'm bringing them to someone.'

'That girl?'

'Yes, Choo. They are for that girl.'

'You should stay away from her. She's a very scary girl.'

'Hot, though, don't you think?'

Virtue stared at him. 'Don't you know there's a quarantine? Where have you been? No one is supposed to go out.'

'A what?'

'A quarantine. That flu going around. Everyone is supposed to stay inside.'

'I've had flu before, big deal,' Sanjit said dismissively.

'Look, if they put on a quarantine they have good reasons. You don't know these people, I think most of them are crazy. You don't know what they might do if they catch you out.'

'I'll be back,' Sanjit said with a jaunty wink. 'Unless I get really lucky.'

'Or she shoots you with that big gun of hers.'

'That's also a possibility,' Sanjit said cheerfully.

He patted Bowie on the head and checked on the others. Then he headed out into the sunlight.

The streets of Perdido Beach had never exactly been busy. It wasn't New York or Bangkok. But they were particularly quiet now. Not a soul in sight.

Maybe Virtue was telling the truth about a quarantine after all. But hey, who better to be with than Lana, the Healer?

He reached Clifftop without seeing anyone.

He pushed through the lobby doors. He knew that Lana had the best room on the highest floor, a room with a balcony that looked down at the cliff and the beach and out at the ocean.

He was confronted with a confusing hallway full of doors, some closed, many showing signs of having been kicked open or battered down so kids could raid the minibars.

He found what he thought was the right door. He straightened his clothes and his flowers and knocked. From inside, Patrick erupted in loud barking.

He saw the peephole go dark as someone looked out.

He smiled and waved.

Soft cursing from inside. Then, 'It's OK, Patrick, it's just some idiot.'

The door opened. Lana had a cigarette hanging from the

corner of her mouth. She had her pistol in her hand.

'What?' she snapped at Sanjit.

'Flowers,' Sanjit said, and held them out to her.

Lana stared at the flowers. 'Are you kidding me?'

'I would have brought candy, but I couldn't find any.'

'Are you retarded? There's a quarantine on. No one is supposed to be outside.'

He had hoped for a little smile. He detected no smile. Instead he smelled alcohol on her breath. Although she didn't seem drunk, her words weren't slurred, and her eyes focused the full intensity of her incredulity quite effectively.

'May I come in?' Sanjit asked.

'In?' Lana echoed. 'Here?'

'Yes. May I come in?'

Lana blinked.

'OK,' she said, and her eyebrows shot up like she was amazed the word had come out of her mouth. She stepped back and Sanjit stepped through.

The room had once been a sterile, anonymous hotel room.

It still was. Lana had hung no pictures, collected no precious possessions. No stuffed animals lay on the bed. The room was filthy, of course, but so was just about every room in Perdido Beach.

It smelled of cigarette butts, whiskey, and dog. A huge shotgun leaned against one wall. Patrick seemed almost as agitated as his owner. Neither Lana nor Patrick was used to receiving guests.

There was a small Sammy sun in the closet so that when the closet door was left open there would be light, and when closed less light.

Sanjit crossed to the glass door. 'Great view.'

'What do you want?'

'I want to get to know you,' Sanjit said.

'Why?'

'You're interesting.'

'Yeah,' Lana said. 'But not in any way you're going to like.'

Sanjit sat down on the desk chair. He laid the flowers on the hutch next to the TV set. He noticed a scratch from a thorn. It was bleeding a little, no big deal.

'No,' Lana said, 'I'm not going to heal your scratch.'

'Good,' Sanjit said.

'Good? Why good?'

'Because when you hold my hand, I don't want it to be work for you.'

'Hand holding?' Lana barked out a laugh. 'That's what you want? Hand holding?'

'Well, we would work up to that. If we like each other.'

'We don't.'

Sanjit smiled. 'You seem awfully sure of that.'

'I know me, and I've met you,' Lana said. She sighed. 'OK,

look, I get it. You're one of those people who thinks they have to help screwed-up people. Or maybe you're attracted to dangerous, unbalanced people. But you're not going to get some kind of contact cool off me, OK? You're a normal kid, I'm a crazy freak, it's not really the basis for true love.'

'Oh. You think I'm normal.'

'Your mom and dad are movie stars.'

'My mom was a teenage prostitute who died of pneumonia after a bout of hepatitis. My father was any one of maybe a thousand guys. If you know what I'm saying.' Sanjit made a fake perky smile. 'Up until I was adopted half of everything I ever ate was stolen, and the other half came from some charity.' He let this sink in for a moment. 'Oh, and see this?' He opened his mouth and pointed to a gap where two molars should have been. 'Got beaten up really bad by a pimp who wanted to sell me to some old dude from Germany.'

Lana glared at him. Sanjit met her gaze and refused to look away.

Finally, she said, 'OK. You want to talk, OK. I'll talk, then you get it through your head and you leave.' Lana lit a new cigarette, puffed it, and looked at him through the smoke. 'I went up there to kill it. The gaiaphage. I drove a tank of propane up there, let it flow into the mineshaft, and all I had to do was light a match. The coyotes came after me. I shot them. I still

187

could have set off the explosion, but I didn't. Is that the story you want?'

'Is that the story you want to tell?'

'It was inside my head. I couldn't kill it. Instead it made me crawl to it. Hands and knees. Like a worm. I gave myself to it. I became part of it.'

Sanjit nodded because he felt like he should.

'It made me shoot Edilio. Bang.' She pantomimed it.

'He survived.'

'Sam and Caine knocked the gaiaphage pretty hard. I was freed.'

'And you saved Edilio. But you don't want to talk about that, right?'

'You know, it's not a big wonderful thing when you save someone you just shot.'

'You didn't shoot him, this monster did. You cured him. That was you.'

Lana's eyes were so penetrating he almost couldn't meet her gaze. But he held steady. She was looking for weakness in him. Or maybe she expected disgust.

'You went up there on your own to kill it,' Sanjit said.

'And failed.'

'But tried. If you were a guy, I'd say you had a big brass pair.'

Lana laughed, caught herself, laughed again. Then she kept laughing, stopping, trying not to laugh again, and failing.

'I don't know why I'm laughing,' she said, almost apologising and definitely puzzled.

Sanjit smiled.

'I don't know why I'm laughing,' Lana said again.

'You're probably a little stressed,' Sanjit said dryly.

'You think?'

Lana laughed again and Sanjit realised he was really enjoying her laugh. It wasn't silly or hysterical. It was, like everything about this strange girl, wise, sardonic. Profound. Mesmerising.

'Oh, dude,' she said, sobering. 'Is that what you're here for? Laughter is the best medicine? Is that it? Am I your act of charity or whatever? Heal the Healer with the power of laughter?'

The full force of her cynicism was back on display.

'I don't think I want to heal you,' Sanjit said.

'Why not?' she snapped. 'I mean, let's not lie, huh? I'm about as screwed up as a girl can be. I am a monument to screwed up. Why don't you want to heal me? I'm a freaking mess!'

Sanjit shrugged. 'I don't know.'

'You think I'm so messed up, it will be easy to get into my pants, is that it? I'm an easy target?'

'Lana,' Sanjit said, 'you carry a pistol and look like you'll use it. You have a dog. You tried to kill a monster all on your own. Trust me when I say, no one. No. One. No one looks at you and thinks, "She'll be easy."'

Lana sighed wearily, but Sanjit didn't believe the sigh or the weariness. No. She wasn't tired of him.

He said, 'I saw you. I heard your voice. I connected. It's not very complicated. I just had a feeling. . . .'

'Feeling?'

Sanjit shrugged. 'Yeah. A feeling. Like the whole point of my life, from the alleys in Bangkok, to the yachts and private island, to coming here like a crazy person trying to fly a helicopter, like all of it, from birth to here, point A to point Z, was all some big cosmic trick to get me to meet you.'

'Whatever,' she said dismissively.

He waited.

'The other day you said I was the second bravest girl you ever met. Who was number one?'

Sanjit's smile disappeared. In the space of a heartbeat he was back there, in that filthy alley smelling of rotten fish, curry, and urine.

'The pimp who knocked my teeth out? He was going to finish me off,' Sanjit said. 'You know? To send the message that you couldn't refuse him. He had a knife. And man, I was already half dead. I couldn't even move. And this girl was there. No idea where she came from. I never saw her before. She, uh . . .'

Suddenly, to his own amazement, he couldn't talk. Lana waited until he found his voice again. 'She came up to the guy and just said, "Don't hurt him any more."'

'So he let you go? Just like that?'

'Not quite. Not quite. She was a pretty girl, maybe eleven, twelve years old. So, you know, a nice-looking young boy is worth some cash to a pimp. But a pretty young girl, well, she was worth more.'

'He took her?'

Sanjit nodded. 'I was sick for about a week, I guess. Thought I was going to die. Crawled as far as a pile of garbage and just . . . Anyway, when I was able to move again I looked for her. But I didn't find her.'

The two of them sat there looking at each other. It seemed to go on for quite a while.

'I have to go to town,' Lana said finally. 'I can't seem to cure the flu thing. So much for being the Healer. But I can at least deal with the usual broken bones and burns and so on.'

'Of course,' Sanjit said and stood up. 'I'll let you go.'

'I didn't say you couldn't come with me,' Lana practically snarled.

Sanjit suppressed the smile that wanted badly to break out across his face. 'Whenever you're ready.'

SEVENTEEN

'**DEKKA.** WAKE UP.'

Her eyes opened. She blinked up at Sam. It was full daylight. Not even early morning, later. She had slept a long time.

A sharp intake of breath. She jumped up and began patting her body, probing, pushing, feeling for anything that shouldn't be there.

The divot in her shoulder burned like fire.

Her stomach growled. Her feet ached. Her scraped shins hurt. So did her back from sleeping on a rock.

'I hurt all over,' Dekka said.

Sam looked concerned.

'I mean, that's good. Hunter couldn't feel much of anything, right?'

Sam nodded. 'Yeah. Yeah, that's good. So I guess burning a hole in you was actually a good thing?'

'Not quite ready to find that funny, Sam. Where's Jack?'

Sam pointed towards the top of a hill. They were in a very dry and empty place. The hill wasn't much more than two hundred feet high and was more of a dirt mound than a mountain.

Jack was at the top, shading his eyes and looking to the north east.

'What do you see?' Sam yelled to him.

'There's a place over that way that looks like it's all burned.'

Sam nodded. 'Yeah. The hermit's shack. What else?'

'Bunch of rugged-looking hills, all rocky and stuff,' Jack yelled. He started to climb down but the dirt was loose, so he slid and slipped and fell. Then he stood up again and jumped.

He jumped thirty feet and landed very near Sam.

'Dude,' Sam said.

'Huh,' Jack said. 'I never realised I could do that.'

'There might be other ways you can use that strength, too,' Sam said.

'I wish I could use it to find some water.'

'Dekka, what do you think? We climb those mountains or go through the burned zone?'

'I kind of hate climbing.'

'The mineshaft isn't too far from the shack,' Sam pointed out.

'Yeah. I remember where it is,' Dekka said. 'We just don't go there.'

It wasn't far to the shack. Or more accurately the few charred sticks that marked Hermit Jim's shack. Sam pulled out the map again. He measured with his fingers. 'It looks like six or seven miles to the lake. I guess we'll all get a drink when we get there.'

The Santa Katrina Hills were on their left now. They were bare stone and dirt, and some of the rock formations looked as if they'd been shoved right up out of the earth, like the dirt was still sliding off them. Off to the right there was the taller mountain, and the cleft in that mountain, which hid the ghost town and the mineshaft.

None of them spoke of that place.

It was an hour's thirsty walk across very barren land before they reached a tall chain-link fence. The dirt was the same on either side of the fence. As far as they could see there was nothing that needed fencing.

There was a dusty, rusty metal sign.

'"Warning, restricted area,"' Jack read aloud.

'Yep,' Sam said. 'We are subject to search.'

'How great would it be if someone did come and arrest us?' Dekka said wistfully.

'Jack. Rip down the fence.'

'Really?'

'The barrier's that way.' Sam pointed. 'We should hit the barrier and follow it to the lake. And like Dekka says: if there was anyone around here to arrest us, it would be great. They'd have to feed us and give us something to drink.'

Sam wasn't sure quite what he expected to find at the Evanston Air National Guard base. He wasn't sure quite what he'd been hoping for. Maybe a barracks full of soldiers. That would have been excellent. But failing that, maybe a giant tank of water. That would have been nice, too.

What they found instead were a series of underground bunkers. They were identical on the outside: sloping concrete ramps leading down to a steel door. Jack kicked the first one open.

Sam provided illumination. Inside was a long, low room. Completely empty.

'Probably kept bombs here or something.'

'Nothing here now,' Jack said.

They opened four more of the bunkers before admitting that there was nothing to be found.

Wandering through the bunker field they came upon a truck with the keys in the ignition. The battery was dead. But there was a litre bottle of Arrowhead water, half full.

The three of them rested in the shade of the truck and shared the water.

'Well, that was disappointing,' Sam acknowledged.

'You wanted to find bombs?' Dekka asked.

'A giant supply of those meals soldiers eat, what are they called?'

'MREs,' Jack said. 'Meals ready to eat.'

'Yeah. Some of those. Like, maybe a million of those.'

'Or at least the truck could have worked so we could drive and not walk,' Dekka grumbled.

They started walking again. Already the half litre of water seemed like a distant memory. They began to notice the blankness of the barrier looming ahead. It rose sheer from the sand and scrub.

'OK, so we hang a left. Let's go find this lake and get back to town,' Sam said.

They kept the barrier on their right. The terrain was getting more difficult, with deep gullies, like dry riverbeds, cracks in the desert smoothness.

Ahead, shimmering like a mirage, was a low building that reminded Sam of the kind of 'temporary' building schools sometimes resorted to. There were few windows and these showed the horizontal slats of ancient blinds. Air-conditioning units poked out of the walls in several places.

In a parking area there were more sand-coloured camouflaged trucks. A couple of civilian cars. All neatly squared away between white lines.

A tall antenna stabbed at the sky. And beyond the building a tumbled mess of huge rust- and ochre- and dust-coloured blocks.

'Hey, that's a train!' Jack said.

Sam checked the map. Only now did he notice the cross-hatched line indicating a railroad track. He hadn't known what it was before.

Sam wished he'd thought to bring binoculars. There was something off about the building. It was too isolated. Although, Sam reminded himself, there might be a whole bunch of buildings just beyond the FAYZ wall. So maybe this one building was just at the edge of a big compound.

But it didn't feel that way. It felt like this place was deliberately far from anything else. He doubted it would even be noticeable from a satellite photo. Everything except the few cars were painted the same ochre colour as the surrounding emptiness.

'Let's check the building first.'

The door was unlocked. Sam opened it cautiously. Dirt and dust had filtered on to the polished linoleum floor. A main room, two hallways leading away, and two private offices behind glass partitions. There were half a dozen gray-painted metal desks in the main room and old-style rolling office chairs, some with mismatched cushions. The computers on the desks were blank. Lights off. Air-conditioning obviously off, too; the room was stifling.

Sam glanced at framed photos on a desk. Someone's family: two kids, a wife, and either a mother or a grandmother. He spotted a stress ball on another desk. There were official-looking binders and racks of ancient floppy disks.

Everything was dusty. Flowers in a tiny vase were just

sticks. Papers had flowed from desks on to the floor.

It was eerie. But they had all seen plenty of eerie: abandoned cars, empty homes, empty businesses.

One thing they had not seen in a very long time: a jar of Nutella was open on one desk, lid nowhere to be seen, and a spoon standing inside.

The three of them leaped as one.

'There's some left!' Jack cried with the kind of pure joy that should have signalled the discovery of something far more important.

Sam and Dekka both grinned. It was a large jar, and it was at least half full.

Jack lifted the spoon. The Nutella dripped languidly.

Jack closed his eyes and stuck the spoon in his mouth. Without a word he handed the spoon to Dekka.

It was like a religious ritual, like communion. The three of them taking spoonfuls, one after the other, each silent, each awed by the wonder of intense flavour, of sweetness after so much fish and cabbage.

'It's been, like, how long?' Dekka asked. 'It's sweet.'

'Sweet and creamy and chocolatey,' Jack said dreamily.

'Why is it still creamy?' Sam asked.

Jack had the spoon. He froze. 'Why is it still creamy?' he echoed.

'This jar had to have been opened months ago, back before

FAYZ fall,' Sam said. 'It would be all dried out. All crusty and stiff.'

'I'd still eat it,' Dekka said defiantly.

'This wasn't opened months ago. This hasn't been open for even a few days,' Sam said. He put the jar down. 'There's someone here.'

Jack had started reading some of the papers strewn carelessly about. 'This was a research station.'

Dekka was tense, looking around for intruders, enemies. 'Research on what? Weapons? Aliens?'

'Project Cassandra,' Jack read. 'That's the header on most of the memos and stuff. I wish I could get into these computers.'

'Someone is here,' Sam said, sticking to the most important fact. 'Someone who can unscrew a jar of Nutella and eat it with a spoon. Which makes it not a coyote. There's a person here.'

'Someone from Perdido Beach?' Dekka wondered. 'Maybe someone left town and found this place and never came back. It's not like we would notice everyone who ever left.'

'Or someone from Coates.' Sam made a motion with his hand, indicating silently that he would go down the hallway to the left and Jack and Dekka should be ready to back him up.

It wasn't a long hallway. Just four doors on each side. Milky light came through a reinforced glass window in the door at the far end of the hallway.

Sam opened doors, one at a time. The first two opened on to empty private offices. The next opened to a dingy room with a metal table and chairs, facing each other. A screen was on one wall. A clipboard was on the floor.

Sam picked it up. 'Project Cassandra,' he read aloud. 'Subject 1-01. Test number GV-788.'

He placed the clipboard on the table and went to the next room.

He opened this room and instantly knew someone was inside. Even before he saw anyone.

This room had a window of regular glass and sunshine poured in. There was a bed, a desk, a large blank TV mounted on one wall. Game players lay dusty beneath the screen.

Books were piled high on a side table.

And one book was in the hands of a boy who sat in a reclining chair with his feet up on the desk. He was maybe twelve. His black hair hung down his back almost to his waist. He would probably be tall when he stood up. Thin. Dressed in jeans, sneakers and a black-and-white Hollywood Undead T-shirt.

'Hi,' Sam said. He frowned.

The boy barely reacted.

'Don't I know you?' Sam pressed.

The boy looked at him with eyes narrowed to slits. He smiled a little. He seemed to want to go back to his book.

'Dude,' Sam said. 'Aren't you Toto?'

The boy's eyebrows went up. His lip quivered. He said, 'Is he real?'

He was speaking to a life-sized styrofoam head of Spider-Man, complete with blue and red cowl, that rested on a shelf.

'I'm real,' Sam said. Then he yelled, 'Dekka! Jack!'

'Why is he yelling?' Toto asked Spidey. 'He could be a Decepticon.'

'I'm not a Decepticon,' Sam said, feeling a bit ridiculous.

'It's the truth,' Toto told Spidey. 'He's not a Decepticon. But maybe he works for the Dementors, for Sauron, for the demon.'

'What are you talking about, Toto?' Sam asked.

Jack and Dekka came rushing up. 'Whoa,' Dekka said.

'He knows what I'm talking about,' Toto told Spider-Man. 'He guesses, he's testing. "What are you talking about, Toto?" he says. Right. He knows. He knows the demon.'

'I don't work for anyone,' Sam said.

'Liar, liar, pants on fire. Someone sent you.'

'Albert, but —'

'They always try to lie, but it never works, does it?' Toto said.

Sam turned to Dekka. 'I think our boy here has been alone for a long time.'

'He means I'm crazy.' Toto addressed Dekka directly, not Spider-Man, though he glanced back at the Spidey head and seemed torn between Dekka and the web slinger. 'The truth teller, truth teller Toto.'

'Are you test subject 1-01?' Jack asked.

Toto didn't seem to hear. But now tears were welling in his eyes. 'One zero one. Yes. One zero two, what happened to her, do you want to hear?'

'Yes,' Sam answered.

'Should we say, Spidey?' Toto bared his teeth and snarled, 'She used to live across the hall. Darla. She was eight. All her stuff was Hello Kitty. She could walk through walls. She didn't want to stay, she wanted to go home, so she tried to just walk right through the wall to the outside and the guards tased her as she was going through and you know what happened?'

'Tell us.'

'He doesn't want to know, not really, does he?' Toto asked Spidey. 'He's seen too many bad things, hasn't he? But I'll tell him anyway, which is that the Taser froze her halfway through the wall. She died. They had to bust out the whole wall to get her out of there.'

'Albert's cat,' Jack said.

Sam nodded. They'd all heard the story of the teleporting cat that misjudged and solidified with a book inside it.

'They aren't surprised,' Toto said. He tilted his head and shook it back and forth, vastly amused by some secret joke. 'They know, don't they?' he asked Spidey.

'Yeah, we know,' Sam said. He raised his hand, palm out, and fired a brilliant green beam at Spider-Man's head. The fabric of the cowl caught fire and the styrofoam within melted.

Toto's pale face went paler. He swallowed hard and looked directly at Sam for the first time.

'Sorry, man,' Sam said. 'But honestly we have all the crazy we can stand. And we don't have all day.'

'Yes, he's telling the truth, he's in a hurry.'

'He's still talking to Spider-Man,' Dekka pointed out. 'He's nuts.'

'Yeah, well, we're all a little nuts, Dekka,' Sam said.

'No, he's not nuts, the Sam boy,' Toto said and he shook his head back and forth. Then, slyly, he added, 'Anyway, he doesn't think he is.'

'We're looking for a big lake. Lake Tramonto. You know how to get there?'

'We don't know how to get anywhere,' Toto said. Suddenly he looked as if he might cry. 'Where's Spidey?'

'How long have you been here?' Sam asked impatiently.

It was Jack who answered. 'A little more than a year. The start date for subject 1-01 was several months before the FAYZ.'

Sam thought it over for a few seconds. Wondering what to do. He couldn't just dump the kid and walk away. Could he? Especially after he'd impatiently burned Spidey.

On the other hand, the very last thing he needed was another person to keep track of. And it didn't look like this kid was going anywhere. Sam could always pick him up later. And in any case, if they found the lake then the whole town would probably be moving, and they'd pass this way again.

'Listen, Toto, I'm going to pretend you're not completely crazy. I'm going to leave it up to you. So you either come with us and start acting at least a little bit normal, or you stay here. Your choice.'

Toto kept glancing back at the brown and black magma that had been the styrofoam head. But in between he looked at Sam and Dekka and even Jack.

'What do you have to eat?' Toto asked.

'Dried fish. Cabbage. Artichokes.'

To Sam's amazement Toto literally licked his lips. 'You have some other things, too, but you don't want to share. That's OK. I've only had Nutella. Ever since.'

'You must have a whole lot of Nutella,' Dekka said, unable to conceal her greedy hope.

'Yes.'

'Show us,' Sam said. 'Show us what you've got. Then we'll go find this lake.'

Sam led the way outside. Jack and Dekka fell in beside him. 'They knew, didn't they?' he asked Jack.

Jack still had a fistful of papers scooped up from one of the desks.

'Yes,' Jack said, still fascinated, reading through printed

sheets of data as he walked. 'I don't think they knew what was causing it. But they knew.'

'What did they know?' Dekka asked.

'Whoever was running this place,' Sam said angrily. 'They knew something was going on with kids in Perdido Beach.'

Jack caught up to him, grabbed his shoulder, and handed him a piece of paper. 'A list of names.'

Sam's eyes went directly to his own name, third on a list of five names. 'Toto, Darla, me, Caine, and Taylor.' He shoved the paper angrily back at Jack. 'Not all of the freaks, but some of us, anyway.'

He didn't know what to say or think. It made him angry, but he didn't even know why it should. Of course they would want to learn about kids who suddenly developed supernatural powers.

And of course they would want to keep it secret.

But still it made him angry and uneasy. 'This means they know. People on the outside, they've been able to guess some of what happened.'

'The real data is on those computers,' Jack said. 'This printout is just a small file. If the power was back on . . .'

Sam glared at the barrier near at hand. And wondered, not for the first time, what kind of welcome they would get if that barrier ever came down.

EIGHTEEN

32 HOURS 36 MINUTES

TOTO LED THEM from the facility to the train.

It was farther than Sam had thought. It had been a trick of perspective in the desert emptiness that had made the train seem to be right beside the building. In fact, they were a ten-minute walk away.

There were two yellow and black Union Pacific diesel engines. Both still stood upright on the track.

Behind the engines was a rust-coloured boxcar, also still on the track.

Behind these came a jumbled mess. There were seven derailed flatbed railcars. Each had spilled two containers – massive steel rectangles – on to the dirt and stunted bushes.

At the far end, the barrier had sliced a boxcar in half. The barrier had snapped into place, bisecting the burnt-orange boxcar, and the sudden shift must have derailed the other cars.

But Sam, Dekka, and Jack were not very interested in such speculation. Dozens of plastic-wrapped pallets had been flung across the tracks and the ground, spilled from the sliced-open boxcar.

Each of the pallets was piled high with flats of Nutella.

'That's, like, hundreds and hundreds of jars,' Sam said.

'Thousands,' Jack said. 'Thousands. We're . . . we're rich.'

If each jar had been a giant diamond, Sam would still have preferred the Nutella.

'This is the greatest discovery in the history of the FAYZ,' Dekka said, sounding like she was witnessing a miracle.

'What is a phase? What do they mean by phase?' Toto asked.

'FAYZ. Fallout Alley Youth Zone,' Sam said distractedly. 'It's supposed to be funny. Dude: what's in the rest of these containers?'

Toto looked uncomfortable. He squirmed so much he looked like he was dancing. 'I don't know.'

'What do you mean, you don't know? Are you lying?' Dekka demanded sharply.

'No lies,' Toto said, eyes flashing. 'I'm Toto the truth teller, subject 1-01. Not Toto the liar.'

'Then what are you saying? You never looked in any of these containers? There's fourteen containers. Plus that first boxcar. What do you mean you don't know?' Dekka found it outrageous.

Toto did his squirmy dance again. 'I couldn't get them open. They're locked. And they're steel. I hit them with chairs, but they wouldn't open.'

Sam, Dekka, and Jack all stared at the strange boy.

Then they stared at the containers.

Then they stared at one another.

'Well,' Sam said, 'I do believe we can get them open.'

Approximately eight seconds later Sam had burned the lock from the nearest container. Jack then pushed the door open.

The contents of the container were wrapped in plastic but still unmistakable.

'Toilets?' Dekka said.

Many of the porcelain fixtures were cracked from derailing, the shards held in place by the shrink-wrap.

A second container revealed more toilets.

The third container held what had to be thousands of medium-sized cartons. The cartons contained baseball caps. Dodgers caps.

'One size fits all,' Dekka said, disgustedly. 'But I'm an Angels fan.'

'This is going to take us a while to go through everything,' Sam said. 'But I think it's probably worth it.'

The fourth held wicker lawn furniture.

'Or not,' Sam said, disgusted.

The fifth container was wicker flowerpots and cracked terra-cotta pots as well as two pallets of plaster yard pretties: cherubs, gnomes, and the Virgin Mary.

The sixth was house paint and deck stain.

The seventh was better, a mixed load, pallets of shrimp-flavoured Cup-a-Noodles, chicken-flavoured ramen, coffee filters and coffee makers, and boxes of mixed teas.

'I wish I'd had some of those noodles,' Toto said wistfully. 'It would have been nice to have noodles.'

'Noodles are fine,' Sam agreed.

'I wouldn't say no to some noodles,' Jack said.

'True, true statement! He would not say no to noodles,' Toto babbled.

The eighth container was empty. Nothing.

The ninth was two big pieces of industrial machinery. 'Whatchamacallits,' Jack said. He searched for the words. 'You know. Like industrial lathes or whatever.'

'Yeah, great,' Dekka said. 'All we need is two hundred and twenty volts and we can set up a machine shop.'

Sam was starting to feel anxious. Nutella and noodles were fine. Great, in fact. Miraculous. But he'd been hoping for more food, more water, more medicine, something. It was absurdly like Christmas morning when he was little: hoping for something he couldn't even put a name to. A game-changer. Something . . . amazing.

When Jack opened the tenth container he just stood, staring.

Sam said, 'OK, what is it?'

No answer.

Sam leaned over Jack's shoulders to look. Pallet after pallet of heavy cartons. Each carton was emblazoned with the Apple logo.

'Computers?' Sam wondered. 'Or iPods?' Neither would be of any use.

At last Jack moved. He rushed to the nearest pallet, then hesitated. He carefully wiped his hands on his pants. Then he tore away the shrink-wrap and gently, cautiously, opened the first carton.

It was with trembling fingers that he lifted out a white box. On the box was a photo of a laptop.

'That would be great if we had internet,' Sam said. 'Or electricity.'

'They ship them fully charged,' Jack snapped, angry at Sam's interruption. Like Sam had started talking in church. 'It's been so long but . . . but they may still have some charge.'

'OK,' Sam said. 'So you can play some games. Let's move on to the next –'

'No!' Jack cried, his voice somewhere between anguish and rapture. 'No. I have to . . . I have to see.'

He spent five full minutes carefully opening the box, lifting out styrofoam packing pieces like they were fragile works of art.

It was like watching some unfamiliar but profound religious ritual. Sam found it almost moving. He'd never seen Jack so emotional.

He picked patiently at the small piece of tape that held the laptop's thin foam sheath in place.

And finally he held up the silver laptop as if holding a baby in his trembling hands.

He turned it over. By now the suspense was even getting to Sam.

Jack closed his eyes, took a steadying breath, turned the laptop over, and pressed the battery indicator light. Two tiny green lights blazed.

'Two!' Jack exulted. 'Two! I was afraid it'd be one blinking light.' Then, in a whisper. 'Two. That's maybe an hour and a half. Maybe two hours even.'

'Dude. Are you crying?'

Jack wiped his eyes. 'No. Jeez.'

'He's lying, he's crying,' Toto called out unhelpfully.

'You need some time?' Sam asked. He doubted any power on earth could convince Jack to move on yet.

Jack nodded.

'OK. Dekka and I will get the next one.'

The eleventh container was more lawn furniture.

The twelfth container was filled from bottom to top with the greatest sight Sam and Dekka had ever seen in their lives.

This time it was they who stood, awestruck. Overcome by emotion.

There was no mistaking that logo.

'Can you put Pepsi in Cup-a-Noodles?' Dekka wondered.

They leaped at the shrink-wrapped pallets and ripped cans free.

Crack psst!

Crack psst!

Crack psst!

The sound that had not been heard in the FAYZ for months was heard once again. Pop-tops were popped, and Sam, Dekka and Toto drank deep.

'Oh,' Dekka said.

'So good,' Toto said.

'It's . . . It's like life is all right again. Like the universe has finally decided to smile at us,' Sam said with a huge smile.

Burp.

'Oh, yeah,' Dekka said. 'Soda burp.'

The three of them were grinning. 'Jack!' Sam yelled.

'I'm busy!' he called back.

'Get over here. Now!'

Jack came running like he was expecting trouble. A grinning Sam held a can out for him.

'Is that . . . ?'

'It is,' Sam assured him.

Crack psst!

Burp.

Jack started crying then, sobbing and drinking and burping and laughing.

'You going crazy on us, Jack?' Dekka asked.

'It's just . . .' He couldn't seem to find the words.

Sam put his arm around Jack's shoulders. 'Yeah, dude. It's too much, isn't it? I mean too much like the world before.'

'I eat rats,' Jack said through his tears.

'We all eat rats,' Dekka said. 'And glad to get a good juicy one, too.'

'True,' Toto muttered with some concern. 'They eat rats. They didn't mention rats before, Spidey.'

The sun was well past noon. Sam said, 'We need to check the last containers. Then get moving. Just because we're living large doesn't mean people at home are.'

'We don't need to find water, we have Pepsi!' Jack said.

'Which is great,' Sam said. 'Might last a few days. If we could get it back to town.'

That sobered Jack. He nodded briskly and said, 'Yes, you're right. Sorry. I was just . . . I don't know. For a few minutes there it was like maybe it was all over.'

Just to do something different they went to the boxcar. The instant they rolled back the door they were assailed by a sickly sweet smell.

The boxcar had been full of oranges. But this was only obvious because of the perky labels on the flats. The oranges themselves had long since rotted in the heat. A sticky liquid covered the floor of the car. Some of the crates sprouted fantastic growths of furry mold.

'A little late on this one,' Sam said regretfully.

'Oranges would have been good,' Toto said.

The very last container was a mixed load: Stanley brand screwdrivers and saws and assorted hand tools, and exercise equipment of various types.

But by then no one cared, because it was the next-to-last container that weighed on their minds.

The thirteenth container had been loaded with shoulder-fired missiles.

The so-called hospital had sounded even worse after the fire. Because then kids had been screaming. Screaming Lana's name.

No screams this time, Lana noted. Coughs. Lots of deep, rasping coughs. Like kids were trying to cough their lungs right out.

Dahra was standing over one of the cots, laying a wet cloth on a kid's head. She hadn't noticed Lana walk in with Sanjit.

Lana did a quick count. Twenty? Twenty-one? Some of them were on cots, some were on mattresses covered in piled-high blankets from a dozen homes, a dozen beds. Some were lying with very little clothing on the cool tile floor.

And most were coughing, coughing, coughing.

Dahra looked up at the sound of their voices. 'Lana. Thank God. You want to try again?'

Lana spread her hands helplessly. 'I'll do whatever. But the magic isn't working on this thing.'

Dahra wiped sweat from her brow. She looked like she hadn't slept. Maybe ever. 'Look, secondary infections, they're called. Someone gets a virus and then something else moves in, too. A lot of times that's what kills people.'

'You're the boss,' Lana said. She meant it, and she meant it only for Dahra.

'Her.' Dahra pointed. 'Start with her. One hundred and six fever. That's what Pookie was before . . .'

Lana went to the girl. She looked familiar; Lana thought her name might be Judith, but it was hard to recognise someone whose face was red from coughing, drenched in sweat, hair plastered down, eyes scared, bleary and defeated.

Lana laid her hand on the girl's head and almost yanked it away. She was hot to the touch. Like touching a plate fresh from the dishwasher.

Lana had no particular ritual for healing. She just touched the person and tried to focus.

'Who are you?' Dahra snapped at Sanjit.

'Lana's boyfriend,' Sanjit said.

'No, he's not,' Lana said.

'You shouldn't be here,' Dahra said to Sanjit. 'We've got

three known dead already. Go wash yourself off in the ocean and go home.'

'Thanks, but I'll stay. I want to help.'

Dahra stared, eyes narrowed, trying to figure out if he was crazy. 'You really want to help? Because I need someone to empty out the bucket. If you really want to help.'

'I do. What bucket?'

Dahra pointed to a plastic trash can with a lid. Around it was a reeking pile of Tupperware containers that Dahra used as bedpans.

Sanjit scooped up the bedpans and balanced them on top of the bucket of urine and feces. The stench filled the room.

'There's a trench in the square. Then, if you're motivated, you could rinse everything out in the surf.'

'I'll be right back,' Sanjit said.

When he was gone, Dahra said, 'I like your boyfriend. Not many guys volunteer to carry ten gallons of diarrhea and vomit.'

Lana laughed. 'He's not my boyfriend.'

'Yeah, well, he can be mine if he wants to be. He's cute. And he carries crap.'

Lana felt the girl under her hand shudder and shake.

Dahra was moving automatically from bed to bed, cot to cot, pile of blankets on the floor to pile of blankets on the floor. She sighed as she wrote down another temperature. She was keeping records. Probably not as good as a doctor would do, but better than the average fourteen-year-old girl with twenty-one hacking, shivering patients could be expected to do.

'Why can't I do this?' Lana wondered aloud. 'The first round of flu it worked, mostly.'

'Immunity, right?' Dahra said. 'The virus gets into you, and then your body fights back. The virus learns, comes back ready for a new fight. So instead of reprogramming to beat antibodies it reprogrammed to beat you.'

'I'm not an antibody,' Lana said.

'Yeah, and this isn't the old world, is it? This is some freak show where nothing works exactly the way it should.'

His freak show, Lana thought. A single match and she could have burned it out, killed it. Maybe. How many deaths had come because Lana had failed?

A boy Lana knew, a first grader named Dorian, suddenly stood up and started running for the door. It was a weaving, unsteady run.

Dahra cursed and made a snatch for him.

The kid was out the door in a flash.

A moment later Sanjit reappeared with Dorian under one arm and the now semi-clean toilet bucket and containers in the other.

'Come on, little man,' he said. 'Back to bed.'

But Dorian wasn't having it. He started screaming and flailing around.

Pandemonium erupted. Two kids started crying loudly, a third rolled off his bed on to the floor, and a fourth was shouting, 'I want my mommy, I want my mommy.'

Then, a cough that was so loud it drew every eye. The little boy, Dorian.

He was standing up. He seemed startled by what had just come from his mouth.

He reared back and coughed again.

'No,' Dahra gasped.

Lana leaped to the little boy's side and pressed her hand against the side of his head.

He coughed with such force it knocked him down, flat on his back.

Sanjit straddled him, holding him down, while Lana lay her hands on him, one on his heaving chest, the other on the side of his throat.

Dorian coughed, a spasm so powerful Sanjit fell backward and Dorian's head smacked against the floor with a sickening crack. Lana kept her hold on him.

'He's so hot I can barely keep my –' Lana said as Dorian convulsed, bent into a C, and erupted in a cough that sprayed bloody chunks over Sanjit's face.

Lana did not waver, did not pull back, but Dorian coughed again, and now blood seeped from his ears and pulsed from his lips.

Lana stood up suddenly and backed away.

'Don't stop,' Dahra begged.

'I can't cure death,' Lana whispered.

Just then two kids appeared in the doorway carrying a third. Lana could see from clear across the room that the girl they were struggling to carry was already gone.

Dahra saw it, too. 'Set her down,' she said to them. 'Just set her down and get out of here, wash yourselves in the surf, and then go home.'

'Will she be OK? She lives with us.'

'We'll do everything we can,' Dahra said flatly. And when they beat a hasty retreat, she added under her breath, 'Which is not a damn thing.'

Lana closed her eyes and could sense the Darkness reaching out for her, questing, a faint tentacle reaching to touch her mind.

So this is how you destroy us, Lana thought. *This is how you kill us off. The old-fashioned way: plague.*

NINETEEN

ORC TOOK A small detour on his way to the beach to tear his old home apart looking for a bottle. He found two.

With one bottle in each hand he headed towards the water. He was drinking from both bottles, a swig from the left, a swig from the right, and very soon he was finding the weight of faeces in his pants almost funny.

'Orc. Man, where you been?'

Howard. Right there in front of him.

'Go away,' Orc said. Not angry, too happy now to be angry.

'Orc, man, what is going on with you? I been looking everywhere for you.'

Orc stared dully at Howard. He drank deeply, tilting the bottle back so far he almost lost his balance.

'OK, that's enough,' Howard said. He stepped forward and reached for the bottle and got his fingers around it.

Orc's backhand sent him flying. He had a sudden savage urge to kick Howard. Howard was looking at him as if he had already been kicked and not just swatted away. A look of betrayal. Of hurt.

Orc closed his eyes and turned his head away. Not up for this. He had turds in his pants, his head hurt, bad memories were bubbling up inside his brain, and he didn't need this.

'Dude, come on, man, this isn't right. I'll take care of you, man.' Howard stood up and made a show of being fine. His voice was soothing, like he was talking to a baby. Or to some stupid animal or something.

'I got what I need,' Orc said. He held the two bottles out like trophies.

Howard stood cautious, ready to jump back. There was blood running from his nose. 'I know you're feeling bad about Drake. I know that, because you and I are best friends, right? So I know how you're feeling. But that's done. Anyway, it was just a matter of time, sooner or later it was going to happen.'

Orc liked this line of reasoning. But he felt like maybe there was a diss hidden in there, too. ''Cause no one could trust me, right?'

'No, man, that's not it,' Howard said. 'It's just, no jail was ever going to hold Drake forever. This is all Sam's fault, if had just done what he should have done –'

'I think I hurt some little kid,' Orc said.

Just like that. Out it came. Not planned. More like it had to escape. Like Drake: it was going to get out sooner or later.

The comparison made Orc laugh. He laughed loud and long and took another drink and was feeling almost cheerful until his bleary eyes settled on Howard's face once more. Howard was grave. Worried.

'Orc, man, what's that mean? What do you mean you hurt some kid?'

'I just want to go wash off,' Orc said.

'This kid you hurt. Where did it happen?'

'I don't know,' Orc growled. He looked around like he might be in the right place. No, this wasn't it. It was . . . He spotted a stop sign at the far end of the block.

There was a pile of rags at the bottom of the sign.

Orc felt an icy cold fill his body. Howard was still talking, but his voice was just a distant buzzing sound.

Orc stood staring, unable to speak, unable to move, unable to look away, unable to breathe. Stared at the little pile of rags that was so clearly, so terribly clearly, a body.

Memory. Orc was back in his old body, the one before, the one made of flesh and not rock. He was raising his baseball bat, intending to teach Bette a lesson. Just a tap. Just a smack to show her he was in charge.

He had never meant to kill her, either.

'I'll get rid of it,' Howard was saying from far away. 'I'll hide it. Or something.'

It. Like the pile of rags wasn't a little kid.

Orc walked away, numb, indifferent to Howard's pleas.

It was a small, sandy area, not quite a cove, not really large enough to be much of a beach. It was just a sandy space between jumbled rocks on one side and a stand of scruffy-looking palm trees and grass on the other.

The five fishing boats – the fleet – were beached, pulled up on to the sand. It was like one of those picture postcards from quaint European fishing villages, Quinn thought. Not that the boats were very pretty, really, they were actually rather scruffy, and lord knew they smelled.

Still, kind of perfect.

Quinn and his fishermen had set up a reasonably pleasant campsite. There was never any rain so the fact that they had no tents or other cover didn't matter.

'We'll camp out old-school,' Quinn had announced as though it was all a fun diversion.

There were nineteen of them all together and they soon discovered that the beach was alive with fleas, tiny sand crabs, and assorted other animals that made sleep really unpleasant.

It was going to be a long night.

Then someone had the bright idea of burning a patch of grass on the theory that the cleared area would be relatively bug- and crab-free.

This of course gave way naturally to a bonfire of driftwood.

It smoked way too much and was hard to keep burning, but it improved everyone's mood and soon they were cooking an early dinner of fish, including some excellent steaks from the shark.

The dinner talk was all about what was happening back in town. Quinn hoped someone would think to update them. Not just forget about them. He made a point of reassuring his crews that Sam and Edilio would be taking care of their siblings and friends.

'This is just so we don't get sick and can keep working,' Quinn explained.

'Oh, goody: work,' Cigar said, and everyone laughed.

None of the fishermen seemed sick. No one had complained. Maybe the fact that they were a sort of self-contained group who mostly hung out together and spent most of their time out on the ocean had kept them safe. Maybe they would be OK.

Quinn watched the sun plunge towards the horizon. He walked out alone on to a spit of rock and sand that stretched a few dozen feet from the shore. Weird how much he had come to love his job and being out on the water. He'd always loved surfing, and now that was gone, but the water was still there. Too calm, too peaceful, too much like a lake, but it was still a remnant of the actual ocean, and he loved being near it and on it and in it.

If the barrier ever came down, what would he do? Wait until he was old enough and move to Alaska or Maine and become a professional fisherman? He laughed. That was not a career path that would ever have occurred to him in the old days.

But now he just could not even pretend to care about college or being a lawyer or a businessman or whatever it was his folks thought he should be.

He had crossed a line. He knew it and it made him a little sad. None of them would ever be normal children again. Especially those who had found ways to be happy in the FAYZ.

A light. Down in the direction of the islands. It would never have been noticed back in the days when Perdido Beach itself was lit up.

Quinn had heard the story about Caine and Diana occupying one of the islands. It was weird to think that the light might be coming from Caine's bedroom. And that Caine might be gazing out at the dark night.

Life would never be totally peaceful as long as that guy was alive.

Quinn turned his gaze south. The Sammy suns in people's homes weren't bright enough to light up the town. But the red glow of the setting sun painted the bare outline of Clifftop, snug up against the nearest arc of the barrier.

Lana. Quinn had liked her. Had even thought maybe she liked him. But something had changed in Lana. She was, in some sense, too large and powerful a person for Quinn.

Like Sam, who had once been Quinn's closest friend.

They were both part of some different class of person.

Sam, a hero. A leader.

Lana? She was grand and tragic. Like someone out of a play or a book.

And Quinn was a fisherman.

Unlike them, though, he was happy. He turned back to look at his crews, his fishermen. They were cleaning their nets, tending to their reels, cutting grass to make beds, complaining, joking, telling stories everyone had already heard, laughing.

Quinn missed his parents. He missed Sam and Lana. But this was his family now.

Roscoe had fallen asleep from sheer exhaustion. He awoke to find persistent itching on his stomach. He scratched it through his T-shirt.

He went back to sleep. But dreams kept him from sleeping soundly. That and the itching.

He woke again and felt the itchy spot. There was a lump there. Like a swelling. And when he held still and pressed his fingers against the spot he could feel something moving under the skin.

The small room was suddenly very cold. Roscoe shivered.

He went to the window hoping for light. There was a moon but the light was faint. Roscoe pulled his shirt over his head. He looked down at the spot on his stomach.

It was moving. The flesh itself. He could feel it under his fingertips. Like something poking back at him. But he couldn't feel it from the inside, couldn't feel it in his stomach. And he realised that his entire body was numb. He could feel with his fingertips but not the skin of his stomach –

The skin split!

'Ahhhh!'

He was touching it as it split, and he shrieked in terror and something pushed its way out through a bloodless hole.

'Oh, God, oh, God, oh, no no no no!'

Roscoe screamed and leaped for the door. His hand clawed at the knob as he babbled and wept and the door was locked, locked, oh, God, no, they had locked him in.

He banged at the door, but it was the middle of the night. Who would hear him in the empty town hall?

'Hey! Hey! Is anyone there? Help me. Help me. Please, please, someone help me!'

He banged and the thing in his belly stuck out half an inch. He was scared to look at it. But he did and he screamed again because it was a mouth now, a gnashing insect mouth full of parts like no normal mouth. Hooked, wicked mandibles clicked. It was inside him, chewing its way out.

Hatching from him.

'Help me, help me, don't leave me here like this!'

But who would hear him? Sinder? No. Not any more.

That was over. All over. And he was alone and friendless. No one even to hear as he screamed and begged.

The window. He grabbed the pillow from his bed and pushed it against the glass and then punched it hard. The pane shattered. He took off his shoe and smashed at the starred glass until most of it fell tinkling to the street below.

Then he screamed for help. Screamed into the Perdido Beach night air.

No answer.

'Help me! Please, please, oh, God, please help me! You can't just leave me locked up!'

But still, no answer.

Fear took hold of him, deep crazy-making fear.

No. No. No no no no, this couldn't be happening. He hadn't done anything to hurt anyone, he hadn't done anything awful. Why? Why was this happening to him?

Roscoe fell to his knees and begged God. God, please, no, no, no, I didn't do anything wrong. I wasn't brave or strong but I wasn't bad, either. Not like this, please, God, no no no, not like this.

Roscoe felt an itching in the middle of his back.

He sat down and cried.

TWENTY

DIANA FED PENNY a little late. But Penny didn't complain. She was off in some dream that had her smiling to herself, smiling at her own illusions.

The bathroom reeked of human waste. Penny was sitting on the tile floor, legs twisted in front of her, just sitting on a plastic exercise mat.

'Hey, you want to take a shower?' Diana asked.

Penny didn't respond, just giggled at something Diana couldn't see.

Diana bent down and tapped her shoulder. She had to do it several times before Penny's faraway eyes focused on Diana.

Penny laughed. 'Oh, that's the real you, isn't it?'

'As real as I get,' Diana answered.

'You come to feed the zoo animal?'

'Here's your food. But I thought you might want to take a shower or bath. I could help you.'

'Is it because I smell like a sewer? Is that it?'

'Yes,' Diana said bluntly. Without waiting for an answer, she went to the tub, a huge oval affair, all pink marble.

How long the water would last, Diana didn't know. But for right now there was water and it was even hot. There was an assortment of Bulgari bath beads, salts, and shampoos. She popped a couple of the bath cubes into the water.

Penny wasn't wearing much, just a dirty yellow tank top and a pair of stained pink shorts. She had two pairs of socks on over her broken ankles.

'How's the pain?' Diana asked.

'Painful. Feels kind of like someone broke my legs and my ankles and my feet. I'll show you what it feels like.'

Suddenly a pack of rabid, vicious dogs were there in the room. Their eyes were red, their breath steamed, they snapped at Diana, ready to launch themselves and rip her apart.

Then they were gone.

'Like that,' Penny said, taking malicious pleasure from the way Diana had leaped back, batting wildly at the illusion.

Diana calmed herself. Getting upset would just give Penny more of a sense of power.

'Sorry,' Diana said for lack of anything else to say. 'Eat something while the tub fills.'

'You don't have to stay here. I can haul myself up into the

tub.' She scooped some of the spaghetti and meat sauce into her mouth with her hand.

'You could drown.'

'Yeah, that would be terrible, wouldn't it?'

Diana didn't answer. There was nothing but pain in Penny's future. There was no way to fix her legs, not without Lana, and nothing to treat the pain but Tylenol and Motrin. It was like trying to put out a forest fire with a squirt gun.

'It's good you have your power,' Diana said.

'Yeah. It's great. Really great. It's like having my own kind of sucky movie theater. You want to know what I was seeing when you came in?'

Diana was pretty sure she did not.

'I was creating monsters with needle teeth. Like vampires, I guess, but more like wolves, like rabid bats, like every scary thing you see pictures of living down at the bottom of the ocean. And you know what they were doing?'

'Let me help get your shorts off.'

Diana knelt and worked Penny's shorts down her thighs. Carefully, as gently as she could. But still Penny made a rising, shuddering cry of pain.

'They were ripping you apart, Diana,' Penny gasped through gritted teeth. 'They were all over you, Diana, doing every horrible thing I could think of.'

'Lift your arms.'

231

Diana pulled the shirt, none too gently, over Penny's head.

'Watching you scream in my head helps keep me from screaming,' Penny said.

'Whatever works,' Diana said.

She put her arm under Penny's, bent low, and lifted her. The girl wasn't heavy. Food had not cured Penny's runway-model thinness.

'Oh, oh, ohhhhhh,' Penny sobbed as Diana lifted her.

Diana rested Penny on the edge of the tub, reached awkwardly to turn off the water.

'Caine could do this easier,' Penny said. 'But he won't, will he? He doesn't want to come in here and see his handiwork. Not the mighty Caine.'

Diana manoeuvred to bear most of Penny's weight and lower her bottom first into the hot water. Her twisted pipe-cleaner legs dragged, then followed their owner into the tub.

Penny screamed.

'Sorry,' Diana said.

'Oh, God, it hurts, it hurts, it hurts!'

Diana stood back. Penny was sweating, even paler than before. But she stopped screaming. She lay back against the tub, up to her chest in water and bubbles.

'There's a sprayer. I'll wash your hair.' Diana turned on the nozzle, tested the water temperature, and played it over Penny's lank hair.

232

She worked in shampoo until it foamed.

'Just like the hair salon,' Penny said.

'Yeah. Probably where I'll end up working someday,' Diana said.

'Nah, not you, you're too smart,' Penny said. She had closed her eyes. Diana rinsed shampoo down Penny's face and neck. 'Beautiful and smart and you have Caine all to yourself now, don't you?'

Diana sighed. 'I'm a loser, Penny. Same as you.'

Caine burst in. He looked startled. 'I heard screaming.'

'Oh, sorry about that,' Penny snarled. 'I hope I didn't wake you up, you piece of –'

'You OK?' Caine asked Diana.

'She's perfect,' Penny said. 'Perfect hair, perfect teeth, perfect skin. Plus she has legs that work, which is really cool.'

'I'm out of here,' Caine said.

'No,' Diana said, 'Help me lift her back out.'

'Yeah, Caine, don't you want to see me naked? I'm still kind of hot. If you don't mind my legs. Just don't look at them. Because they'll kind of make you sick.'

To Diana's surprise Caine said, 'Whenever you're ready.'

Diana popped the drain.

'Why don't you just kill me?' Penny demanded. 'You know you will sooner or later, Caine. You know you can't take care of me forever. You want to do it, don't you?'

Diana tried to read the answer in Caine's eyes. Nothing. There were times she was sure she saw human decency there. And other times when his dark eyes were as pitiless as a shark's.

'OK, raise her up,' Diana said.

Caine stepped closer and lifted up his hands. Penny rose from the water like some awful parody of a surfacing dolphin. She rose and the water fell and bubbles slid off her.

Diana took the nozzle and sprayed Penny off as she floated a few feet in the air. Even the touch of the water on her legs made Penny wince and grit her teeth.

Diana spread a clean towel over the mat and Caine set Penny down slowly. Gently.

'I could fill your head with living nightmares,' Penny said to Caine. 'I could make you scream like I scream.'

'But then I would kill you, Penny,' Caine said coldly. 'And I don't think you're quite ready to die.'

Albert stared at the ledger book like it could answer his worries. But it was the source of his worries. The columns where he normally entered the amount of produce coming in from the fields, the number of pigeons or gulls caught by Brianna, the number of rats sold to him, the quantity of birds, raccoons, opossums, squirrels or deer brought in by Hunter, were all empty for this day.

Albert reminded himself to get someone down to the dock

to bring up the catch. He should have done it earlier, but it had been a hectic day. Maybe he could send Jamal. Speaking of which, where was Jamal? He was supposed to be back by sunset and it was well after that.

Albert made a mental note to himself: give Dahra something nice as a reward for her quick thinking. If Quinn and his people had been brought down by this flu, the situation would be even more desperate.

Albert had a page for water. Bottled water found in homes or cars: nothing in days. Water trucked in: nothing in a day.

Just like that, in the blink of an eye, Perdido Beach had gone from self-sufficient at a very, very basic level to disaster.

Albert glanced around the room. His natural caution had become something closer to paranoia lately. The house was empty – even the maid was away. But what he was about to do would have been troublesome if observed: he opened his desk and pulled out a bottle of water.

It made a snapping sound as he broke the seal on the bottle of Arrowhead water. He drank deep, then carefully sealed the bottle and hid it away again.

He closed the ledger. Nothing to add to the incoming columns.

Then an unmistakable noise: shattering glass.

Albert froze. The sound was from close by. The kitchen?

He hesitated only a moment, running through his options.

Then he reached under the desk, fumbled for and found the pistol taped to the underside.

A door opened. He heard the sound of it and felt the air pressure change and pushed back his chair and tried to rip the tape free so he could hold the gun properly as he'd been shown by Edilio, but he was too slow, too late, they were in the room and on him.

Turk, Lance, Watcher and Raul. All armed.

It was Watcher – a quiet eleven-year-old who had been caught stealing – who whacked his knee with a crowbar.

'Aaahh!' It hadn't been that hard a swing but the pain shot up his leg and for a second he could think of nothing else. He'd never felt pain like that. His ankle and foot were tingling like he'd stepped on a downed power line.

'Get him!'

'Yeah!'

'Hit him again!'

'No!' Albert yelled, but the next blow came from Turk. His nose gushed blood. This was more numbing than painful. His thoughts were scattered, ripped into fragments.

'Wha . . .' he said.

His pistol, gone. Where? He squeezed his hand, stupid for a few seconds, not able to figure out –

Turk grabbed him from the back and slammed him down on the ledger. A distant part of Albert's mind worried that his blood would seep on to the pages and make them hard to read.

He groaned as someone punched him in the back and in the side and ground his face savagely against the ledger.

Turk yanked him back and shoved him against the wall. Albert's legs gave way and he fell on his rear end.

The four of them loomed over him. Albert knew he was crying as well as bleeding. And he knew that both his tears and his blood would make the creeps happy.

'What do you want?' he said, slurring his words, realising a broken tooth was stuck into his tongue.

'What do we want?' Turk mocked. 'Everything, Albert. We want everything.'

After cleaning Penny, Diana felt the need for a shower herself.

She shampooed. She conditioned. She shaved her legs and armpits. So normal. So like being home. Except that here her mother's creepy boyfriends didn't sneak in to get a look at her and pretend they'd come looking for aspirin or whatever.

She turned off the shower with great reluctance. She could stand there under the spray forever. But in the back of her mind was the knowledge that they had all wasted food until they were starving. She had learned a deep lesson about waste.

She wrapped one of the soft bath sheets around herself and brushed her teeth.

She went towards her bed and found Caine waiting there for her. He was standing awkwardly, chewing his thumbnail.

'Napoleon?' she asked him.

'No,' he said, and looked down at the floor.

'Uh-huh.'

'I helped with Penny.'

'Yes, you did. And you only threatened to kill her once.'

A flicker of a smile. 'Even Sam would have threatened her.'

Diana went to him. They did not touch. But they stood just inches away. Close enough for Diana to feel his breath on her face.

'Why did you save me?' Diana asked.

Caine sucked in a deep, steadying breath, like he was getting ready to dive into a pool. 'Because I . . .' He paused, blinked, seeming surprised at the words coming out of his own mouth. 'Because what would I do without you? How would I live without you? Because.'

'Because?'

'Because you are the only human being I need.'

Diana looked at him sceptically. Was he changed? Even a little? Or was it all just manipulation?

She might never know. But at that moment she also knew this was all she would get from him. And she knew that it was enough. Because she was not going to turn him away.

She grabbed his head in both hands and drew him to her.

She kissed him hard. It was a hungry, needy, wild kiss. No time to breathe, no time to be gentle, no time for any more stupid questions or doubts.

Diana took a step back, unwound the towel, and let it drop.

Caine made a sound like a strangling animal.

She pushed him hard. He landed on his back on the bed.

He began to fumble with his shirt, trying to get it off.

'No, I'll do that,' Diana said.

PETE

SOMETHING WAS NOT right. He could no longer balance atop the sheet of glass. He had fallen. He was falling still.

There was a ringing in his ears. A fire burned inside his body and that body was almost all he saw now. The sister was a faint echo. The Darkness was far away. He was inside himself, burning, twisting and falling forever and forever.

He tried to make his mother appear, but she wavered and slipped away.

The cool breeze could not reach inside him, it sliced his skin but did not put out the fire.

He felt his body empty out. Wrong. Wrong even to see himself, wrong to have his body be so big a part of his mind, pushing everything else aside.

Pain. An explosion, one of many, erupted from him and shot white-hot spears into him again and again.

His sister was upset, her distraught, too-bright, too-blue eyes swam around like fish in an aquarium.

The pale tentacle reached, quested, but could not find him because he was no longer high atop it all, perched and balanced, he was falling, spinning downwards into thirst and burning and pain.

He had to make it stop.

But how?

LITTLE PETE LICKED his lips. They were dry and cracked.

Astrid was thirsty, too. She'd gone out a couple of times, defying the quarantine, to look for water.

Her plan now was to wait for dawn when the dew would settle on the leaves of the trees, on the siding of the house.

She had a squeegee and a bucket and some fairly clean rags. She had to get water. She had to get Pete something to drink.

No one to call on for help. Sam was gone. She had looked for Edilio but not found him. Who could get her anything? Who could help her?

Little Pete coughed hoarsely and licked his lips as he hung in mid-air, twist slowly, like a chicken on a rotisserie, hovering in the breeze that blew strong through the window.

Afterwards Diana lay alone in her bed. She'd kicked Caine out and Caine was relieved to go.

Diana would not have minded him staying. But she sensed

he needed to go off and think, wonder what he'd gotten himself into, and regret any implication that he had cleaned up his act and accepted her terms.

It was all a fantasy, of course, the idea that he would change. Maybe someday. Maybe when he was older. Maybe when he got a career and a house and a wife and all the other things that cause wild boys to turn into men.

Not that men were always better behaved than boys.

Diana stayed on her side of the bed, just as if Caine was still there. That had become his side of the bed. It belonged to him.

Of course if that was true she was going to have to find some condoms. From just the two times the risk of pregnancy wasn't great, especially given the fact that her body was half wrecked. But still. The last thing anyone wanted was a baby.

What chance would any kid have with Caine as father and Diana as mother? Diana laughed softly. And could not later recall the exact moment or the exact reason that her laughter turned into bitter tears.

Edilio stood completely still in the hallway outside of Roscoe's room.

He could barely breathe.

What could he say? What could you say to a boy who was going to die? The terrible truth was that he could do nothing for Roscoe. It was good that Roscoe was calling to God because only God could save him. Edilio could not.

And what Edilio had to do next would destroy Roscoe's last hope.

Edilio looked at the plywood. Three half sheets, each four by four feet. A hammer and nails. Two-by-fours.

It had to be done. It had to be. Roscoe – the things inside him – could not be allowed to escape.

Edilio dragged the first sheet across the dark hallway and propped it against the door.

'I hear someone out there!' Roscoe yelled.

'It's me, Roscoe. It's Edilio,' he said.

'Edilio! Please, can you help me?'

Edilio opened the box of nails, grabbed the hammer, lined the nail up so it would go through the plywood into the door molding.

'Roscoe, there's nothing I can do, brother. I have to . . . You're going to hear some hammering.'

'What?'

Edilio slammed the hammer into the nail. He had to be careful; it was dark, and operating by feel alone was a bad way to hammer nails.

This was going to take a long time.

'Roscoe, I have to do this, man,' Edilio said.

'You're going to lock me in here and let me die?'

Edilio hesitated. 'Yes.'

'No way. No way. No!'

'And I have to do the same thing to the window, man.'

'Edilio, no. No, man. You don't want to do this.'

'No, I don't want to do this,' Edilio said.

Roscoe fell silent as Edilio nailed the remaining plywood in place. Edilio propped the two-by-four against the plywood and nailed it into place. The other end he nailed into the floor with massive long nails that took forever to hammer in.

Outside in the fresh air, Edilio steeled himself for what came next. He leaned the ladder against the building and with some difficulty wrestled a sheet of plywood up the ladder. He was going to fall and kill himself, he thought, and it would be justice, wouldn't it?

Roscoe was there at the window. His face was ghostly in the pale moonlight. 'Isn't there anything . . .?' Roscoe pleaded.

'Sam can't even kill the things,' Edilio said. 'He tried but he couldn't. I can't let them hurt more people.'

'Yeah,' Roscoe said. He nodded, jaw so stiff his teeth were cracking audibly.

'Sorry, man,' Edilio said. He slapped the wood into place against the window, resting it precariously on the narrow sill.

'Tell everyone I was ever mean to that I'm sorry,' Roscoe said, his voice muffled now.

'You were never mean to anyone, man. You were a good guy.'

Edilio winced, realising too late that he was using the past tense. He quickly drove in the first nail. He hit his thumb with the hammer. The pain was stunning.

He welcomed it.

Orc woke to a headache and shivers.

He was facedown. On the sand. The surf was lapping at his legs, covering his feet, gently surging to wash over his calves.

His head was a single giant ball of pain.

There was sand in his mouth. Sand in the cracks between the pebbles that formed his skin.

He could see the bottles. Just a few inches from his head, empty. Not even a tiny little drop left.

He was still drunk, he had not slept long enough to sober up. But he was no longer blacked-out, brain-dead drunk.

He was naked. That surprised him a little. But he had vague memories of ripping his stained, filthy clothes off and rampaging like a wild animal through the water. Bellowing.

There was no one to see him anyway. No one around. No one was going to hang around when Orc went crazy.

Scared of me, Orc thought. Surprise, surprise. Orc the monster, all covered in his own crap and staggering and lurching through waist-high water trying to get clean, scared people.

He decided to go look for another bottle, quick, before it all came rushing back into his head but it was too late because it was all coming back now.

He got to his knees. He might be a filthy, disgusting drunk, but he was still strong.

He'd have to walk naked through the dark streets. What did it matter? He wasn't a boy, he was a monster. A naked Orc was just a curiosity for people to laugh at. One more thing for people to find disgusting.

He tried to stand up but somehow ended up rolling on to his back. He vomited. It dribbled over the side of his face, over the last patch of human skin.

There were stars in the sky. They kind of swam around and sometimes doubled and blurred.

Here he was: Charles Merriman.

He hated himself. Hated himself so much. He had what he deserved: cold sand and colder water and pain.

Why couldn't he just die? He deserved to die. He needed to die. If there was some kind of God up there looking down at him, then God was wanting to throw up.

Of course God probably liked doing stuff like this. Charles Merriman was probably, like, his favourite person to beat on. Yeah, it was, like, *I'm going to give this kid a violent drunk for a daddy, and a dumb dishrag for a mother, and I'm going to make it hard for him to even learn to read, and then, just when he's starting to finally get some respect, I'll turn him into a monster.*

No one ever treated Charles Merriman like he might be a kid. Like he might not be totally worthless. Except Howard, and that was just so Howard could use him.

The only other person who had been nice to him was Astrid. Not like she liked him, but she didn't think he was scum. Like he wasn't just some nothing.

He had saved her life once. But even before that she'd been nice to him. One person. Ever.

With a supreme effort, Orc got to his feet.

In the end Sam decided to camp for the night by the train. They had crates to burn and a reassuring fire roared high into the night sky.

They made a camp out of lawn furniture. They ate Nutella and drank Pepsi, nowhere near tired of the sweetness.

They stared into the flames and up at the sparks.

'If we bring kids here, they're going to find out about the missiles,' Dekka said.

'Yeah,' Sam agreed. He made a *keep it down* gesture and added a significant glance at Toto, who was dozing fitfully on a wicker chaise lounge.

'We can't get all this to town. They have to come here.'

'Yep,' Sam said.

'What we need right now is a bunch of . . . what were they called?'

'M3-MAAWS,' Jack said. 'Multi-role Anti-Armour Anti-Personnel Weapons System.' He was reading the instruction manual by the light of the fire.

Sam rolled his eyes. 'M3s. Yeah, this would be, like, the last thing I would want to see getting into a kid's hands.'

'Can we hide them?' Dekka suggested.

'I won't tell anyone,' Jack said distractedly. 'I don't want kids coming here and stealing my 'puters, anyway.'

'We have a new member of our little band,' Sam said. 'Toto the truth teller. I don't think he's great at keeping secrets.'

He got up to throw another wooden crate on the fire. The fire would most likely keep the coyotes away. He yawned and flopped into the wicker rocking chair and hefted his sore feet on to the little table.

'You know what?' Sam said. 'I keep forgetting: I am not the guy in charge.' He laughed contentedly. 'I'll tell Albert. I'll hand Toto off to Edilio. Then? Not my problem.'

'Yeah, that's totally going to work, Sam,' Dekka said.

Sam noticed her feeling her stomach, pressing in on it, frowning.

'Anything the matter?' he asked.

Dekka shook her head. 'I think I'll get some sleep.'

Sam nodded off. At some time in the night he woke to see the fire had burned down to glowing coals. He saw Dekka some distance away, just outside the circle of firelight. She had her back to him, her shirt lifted up to expose her stomach, which she prodded and poked.

Sam went back to sleep and came fully awake what felt like mere seconds later, though the fire was almost entirely out and Dekka was on her own chair, snoring.

Something. Something out there in the dark.

Coyotes? He didn't want a fight with coyotes – if he or one of the others was badly hurt, there was no easy way to get back to Lana.

He raised his hand and tossed a Sammy sun into the air. It hovered ten feet up, casting a sickly light over the camp. Jack and Toto asleep. Dekka, no longer.

'What is it?' Dekka hissed.

'Don't know.' He pointed to the direction he thought the sound had come from. Then, in a voice pitched loud enough to be heard but not loud enough to wake his sleeping companions, he said, 'If anyone's out there, I am Bright Hands. I will burn you if you bother us.'

No answer.

A faint but definite rustling sound. Maybe a clicking. Maybe not. Then silence.

'So much for sleep,' Sam said.

'I'll sit watch,' Dekka said.

'Dekka: you have anything you need to tell me?'

He heard her sigh. 'Just being paranoid, Sam. Just, you

know, making sure. My stomach was just rumbling and I thought maybe . . . You know.'

'Dekka, the last time you had anything even a little bit sweet was months ago. It's not a surprise your stomach would be a little off.'

'Yeah. I know. Is yours?'

'Sure. A little,' Sam lied.

Jack woke with a loud snort and a crash as he smashed his arm down, crushing a table.

'What?' he yelled. He sat up. Rubbed his face. Found his glasses. 'Why are we awake? It's still night.'

'It's true: it is night-time,' Toto said.

'Well, if we're all up, we might as well push on. Sooner the better,' Sam said with a sigh. 'Let's go find this lake.'

Sanjit was slight in build. But he was strong. So when Lana collapsed he was able to catch her and hold her.

Dahra saw it happen. 'She needs sleep,' she said to Sanjit. 'Get her out of here.'

'What about you?' Sanjit asked.

'I've gotten really good at grabbing power naps,' Dahra said. 'Besides, Virtue is almost as much use around here as you are.'

'Almost?' Virtue grumbled.

He had come to the so-called hospital with word that Bowie

was doing much better. He had tucked the rest of his brothers and sisters into bed with too little water and too little food. And now he was helping Dahra.

Dahra put a hand on his shoulder and said, 'You're a lifesaver, Virtue.

'I can't carry Lana to Clifftop,' Sanjit said. 'But I can get her a place to lie down.'

Lana woke up long enough to say, 'Urrhh. Wha?' And then her eyes rolled back in her head and Sanjit lifted her in his arms. Virtue brought him a couple of blankets and draped them over his shoulders.

He carried her up out of the basement, up through the hallway crowded with hacking, miserable kids, and out to the plaza.

Five unburied bodies lay there side by side. Mismatched blankets covered each one, corners tucked underneath, faces covered by chenille or satin or tartan wool.

They'd given the plague a name, a callous nickname. The SDC they called it: Supernatural Death Cough.

But at some point during the day they'd begun to notice that some kids were getting better, too. The flu was awful. But it wasn't a death sentence to everyone who caught it.

They'd been unable to keep complete records, but according to Dahra's hasty notes and frazzled memory about one in ten progressed to full-blown SDC.

Sanjit was struggling a bit to carry Lana, but he was unwilling to lay her down near the dead or within sound of the hacking coughs.

She wasn't just going without sleep. She was going without love and hope. She was living with guilt for having failed to be Superwoman, having failed to kill the evil in the mineshaft, having failed to see what was happening to Mary.

He took her to the beach and laid her down on one of the blankets, which he spread on the soft, dry sand. She was lying on top of the gun in her belt, so he slid it out and lay it on her stomach. Then he covered her with the other blanket.

Her faithful dog had followed them the whole way and now Patrick snuggled beside her. He looked up at Sanjit, questioning.

She would almost certainly be safe here alone. No one wanted to hurt the Healer. And Patrick would bark if anyone came close.

But Sanjit couldn't just leave her here all alone. So he settled into a sort of yoga sitting posture, sighed, and decided to await sunrise.

Albert did not resist. Maybe, he thought, a braver kid would have. But he wasn't that kid. When Turk demanded to know where Albert's secret stash was, Albert told him.

Simple as that.

Albert had wet himself. He had cried. Still was crying.

He was going to die. He knew that. They would figure out pretty soon that there was no safe way to release Albert.

They would know that. He knew it, so how could they not know it?

But he could negotiate, maybe. Maybe now that they had all his stuff, his stash of canned food and bottled water.

It didn't look like much. It wasn't, although it was untold wealth in the FAYZ. They had filled two small boxes with his things and filled their hoodie pockets as well.

'You got what you wanted,' Albert said, trying desperately but failing to keep the sobby quaver out of his voice. 'Just go away. I won't tell anyone.'

'Man, you were hiding cans of Beef-a-Roni,' Raul said. He was disbelieving. 'You had three cans!'

'Take it,' Albert pleaded. 'Take it all.'

Turk glanced at Lance. Even in his despairing, shattered state, Albert knew they weren't quite sure just yet. Hope rose like a tiny flame inside him. Maybe. Maybe they wouldn't.

'Look, you want food and water, right?' Albert pleaded.

'You have more?' Lance demanded angrily.

'Not-not-not here.'

'Not-not-not,' Lance mimicked.

'N-n-n-n-not h-h-h-here,' Watcher said, and laughed.

'So where is this other stuff?' Turk asked, and kicked him almost tentatively. It was enough, though, to send a breathtaking spike of pain up Albert's leg from his broken knee. The knee was already swelling to twice its normal size. It was the worst of many agonies in his body.

'I don't have anything else here,' Albert said. 'But listen, I make more, right? I buy more. I control what gets made and picked and all.'

'Yes,' Turk said, mock-serious. 'You're a big man, Albert. Too bad you peed yourself.'

That set off another round of laughter.

'You think we're stupid?' Lance demanded. 'You think we're just some stupid white boys who don't know you can snap your fingers and have Sam or Brianna or one of those freaks come after us?'

'I wouldn't do that,' Albert said. His jaw was quivering so bad he almost couldn't speak. 'I wouldn't. Because if I did that, you'd, you'd, you'd tell people I cried.'

'And wet your pants.' Watcher seemed the most likely to let him go, but Albert knew the decisions were being made by Turk and Lance.

There was no pity in either face. Lance was aglow with hatred. Turk was less emotional.

'You know what we ought to do?' Turk suggested, laughing in anticipation of his punch line. 'We ought to throw him in one of the slit trenches we dug for him.'

'No, no, don't do that,' Albert begged. A dunking in excrement was infinitely better than being killed. 'No, don't, I'm begging you.'

Lance squatted down, brought his handsome, chiselled face right down to Albert's level. 'You just think you've got it all, don't you? Yeah, it would be fun to see you wallow around in the crap like you made us do. But then you'd just climb out and next time one of us turned around, there'd be Sam Temple. Flash of light and *zap*, we'd be dead.'

'I'm not . . . That's not . . .' Albert said. 'Please. Please don't kill me.'

Turk looked offended. 'Did we say we were going to kill you?' He turned to Lance. 'Where did he get that idea?'

Lance played along. 'I have no idea, Turk.'

'Maybe because of this,' Turk said. He levelled his rifle at Albert's face.

Something exploded.

Albert heard no sound.

He was on his side.

Blood covered his right eye, blinding him. Or maybe his eye wasn't there any more, he didn't know.

He tried to breathe and heard gurgling in his lungs. Heard his heart slow . . .

Turk looked at once alarmed and ecstatic. Lance's face

became sullen. The two younger kids backed away, tripping over each other, and ran.

Lance punched Turk's shoulder in rough congratulations.

Albert's one good eye went dark.

'**THAT** IS A lake,' Sam said. 'That is definitely a lake.'

'I can't believe we didn't even know this was here,' Dekka said.

The sun was still not up, but a pearly gray light showed a long slope heading down to a vast body of water. Bigger than anything Sam had seen outside of the ocean.

Dry grass grew in tufts. Amazingly scraggly, stunted pine trees showed here and there, but the shore itself was formed by a line of large jumbled rocks broken up by narrow, halfhearted sand beaches.

At the limits of their vision was a small marina with perhaps two dozen boats at the dock.

The barrier sliced right across the lake, but the part on the inside was more water than the kids of Perdido Beach could ever need or want.

'You think it's drinkable?' Dekka wondered.

'Let's find out,' Sam said. He jogged downhill towards the

shore, careful not to trip, but anxious to see and taste. It would be too cruel to get here and find that it was salt water. That would be one more dirty trick, one more disappointment. Not to mention the fact that it might doom them all.

He reached the lakeshore with the others close behind. The pale rock was shifting and unsteady, so he felt his way gingerly.

He pulled off his shoes and then impulsively dived in a flat arc into the water.

It was shallow near the shore and he scraped his chest on submerged rocks, but with two strokes he was out in water over his head.

Sam gulped a mouthful. Treading water he looked back to see Jack, Dekka, and Toto standing uncertainly on the rocks. 'Ladies and gentlemen,' Sam said, his face split by a huge grin, 'we have fresh water.'

In something less than five seconds, the three of them splashed in after him.

'It's water!' Jack cried.

'It is so totally water!' Dekka agreed.

'She's telling the truth, Spidey!' Toto said.

Sam turned a joyful somersault. The lake was cold but not bone-chilling. The surfer part of his brain calculated he'd have been warm and toasty enough with a 3/2 wetsuit.

He gulped some more water and swam over to his friends.

'Fresh water,' Dekka said. 'Cold fresh water. Brrr.'

Sam scanned the shore. 'This isn't a great place to set up a new town, really. We'd need something flatter. And then we'd have to be careful about not having everyone's sewage end up flowing into our drinking water. I guess we . . .' He stopped himself. Albert and Edilio could figure out the details. He had done what he needed to do.

'I saw boats,' Jack remarked. 'I wonder if there are fish.'

Toto said, 'Fish, yes, fish.'

'You know something?' Sam asked him.

'My dad used to take me fishing.' Then, as if puzzled by his own words, he looked for the Spidey head that wasn't there and said, 'This isn't that lake, is it? No, that was Lake Isabella.'

'OK,' Dekka said patiently. 'Were there fish in that lake?'

'Trout,' Toto said. 'Bass. Also crappie. Fish.'

'If we find fishing poles and stuff on the boats, it means there are fish,' Jack pointed out.

'It's only, like, half a mile. We could swim,' Sam said.

'You could swim half a mile,' Dekka said. 'Me, I'll walk.'

They climbed out, Sam with great reluctance. It was invigorating, this new and unexplored body of water. Who knew what might be found on or around the lake?

But he understood that Dekka and the others might not be thrilled by a long, cold swim.

The shore was a series of curves, like the edge of a lace doily made with sketchy sand beaches and rocky promontories.

They soon came upon a trail and were laughing and chatting lightheartedly.

Sam knew logically that without gas – and a lot of it – they'd never get enough water down to –

He stopped dead. 'Marinas,' he said. He felt a chill that had nothing to do with temperature. 'Marinas. You know what they have?'

'Boats?' Jack suggested, like he was afraid it was the wrong answer.

'Boats.' Sam grinned. 'Sailboats, maybe. But you know what else? Motorboats. Jet skis.'

'You want to jet ski?'

'What do jet skis run on, my friend?'

'I want to say water,' Dekka said.

'Gas!' Jack cried.

Sam slapped him on the shoulder. 'Yes! A marina isn't a marina if they don't have fuel.'

He grinned and started to run toward the marina. A nagging voice in his head warned him not to hope, not to expect a good answer. *It's the FAYZ*, the voice said.

It's still the FAYZ.

But after so much pain, so many disappointments, and so many horrors, surely they were due for some good news?

Surely.

* * *

Lana opened her eyes.

Patrick licked her face. Which was probably why she opened her eyes.

Something heavy lay on her chest. A head. Long, dark hair.

She pushed it away and it groaned, and said, 'I'm awake.'

Sanjit sat up, looked at her, and wiped drool from the corner of his mouth.

Lana was on the beach. The sun was up but had not yet cleared the mountains. How she had come there she did not know. Instinctively she felt for her gun. It was not in her waistband. It had become tangled in the blanket.

'How did I get here?'

'I brought you here.'

Lana absorbed that. 'Why?' she demanded suspiciously.

'You passed out.'

Lana ran her hands through her tangled hair. She wiped her mouth and made a face, tasting the inside of her mouth. 'You have any water?'

'Sadly, no,' Sanjit said.

She sighed and looked at him with tired eyes. 'What is it with you? You don't even have a blanket,' Lana said.

'I wasn't going to sleep.'

'Tell me you weren't watching me sleep, because then I'd have to throw up.'

Sanjit grinned. 'I did. I watched you sleep. And heard you sleep, too.'

'What does that mean?'

'Well, you farted once. But mostly you talk in your sleep. Groan in your sleep.'

'What did I say?'

Sanjit made a show of trying to recall. 'Well, mostly it was, urrgh, mmmm, unh, unh, don't try to . . . urggh. And the fart was very, um, genteel. Like: *poot-poot!* Almost musical.'

Lana stared at him.

He shivered.

'Are you cold?' she asked.

'Just a little chilly. You know, from just waking up.' He shivered again and wrapped his arms around his drawn-up legs.

She pulled her top blanket off, balled it up, sand flying, and shoved it at him. He draped it over his shoulders.

'How many more dead?' she asked.

'It was five total when we left.'

Lana hung her head down for a moment and Sanjit remained silent. Then she stood up. She walked down to the water's edge. She stripped off her outer clothing, leaving only her underthings.

Then, gritting her teeth, she ran into the surf, and as soon as the water was up to her knees, she dove headfirst. It was freezing. But it was clean. It washed away the blood and the grime.

She rinsed her mouth with salt water.

Then, shivering, she came back out of the water and ran back to Sanjit.

'You're staring,' she said.

'Beautiful girls in wet underwear have a tendency to cause staring in teenage boys.'

She bent down, picked up the blanket, shook the sand out of it, and wrapped it around her. Sanjit stood up.

She kissed him on the mouth.

A real kiss.

He cupped her wet head in both hands and kissed her back.

'That wasn't as bad as I thought it would be,' Lana said.

For once, she noted with satisfaction, Sanjit did not seem to have a glib comeback. In fact he looked just a little sick, and very much as if he meant to kiss her again.

'Back to the hospital,' she said.

Brittney rose to consciousness on a narrow dirt path. Seven-foot-high dirt and stone walls hemmed her in, towered over her. And perched atop those walls, coyotes leered down, their mouths open, tongues lolling out.

Jamal was behind her, checking the wire that held her arms pinned together at wrist and elbow.

Her ankles, too, were tied, but with a loose rope so that she could take short steps, but not run.

'Where are we?' Brittney asked.

Jamal shrugged with his one good shoulder. 'Somewhere Drake wants us to go.' He yawned, glanced up nervously at the coyotes, and yawned again.

'You should get some rest,' Brittney said. 'You're in pain and tired.'

'Here?' He laughed bitterly. 'This feel like the place for a nap?'

No, Brittney acknowledged silently. There was something dark about this place, even though the sun was up in the sky. Something about the air. Something about the look in the eyes of the coyotes. A darkness that reached inside to her un-beating heart.

'I want to go back,' Brittney said.

'Yeah? Me, too,' Jamal said. 'But if I do, old Drake will whip the skin off me.'

He shoved her forward. She stumbled when the rope snapped at her ankles and almost fell. But she caught herself and shuffled on, not knowing what else she could or should do.

What must I do, Lord, to earn my true death and my place in your heaven?

'This is a bad place, Jamal,' Brittney said. 'I can feel it.'

'Yeah,' he said. 'Drake is a bad boy, and he goes to bad places. But better off with him than against him, I figure.'

They emerged from the cut-through in view of a half-ruined

hole in the side of a sheer rock face. There was just enough pale pink light to see that the mineshaft was blocked by tons of fallen rock. The massive timbers that framed the hole were splintered and looked as if they might snap.

Whatever evil Brittney felt, it came from there, from that hole, that pile of rocks.

'Where are we?'

'The mineshaft,' Jamal said. 'Haven't you heard all about that? In there? That's the thing that gave Drake his whip.'

'In where?' Brittney said. 'It's all collapsed. It's sealed up.'

'That's probably good, huh? 'Cause if that thing feels this bad from out here, I don't want to know what it feels like up close.' He bit his lip and in a low voice said, 'Like a big claw holding your heart. Like icicles in your brain.'

'Jamal, if you ran away . . .'

He shook his head. 'Drake would come after me. Look, you can't be killed, right? And he can't be killed, right? Which means, I betray him, sooner or later he gets me.'

'Maybe fire,' Brittney said softly. 'Maybe God's holy fire can destroy us both.'

'Yeah, well, I don't happen to have any of that.'

'Only Sam can end this.'

Jamal put up his hands in a *who, me?* gesture and said, 'I am cool with that. If big Sam wants to take Drake out, I'm not going to say anything to stop him. But listen: all you're trying to do is slow Drake down, girl. Him and Sam, they're going to get into it eventually, right? So maybe you should be trying to speed him up, you see what I'm saying?'

Brittney stared at Jamal. Was it a trick?

Is this the devil tempting me?

'What did the demon Drake ask you to do?'

Jamal nodded at the cave. 'He just said be here. He's got in his head that he can talk to that thing in there. Or at least hear what it says.'

Brittney could believe that. How could she not believe in things that seemed supernatural? Her brother sometimes spoke to her as an angel. And God was with her always. Wasn't He?

And she herself, this gruesome remnant of the girl she once was, she herself was something outside of nature.

Was Sam the Lord's servant? The very tool God had chosen to liberate Brittney? She'd begged Sam often for liberation. But God's ways were not knowable to her. His time was not her time. His will be done.

'What does Drake want of me?' Brittney asked.

'Just, you know, don't always be trying to run away so I have to tie your legs and slow us down and all.'

'Is he going after Sam? Is that his plan, to go after Sam?'

She thought she caught just the slightest falseness in Jamal's eyes as he said, 'That's exactly his plan. Straight for Sam, as soon as he checks in with . . . you know.'

'You can sleep, Jamal,' Brittney said. 'Sleep until Drake comes back. I won't run away.'

'How am I going to trust you?'

'Because I swear it. On the blood of the Lamb, I swear it.'

Jamal woke to the pain of Drake kicking him.

'What?'

Drake was actually smiling. It wasn't a good look for him.

'You were asleep,' he said. 'And I'm still here.'

Jamal jumped up and quickly untied Drake. 'Yeah, I did just what you said, Drake. Just like you said. I told her that you would go after Sam first thing. Then Sam would burn you both up and . . .'

He gulped, suddenly realising that this might be taking it too far.

But Drake was in a charitable, expansive mood. He patted Jamal lightly on the cheek with the tip of his whip. 'You did good. And I will get Sam Temple. Sooner or later.'

Drake gazed at the mineshaft. What he felt towards the Darkness within was something very much like love. Fear, yes, but the Darkness deserved his fear. His fear and his devotion.

If he had to pull the rocks out of there one by one, and if it took weeks, he would reach the Darkness and free him.

'My old body's down there,' Drake said, realising it for the first time. 'My old body is down there with him.'

Drake felt a sudden pang of longing. He wanted to press his body against the rocks in the mine's mouth. It would bring him closer. Maybe the Darkness would reach out to him, touch his mind, tell him what to do next.

But he couldn't do that in front of Jamal.

'Start hauling rock,' Drake said. 'You have to pile it, like, back over there.' He pointed at a relatively flat space. 'I don't know how far the rock fall goes. It may take us a while. Put Brittney Pig to work when she comes back.'

For two hours or more they lifted and carried. It would have helped if they had a wheelbarrow. It would have helped if Jamal's arm weren't broken. They had to lift each chunk of stone, each shattered timber. Some were big enough that they had to each take an end. Some were so big they couldn't even budge them and had to just go around them.

At the end of two hours they'd moved no more than a foot and a half deeper into the shaft.

Brittney had reappeared once during that time and she had bought into the idea of helping with the digging. But Drake couldn't kid himself: they weren't getting anywhere. It could take months. Years. Forever.

The coyotes came and went, watching, no doubt thinking about eating Jamal. So when Drake heard the sound of movement coming from around the bend in the road, he assumed it was coyotes.

Only it wasn't the usual stealthy *pad-pad-pad* of coyotes. This was a sound with clicks and sudden rushes.

Drake wiped his brow and turned warily towards the sound.

It looked like something from a science fiction movie. Like an alien or a robot or something, because it was way too big to be just an insect.

It was silver and bronze, dully reflective. It had an insect's head with prominent, gnashing mouthparts that made Drake think of a Benihana chef flashing knives ceremonially. Its wickedly curved mandibles of black horn or bone protruded from the side of its mouth.

It smelled like curry and ammonia. Bitter but with a tinge of curdled sweetness.

More came now, scurrying up beside the first. They had eyes and antennae. The eyes were arresting: royal blue irises that could almost pass as human. But with nothing of human awareness, nothing of human vulnerability or emotion. Like ice chips.

They ran in a rush on six legs, stopping, starting, then skittering forward again at alarming speed. Their tarnished silver wings folded back against bronze carapaces, like beetles or cockroaches. The wings sometimes flared slightly as they ran.

Bugs. Maybe. But each at least five feet long and three feet tall, with antennae adding another foot.

Drake stared into the soulless blue eyes of the first bug.

He was ready with his whip hand, and Jamal was ready with his rifle, but Drake didn't like his chances much if they were looking for a fight. There were a dozen of the creatures, jostling around one another, like ants pouring from a mound or wasps storming angrily from a disturbed hive.

Drake felt a stab of fear: could he survive being eaten? Chopped into chunks by those gnashing mouths and swallowed?

A coyote, keeping a cautious distance, loped to the top of the rise and spoke in the strangled speech his species had achieved.

'See the Darkness,' the coyote said.

'Them?' Drake asked. The coyotes and these monstrosities could communicate? 'They want to see the Darkness? Fine,' Drake said. He jerked his thumb over his shoulder toward the mine. 'Go for it.'

'They hungry,' the coyote said.

Drake didn't have to ask what he was supposed to do about that. Because now the same foul, insinuating voice that was speaking through the coyote reached him directly, touched his willing, submissive mind and flooded it with a deep and awful joy.

Drake closed his eyes and rocked slowly back and forth, feeling the touch of his master.

Soon Drake would be with the Darkness. The Darkness

would give him all he needed. And Jamal had served his purpose.

'So tell them to eat something,' Drake said. 'Sorry, Jamal.'

'What?' Jamal waited for Drake to laugh, like it was a joke. But Drake just smiled and winked and said, 'Dude, sooner or later I was going to kill you anyway.'

'No, no!' Jamal gasped. He backed away. He turned and ran.

The nearest bug, icy blue eyes focused with terrible intensity, flashed out something that might have been a tongue. It was black, and as thick as a rope with a barbed tip like a cluster of fishhooks. The tongue caught Jamal's leg and Jamal fell facedown.

'Drake! Drake!' Jamal yelled. 'Please!'

Drake laughed. He gave a little wave as the rope tongue yanked Jamal towards his doom.

Jamal fired. *BLAM BLAM BLAM.* At close range, then closer range, then inches from the bug's hideous face.

The tongue released and snapped back. Then scimitar mandibles cut Jamal in half and there was no more firing.

The massive bugs surged, and within seconds nothing was left of Jamal.

Then, without a pause, the blue-eyed monsters went to work moving rocks at dazzling speed, pushing with their mandibles, rising on their hind four legs and gripping with their front two.

Drake felt Brittney returning. But that was OK, because now his Lord and Master, the Darkness, Drake's one true God was with him, filling his heart and soul.

And It would not be thwarted.

TWENTY THREE

ASTRID WAS IN the backyard using the slit trench when it happened. She had sat by Little Pete's bed for two days, waiting, fearing.

But even dehydrated, she still had to go eventually. She'd hoped it would be safe. She'd hoped to see that Albert's people were delivering water and food and the epidemic was past.

But the streets were abandoned. She heard no distant sounds of truck engines, nor even the squeaky wheels of hand-drawn wagons.

So she did what she had to do at the slit trench in the yard and continued to pray as she had almost constantly.

Whooosh-craaack!

The entire upper floor of the house blew apart.

There was no fire. No flame.

The top floor – the tile roof, the siding, the walls, wood, and drywall, all of it – blew apart almost quietly. A big chunk of roof spun over her head, throwing off red tiles as it spun and dropped with a massive crash against the wall of the house next door.

She saw a window, the glass still somehow in place, go whirling straight up like a rocket. She followed it with her eyes, waiting for it to come spiralling down at her. It crashed into the branches of a tree and finally then the glass shattered.

The bed from her own bedroom was on a roof two houses down. Sheets and clothing fluttered to the ground like confetti. It was almost festive, like someone had set off a Fourth of July rocket and now she could oooh and aahh as the sparkles came down.

But no fire. No loud explosion. One second it had been a two-storey house and now it was a one-storey house.

One of Astrid's kneesocks from her dresser landed on the grass, draped over the lip of the trench.

Astrid remembered she could move. She ran for the house yelling, 'Petey! Petey!'

The back door was partly blocked by a small piece of siding. She threw it aside and ran through the kitchen and up the debris-strewn stairs.

The full weirdness struck her then. The handrail of the stairs stopped as it reached the level of the upper floor. The steps themselves ended on a splintered half riser.

Astrid stepped out on to what was now a platform, no longer the second floor of a house. Everything was gone. Everything.

It was as if a giant had come along with a knife and simply sliced off the top, cutting through walls and plumbing pipe and electrical conduit.

All that was left was Little Pete's bed. And Little Pete himself.

He coughed twice. He licked his lips. His eyes stared blankly up at open sky.

Astrid followed the direction of his gaze. And there, in the blue morning sky, a puff of grey cotton. Directly above the house.

Brianna was seething. She seethed a fair amount at the best of times, but she was still doing a long, slow burn over the fight with Drake and the fact that Jack had left town without even telling her so she had to hear it from Taylor.

She didn't much like Taylor. She had once suggested that Taylor should adopt a cool name, like Brianna had with 'the Breeze'. 'The Teleporter,' maybe. Taylor had laughed at her.

Brianna wasn't supposed to be on the street. The quarantine was still in effect. But she was thirsty, hungry, humiliated, and furious, and she was looking for trouble.

Or at least a sip of water.

She was giving this whole waiting-around thing a few more minutes and then she was going to run up to Lake Evian herself for a drink. Taylor said the road was dangerous, that the greenies were there. But Brianna didn't fear flying snakes. Not even flying snakes that peed green bug eggs, or whatever that was all about. She was too fast for some stupid snake, flying or crawling.

Someone had nailed plywood up over a window in town hall.

'What's that about?' she wondered aloud.

She shrugged and was getting ready to zoom when she heard a sound like chewing. Like a lot of chewing getting rapidly louder. And coming from the window with the –

Splinters pushed out through the bottom of the plywood. They were pushed by something silvery that moved with respectable speed.

Brianna stared up at it for a few seconds and then, quite suddenly, metallic-looking insects, each the size of a small dog, began to force their way through the plywood.

The first to emerge spread beetle-like wings and floated to the ground.

Brianna had plenty of time to observe its gnashing mouth and its antennae, and to be utterly creeped out by eyes the colour of rubies.

She could guess what they were. These were the things that Taylor had gotten all freaked out by. The things that had supposedly come out of Hunter's guts. Only now they were right here and pouring down the wall from the second floor of town hall.

The instant the first bug landed it launched itself at Brianna.

She sidestepped it like a matador with a bull.

'You're quick, I'll give you that,' Brianna said. 'But you're not the Breeze.'

As one the swarm raced towards her, scythe mandibles slashing and mouthparts gnashing and red eyes blazing.

This was more like it. She could just zoom far away, of course, but she was enjoying this game.

Until Edilio came at a run, unlimbering his automatic rifle and yelling at the top of his lungs.

'Oh, well,' Brianna said. 'Time to end this, I guess.'

She unsheathed her big knife and sliced the antennae from the nearest bug. Then, just for show, just because it was a cool move, she somersaulted and landed almost astride another bug. She stabbed it, aiming for the space between its hard-looking wings. Her blade bit the wing instead and did not penetrate.

The bug twirled, fast, very fast. Not fast enough. Brianna stabbed straight for the blood-red eyes and the blade sank deep into one.

The bug stopped moving.

'That's why you don't bug the Breeze,' Brianna said.

Edilio had almost arrived and Brianna was pretty sure he would spoil her fun. So she awaited the charge of another bug, dropped low, swept her knife, and sliced through its two front legs. It crashed forwards on to its horror-movie face.

BLAM! BLAM!

Edilio fired at one of the bugs that had evidently had enough and was running from the Breeze.

Brianna saw the bullets hit. And she saw them ricochet off the hard wings.

'Head shots!' she yelled to Edilio. 'You have to get 'em in the head!'

She had meant to point to the one she killed as an example. But the dead bug was moving.

So was the bug from whom she had subtracted the front legs.

With a frown she pulled out her shotgun. She caught up to the wounded bug, placed the muzzle right in its eerie eyes, and pulled the trigger.

The bug head blew most of the way off. Greenish-black brain goo sprayed.

The bug shook itself like a wet dog. Then kept moving.

'No, no, no,' Brianna said. 'I may lose to Drake, but I do not lose to a bunch of bloodshot roaches.'

BLAM! BLAM!

Edilio shot his bug twice more. Then, seeing Brianna hesitate, he yelled, 'Try to crush them!'

'With what?'

Edilio looked around helplessly. 'I don't know.'

'They're getting away!'

The bugs, half a dozen of them, were ignoring Brianna

and Edilio now and racing off down the street, away from town.

'They're too fast for you,' Brianna said.

Edilio looked like he was going to have a stroke. He glanced at the window above, the bugs racing away, and Brianna could have sworn his next move would be to throw up his hands and say, 'Forget it, I'm outta here!'

But he gritted his teeth, took a deep breath, and visibly steeled himself for a decision he knew might be wrong. Might even be fatally wrong.

'Breeze,' he said grimly. 'Listen to me before you go tearing off. I want you to follow them, see where they go. But this leaves us with, like, no one playing defence. Orc's off on a drunk, Sam and Dekka and Jack are out of town, kids are falling out sick all over the place, and Drake may still be lurking . . .' He stuck his finger at her. 'Don't take risks, don't be your usual reckless, stupid self: come back as soon as you can, as soon as you see where they're going.'

Brianna executed a mock salute – she didn't mind being called stupid so long as he was acknowledging her bravery – and loped off at an easy sixty miles an hour to catch up with the swarm.

'Don't sweat it, Edilio,' she called over her shoulder. 'The Breeze is all over these bugs.'

* * *

Orc was running dry. He stared balefully at the bottle in his hand. Shouldn't he be dead by now? How much booze did it take before you just died already?

His mind laboured to work out solutions to the problem. Probably still a couple of bottles back at the house, if kids hadn't looted them. If not, he had another option, but it was a long walk and he wasn't really in the mood for a long walk. A long walk would sober him up.

He was on his way to the house and drowning his brain in booze again when he thoughtlessly walked past the stop sign.

No body lay crumpled there.

For a moment he thought he might be in the wrong place. Or that maybe he was mistaken about the body. But then he vaguely recalled running into Howard and Howard promising to fix things.

So now the little boy's body would be rotting in an unused house. Probably not the only body lying around. Probably.

Orc took a drink. He was shaky in body and mind. He was used to booze, but even by his standards he had punished his body in the last day. His stomach burned. His head hammered. Now he had to fight down an urge to run and run and run until . . .

Until what?

Run where?

They would figure it out, sooner or later. That he had slammed that little boy, that little boy who never hurt Orc or probably anyone else. Just some sick kid.

Someone would have seen it happen, or one of the smart ones – Astrid or Albert or Edilio – would figure it out. And he wouldn't even be given a chance to explain. They would make him leave, go live outside town, like they had Hunter.

But he wasn't Hunter. He couldn't live out there. Out there was where the coyotes were.

Orc remembered the coyotes. He remembered the way they had sunk their muzzles into his living guts and ripped and torn his insides out.

That's when it had started. That's when the ripped-up flesh had turned into gravel and the rocky, pebbly, monster skin had grown to take over his whole body.

No. They couldn't make him live out there.

Astrid had rules, though; she had made them up and that's what they would do, push him out, *Go away, Orc, go away and die, you freak.*

Yeah, well, Charles Merriman was inside this monster. He was not an orc. He was Charles Merriman.

He had to talk to Astrid. She'd always been nice to him. The only one who'd been nice to him. They were her stupid rules, so she would be able to figure out something. She was smart, after all. And nice.

With that vague thought sloshing around in his brain, Orc stomped off towards Astrid's home.

Two blocks away he noticed something very strange. So strange he thought he might be imagining it. Because it wasn't right, that was for sure.

There was a cloud. Up in the sky. As he gaped up at it the sun started to slide behind it.

Cloud. A dark, grey cloud.

He kept moving. Kept drinking. Kept looking at that crazy cloud up in the sky.

He stepped on to Astrid's street. From half a block away he saw the wreckage strewn out over trees and yards and draped over fences.

Then the house. That stopped him dead in his tracks. The top of the house was gone.

And there stood Astrid, right up on top, right out in the open because the walls were all gone, and there was her 'tard brother, only he was kind of, like, floating in the air above a bed.

Orc gaped up at Astrid, but she didn't notice him. She was looking up at the sky, up at the cloud. Her hands were at her side. In one hand she held a huge-looking pistol.

A brilliant flash lit everything up.

A tree not ten feet away blew apart.

CRRR-ACK!

BOOOOM!

Lightning. Thunder.

Splinters and leaves from the tree came down in a shower all around Orc.

And suddenly the cloud seemed to drop from the sky, only it wasn't the cloud itself, it was rain. Grey streamers of water, pouring down.

It was like stepping into a cold shower. The rain fell on Orc's marvelling, upturned face. It pooled in his eyes, it ran in streams through his quarry of a body.

Astrid cried out, words irrelevant. Orc heard the despair, the fear. She was soaked through, standing there with her big gun, screaming at her brother, sobbing.

Orc opened his mouth and water flowed in. Clean, fresh, as cold as ice water.

TWENTY FOUR

BRITTNEY SAW THE huge, blue-eyed bugs. She saw the cave. And she understood none of it.

Then she saw Jamal's gun. Shreds of his clothing. The blood that soaked them.

Nothing left but his clothing, his shoes and his gun.

The bugs skittered madly past her carrying rocks eight, nine, ten times their own size. Like busy ants. But ants the size of wolves or Shetland ponies.

Coyotes watched. They were anxious, skittish, scared of the massive insects.

She wished she could ask Jamal what was happening. But Jamal would not be answering any more questions.

She wondered if she could flee. She wondered if she should flee. But what difference would it make?

The bugs had piled up a small mountain of rocks. Bigger and bigger stones were being hauled out.

She stepped in front of one of the insects. It was carrying a rock that could easily crush her. It would be nothing for these bugs to attack her, tear her apart as they'd apparently done to poor scared Jamal.

But the bug just scuttled around her.

Why? Why would they eat Jamal and not her? Because they ate only truly living flesh? Or because they knew that she was Drake and Drake was she and they could not harm Drake?

What was stopping them?

Who was stopping them?

But Brittney already knew the answer. She knew that something, someone, some mind was touching hers. It was as if she'd always known it. As if that cold consciousness had always been there in the background watching her even as she averted her eyes and looked to heaven.

When she was still in her grave, clawing at the dirt, she had felt it.

When she looked deep into the eyes of her brother, Tanner, she could sometimes catch glimpses of it, in layers down beneath his disguise as an angel.

She had known but had not wanted to know that Drake was its creature, the creature of this devil, just as she was God's creature.

She looked at the mineshaft, stood there as the insects cleared the rocks. Like a rock herself in the midst of rushing waters.

They were freeing the evil one. She could do nothing to

stop them. She would do nothing to stop Drake from going to be with it. The devil would win this battle.

The dark mind teased at the edges of her own muddled thoughts. In faint, wordless whispers it made promises.

'What do you want with me?' she asked.

To give you what you want.

'I want to die,' Brittney said. 'To go to heaven.'

When she closed her eyes she felt, rather than saw, something very like a glowing smile from a deep pool of darkness.

She had begged God to free her. Maybe this was His way. Maybe it wasn't Sam who would free her, but this devil inside the mountain.

Brittney walked into the mineshaft, lifted a small rock, and carried it away.

'Can you make any sense out of that?' Sam asked Jack.

They were in the marina's office. Two dozen boats sat placidly in the water. Several dozen more were raised out of the water in a long boathouse. There were papers on a desk, books in grey steel shelves, two broken-down rolling office chairs. The out-of-date calendars were reminders that no one had been here in a very long time.

The computers were useless, of course, without electricity. But Jack had insisted on carrying three of the half-exhausted laptops from the train. And a search had turned up a flash drive.

'It's some kind of proprietary software. I had to open it in Preview and it's hard to make sense of.'

Toto was rummaging through cupboards, finding nothing much. Dekka was sitting in one of the chairs with her feet up, gazing gloomily out at the lake. From time to time she surreptitiously ran her hands over her stomach, shoulders, thighs, checking for any sign of infestation.

And from time to time she would pull her shirt back to check the cauterised wound from Sam's fire.

'Hah!' Jack said. 'I think I've got it. They had a truck deliver marine gas just a week before the FAYZ. A thousand gallons in round numbers. That should have brought them up to about twelve hundred gallons total. And they have diesel, too. I just can't find those . . .'

He trailed off, lost in the numbers again.

This, thought Sam, *is why I brought Jack.*

Sam was feeling amazingly contented. He'd had a sudden flood of good news. They had found food. They had found soda. They would undoubtedly find beer and more soda and maybe a few bags of ancient chips once they searched the boats, the kind of stuff people took for a day on the lake.

Best of all, the lake was huge and filled with fresh water. More fresh water than they could ever use in a thousand years.

They'd also found a clipboard with scrawled figures indicating that the lake had recently been restocked with trout and bass.

It was like stumbling into the Garden of Eden. They could move the whole population up here. Use the boats as housing. Fish the lake. Drink the water. Use the gas to haul the crops from the fields up here.

It wasn't perfect. But for the FAYZ it was heaven.

If only Astrid were here.

He tried to push that thought aside. He was mad at Astrid. He was sick of Astrid. And yet, all he could think of was her face when he handed her a jar of Nutella and a can of Pepsi.

'Why didn't they do something?' Dekka wondered aloud.

'Who?' Sam asked.

'The people who were studying crazy boy over there.' She jerked her head towards Toto.

'What were they going to do?' Sam asked with a shrug.

'How about warn people what was happening?' Dekka said. 'Like, "Hey, people of Perdido Beach, something very weird is happening"?'

'They were scientists,' Jack mumbled, no longer deciphering boring documents but searching the laptop's hard drive, revelling in the sheer visceral pleasure of opening applications.

'So they were scientists,' Dekka snapped. 'So what?'

'So they were studying, right?' Jack said. 'They had to understand it first. Can't just run around . . . Hey, look, there's this cool Easter Egg if you press –'

'Means people on the outside know what's happening,' Dekka said.

'What do you think happens when the barrier comes down?' Sam wondered aloud. 'I mean, to all of us?'

Jack said, 'Most likely all our powers go away.'

'Most likely,' Sam agreed.

'But not for sure,' Jack said.

'No.'

Dekka said, 'They don't even let you carry a Swiss Army knife at school, what are they going to do with you, Sam? You're like a guy carrying two massive lasers.'

'Like Jack said, most likely our powers will be gone. That will be a relief.'

'Not true,' Toto said. 'He says it will be a relief, but that's not what he believes.'

Sam glared at Toto. 'OK. I would probably miss it.'

'Truth,' Toto said. Then, communing once more with his imaginary Spider-Man head, he added, 'It's the truth.'

'Look what they did with Toto and subject number two,' Dekka said.

'Locked us up,' Toto said. 'No family. Stole us away and locked us up.'

'That's not going to happen,' Sam said. 'Everyone in the world probably knows about us. We'd be too well-known.'

'He believes it,' Toto said.

'But he's not sure,' Dekka said dryly. 'Sam, you've never been a freak out in the real world. Me? To a lot of people I was a freak before I ever got here. If my parents would send me away to Coates just for being a lesbian, imagine how happy they would be to see that I can also cancel gravity.'

She laughed to take the edge off it. But Sam did not join in.

'I still want the barrier to come down,' Sam said.

'Not the truth,' Toto said.

'Yes it is,' Sam protested. 'You think I like things like this?'

Toto started to answer, but Dekka cut him off. 'Sam, maybe you haven't spent much time thinking about this, but I have. And trust me, lots of kids have, and not just freaks with powers. I mean, you think Albert wants this all to end so he can go back to school and to being some little nerd?'

'Astrid wants it to end,' Sam said.

Dekka nodded. 'No doubt. And Jack here wants it to end so he can get back to his computers and all because half the time he doesn't even remember he has super-strength. Edilio wants it to end, too, I guess, unless he starts thinking about getting deported back to Honduras. But do you honestly think Brianna wants to stop being the Breeze?'

'Brianna would hate it,' Sam admitted.

'There's kids who pray every night for all this to be over. There's other kids who pray every night that the barrier stays right where it is. And now that we're going to show them all this lovely fresh water, this nice place up here . . .'

'You believe that,' Toto confirmed.

'Thanks,' Dekka said sarcastically.

Sam gazed out at the lake with a very different feeling now. If they had water, if they had food, if peace could be kept between him and Caine, and especially if they could get power flowing somehow, how many kids would stop hoping for an end to the FAYZ?

'You need to think about all that, Sam,' Dekka said. 'You're the leader, after all.'

'Not any more,' he said.

Dekka laughed. She stood up and stretched. 'Sam: you're still the leader. You're always going to be the leader. It's not something you choose: it's something you are.'

She took his arm and guided him out of the building, out on to the dock.

Her mood was different now. Sam was shocked by the suddenness of the change. She'd been putting on an act. But now her eyes were dull and her mouth turned down at the edges. She stood close to him, took his hand, and pressed it to her shirt over the top of her abdomen. 'Feel that? That lump?'

He nodded.

'My mom had a benign cyst once, so maybe that's all it is,' Dekka said gravely.

'You think it's . . .'

'Maybe I just noticed it because I'm looking for it, but maybe it's one of them,' Dekka said.

'Don't jump to –'

'I'm not,' Dekka said. 'But if that's what it is, if it's those things, I'm going to ask you to take care of me.'

'We've been over this,' Sam said, pulling his hand away.

'If I tell you it's time, you do it, OK, Sam?'

He couldn't answer.

'I'm not afraid to die,' Dekka said.

Sam was glad Toto wasn't there to hear.

'And you have to promise me something,' Dekka said.

'What?'

'Don't you ever tell Brianna what you know about how I feel. It would only bring her pain. I love her and I wouldn't want to make her hurt.'

'Dekka . . .'

'No,' she said briskly. 'Don't argue, OK? Maybe I'm wrong and this is nothing. So let's not argue about it.'

'Yeah,' he said. They stood awkwardly for a while, then Sam said, 'I don't want to sound weird, but you know I love you, right?'

'Love you, too, Sam.'

Sam made a move as if to hug her, but stopped himself.

She smiled. 'Yeah, we're not the huggy type, are we?'

Sam said, 'Let's go see what we can find down in the boats.'

ONE THING WAS crystal clear to Astrid as she stood in the drenching rain: the secret she had kept for so long was no longer a secret.

She looked down at the street and saw Orc there. He was staring up at her, his stone-and-flesh jaw slack.

And coming up the street behind him were four other boys. She recognised Lance and Turk. The other two she barely knew.

All four were armed. Orc didn't need a weapon.

She scanned in every direction, frantic, looking for some source of support. Maybe Sam had come back. Maybe Brianna. Maybe Edilio and some of his soldiers.

But no, the streets were abandoned but for a sick-looking girl, crouched and weary, moving in the general direction of the plaza, stopping to cough, staggering on.

Orc had defended Astrid once before, rescuing her from Zil and his Human Crew thugs. Now four of those thugs were pointing at her, at the amazing rain cloud, then breaking into a run, all eager malicious energy.

The cloud was growing. The rain was spreading.

Orc was standing in it, an animated gravel heap under a deluge.

The others slowed and then stepped gingerly into the rain and, like Orc, tilted their heads back and drank in the wondrous fresh water.

She had a gun. Would she use it?

'It's the 'tard,' Turk yelled. His face broke out in a grin. He was standing beneath a tree that was decorated with a yard sale's worth of clothing and bits of broken toys. 'It's that dumb brother of hers, Petard!'

Turk circled past Orc and hopped the fence into Astrid's yard. His friends followed warily, eyes darting from Astrid to Orc. Orc did nothing.

Then, in a sudden rush, Turk was up the stairs and standing on the platform. The others crowded beside him.

Turk laughed loudly, gleeful. 'It's the 'tard! He's the one making it rain.'

'Orc!' Astrid cried.

'That little kid must have some mad powers,' Lance said.

'Go away,' Astrid said.

She was aware of the fact that her drenched nightgown clung far too closely to her body. The gun in her hand weighed a ton.

'Grab the kid,' Lance said. 'If we have him, we control the rain, right?'

There was blood on Turk's shirt. Too much of it.

'What have you done?' Astrid demanded.

Turk looked down at the blood. He seemed surprised by it. 'Oh, that?' He laughed savagely. 'That's nothing much. Just means we run this place now, Astrid. No Sam around, huh? Where's mister light hands?'

'Orc!' Astrid cried out. She didn't want to reveal the depths of her fear. But she knew what Turk would do. And she did not want to use the gun. Not even now, not even for Petey.

'What other tricks can the 'tard do?' Lance demanded. 'Float in the air, make rain. What else?'

'Mutant retard. Freaktard,' one of the other kids said, and laughed tentatively like he wasn't quite sure it was funny.

'He doesn't know what he's doing,' Astrid said. She was chilled now and beginning to shiver. 'He was just thirsty. He has the sickness, the flu, and he was thirsty.'

On the street below, other kids were coming out of their homes, carrying bowls and buckets. They advanced with wondering eyes, edging toward the rain curtain as it edged toward them.

'The 'tard must be some kind of serious moof to do this,' Lance said. 'Blow off the top of the house? Call up a rain cloud? That's, like, at least three-bar powers there. Maybe four.'

297

'If you bother him, he may stop.' The threat was a sudden inspiration and it worked. Lance's eyes narrowed even further and Turk was suddenly very still. Drinkable water was important, even to such sub-geniuses as Turk and Lance.

Then Turk shook his head and said, 'Nice try, Astrid. But if the freaktard makes rain whenever he gets thirsty, all we gotta do is keep him thirsty and we own the rainmaker.'

'Wonder what he does when he gets hungry?' Watcher asked.

The rain beat on the carpet. It was already pooling around their feet. Shallow puddles in dirty carpet.

Turk made his decision. 'I think we're just going to take old Petard with us.' He motioned to the two younger boys. 'Grab him.'

The pistol came up suddenly, almost as if the gun itself had made the decision. Astrid aimed it at Turk.

Despite the rain her mouth was dry as parchment. Her throat wouldn't make sounds. Her finger was on the trigger, stroking the grooves, feeling it. Her thumb was on the safety.

She clicked it off.

All she saw now was Turk's face, and the v-sights of the pistol.

'You aren't going to pull that trigger, Astrid,' Turk said.

A sound from the steps. Running feet.

Edilio emerged. He had an automatic rifle aimed at Turk. 'It's over, Turk,' Edilio said.

Astrid dropped the pistol to her side. She breathed a huge, shaky sigh of relief.

'You going to let Astrid just own this freak?' Turk demanded of Edilio.

'Drop all your weapons. Right now!' Edilio yelled.

The two younger kids looked to Turk for guidance.

Lance was the one who moved. He raised his own pistol and pointed it at Little Pete. 'Anyone shoots anyone, the 'tard takes one in the head.'

'Man, you don't want to do this,' Edilio warned.

'Yeah? Well, listen up, Edilio: Albert's dead.'

Edilio's eyes opened wide.

'See, the situation has changed rapidly,' Lance said in a parody of a newscaster's voice. 'So, now, ladies and gentlemen, what we have here is a Mexican stand-off. You squeeze one off, Edilio, chances are I can still get the kid. Bang.'

'You should understand what a Mexican stand-off is,' Turk mocked. He raised his own gun and aimed it at Astrid. 'See? Now it's even more complicated. Lance is right: Albert is, uh, not feeling well. Forever. So no one is even paying you, wetback. You need to walk away. Run before the immigration cops get here.' He laughed.

A terrible thought formed in Astrid's brain: if Little Pete was killed it might all end.

A simple act of murder . . .

What kind of life did he have? Was Little Pete's life worth all of this? Was it worth Edilio dying? Was it worth the many more deaths that would surely happen? Was it worth all of them dying in this violent, foul, God-forsaken FAYZ?

'Go ahead,' Astrid said flatly. She let her pistol drop to the sodden carpet. It splashed. 'Go ahead. Shoot him. Kill Little Pete.'

Diana and Caine had made love several more times. In her bed. In his bed. In the big bedroom with its ego wall of the two movie star parents grinning out from photos taken with a bunch of people who were probably famous but looked more like they were businessman types.

Diana was in the kitchen, wearing a robe and slippers and heating some food for Penny. New England clam chowder. A quesadilla. A mismatched kind of meal, she supposed, but Penny wasn't going to complain. They were all still a long, long way from complaining about food.

Diana had not intended it to be this way with Caine. Somehow she'd imagined the one time, but not an endless series of sequels. But Caine's appetite had not been sated. He had come back to her bed in the night. And then, this morning, before the sun was even up.

Something was happening to her. She was coming to like Caine. Love? She didn't even know for sure what that meant. Maybe she loved him. That would be strange. He wasn't exactly lovable. And once you knew the real Caine, he wasn't even likable.

Diana had always found Caine fascinating. And she'd always found him attractive. Hot, she would have said when she was younger. Hot in a cold sort of way, if that made any sense.

But this was different. She wasn't using him now. That was her usual attitude towards Caine, at least that's what she'd always told herself: he was useful. A girl like Diana, a girl who enjoyed taking risks, who enjoyed sticking a knife of wit and cruelty into other girls at school, who enjoyed taunting the panting hormonal boys and leering old men, a girl like that could use a strong male protector.

And Caine was definitely a strong protector. It would take a suicidal guy to cross him. Even before Caine had started to develop powers, he was the kind of boy other boys steered clear of. He wasn't always the biggest or the toughest-looking, but he was always the most determined. The most ruthless. You knew if you messed with Caine, you'd suffer for it.

She supposed, if she had to be serious, that she'd long ago developed genuine emotions for him. Of some sort. Not love. Not even like. But something. Something normal people might have thought was sick, in a way.

Emotions. But not what she felt now – whatever this was.

Diana plated the quesadilla and poured the soup into a bowl. She set it all on a tray and carried it upstairs. She knocked, opened the door, and placed the tray of food in front of a sleeping Penny. It was like feeding a dog.

She found Caine out on what had once been a well-manicured lawn that covered the ground from the house to the cliff. It was now wild with weeds, some as much as head-high. He was looking towards the distant town through his telescope.

He heard her approach. Without looking back he said, 'Something's happening in town.'

'I don't care.'

'A cloud. Like a rain cloud. In fact, I think it is raining. It's just a small cloud. Way down low, though, not an illusion in the barrier.'

'You're probably seeing a reflection. Or an illusion.'

Caine handed her the telescope. She wanted to refuse it, but she was curious. She looked. The town leaped closer. Not enough to see people, but enough to see that there was indeed a cloud, just one, hanging far too low, staying put in one place. The grey smudge beneath it might be falling rain.

'So?' she asked. 'So some freak has developed the power to make a cloud.'

'You don't wonder who? That's a pretty major power.'

Diana sighed theatrically. 'What do you care?'

'I don't like the idea of there being another four bar. Two of us is already one too many.'

'It doesn't mean it's a four bar,' Diana said. 'Brianna and Dekka and Taylor are only threes. They have greater powers than that.'

'At least a three bar, though.' He took the scope back. 'You don't think if they can find a way they'll come after us? If Sanjit made it there alive, then Sam knows what we have here. You don't think he'll come after it?'

'No,' she said honestly. 'I don't think he'll look for a fight with you. He's not as insecure as you are.'

Caine snorted a laugh. 'Yeah, that's my problem: insecurity.'

'It doesn't matter anyway. There's no way for us to get back even if we wanted to.'

'There's always a way, Diana. There's always a way.'

'Don't,' she said. 'Don't find a way.'

TWENTY SIX

'**YOU** WANT US to shoot your brother?' Turk was incredulous.

'Don't even think about it,' Edilio said. He had a tight grip on his rifle, finger on the trigger. The sights were centred on Turk's anxious face. But his eyes were bleary and he was stifling a need to cough. 'She doesn't mean it.'

'Too many dead kids,' Astrid said wearily. 'There just can't be any more dead kids. It's time to end it.'

Edilio felt panic rising within him. What was he supposed to do now? Was Astrid losing her mind like Mary Terrafino?

'I know how many kids have died,' Edilio said. 'I buried most of them.'

'It's all because of Little Pete,' Astrid said.

'No. You don't know that.' Edilio aimed a furious look at her.

She blinked. Shook her head slightly. Her long hair, soaked, hung like golden snakes. 'You aren't the one taking care of him, Edilio. You're not the one responsible.'

Edilio coughed, fought it back, coughed again. He tried to steady his mind and calm himself down. Had to keep focus.

'What are you two talking about?' Turk demanded. He was clearly confused.

Edilio felt the house rumble. Heavy footsteps. Orc. It had to be Orc. Orc on whose side? That was the question.

The boy-monster emerged on to the platform. He made a strange slushy sound as he moved, like someone shuffling their feet on wet gravel.

He pushed past Edilio. His head sagged to his chest, and for a moment Edilio had the incredible thought that Orc might have fallen asleep.

No, he was just hammered, Edilio realised. 'Drop your guns.'

'No, no, no. What are you two talking about? That's the first question,' Turk demanded, sensing an advantage he couldn't quite put his finger on. His gun was still aimed at Astrid.

'Shut up, Turk, and drop your gun. If you murdered Albert, you're going into exile.'

'What happens if I shoot the 'tard?' Lance demanded.

'You know the law. You kill someone, we give you a trial. And if you're guilty, you leave town and never come back.'

'That's not what I'm asking, and you know it, Edilio,' Lance snarled. 'Tell me, Astrid. Tell us all. What happens if we shoot the 'tard?'

Panic. It was eating at Edilio's mind. What was he supposed

to do? He had to get control of the situation. He had to be in charge. But what should he do?

Edilio stared down the barrel of his rifle at Turk. His head was swimming. His neck and face were hot.

He shifted his aim, traversed the gun just an inch of arc to bring Lance into his sights.

The first one to decide would win.

'If –' Astrid said.

BLAM!

The rifle kicked against Edilio's shoulder. The side of Lance's handsome face erupted in a fountain of blood.

'Lance!' Turk cried.

Lance brought his own gun around, not aiming at Little Pete now but at Edilio.

BLAM!

Lance's aim was off. Nowhere near Edilio. Instead the bullet struck Orc in his thigh and ricocheted off.

Turk, his face a mask of fury, aimed at Edilio. But Edilio had already shifted his aim and his sights were back on Turk.

'Don't!' Edilio warned.

Turk hesitated. But Edilio didn't see the hesitation, he saw Turk's gun and only his gun, the round black hole of the barrel, and without thinking he squeezed the trigger.

Another loud bang.

Another kick against his shoulder.

Turk was on his back. His gun was beyond his reach, although he was struggling to get to it.

'I said, don't!' Edilio yelled again.

Turk held his stomach with one hand and reached for the gun with the other. Edilio's finger was slippery on the trigger. He could feel something awful inside him, a tidal wave of awful, barely held in check as he aimed at Turk's head.

Orc crunched Turk's gun beneath his foot.

Edilio breathed. Sobbed for breath. Coughed.

He lowered his weapon.

Lance shrieked. It was a sound made up of fear and shock and pain. The bullet had struck his cheekbone and come out through his ear. Quivering red flesh hung loose.

Turk groaned more quietly. His throat convulsed. Like a fish on dry land, he was gulping, trying to breathe. His hand still stretched towards his now-useless gun.

Neither boy was dead.

Edilio formed the thought that would shame him later: he should finish them. He should do it now. Just walk up close and *bang!* If he didn't, they might live, with Lana's care. And if they lived they'd be back for revenge.

Orc and Astrid were both watching him.

It seemed terribly unfair that even now they were looking to him for some kind of answer.

'I'll get Lana,' Edilio said.

MICHAEL GRANT

He turned and ran, and fell down the steps. Heaving with sobs, blinded by rain and tears he ran for Clifftop.

It took Sam and Jack working together to start one of the motorboats. Almost all had dead batteries. But one of the boats had just enough power left to fire the engines.

They roared to life with a deep, wet growl.

'You know, this boat has power enough that it could pull water skiers,' Sam observed.

Dekka smiled fondly at him. 'You want to water ski?'

'Not right now. I'm just saying . . .'

'That's a lie. He wants to go now,' Toto said.

'Yeah, well, I don't always do what I want,' Sam grumbled. 'We need to explore the rest of the lake, then we can head back to town and be welcomed as heroes.'

He'd meant that last part to be self-deprecating, but a part of him actually was looking forward to striding into town to announce that they had found all the water they could ever need, and a fair amount of sugary snacks besides.

Then he would go see Astrid.

And then what would happen?

Then nothing would happen. They would still be right where they'd been.

'Cast off,' Sam called to Jack. Then, with the ropes aboard, he pointed the boat towards the west and roared out of the marina.

The feel of spray on his face and a throbbing engine beneath his feet was intoxicating.

Later they would run out of fuel, and later all the Pepsi would be drunk, and all the noodles would be eaten. But it wasn't later yet.

They could build a better life here at the lake. Leave behind all the reeking sewage and trash and memories of Perdido Beach. Leave behind the wrecked church and the burned houses. Leave behind that awful cemetery.

This time they would do it right. They'd organise before they ever started to move anyone up here. Form little families that could live aboard the boats or use the boathouse or the marina office. He frowned, trying to count in his head how many of the boats had any kind of superstructure. Maybe half a dozen of the small sailboats, a dozen of the motorboats. And then there were the four or five houseboats.

That wasn't enough, obviously, but they could set up tents and maybe build small shelters. It's not like it ever got cold in the FAYZ, not like anyone needed insulation. Just a roof to keep the sunlight off them.

He scanned the shoreline, hoping to spot a campground. Logically there had to be one, there were always campgrounds at a lake. It just stood to reason.

Of course they could be on the other side of the barrier . . .

Never mind, it was all good. They had enough gas to drive

the various Winnebagos and campers and trailers up here from Perdido Beach – there were at least a dozen parked in driveways, although a lot had burned in the big fire.

He would have a boat. Big enough for himself and Astrid and Little Pete. Maybe he would ask Dekka to live with them, too. Assuming he got dibs on one of the houseboats. And why shouldn't he?

One of those forty-six-footers would probably sleep six. Him and Astrid . . . It occurred to him that in his head he had them sharing the master's berth. Which wasn't likely to happen.

Was it?

Maybe. Maybe if they got away from Perdido Beach, maybe . . . A new thought occurred to him. He pushed it aside. But back it came.

What if they got married?

Then they'd be like a family. Him and Astrid and Little Pete.

There was no telling how long the FAYZ would last. Maybe forever. Maybe they would never get out. In that case, what were they all going to do? He was fifteen, Astrid was fifteen, they'd both survived the poof. That was young in the outside world, but it was old in the FAYZ.

'Yeah, but who can marry us?' He spoke the question aloud, not meaning to. He glanced nervously over his shoulder to see if anyone had overheard. Of course not, with the engines roaring and the *boosh-boosh-boosh* of the bow smacking the wavelets.

Dekka was sitting on one of the cushioned seats in the stern, gazing wistfully toward the land. Jack was hunched over one of the laptops, fingers flying over the keys, grinning. Toto was talking to someone who wasn't there.

'Ship of fools,' Sam said to himself, and laughed.

Water and gas, noodles and Pepsi and Nutella, a crazy truth-telling freak, and despite Dekka's fear, there was hope.

Quinn. He would make a good justice of the peace. That's all you needed to perform a marriage, right? That's how his mom had married his stepfather. If they could elect someone mayor, why not elect someone justice of the peace?

'Marry me and live on a houseboat,' he said.

'I like you, Sam, but not in that way,' Dekka said.

Sam jerked and yanked the wheel to one side. He steadied and tried to ignore the blush that was spreading from his neck up to his cheeks. She was standing next to him.

'How's the shoulder?' Sam asked.

'See, this is why it's good that Taylor isn't still with us,' Dekka said. 'If she'd heard you, the news would have spread faster than the speed of light.'

Sam sighed. 'I was having a moment of optimism.'

Dekka patted him on the back. 'You should, Sam. The FAYZ owes you some good news.'

* * *

Orc stood staring.

The kid, the Petard, he was still just floating there in the rain, like it was all nothing.

Astrid looked like a zombie or whatever.

The two shot kids were yelling and spazzing. Grinding Orc's last nerve. He didn't care about them. They were no better than he was. Let them scream, but not now, with his head banging like a drum, with the echo of gunshots still bouncing around in his skull.

Edilio had said to get out of town. That's what was rattling around in his brain, too. Killers had to get out of town.

Astrid's laws. She made them up.

'That true, right?' he asked her without preamble.

'What?'

'Anyone kills anyone, they have to go away for good.'

'Are you going to kill them?' She meant the two hurt kids. It took him a while to realise that.

'What if . . . what if you didn't mean to kill some kid.'

'I have to get him away from here,' Astrid said. But Orc didn't think she was talking to him.

'I mean, if you didn't even mean to. Like it was just an accident?'

'I don't know what you're asking,' Astrid said.

Orc was out of words. He felt so tired. He hurt so badly.

'Can you pick him up? Can you carry him?' Astrid was asking

him something. So maybe she didn't care what he'd done.

'The 'tard?'

'Little Pete. Can you carry him, Charles?'

'Where to?'

'Away,' Astrid said. 'That's the law. Killers have to leave. That's what he is, you know. He's the worst of us all. Every death from the FAYZ . . . All those kids . . .'

Orc seized on an idea that drifted through his slow brain. He lost focus when Lance started howling louder than before.

'Shut up or I'll shut you up,' he yelled. He struggled to regain his thought. Little Pete. Killing. 'Yeah, but he don't know what he's doing, right? People who don't know what they're doing, it's not their fault.'

'Please, Charles. Pick him up. Edilio will be back with Lana soon. We have to be gone by then.'

Orc stepped over Turk. The boy was shivering uncontrollably now, his legs stuck straight out, feet twisted, shivering an shaking.

Lance was still screaming, he hadn't stopped, but now he was mixing in curses, raging at everyone, spewing every hateful word he could think of.

Orc looked down at Little Pete. Astrid said he had killed people. Orc didn't see how that was possible. He couldn't even move much, it didn't seem.

Little Pete coughed three times real fast. He didn't cover his mouth or anything. It was like he didn't even know he'd coughed.

Orc plucked Little Pete out of mid-air. He didn't weigh much. Orc was strong.

Astrid watched it all like she was a million miles away. It was as if she was seeing everything through a telescope.

'Where to?' Orc asked her.

Astrid knelt and picked up the gun she had dropped. 'Away,' she said.

Orc shrugged and headed down the stairs and walked north, toward the hills, and away from the sound of screams.

TWENTY SEVEN

DRAKE EMERGED.

He was holding a stone. Which meant Brittney had been holding the same stone.

It must have been heavy for her but his tentacle wrapped around it and held it without much strain.

Around him the bugs were looking less and less like insects. Not even like really large insects. The least of them was as big as a Dalmatian. The largest were as big as ponies. They reminded him more of Humvees or tanks.

They seemed more fragile at this size, as though the same weight of burnished exoskeleton had been stretched to make a much larger creature. Only half of them were still carrying out debris. The rest, the larger ones, had stepped aside and now waited with an impression of impatience about them. Like jets waiting for takeoff.

That's what they reminded him of: fighter jets. They had a predatory, dangerous air about them. Like all they had to do was get the word and they'd go blasting off, dealing out death and destruction.

Who was to give them the word? Him?

The coyotes had disappeared. Had they decided to leave? Or had the bugs eaten them finally? Drake noticed a smear of blood on a slab of rock and thought he knew the answer.

Had the Darkness made the coyotes sacrifice themselves to feed his new servants?

Drake tossed his rock on to the pile. Then he turned back toward the mine shaft. Back to the welcoming shadow of that hole in the earth. His step was light. His heart beat fast, but from joy, not fear.

He felt the mind of the Darkness touching his. Felt that powerful will. It wanted him. And he was sure now what the Darkness would ask of him, and what weapons it would give him.

The mineshaft was clear but still a dangerous place. The supporting timbers had not been replaced and now the stone roof was jagged, hanging precariously in some places, while in others it had been hollowed out into dark cathedral domes by the collapse.

'I'm coming,' Drake whispered. But why whisper? 'I'm coming!' he yelled.

He left the last of the light behind. Total darkness now. He felt his way forward, step by step, hand and whip hand outstretched. He scraped against jutting rocks, stubbed his toes dozens of times. The air smelled stale. It was hotter than it should have been in the shaft, warmer than the outside.

'I'm coming!' he shouted again, but his voice now was metallic and flat and did not carry any distance. He tripped and fell to his knees. When he stood up, he banged his head.

He was going down a long, long slope. How far had he come? He couldn't say. He heard the rustle of the bugs coming behind him. In tight places they had to squeeze through, like massive cockroaches, flattening themselves to squeeze beneath low-hanging ledges, squirming on to their sides to edge past piers of solid rock.

They were following him. His army. Yes. He was certain of it. They would be his to command, his to use.

His army!

He could no longer breathe the air. But this was not his first time without oxygen. He still could see in vivid flashes the long, slow claw up through the mud of his grave.

No, Drake did not need air. Air was for the living, and Drake was something so much better than alive.

Unkillable.

Immortal.

The immortal soldier of the gaiaphage. His head swam with the joy of it.

Suddenly the floor ended and he pitched forwards,

face-first. He fell for several stretched seconds. He slammed into unyielding rock, bounced, rolled over, and laughed a sound-less laugh.

He felt around with his hands and knew he was on a narrow ledge on one side of a deep vertical drop.

He stood up, put his toes on the edge, and looked down. Far below, a dim green light glowed, the only light in this pit of blackness. It might be a hundred feet, it might be a mile, it might be a hundred miles. There was no way to know.

Tumbling off the ledge he fell and fell, like Alice down the rabbit hole. It seemed to go on forever. Not seconds but minutes. An eternity.

WHUMPF!

He hit with such force that it should have snapped his calves and thigh bones and burst his knees and jackhammered his spine and cracked his head open like an egg.

Instead, after lying crumpled for a moment, he unwound his twisted limbs and pushed himself back on to his feet.

The walls around him all glowed. With his eyes fully adjusted to the pitch black he could see fairly well now with nothing but the toxic radioactive glow.

Was he there? Was he at the end of the trip?

Come.

Farther still, down a sloping ramp. He realised that this was a different type of tunnel, no longer a man-made mining shaft but a natural cave deep, deep in the bowels of the stifling earth.

He entered a cavern that soared hundreds of feet above him. Green-tinged hanging stalactites met stumpy stalagmites. Like walking into the jaw of a gigantic shark.

Through the cavern and ever downwards, following the faint trail of green. The creatures kept pace behind him. They had fallen after him, one by one, slowing their descent with their wings, spiralling down like helicopter seedpods.

An army! His army!

How far had he fallen? He could not know. How deep was he now? Miles.

Closer and closer.

And then, even as he felt his journey drawing to a close, his desperate goal coming close, Drake felt the familiar disturbance and swift onset of stumbling awkwardness that accompanied the transformation.

'No!' he moaned. 'No, not now!'

But he had no power to stop the transformation.

It was not Drake but Brittney who finally came to the place where the gaiaphage lay. It was like living green sand. Billions of particles, each almost invisible to the eye, but together forming a single living thing, a hive.

The cavern was vast, impossibly huge. As if someone had sunk a sports stadium into the earth. The green, glowing mass of the gaiaphage covered stalactites and stalagmites, granite walls, and sandstone rock skyscrapers.

But beneath Brittney's feet the floor was strangely level and smooth. The gaiaphage had left an uncovered space for her to see and to understand.

She knelt and pressed her hand against a clear patch of translucent, pearly grey beneath her. The searing pain a living person would have felt was only an interesting tingle to Brittney.

She knew what it was and where she was. This was the bottom of the FAYZ wall, the bottom of the giant bubble. She was ten miles down, at the lowest depths of the enclosed universe of the FAYZ.

She stood and looked left and right, in every direction, turning slowly to see. It was all resting on the barrier, she realised. The rock walls, the jutting stalagmites, all of it rested on the barrier itself.

And everywhere but in this one patch, the gaiaphage covered the barrier. It touched the barrier and did not feel pain.

Then, as Brittney looked down, she saw the colour of the barrier change. The eternal blank greyness was crossed by fingers of dark green, the colour of late summer leaves.

She understood: the gaiaphage could touch and alter the barrier itself.

She knew it was conscious. She knew it because she felt now the dread touch of that awful mind in hers. There could not be the slightest doubt.

Brittney fell to her knees.

She laced her fingers together and squeezed her eyes tight. But she could not block out the green glow. She could not stop herself seeing. She could not keep her mind safe from its terrible touch.

She felt her every thought opened, like so many files on a computer, each opened, observed, understood.

She was nothing. She saw that now. She was nothing.

Nothing.

She tried to call on her God. But her prayers would not form in her brain, would not whisper from her numb, trembling lips.

She saw it all clearly, the whole of it. A race of creatures who worshipped life. A virus designed to spread life wherever it reached. The planet first infected, then deliberately blown up so that seeds of life would spread throughout the universe in a billion meteors.

The endless, endless blackness of space, of millennia during which one of those rocks spun along a path that might never reach an end.

It was caught in the gravity well of a small star.

And then of a small planet.

The shattering, fiery impact.

A death. A man obliterated.

And the absorption into that alien virus of something new and incredible: human DNA.

A new life-form. The unintended consequence of a noble plan.

No God in His Heaven had created the gaiaphage. And here, now, in the airless pit, no God could save her.

It was then in her despair that Brittney prayed, not as she always had, but to a new Lord. A saviour who waited to be born, to break free.

Brittney bowed her head and prayed to the gaiaphage.

Tanner appeared to Brittney as she prayed.

Her dead brother was an angel. Not with wings and all of that, but she knew he was an angel. And now he appeared to her and spoke in a soft, soothing voice.

'Don't be afraid,' Tanner said.

'Let me die,' Brittney whispered.

'Who do you pray to?' Tanner asked.

'To you,' she said. Because she had no doubt that Tanner was speaking for the gaiaphage.

'I cannot give you death,' Tanner said. 'You are two in one. Your immortality is his. And he is necessary to me.'

'But who made me this way? Why? Why?'

Tanner laughed. '"Why" is a question for children.'

'I am a child,' Brittney said.

There was softly glowing magma dribbling from Tanner's cruel mouth. He bent down and touched her with fingers of ice.

'I must be born,' Tanner said. 'And then, at the ending of my beginning, you will die.'

'I don't understand.' With piteous eyes she looked up at the angel-turned-devil. 'What do you need me to do?'

'Nemesis must be mine,' Tanner said. 'Nemesis must serve me and me alone. All who defend him and protect him must be destroyed. He must live to serve me.'

'I . . . I don't understand.' She knelt with bowed head, unable to look at Tanner, knowing now that he had never been an angel, that he had never been God's servant, that he was nothing real at all, just the voice of the evil one.

'Nemesis,' Tanner said, hissing the word. 'We are two in one, like you and the whip hand. Two in one, waiting to be born. Only when he is alone, utterly alone, will he serve me. And then I will be burst from this cocoon.'

'I don't know anyone called Nemesis,' Brittney whispered.

She could feel her consciousness fading. Already her fingers were melting together to form the whip.

In the moments before she lost sight and sound, as she spiralled down into the blackness and Drake surged upwards, Brittney's tortured mind saw the image of Nemesis.

She knew his name.

Peter Michael Ellison. Who everyone called Little Pete.

PETE

HE FLOATED ABOVE the ground in the arms of a monster. His cheek lay against a stone shoulder. Rain no longer fell. Wild colours – green and yellow, brown and red, jagged edges of colour scraped at him, wounding his ears.

The sister walked behind him. Her face was as stony as the monster's. Lips too red, eyes too blue, the sound of her breathing too loud.

At each step the monster's pebble skin rubbed against Pete's raw flesh, like sandpaper, like a thousand saw blades drawn slowly over tender scabs.

He wanted to scream, but if he screamed the loud colours would get louder.

He was no longer high atop the sheet of glass. He had fallen, fallen, down into the world of noise and blazing light. The Darkness was only a distant echo now. Now was now, utterly now and here and like needles under his skin, like knives in his ears. His eyes ached and throbbed.

He coughed and it was a cannon firing out of his chest, up through his throat, his mouth, burning him like blazing lava.

Why was he here? Why in a monster's arms? What was happening to him? After a long and peaceful escape he had been recaptured by the too-much world of furious activity and disjointed images.

His body, his body, that was all he could see or feel, the pain and the ache and the shivering that made him feel as if parts of him might come loose and fall, his body, forcing his attention away from the pristine glass cliff. Forcing him to feel every shiver, recoil at every cough, to feel, really feel, the sickness that was overwhelming his defences.

TWENTY EIGHT

DRAKE DID NOT see Tanner.

The gaiaphage needed no angelic illusions to reach into Drake's fevered mind. Drake knew all he needed to know. The bugs, the creatures would serve him. He had his army.

And in his head he had a list of names. The freaks first. The normals next. All of them.

All but one, the gaiaphage told him. Kill until there is no one left to kill. But don't harm Nemesis.

Drake was filled with a pure joy he had never known. He felt a wild energy. All his life he had waited for this kind of moment. It was as if every single thing he had ever done – the beatings he had suffered, the much more numerous beatings he had delivered, the pleasure he had found in burning frogs and microwaving a puppy and drawing all those endless loving pictures of weapons, spears, knives, torture devices, all of it, all the hatreds, all the burning lust, all the madness and rage, had come together to form this perfect, ultimate moment of crystalline joy.

He thought he might die from the pleasure he felt, so much emotion, a flood, a storm, a crashing of planets! Death! He was death, unleashed at last.

He snapped his whip and threw back his head and howled till his throat was raw.

Then he ran, leaped, cavorted through the swirling tides of insects, running and climbing, indifferent to the sharp rocks that lacerated his undead flesh.

Kill them all!

He raged when he reached the heights he couldn't climb but then the creatures rushed to lift him up and sped him up and up at dizzying speed through the endless caverns.

An army!

His army!

They vomited from the mineshaft and Drake leaped on to the rock pile. A single coyote waited there.

'Where is he, Pack Leader?' Drake demanded.

'Not Pack Leader. Pack killed.'

'I don't care what you call yourself, where is he?'

'Who?' the coyote asked.

Drake grinned. 'The one with the killing hands, you stupid dog. Who do you think? Sam!'

'Bright Hands is far. By the big water.' He simpered and turned in a circle and then with his muzzle pointed to the west.

'Excellent,' Drake purred.

Just then a rush of bugs, a new column of the creatures came over the ridge and poured into the mass of Drake's army. Different. These had blood red eyes.

They were not alone.

Brianna stood, arms on hips, glaring down at him.

'You!' Drake said.

'Me,' Brianna said.

To the creatures he said, 'Red eyes, serve me! To the town. Kill everyone but Nemesis!'

'You talking to these bugs now?' Brianna said. 'I have to tell you: I don't think they speak psycho.'

'Blue eyes, with me!' Drake said. 'Two columns, two armies: blues with me, reds back to town and kill. Kill!'

'What exactly do you think you're doing?' Brianna demanded.

'Me?' Drake laughed loudly. 'I'm going on an epic killing spree.'

'You'll have to go through me,' Brianna said.

'I wouldn't have it any other way,' Drake said.

They walked out of the rain. Astrid and Orc and Little Pete. The cloud did not follow them. No new cloud appeared. The cloud remained, no longer expanding, but still pouring rain on the street and the ruined house.

Little Pete coughed directly against the side of Orc's face. It was getting worse, the cough, slowly but steadily worse.

Maybe it would kill him.

Go ahead. Shoot him. Kill Little Pete.

Astrid told herself she hadn't meant it. It was just a tactic. After all, if someone was using a threat you had to devalue the importance of the threat, pretend it didn't matter.

Lance's face exploding. Some of it had hit her.

Turk moaning in pain, writhing on the wet carpet.

It had to stop. It had to end. One death to save dozens, maybe hundreds of kids?

A simple act of murder . . .

Astrid saw herself choking Nerezza. She felt again the way her fingers dug into the soft neck, fingertips finding the spaces between tendon and artery.

Astrid had never felt anything like that red-misted rage before in her life. She had hated before – she had hated Drake. She had feared before – many, many times. But she would never have believed herself capable of that murderous rage.

The true revelation was the joy she'd felt at that moment. The sheer, vicious, uncomplicated joy of feeling the blood pounding to get past arteries blocked by Astrid's own hands. Feeling the spasms in Nerezza's windpipe.

Astrid let loose a whimper. It had to end.

'You OK?' Orc asked.

Would she ever be herself again? Or had Astrid, the old Astrid, died, to be replaced by this new creature, this angry, frightened witch?

Not for the first time she realised that this had been Sam's life since the coming of the FAYZ. How much rage and fear had he endured? How much bitter shame for his failures? How much guilt ate at his soul as it now ate at hers?

She wished he were here now. Maybe she would be able to ask him how he lived with it.

No, she told herself, it's not Sam you need. A priest. You need to confess and do penance and be forgiven. But how could she be forgiven when even now she was watching Orc as he laboured uphill, seeing Petey's lolling head, and asking herself over and over again if she had meant it.

Go ahead. Shoot him.

God hears prayers, even from those who have not repented, she told herself. She wanted to pray. But when she tried she couldn't see the face of a patient Christ as she had in the past. She could see memories of crucifixes, paintings, statues. But the God she had believed in was not there any more.

Was she losing her faith?

Had she lost it already?

A simple act of murder . . .

Leslie-Ann knew about the quarantine. But she also knew she couldn't stand being thirsty and hungry any longer and her two brothers couldn't stand it, either.

The one good thing about being Albert's maid was that Albert made sure she had enough to eat. Albert always had food and water. He wouldn't let her starve.

So Leslie-Ann made her way from the house she shared with her siblings to Albert's much fancier house.

She noticed a strange thing over towards the west: a cloud. Leslie-Ann frowned, wondering why that seemed so strange.

But she had no time to wonder: the FAYZ was full of weird stuff. If you'd seen Sam shoot light from his hands – and she had – you stopped being amazed by strange things.

Albert's front door was open. That in its way seemed weirder than the cloud. Albert never left his door unlocked. Never. Let alone open.

Leslie-Ann approached cautiously. She felt for the hilt of the knife she carried. She was nine years old, and not exactly big or scary. But once she had waved the knife at a kid who wanted to steal her cantaloupe and he had run away.

'Albert?' she called out.

She pushed the door all the way open. She drew her knife and held it out in front of her.

'Albert?'

She thought she heard something coming from the living room. Her foot slipped on the Spanish tile. She looked down: a red smear.

Blood. It was blood.

She turned and ran back to the door. Ran outside, waving the knife around her.

She looked around, wishing Edilio or someone would come along. But if they did she'd be in trouble for going outside during the quarantine. Her brothers would still be thirsty and hungry, and so was she.

Leslie-Ann steeled herself and headed back inside, knife first. She stepped over the blood smear.

Her foot kicked a can. It rolled noisily. A can on Albert's floor? Who would have made that kind of mess? She would have to clean that up or Albert would fire her.

She bent down and snagged the can with her free hand. It smelled of food. Her mouth watered. She held the knife awkwardly as she ran her finger inside looking for anything that might be left. She came up with maybe a tablespoonful of tomato sauce and licked it greedily from her finger.

It tasted like heaven.

She carried the can with her to the living room. And there the full extent of the mess became clear: cans and wrappers everywhere. And tomato sauce all over the white carpet.

Only here it wasn't tomato sauce and Leslie-Ann knew it.

Then she saw Albert. He was sitting with his back against the wall.

His eyes were closed. He wasn't moving.

'Albert?'

She fought the desire to run and run and keep running. Only, she was still thirsty and hungry. And there lay a water bottle with a few precious sips still. She drank it. Not enough, but something.

She went to the kitchen and with shaking fingers dug out the plastic trash bags. Then, quick, quick, before someone stopped her, she gathered all the cans and bottles and thrust them into the bag. It wasn't much, but her brothers could find a couple of ounces of food.

She glanced at Albert, feeling sorry for him and a little guilty and . . .

His eyes. They were open.

'Albert?'

She went closer. Were his eyes following her?

'Are you alive?'

He didn't answer. But slowly, slowly his eyes closed. And then opened again.

Leslie-Ann ran from the room and from the house. But she did not drop her bag.

TWENTY NINE

BRIANNA DREW THE bowie knife she had retrieved from the church. 'Cutting you in three pieces didn't do it,' she said to Drake. 'So this time I'm going to dice you like an onion.'

She blurred and Drake split open at the waist. Not clean-through, but she'd finish it with the next one.

'Get her!' Drake yelled.

She twirled in midair, kicked off the back of a bug, and brought the huge knife down again, chopping Drake's whip hand and leaving it like a reddish python, squirming but no longer attached to Drake.

She struck! Again! Again! In the blink of an eye.

But the creatures were reacting now, a mass of them, rushing her. Slow, too slow, but still she had to sidestep them, and that cost her a precious second.

And Drake was still alive. Or something like alive.

She threaded past gnashing mouthparts and scything

335

mandibles and buried the knife in Drake's skull. The blade sank into the bone, stuck.

She yanked on it, but Drake's upper body came with it. The blade would not come free.

Speeeewt!

Something slapped her calf. She twisted to look and saw a long, barbed, black rope extending from the mouth of the closest bug. She shook her leg but it did not come off.

'Gross!'

Another bug tried the same thing and she somersaulted out of the way. Still that first tongue was attached to her and she could feel hooks buried in her skin.

She needed her bowie knife. But now it was out of range as Drake wrenched it free and tossed it away.

Brianna spotted a stone with a dull edge. She slammed it down on the tongue with all the force her speed afforded. The tongue bled but did not break. Blue bug eyes fixed on her with what now looked like triumph.

'Oh, no you don't.'

She hit the tongue fast, twenty times in a second with her rock and it yanked away, quick as Drake's whip hand.

Shwoop!

But now the bugs were around her, snapping at her with their creepy froggy tongues and those tongues were fast, fast even by Brianna's standards.

The bugs had played her. They'd concealed this weapon in their arsenal and she'd gotten cocky.

Speeewt!

Brianna kicked and squirmed, but two of them were on her. She used the rock on the tongue that latched on to her stomach and knocked it loose but it was instantly replaced by three more.

Speeeewt! Speeewt!

They had her! She was held in a web, yelling, cursing, smacking.

Drake was putting himself back together, but his whip hand was still squirming by itself like a snake on hot pavement.

She was pinioned by half a dozen of the tongues and now the rest of the bugs were closing in to chew her up, mandibles slicing the air like scimitars.

Brianna felt a sudden wave of fear. Was it possible she could lose this fight?

'Don't kill her,' Drake said. 'Hold her! She's mine!'

He was on his feet and searching through the wild melee for his whip arm.

Suddenly, the coyote was in the fight. He leaped for her, jaws open, teeth flashing yellow.

'Really?' she cried.

She shoved back against the greedy muzzle with all her strength. The move stretched one of the lashing tongues taut.

The coyote's powerful jaw, missing Brianna's arm, clamped hard on the tongue, which snapped back like a cut high-tension cable.

She was pinned, but she still had her speed.

She grabbed the coyote's ruff and swung it around to clamp on a second tongue.

Now just four tongues still pinned her. She didn't have the strength to hold on to the coyote. The creature, maybe fearing the bugs would retaliate, took off yelping as if it had been kicked.

Four lines held the Breeze, all more or less on her left side, so she kicked off, pushing straight towards the insects. The tongues slackened. Brianna somersaulted. It was a sketchy manoeuvre, poorly executed, and she landed hard on her back, but the four tongues had been twisted around and now, as one, they released her.

Even as they released others struck. She could see them flying toward her like striking cobras.

She kicked a bug in the face, kicked hard against a slashing mandible, then *boom boom boom*, three hard kicks and she was out of there.

She caught her breath on a rise a hundred feet away, her bowie knife glinting in her hand once again. Her body was blistered wherever the tongues had touched. But she was alive.

She watched, panting, shaking, as Drake's tentacle melded seamlessly into his shoulder.

'Come on, Breeze,' Drake taunted. 'Come and get me. Here I am!'

Brianna had never been one to ignore a taunt. She had never run from a fight. But she had escaped by inches. By millimetres.

'It's the end, Breeze,' Drake crowed. 'I'm going to kill all of you. Every last one of you!' He danced in a circle, twirling in wild glee. 'Run, Breeze! Ruuuuun! Because when I catch you, I'm going to make you suffer!'

Brianna ran.

Leslie-Ann fed her siblings the scrapings from the cans and let them drink the water.

OK, she told herself: You did all you could.

Except that she hadn't done all she could. Not yet.

She had never liked Albert much. He was kind of a jerk to her. He never said anything nice like, 'Good job, Leslie-Ann.'

But he didn't deserve to just die like that. Maybe he was still alive.

'I'm just a kid,' she said aloud to no one.

But she knew what she felt, and what she felt was that she hadn't done right.

She went out into the streets, not knowing exactly who she should locate, or who she should tell, but she knew she had to tell someone.

From where she stood she could see the big, weird cloud

more clearly. It looked like it was raining. And just then two kids came past. They were walking in tandem, sharing the load of a heavy plastic tub. It was sloshing water over the sides and they were soaked through.

One of them noticed her and grinned. 'It's raining!'

'No one's s'posed to go out,' she said.

The kid snorted. 'No one's telling anyone what to do right now, and there's water. If I was you, I'd get some fast.'

Leslie-Ann ran back inside and located a bucket in the garage. Then she walked as fast as she could towards the rain cloud. If everyone was there, maybe she could find someone to tell about Albert.

As she drew nearer she noticed something that was, in its own way, as weird as the cloud, which was now almost overhead: there was water running in the gutter. Actual water. Just running down the gutter.

She broke into a run and saw a crowd of dancing, cavorting kids ahead of her. Buckets sat under the downpour. Kids stood with their mouths open, or tried to shower, or just shoved and played and splashed.

A very unusual sound for the FAYZ: the high-pitched laughter of children.

Leslie-Ann set down her own bucket and watched, marvelling, as a quarter of an inch of water covered the bottom.

When she looked away, she saw an older kid. She'd seen him

around. But usually he was with Orc and she was too scared of Orc ever to get near him.

She tugged on Howard's wet sleeve. He seemed not to be sharing in the general glee. His face was severe and sad.

'What?' he asked wearily.

'I know something.'

'Well, goody for you.'

'It's about Albert.'

Howard sighed. 'I heard. He's dead. Orc's gone and Albert's dead and these idiots are partying like it's Mardi Gras or something.'

'I think he might not be dead,' Leslie-Ann said.

Howard shook his head, angry at being distracted. He walked away. But then he stopped, turned, and walked back to her. 'I know you,' he said. 'You clean Albert's house.'

'Yes. I'm Leslie-Ann.'

'What are you telling me about Albert?'

'I saw his eyes open. And he looked at me.'

Albert dead.

Sam gone, and no telling when he would get back.

Astrid gone with Little Pete and Orc.

Dekka away with Sam and Jack.

And now Edilio, numb with the scale of the disaster, sat exhausted on the steps of the so-called hospital. He didn't need

Dahra's thermometer to tell him what he already knew: he was hot, flushed, weak.

He coughed. And stared blankly at Brianna, who buzzed and vibrated to a wild halt before him.

'Bugs!' she yelled. 'I passed them heading this way. Drake and a bunch more bugs are still back at the mineshaft. I saw them heading west but I think it's just a fake; he's probably coming here, too.'

'How do we stop them?' Edilio asked and coughed into his hand.

'We need Sam,' Brianna said.

'We –' He coughed again and fought off a wooziness that made him desperately want to lie down. 'I don't know where he is.'

'I'll find him,' Brianna vowed.

'You're all I've got left,' Edilio said. 'You're the only freak with any serious powers. I don't think the Siren would be much help against' – he coughed – 'those creatures.'

'She might work on Drake, though,' Brianna said, and laughed at the thought of little Jill pacifying Drake the monster with the power of song.

As Edilio coughed again, she blinked, frowned, and said, 'Are all these kids sick?'

Edilio coughed hard. It hurt his chest. He was sick. Sick in his body and sick in his heart.

He had seen so many terrible things and done so many terrible things since the coming of the FAYZ. But nothing so cold-bloodedly awful as lining up the sights on Lance's head and squeezing the trigger.

It was the right move. Probably. It was the winning move, it seemed, since Astrid and Little Pete had both survived.

It was the ruthless move. The lesser-of-two-evils move. It was what Sam would have done in his place.

But it was poison in Edilio's heart.

'I can't save us,' Edilio said. 'Neither can you, Brianna. And Sam . . . I don't know if he can, either. So maybe this is the end. Maybe this is it and we lose.'

Brianna slapped herself in the chest. 'I don't lose!'

'You can't beat them alone, Breeze.' A coughing fit, the worst one yet. It was several minutes before he could continue. 'I'm done for. I don't know if this will kill me or not but I can't even stand up.'

'Hey, we can't just give up,' Brianna said. 'Those things are the size of ponies now, some of them. And they're growing! You can't give up, Edilio. You're the one in charge.'

He aimed his eyes at her, but they were swimming. She was an angry, unfocused face.

'Get me a piece of paper and a pen,' Edilio said.

She was back in less than a second.

His fingers were trembling as a fit of chills racked his body.

He had a hard time steadying the pad and holding the pen. But with supreme effort he scribbled something, folded the paper, and handed it to Brianna.

'Quinn,' he said.

She read the message and flushed furiously. She threw the paper at him. It hit him in the face. 'Are you nuts? I'm not doing this!'

'I'm in charge,' he whispered. He bent with shaky fingers and retrieved the note. 'My call. It's the only way. Do it, Breeze: do it.'

'No, no. No way.'

Edilio grabbed her arm and squeezed it with the last of his strength. 'For once in your life, think. Can you stop them? Can you stop those bugs from reaching town and killing everyone here? Yes or no?'

'I can try.'

'Yes or no?'

She stifled a sudden sob. She shook her head. 'No.'

'OK, then,' Edilio rasped. 'Do you want to be responsible for the lives of everyone who will die just so that you can act all tough?'

She had no answer. She glanced around as if seeing the sick and the dead, the wrecked church, and the sad graveyard for the first time. 'No,' she said.

'Then go, Breeze. Go.'

THIRTY

SAM HAD RUN the boat all the way up the lake and all the way back. They had found two small campgrounds in all, but had not explored them carefully. Maybe a dozen big campers, a few ragged tents in various states of collapse. No doubt some camp food, soda, beer, coffee, all the things people brought camping.

And gas in some of those tanks. Lovely, lovely gasoline.

He was already imagining the steps they'd have to take. They would drive the campers to the marina area and form them up in a rough circle or maybe two concentric circles. They would have to dig some serious septic tanks well away from the lake so there wasn't any seepage into drinking water.

They would need to ration the gas carefully, carefully, saving it for moving produce from the fields and fish from the ocean. They would still need Quinn's steady supply of blue bats to pacify the zekes. Besides, they would need to be cautious about overfishing the lake.

No more stupid mistakes. This time they would have to get it right.

That was a job for Albert, Sam had to concede. No doubt Albert would get richer still, but he was the only one with the organisational skills for the job.

Yes, it would work. They would build it and organise it and this time they would get it right.

For his part he had to find a way to destroy the flying greenies. But surely with Jack's strength and Dekka's powers and maybe Brianna – who could probably run through a cloud of greenies without getting hit – they could seal up that cave and crush or burn whatever survived.

They were heading back towards the marina now, chugging along slowly, taking their time. It was getting late in the day and Sam was trying to decide whether they should try to start one of the vehicles parked at the marina and drive back tonight, or plan a little more carefully and go in the morning.

The last thing anyone needed was three hundred or so kids tearing off in a mad search for sweets. Half would end up lost in the desert or the hills and end up being coyote food.

The news needed to be handled the right way. Edilio and the rest of the council would have to plan a little.

To Dekka he said, 'I think maybe we should load as much water as we can carry in an SUV and drive back tonight.'

'I guess you've noticed there's no road that goes straight back.'

'According to the map the road that follows the lake curves up around, hits the barrier. Right? But there has to then be a road that goes down through the Stefano Rey and hits the highway, right?'

Dekka shrugged. Her mind was elsewhere.

He couldn't blame her. But he had convinced himself she was worrying for nothing.

He indulged himself with a moment of fantasy. They would be heroes, showing up in town with water, even if it wasn't that much water. That would be one very welcome sight, an SUV full of water bottles. Maybe a few jars of Nutella, too, if they drove east to the train before cutting south.

Then, a meeting with the council. They could start trucking water right away. That would keep everybody calm until a plan was worked out.

'We'll go in . . .' His words died as his gaze travelled to the marina. 'Dekka. Jack. Look.'

They looked.

Creatures, like giant silvery cockroaches, cockroaches the size of mini-vans, clustered on the shore. Maybe a dozen.

It had to be an illusion. A trick. They were impossible. Like a nightmare out of some ancient science fiction movie.

Sam reached for the binoculars he'd found in a locked case on board. He raised them, focused.

'It's Hunter's bugs,' he said. He couldn't keep the awe out of his voice. 'But they're huge.'

He traversed his binoculars and then saw a human standing atop one of the creatures. He could not see the face well enough to identify it. But there was no mistaking the long, jauntily waving tentacle.

Drake. No longer locked in his basement prison.

Sam's Garden of Eden had its own snake.

Howard's first impulse had been to go to the so-called hospital and find Lana. But what profit would be in it for Howard?

Orc was off somewhere, freaking out, hammered, faced, blasted. He'd come back when he ran out of alcohol, but for now, Orc was gone, and Drake's escape was a sort of black eye for Howard.

In the back of his calculating mind, Howard wondered if Orc was just determined to pull a Mary and off himself. He was nowhere near the deadly fifteenth birthday, but Orc might one of these days pick a fight that would get him killed.

Or he might just drink himself to death. And then what? What did Howard have if he didn't have Orc?

On a level still deeper was a genuine sadness that Orc would abandon him. They were friends, after all. Amigos. They'd been through everything together. Orc wasn't just Howard's main asset, he was Howard's only friend.

He cared for Orc. Genuinely cared for him. Obviously Orc didn't care much about him.

Howard took his time making the decision. Took his time and a fully clothed shower, too. But finally he made his decision and sauntered away from the cloud, soggy but moderately clean, unnoticed by frolicking kids.

It wasn't far to Albert's place. He found the door open, and quickly located Albert. The young mogul's eyes were closed. He definitely looked dead. Very definitely dead.

He advanced cautiously, as though Albert might suddenly rise up and start yelling at him for intruding. He pressed two fingers against Albert's neck. He didn't feel a pulse.

But he did feel warmth. The body should be colder.

He squatted in front of Albert and with his finger pushed up one eyelid. The dark iris contracted.

'Yaaah!' Howard said, and fell backward. 'Are you alive, man?'

No answer. Nothing.

Howard was frustrated because he'd hoped – if Albert was still alive – to negotiate a deal. After all, if Howard saved Albert's life then it stood to reason that he owed Howard a little somethin'.

Howard hesitated. He could do nothing and sooner or later Albert would be a hundred per cent, stone-cold dead. Or he could try to find Lana. And maybe there would be some reward.

Albert was tight with his money, but surely if Howard saved his actual life . . .

'OK, I don't know if you can hear this or not, Donald Trump, but if I save your butt, you owe me.' He frowned and decided he'd better add, 'And oh, by the way, this is Howard talking. So it'll be Howard you owe.'

Howard arrived at the so-called hospital to see a very disturbing sight: Edilio, shivering and muttering on the stone steps, ignored. He was just one of dozens of sick kids with various degrees of illness. Coughing, hacking, shivering.

The last thing Howard wanted to do was get any closer.

'Hey!' Howard yelled up the steps.

No one answered. He winced, turned away, turned back, doing a little dance of indecision. Without even knowing what his reward might be, it was hard for Howard to decide to risk his life. A man needed to know what he was getting paid, after all.

Kkkrrraaalff!

A kid at the top of the steps suddenly coughed with a force Howard had never seen or heard or imagined. The cough blew the boy backwards. He landed hard, head smacking granite with the sound of a melon dropped on a floor.

The boy rolled over, got to his knees, then coughed a spray of blood all over a girl nearby.

'No way,' Howard said. 'No way.'

The new kid, Sanjit – Helicopter Boy – appeared at the top of the steps. He rushed down to the coughing kid and grabbed his shoulders from behind.

He spotted Howard standing there. 'Give me a hand, I need to get him off these steps.'

'I'm not touching that little dude,' Howard said.

Sanjit shot him an angry look. But then softened, like he understood.

Sanjit tried to walk the boy back up the stairs, but then the kid started coughing again with such violence that he threw Sanjit off and went flailing back again.

This time he rolled down the stairs to stop at Howard's feet. He lay there, shivering and moaning. A fountain of blood flowed at once from his ears and nose and mouth.

Sanjit came down and stood over him. 'Get out of the way,' Sanjit said to Howard. 'I have to drag him across the street.'

'Is he dead?'

'No, he's in perfect shape,' Sanjit snapped. He grabbed both of the boy's wrists and started to haul him towards the plaza.

'You see Edilio there?' Howard demanded.

'Yes, I saw Edilio there,' Sanjit said.

'Shouldn't you . . .' Howard motioned vaguely.

'Yeah, I should call for a stretcher and get him straight to the intensive care unit,' Sanjit said with contained fury. 'I'll get him on an oxygen machine and pump him full of antibiotics.

351

Or maybe I'll just see if he lives or dies because that's really all I can do. All right?'

Howard took a step back in the face of the slender boy's anger.

'Didn't mean to . . .' he said, and followed at a safe distance as Sanjit dragged the body off the curb and on to the blacktop.

Sanjit stopped halfway across and stared at the sky.

'What's that? Is that a cloud?'

'Oh, that? Yeah, it's raining. More weirdness,' Howard said.

'What? It's raining? Like, water?'

'Yeah, water. It was a shock to me, too,' Howard said. 'This being the FAYZ you'd expect it to be raining fire or dog turds or something.'

'Choooooo!' Sanjit yelled at the top of his lungs. 'Chooooo!'

A few seconds later, his chubby African brother came running down the stairs, looking alarmed.

'Water!' Sanjit said.

'Where?' Virtue demanded.

Sanjit pointed with his chin. 'Get a bucket. Get every bucket you can find!'

Virtue gaped, then ran.

Sanjit resumed dragging the corpse.

'Listen, dude,' Howard said. 'I need Lana. You know who I mean? The Healer.'

'You have a boo-boo?' Sanjit snarked. 'She's kind of busy trying to save a couple of creeps Edilio shot.'

'Where?'

'Astrid's house. I don't know where it is. How about you either help me or get lost?'

'I'll choose B.'

Astrid's house. OK. That would be . . . pretty much right directly under the cloud.

'Well, well,' Howard said as the truth dawned on him. 'Little Pete's secret is out, then. Well, buckle up, Howard, buckle up.'

Quinn and his crew were pulling towards shore, far later than usual. They'd had a tough day of it. After a miserable night in camp, they'd had trouble getting one of the boats floating again. They had unknowingly run it ashore and scraped a hidden rock. A gash had been gouged in the bottom, which meant hours of finding a way to patch it.

Fortunately it was one of the wooden hulls, not one of the metal or fibreglass; those would have been impossible to patch without going back to town for equipment.

Still, they'd had to use just their Swiss army knives to whittle some driftwood into fairly flat, fairly smooth planks. Then they'd found they had no screws, so they had to remove bolts from other boats, drill through the repair patch and the hull, and use the bolts to attach the patch. They had scraped and then melted some paint to use as a sealant.

When they were all done the boat was surprisingly seaworthy. They'd all felt pretty well pleased with their work, but a day of fishing was still to be done.

Harder later in the day. As the sun heated the top layer of seawater, some of their most reliable catch went deeper or stopped feeding.

So there were none of the jokes or laughs or bits of song that often accompanied their homeward row.

'They still haven't picked up yesterday's catch!' Quinn yelled when they drew close enough to see.

And sure enough, most of the fish they'd worked so hard to land the day before were still on the dock, rotting in the heat.

This revelation set off a round of angry curses from the crews, followed by a more disquieting worry. It was hard to imagine how Albert could have let this happen.

'Something's wrong,' Quinn said. 'I mean even more wrong than we knew.'

They were still two hundred yards out when Quinn saw a blur that froze and became Brianna. She was at the end of the dock.

There was something in her hand.

'You guys hang back,' Quinn yelled to the other boats. 'We'll go in and see what's up.'

Quinn's boat touched the dock and he tossed a loop over one of the cleats.

'About time,' Brianna said.

'Hey, sorry, we were kind of busy,' Quinn snapped. 'And I didn't exactly realise I was on a schedule.'

'I don't like what I have to do here,' Brianna said. She handed Quinn the note.

He read it. Read it again.

'Is this some kind of joke?' he demanded.

'Albert's dead,' Brianna said. 'Murdered.'

'What?'

'He's dead. Sam and Dekka are off in the wilderness somewhere. Edilio's got the flu, he might die, a lot of kids have. A lot. And there are these, these monsters, these kind of bugs . . . no one knows what to call them . . . heading towards town.' Her face contorted in a mix of rage and sorrow and fear. She blurted, 'And I can't stop them!'

Quinn stared at her. Then back at the note.

He felt his contented little universe tilt and go sliding away.

There were just two words on the paper: 'Get Caine.'

THIRTY ONE

SAM PULLED THE boat to within thirty yards of the shore.

'I guess you wish you'd burned me all up, huh?' Drake called to him.

'I do,' Dekka growled.

'That's true,' Toto said. 'She does wish it.'

Sam had to master a furious anger that burned within him. How had Drake escaped? Had he found a way to bribe Howard?

'He wouldn't be standing there taunting us unless he thought he could beat us,' Sam said quietly. 'Those bugs: I couldn't kill them when they were a lot smaller.' He looked at Toto. 'All you've got is the truth-telling thing, right? You don't have some other power?'

Toto gave his answer to the missing Spidey head. 'No weapons.'

'Can those things swim?' Jack wondered.

'If they could they'd already be after us,' Sam said.

'Do you think Drake can control those things, make

356

them do what he wants?' Jack wondered.

'I guess we'll find out sooner or later,' Sam said.

They all fell silent, gazing at him expectantly.

For the moment they were probably safe, Sam reasoned. Otherwise Drake would have come after them. If they went ashore it would mean a fight. And Drake was pretty cocky, swaggering around and taunting them from shore.

He could head the boat back up the lake. He could land and get around Drake's insect army. They could make it to someplace where they could fight without destroying the marina.

'We need to get away from here,' Sam said.

'Hey, Sam,' Drake shouted. 'I thought you'd like to know this isn't my whole army.'

Sam didn't doubt it.

'Your girl Brianna tried to stop us.' Drake waved a bowie knife in the air. 'I took this from her. I whipped her, Sam.' He snapped his whip hand. The crack was like a pistol shot. 'I broke her legs so she couldn't run. Then . . .'

Dekka was halfway over the side, ready to swim ashore. Jack grabbed her and held her.

'Let me go!' Dekka yelled.

'Hold her,' Sam ordered Jack. 'Don't be stupid, Dekka. He wants us to come rushing at him.'

'I can beat him,' Jack said. 'Dekka and me together, we can kill him.'

357

Sam registered the fact that Jack was actually making a physical threat. He didn't remember ever hearing that kind of thing from Jack. But Dekka was Sam's greater concern.

'I'm going to kill him,' Dekka said in a voice so deep in her throat she sounded like an animal. 'I'll kill him. I'll kill him.' Then she shouted, 'I'm going to kill you, Drake. I'm going to kill you!'

Drake grinned. 'I think she liked it. She was screaming, but she liked it.'

'He's lying,' Toto said.

'Who?' Sam snapped.

'Him.' He pointed at Drake. 'He hasn't killed that girl or hurt her.'

Dekka relaxed and Sam and Jack let go of her.

'Truth-teller Toto,' Sam whispered. 'He can tell when people are lying.'

'I just decided I like you,' Dekka said to Toto. 'You might be useful.'

Toto frowned. 'It's true: you just decided you like me.'

'Keep listening, Toto,' Sam said. He thought for a minute. Then he yelled, 'Brianna may be dead, but we still have more than enough muscle to deal with you.'

Drake threw back his head and laughed. 'Yeah, the rest of my army is finishing off the last few kids in Perdido Beach. It was a beautiful massacre, Sam, you should have been there.'

Sam made a motion to Dekka not to answer. The more Drake talked the better.

'But I still have Astrid alive, Sam,' Drake shouted. 'I have her somewhere safe. I want to take my time with her.'

Sam waited, held his breath.

'Those are lies,' Toto said.

'All of it?'

'All of it.'

Sam breathed.

'Well, Drake,' Sam shouted across the water. 'I'm sorry to hear about that. I guess there's nothing left but for you to come and get me.'

His tone was so casual, it left Drake gaping open-mouthed. It took the psychopath a few moments to regroup.

'What's the matter, Sammy? Scared? Chicken?'

'No, actually we were thinking we might catch some fish,' Sam yelled. 'I hear the trout from this lake are delicious. Would you like to join us? You can swim with that whip hand, can't you?'

Drake stared. He looked at the knife in his hand as if it had somehow betrayed him. Then, eyes narrowed, he glared at Toto.

'Come on, Drake. Don't be a baby. Come and get us.'

All the while Sam had been letting the boat edge closer, closer while not grounding. He was within ten yards of Drake. He didn't have to raise his voice to be heard.

Without turning towards her, and speaking in a whisper, he said, 'Dekka, can you reach him from here?'

'Barely,' she said. 'The sharper the angle, the less I can do. But yeah.'

'On one,' Sam said. 'Three . . . two . . .'

Dekka raised her hands and Drake rose feebly from the ground. He felt it immediately, knew what was happening, and kicked against the air like a marionette.

Sam raised his hands. Twin beams of green light fired. They hit one of the creatures, two feet to the left, but Sam swung right and caught Drake's leg.

The leg turned bright and smoke swirled.

Drake lashed with his whip and caught one of the creatures. He yanked himself out of Dekka's field and tumbled among the creatures, blocked from Sam's beams.

'Will he die?' Toto asked.

'Sadly, no,' Dekka said.

From shore they heard Drake bellowing in outrage, then: 'Get them! Go!'

The creatures responded instantly. They rushed to the water's edge. It was almost impossible for Sam to see them as living creatures, they seemed more like robots. Insects simply were not that big. Couldn't be that big.

They rushed in a swarm to the water. And kept running straight in.

'They float,' Jack said. 'That's bad.'

'Yeah, but they can't swim very well,' Sam pointed out. He threw the engine into reverse and chug-chugged slowly back to a safer distance. The creatures had stopped rushing into the water. Those that could reach bottom scurried ignominiously back to dry land. Two of the creatures floated like unmoored rafts, or like trailers caught in a flood, twisting slowly, helpless.

Then one of the creatures on shore opened its wings. Beneath the hard carapace were wings like a dragonfly's.

'They can't actually fly, can they?' Dekka wondered.

The creature lifted off. It was awkward and slow. But it flew. It flew towards the boat.

'Go back to camp after you offload the catch,' Quinn instructed his crews. 'I'll catch up with you later. And if I don't . . . well, keep up the routine.'

He felt worried eyes following him as he walked down the dock. There was one motorboat that still had a few gallons of fuel. They had designated it for emergency use only. He supposed this was emergency enough.

'You coming?' Quinn asked Brianna.

She shook her head. 'I can't beat these things, but I can at least fight them.'

'What if he won't come?' Quinn asked.

'He'll come. It will be his big moment.'

'Will he be able to stop these creatures?'

'How would I know?' Brianna demanded. 'It wasn't my idea. I'm not the one saying we should bring him back. Maybe he and Drake will go back to being best buddies. How would I know?'

'Well, I guess Edilio thinks Caine can save us.'

Neither of them spoke for a while, both thinking of Edilio, wondering if he would survive. Right from the start Edilio had been one of the good guys. Probably the best of them.

He and Mary: two selfless, loyal, decent people. One dead after betraying everything and everyone. The other maybe dying right now, ignored and alone.

'One more question for you, Brianna. It's serious. So don't just give me your automatic tough-chick answer, OK? Because I want the truth.'

'Yeah?'

'Can you beat Caine? If he starts in with his usual, starts pushing people around, hurting them . . . Can you take him?'

He saw the beginnings of a cocky smile. But then she dropped the act, sighed, and said, 'I don't know, Quinn.'

Still he hesitated. He didn't want to go. And he knew why. 'Everybody kind of likes me now because I fish. I have this thing I do, right, and it's necessary and so people respect me.' He sighed and unwound the motorboat's rope from its cleat. 'Now I'll be the guy who brought Caine back.'

Brianna nodded. 'Sucks to be you. Sucks worse to be me.'

Impulsively, Quinn hugged her. Like a brother. She didn't return the gesture, but she didn't blur away either.

'Hang in there, Breeze.'

'You too, Fisherman.'

Quinn stepped down into the boat. Brianna was out of sight before he could fire the engine.

He headed out of the marina, chugging along slowly until he was away. Then he pushed the throttle to full speed and pointed the bow towards the distant island.

Astrid looked around, wondering where they were and where they were going. Orc seemed to have someplace in mind. But he also seemed confused. They were in an area of tangled woods and sharp, sudden, brush-choked valleys.

'Are you taking us to Coates?' Astrid asked.

'Yeah,' Orc answered.

'Why there?'

'You wanted to get away, right?'

'I want my brother to be somewhere safe,' Astrid said, conscious of the hypocrisy.

'It's safe there,' Orc said.

'How do you know?'

'It's a secret,' Orc grumbled. 'I mean, there's no one there. None of those kids anyway. Caine and all them guys.'

'What if Drake goes there?'

Orc shrugged, which caused Little Pete's head to fall from his shoulder and loll back. 'If Drake's there, I'll take care of him.'

Astrid stepped quickly to catch up with Orc. She put her hand on his shoulder. He slowed down and moved aside so she could walk beside him.

'Are you looking for Drake?' Astrid asked. 'Because I don't think that's a good idea.'

'I don't care about Drake,' Orc said angrily. 'I had enough of him. But I have to be away from town. Where else am I going to go?'

Astrid felt sure that was part of the truth. But not all of it.

'Thanks for helping us,' she said. 'But you don't have to stay away from town. It's not your fault Drake escaped.'

'Didn't say it was.'

'Then why?'

Orc said nothing, just walked on heavily, stone feet trampling the undergrowth like some undersized Godzilla. Then, 'This kid,' he said.

'What kid?'

'This kid, this little kid, was all sick or whatever, and I was . . . I guess I was drunk.'

'What happened with the kid?'

'Got in my way,' Orc said.

364

It was hard to read Orc's expression. But she heard anguish in his voice.

'Oh,' Astrid said.

'Gotta leave town. Like Hunter. That's the law. You oughta know, you made up that law.'

'I didn't come up with "thou shalt not kill",' Astrid said defensively. The sanctimony in her own voice made her sick. The same Bible that said 'thou shalt not kill' also said 'he who hateth his brother is a murderer'.

Didn't she hate her brother? Hadn't she contemplated murder? Hadn't she dared Turk and Lance to do it for her? If Orc had to go into exile, then didn't she as well?

Would she wish her brother dead and live with that mortal sin, and yet draw the line at sleeping with Sam? How absurd was that? Murder, sure, but fornication? No way.

Astrid had never felt so low. She dropped back so Orc wouldn't see the tears in her eyes. Oh, God, how had she become this person? How had she failed so utterly?

Hypocrite. Murderer in her heart. A cold, manipulative witch. That's what she was. Astrid the Genius? Astrid the Fraud.

And now she slogged through darkening woods to find a cold shelter with a drunken killer and her brother. One who killed from rage and stupidity; the other who killed from what? Ignorance? Indifference? From the simple fact of too much power for anyone to handle, let alone an autistic child? She laughed, but it was not a happy sound.

'What's funny?' Orc demanded suspiciously.

'Me,' Astrid said.

They spotted the dark gabled roofs of Coates through the trees and then struck the road that led up to the front gate.

It was a gloomy place, a haunted place. Pale whitewashed stone that showed evidence of violence. A massive hole in the facade was like a fatal bullet wound. The door had been ripped apart, shredded.

Orc stomped steadily forwards, climbed the steps, and yelled, 'Anyone here?'

His voice echoed in the arched entryway. 'There're beds upstairs. Gotta take the back stairs.'

He led the way, obviously familiar with the layout. Astrid wondered how he had come to know the place so well. Orc was not a Coates kid.

They found a dorm room that hadn't been burned or shredded or used as a toilet.

Orc tossed Little Pete negligently on to a bare mattress. Astrid searched for and found a tattered blanket, which she spread over him.

She felt his forehead. Still feverish, but perhaps no worse than before. She had no thermometer. He was coughing in fits and starts. Not worse, not better.

'What's next, Petey?' she asked him.

If Lance had squeezed the trigger, would the bullet have killed Little Pete? Would he have had the power to stop it? Surely. But would he have known what was happening?

'How much do you know, Petey? How much do you understand?'

He would need clean bedding after he wet himself. And she herself needed clothing, she was still in just a nightgown. And although there would be no food left in this place, surely there might be a few drops of water.

Astrid called to Orc, but he didn't hear. She heard his heavy footsteps reverberate in the eerie silence.

Best to leave him be. In another room she found clothing that was close to her size. Close enough. It wasn't clean, but at least it had not been worn recently. Coates had been abandoned for a while. She wondered if it belonged to Diana.

She went in search of water. What she found was Orc. He was in the dining hall. His massive legs were propped on a heavy wooden table. He had pushed two chairs together to bear his weight and spread.

In his hand he held a clear glass bottle full of clear liquid.

The room smelled of charcoal and something sickly sweet. The source was obvious: in the corner, next to a window, was a contraption that could only be a still. Copper tubing probably salvaged from the chemistry lab looped from a steel washtub that rested on an iron trestle over the cold remains of a fire.

'This is where Howard makes his whiskey,' Astrid said. 'That's how you know the place.'

Orc took a deep swig. Some of the liquor sloshed out of his mouth. 'No one ever comes here since Caine and all them took off. That's how come Howard set up here.'

'What does he use?'

Orc shrugged. 'Don't matter much as long as it's any kind of vegetable. There's a patch of corn only a few people know about. Artichokes, too. Cabbages. It don't matter.'

Astrid took a chair at some distance from him.

'You changed clothes,' he said.

'I was cold.'

He nodded and drank deep. His eyes were on her, looking at her in detail. She was very glad to no longer be wearing her nightgown.

She wondered whether Orc was old enough for her to worry about in that way. She thought not. But it was a frightening possibility.

'Should you be drinking that so fast?'

'Gotta be fast,' Orc said. 'Otherwise I pass out and can't get enough to do the trick.'

'What trick?' Astrid asked.

Orc made a sad smile. 'Don't worry about it, Astrid.'

She didn't want to worry about it. She had enough of her

own worries. So she said nothing as he gulped and gulped until forced to take a breath.

'Orc,' she said softly. 'Are you trying to kill yourself?'

'Like I said, don't worry 'bout it.'

'You can't do that,' she said. 'It's . . . it's wrong.'

She noticed two more bottles down on the floor, right where he could reach them without moving.

'It's a mortal sin,' she said, feeling like a stupid fool. The very word 'sin' felt like a sin when she spoke it.

Hypocrite, she berated herself silently. Fraud.

'If you do this, you'll have no chance to repent,' Astrid said. 'You'll die with a mortal sin on your conscience.'

'Got that already,' Orc said.

'But you're sorry for that. You've thought about it. And you're sorry for it.'

Orc sobbed suddenly, a loud sound. He tilted his head back and she saw the last of the bottle drain into his mouth.

'If you've asked for forgiveness, and if you felt truly sorry, then God has forgiven you for that little boy.'

The bottles weren't corked, just sealed with a piece of Saran Wrap and a rubber band. Orc pulled the plastic off a second bottle.

'There's no God in the FAYZ, didn't you know that?' he said.

THIRTY TWO

SAM FIRED. THE beams of light hit the hovering bug squarely. The rays of light bounced and fragmented, steaming the water.

'Dekka!' Sam yelled.

She killed gravity beneath the hovering bug so that it shot suddenly upwards followed by a swoosh of rising water.

But it was no good. More of the creatures were opening their roach-like wings and flying awkwardly out toward the boat.

Sam cursed. He threw the engine into gear and spun the wheel. The boat zoomed towards the middle of the lake.

The bugs tried to chase, but they were insects, not eagles, and their flight was jerky and poorly controlled.

'I can maybe crush them,' Jack said over the roar of the engines.

'He believes he maybe can,' Toto commented.

'But they scare me.'

'That is true, too,' Toto said.

'Yeah, I could have guessed that,' Sam yelled as they dodged another lumbering creature.

They could keep dodging the bugs, maybe forever, but when Sam tapped the gas gauge it showed just an eighth of a tank.

There was a hand pump built into the dock's gas tank. But it wasn't as if Drake would let them pull in and refuel.

'We need gas,' Sam said.

He headed the boat away from the marina, keeping close to the shore, hoping Drake's creepy army would follow. They were faster on land than in the air so they zoomed in their crazy bumblebee way back to land on shore.

He looked back and saw Drake urging the creatures on. They were quick, skittering on their insect legs. But not quite as fast as the boat. At top speed he could pull away.

'Are we running away?' Toto wondered.

'Yes,' Sam snapped.

'That's not true.'

'Is there any way to shut you off?' Sam demanded. 'We're faster than they are. So we're going to draw them off, double back, and beat them back to the marina.'

'Then what?' Dekka asked.

'We gas up and drive around out here forever,' Sam said.

'Great plan,' Dekka said.

'Sooner or later Drake gives way to Brittney. We might have a shot then.'

It didn't take long at full speed to reach the end of the lake. The huge roaches swarmed along the shore, rushing eagerly to catch up. None were airborne now.

'Where's Drake?' Jack asked.

Sam scanned the insect army. No sign of Drake. Sam killed the engine, saving gas for the mad dash back to the marina. In the sudden quiet he heard a different engine.

A sleek boat with two big outboards was throwing up a cloud of spray and *whump-whump*ing toward them. There could be no doubt as to who was driving the boat.

The bugs on the shore. Drake on the water.

'If he has a gun, we're in trouble,' Dekka said.

'He doesn't need a gun,' Sam said grimly. 'He can ram us. He's unkillable, we're not.'

'What do we do?' Jack asked. Then, more panicked, 'What do we do?'

Dekka put a calming hand on his shoulder. 'Take it easy.'

Sam measured the shoreline, checked the gas supply, glanced at his two friends, and finally appraised Toto.

'Dude, do you think you can pump gas?'

Toto looked away and passed the question along to the imaginary Spidey head. 'Can I pump gas?' Then, apparently hearing an answer, he said, 'Yes.'

Sam fired the engine up. He turned the wheel, waited, waited, as Drake's bow wave grew large.

'Jack. Grab that boathook. And be ready.'

'What?'

'You ever see that movie where Heath Ledger was a knight?'

'Not his best movie,' Dekka said.

'True,' Toto agreed.

'Hold on,' Sam warned. He put the engine into gear, pushed the throttle all the way, and flew towards Drake.

Lana did not run, she was too tired for it, and anyway Howard was probably wrong. Turk and Lance surely did believe they'd killed Albert. As he'd laid there, shrieking in pain beneath Lana's healing touch, Lance kept babbling something about forgiveness, praying to be saved, saying he was sorry for Albert. 'It was Turk, it wasn't me!' he'd said, his destroyed cheek flapping bloodily with each word as the drenching rain swept the blood down to the carpet beneath his head.

Lana had mostly healed Turk and Lance. They wouldn't die, at least. She hadn't much seen the point: they were scum and someone would only have to kill them all over again, sooner or later. But she supposed it wasn't her decision to make. She was just a player in the madness.

She had missed her chance to be a hero by destroying the gaiaphage. And she had failed to stop the virus that now claimed nine bodies. Instead she'd saved a couple of creeps. Yay for her.

She and Howard found Albert just as he'd said: sitting with his back against the wall.

Lana noticed an awful lot of blood. A small, sticky sea of it around Albert.

'He didn't die right away,' Lana observed. 'Dead people don't bleed as much. And see how the wall is smeared? He sat up.' She knelt and placed her fingers on his neck. 'Then he just sat here and bled to death.'

No question in her mind. He had a bullet hole in his face. And a much larger exit wound out the far side. It looked as if some wild animal had taken a messy bite out of his skull.

'I don't raise the dead,' Lana said.

'No, wait,' Howard insisted. He knelt beside her and lifted one eyelid. It was dark, there wasn't much light for an iris to react to. So Howard fished out a lighter and flicked the flame.

Lana's eyebrows went up. 'Do it again.'

Howard lifted the other lid. That iris, too, responded.

'Huh,' Lana said.

She pressed both hands against Albert's head. After a few minutes holding that pose she bent his head forwards to see the awful exit wound. Around the jagged, ripped edges, flesh was growing.

'The brother's not dead,' Howard said.

'About as close as you can get,' Lana said. 'But no: he's not dead. And this kind of thing, at least, I can heal.'

'Boy's going to owe me,' Howard said.

'You're a trip, Howard, as my dad would say,' Lana said. 'You are definitely a trip.'

'You'll tell Albert I brought you, right? You'll tell him it was me, right?'

'Why? Are you leaving?'

Howard stood up. 'Gotta go find Orc. I just figured out where he'd go.'

Lana got herself into a more comfortable position. Patrick went off to scavenge around in the house.

'You find anything, you better share,' Lana called after her dog.

The two boats raced towards each other.

Six seconds to impact.

Sam's mind was racing. Drake would know he was bluffing. Drake didn't fear an impact, he would know Sam was bluffing and he would expect Sam to suddenly veer aside.

Four seconds to impact.

'Jack!' Sam yelled. 'Up on the bow!'

'What?'

'Do it!' Sam bellowed.

Jack sprang straight from the stern to the bow. He was holding the boathook like a lance. Like he really was a knight. Hopefully Drake had noticed.

One second.

'Now, throw it!' Sam shouted.

Jack threw it with all his desperate, supernatural strength.

Sam had not expected the boathook to impale Drake – and it didn't. But even an unkillable killer had instincts, and Drake instinctively dropped to let the boathook fly harmlessly over his head.

Sam had already twisted the wheel.

They blew past Drake's boat, spraying it with their bow wave and taking a drenching spray in return.

Dekka grinned at Toto. 'See, this is what makes Sam, Sam.'

It took a furious Drake ten seconds to turn his boat and come after Sam.

The bugs were even slower to catch on. Now they were racing back along the shore, but neither Drake nor the bugs would get to the marina before Sam.

'OK,' Sam yelled over the throb of the engines. 'Toto, when we get there you pump like crazy, right? I'll show you how. But Drake will be on us quick and he may try again to ram us, so Jack? You and Dekka be ready.'

'Ready to do what?'

'Hang on!' Sam yelled. He aimed the boat for the dock, threw it into reverse, the water boiled, the engine roared, and the boat scraped harshly to a stop by the gas pump.

Sam grabbed Toto and shoved him bodily up on to the dock.

'Dekka! Tie us off.' He unlimbered the hand pump, thrust the nozzle into the gas tank and physically placed Toto's hands on the pump. 'Up and down, up and down, and don't stop until I tell you to.'

Sam ran to the end of the dock. Drake was roaring down on them. Sam glanced left, right, looking for what he needed. A low-slung sailboat. That would do.

'Dekka! Float that boat!'

Dekka raised her hands and the boat rose from the water, dripping all over them, tilting to one side so that for a moment Sam was afraid it would roll over and smash its mast down on their heads.

'OK, Jack. You missed with the boathook. Try this!'

Jack had to skirt Dekka's field, and for a second he lost his footing and almost fell into the water. Sam grabbed his hand and hauled him upright.

Jack backed up twenty feet, took a deep breath, and ran straight at the boat that now hovered over the end of the dock.

Sam had the pleasure of seeing the sudden realisation dawn in Drake's eyes.

Jack rushed forwards, jumped, and hit the stern of the sailboat.

The boat flew, twisting crazily through the air. Not far, just twenty or thirty feet before it exploded into flames as Sam aimed and fired.

The boat fell, hit the water, and Drake's boat smashed into it at full speed.

Both boats shattered, flaming wood splinters flew, bits of metal railing and big pieces of the engine spiralled and landed like shrapnel all around them.

Toto cried out in pain. His hip had been hit and he was bleeding and screaming and not pumping any longer.

'Jack! Pump! Dekka, get Toto.'

Sam dropped back into his boat and began snatching up and tossing out bits of flaming debris.

'Be dead, be dead,' Sam muttered under his breath.

A sudden sound and Sam felt a burning pain. A red lash mark appeared on his arm.

Drake was holding the dock with his real arm, whip hand drawn back to strike again.

Sam fired. Missed. Bought two seconds as Drake sank beneath the disturbed water.

He shot a look up the shore. The racing creatures pelted through the parking lot, swarmed over and around the cars, would be on them in seconds. Now or never.

'Enough! Back in the boat!'

No one needed to be told twice. Toto and Jack were first in. Dekka stumbled as she ran, slapped her belly, and for a moment Sam thought something had hit her.

Drake was up and his whip hand found Jack. Jack howled

and grabbed at the tentacle but missed.

Sam gunned the engine. But he had forgotten the rope. The boat roared, shot forward, and snapped the cleat off the dock. The resistance was enough to yank the boat around.

It smashed into another parked boat and sent everyone tumbling.

By the time Sam cleared his head, Drake had his hand on the gunwale and his whip hand was flailing madly into the boat, striking Jack again and Toto.

Sam threw the boat into reverse, pushed the throttle, twisted the wheel, and ground Drake between boat and dock.

Then he changed gears and roared off, leaving Drake cursing in the water as the bugs raced down the dock, their mandibles slashing at the air.

Sam drove to the middle of the lake and killed the engine. The gas gauge showed a hair over a quarter tank. Enough for now. But at the cost of Toto screaming in pain.

'It's bad,' Dekka reported. 'But he'll live.'

She lifted Toto's shirt to show Sam a nasty gash. 'Jack, see if there's a first aid kit aboard.'

Sam sagged, very tired now. 'You OK?' he asked Dekka.

She didn't answer.

He looked more closely at her. 'Dekka?'

She looked sick. She bit her lip. 'I am sorry to add to your problems, boss,' she said. Then she raised her own shirt and Sam saw the tiny mouthparts poking through her flesh.

The light died and night fell as the boat rocked on the gentle waves.

THIRTY THREE

3 HOURS 47 MINUTES

DIANA ROLLED OUT of the bed, accidentally pulling the covers off Caine as she did.

'Hey!' he protested.

'It's nothing I haven't seen. Repeatedly.'

Caine grinned and laced his fingers behind his head. 'I could get used to this life. I think I'll have another can of peaches.'

Diana took a quick shower and stepped out, dripping wet, to find him waiting for her, holding a towel.

'Seriously: no,' she said. 'We're done.'

'Well, until we get something to eat,' he said.

She dried off and combed her hair while he watched. The lack of privacy was a little irritating, but she told herself it was a small price to pay for peace. In any universe this would be a lovely room, in a lovely house, on a lovely island. But in the FAYZ every part of it was exquisite, a miracle of beauty and comfort. She remembered Coates all too well. Especially the

381

last months there as the food ran out and the fear and depression and self-hatred set in.

This was a beautiful place. And Caine was a beautiful boy – a young man, she supposed – at least on the outside.

If comfort and luxury and Diana herself could keep him pacified, maybe life would go on this way: peaceful.

Even caring for Penny and dealing with Bug were small problems compared to what she had survived. Panda: she shuddered at the memory and felt sick.

'What's the matter?' Caine asked.

'Nothing.' She forced a smile. 'I guess I'm hungry.' Then, seeing his expression, amended the statement. 'For food.'

They pulled on underwear and wrapped themselves in soft, expensive robes bearing famous, embroidered initials. She slid her feet into silk slippers and together they headed down to the kitchen.

Bug was there, looking even more disturbed than usual. He was breathing hard. Diana glared at him, wondering whether he had been spying on them.

'There's a boat coming,' Bug said.

'What do you mean?' Diana asked.

'A motorboat. It's real near.'

Caine was out the door in a flash and Diana had to run to catch up. The sky was near dark, the sun setting gorgeously and sending fingers of gold and red across the water below them.

And there, shockingly close, was a motorboat. She saw one person aboard, a boy, but could not make out his shadowed face.

She looked searchingly at Caine. On his face she saw the expression she expected to see, the expression she dreaded.

His eyes were alight, his mouth in a feral grin. His whole body seemed to lean forward, anticipating, ready. Excited.

'Whoever it is, just tell him to leave,' Diana said.

'Let's at least find out who it is,' Caine said.

'Caine, just get rid of him.'

The boat scared Diana. She wrapped her arms around herself as if shielding herself from cold.

Now the boy in the boat looked up.

'It's Quinn,' Caine said. 'What's he doing here? I expected it to be Zil or one of his losers.'

'You expected?' Diana frowned. 'What do you mean, you expected?'

Caine shrugged. 'Sooner or later one of them was going to come to me.'

'But . . . Why would you . . .?'

He laughed. A smug, cruel laugh. 'There are only two four bars in the FAYZ, Diana. Sooner or later someone would get sick enough of Sam lording it over them that they'd come to find me.'

Diana felt something twisting inside her.

'Hey, Quinn. Up here!' Caine yelled. Then, in an aside, 'Bug, disappear. Stay ready. It might be some kind of trick.'

Bug faded from view.

Quinn killed the engine. He stood up, moving easily with the rocking of the boat. 'Caine. Where do I land the boat?'

'No need,' Caine said. He was grinning hugely now. 'Sit down and hold on.'

Caine stepped to the very edge of the cliff. He raised his hands. The boat began to rise from the water. Dripping, and trailing a fringe of algae, it floated up and up and came to rest on the overgrown grass. Caine released it and it tipped on to its side. Quinn jumped to avoid being spilled out of the boat.

'Well, Quinn, what brings you to Fantasy Island?' Caine asked.

'Hey, Diana,' Quinn said.

Diana didn't respond. She knew. Just like Caine knew. Somehow, despite everything, Quinn was here to bring Caine back.

'Edilio sent me,' Quinn said.

Caine smiled sceptically. 'Edilio? Last guy on earth I expected to be sending me messages.'

'Edilio's mayor now.'

Diana felt a pang. 'Is Sam dead?'

Quinn started to answer, but Caine interrupted. 'No, no: let me guess. I'm going to say . . . Sam got tired of doing everyone's dirty work, taking all the risks, and then catching all the blame when things didn't go perfectly.'

Caine relished the mute confirmation on Quinn's face. He laughed and said, 'Come on, Quinn. Come inside and have something to eat.'

'I'm just here to –'

Caine waved this off and said, 'No, no, no, you have to come in. I don't want to stand out here in a bathrobe. After all, this is a big moment in the history of the FAYZ.'

'A big moment?' Diana said.

'My triumphant return, Diana. That's why Quinn's here: to beg me to come back.'

'Well, he's wasting his time,' Diana said, but even she didn't believe it. She followed Caine and Quinn back to the house.

'Would you like some crackers and cheese?' Caine suggested brightly. He could barely contain himself. He was grinning hugely. Cocky. Swaggering. Even as Diana felt the small hope she'd nurtured die inside her.

They brought Quinn some crackers and cheese and a cookie. He didn't resist but ate them quickly with pleasure he could not conceal.

'You know, we have a very nice life here,' Caine said expansively. 'Plenty of food. Water. Even hot water for showers if you can believe it. In fact, we were just lying in bed talking about it.'

'Yeah. It's nice,' Quinn said with an embarrassed glance at Diana.

Caine watched him eat, considering. 'Diana, I think you'd better do a reading on Quinn. Just in case something has developed.'

Diana hadn't done a reading in a long time. It was her power: an ability to read whether a person was a freak or a normal. And then to know how much power the person had. Diana was the one to invent the half-mocking bar system. One bar, two bars, like a cell phone.

Diana stood next to Quinn and laid a hand on his shoulder. She concentrated, forming the picture in her head.

'Nothing,' Diana said.

'Could have told you that,' Quinn said, voice muffled by cookie.

Diana dropped her hand to her hip. 'You're normal, Quinn. Now . . .' She stopped in mid-sentence. She'd been about to tell Quinn to go home, leave, get off the island right now, this instant.

But something . . . she felt something. Something registered, some power.

A freak.

Bug was close by, still invisible, but not touching her, not making physical contact. Nor was Caine touching her. The power to read freaks only worked on direct touch.

Was she sensing her own power? No. No, this was something different. It was faint but persistent.

She turned away and placed her hand on her stomach.

'So, Quinn, tell me: what's the big crisis?' Caine asked.

Diana nearly fainted. There it was, clearer than before. A reading. Two bars. Definitely. Clear, unmistakable.

'There's a sickness,' Quinn was saying. 'Like a flu or something, but kids are coughing their lungs out, dying.'

No, Diana thought. *Please, no.*

'And there are these creatures, like, well, people are calling them roaches . . . And Drake . . .'

'Old Drake's alive?' Caine stood suddenly.

'In a way,' Quinn said darkly.

'I have to . . .' Diana said faintly. 'I have to go to the bathroom.'

She fled the room and held it together until she reached her room. There she threw herself on the bed and lay both hands on her belly. She read her own power – as always, two bars. But there it was still, definitely there. A second power.

Not possible. It didn't happen this quickly. She tried to recall half-remembered lectures from sex ed. a million years ago. Words like 'blastocyst' and 'embryo' swam in her brain.

It had been just twenty-four hours since the first opportunity for fertilisation. She knew from past experience that a home pregnancy test wouldn't even work until ten days after.

Absurd. She was panicking. She was misreading. There was no way, none. Impossible, not this quickly.

Impossible, some cruel voice inside her said, as impossible as an impenetrable dome. As impossible as everyone over the age of fourteen disappearing. As impossible as coyotes who could speak.

As impossible as a boyfriend who could mock the laws of physics by raising a boat from the sea with nothing but a thought.

Little Pete's fever was spiking again. Astrid had found a thermometer in the former nurse's office at Coates.

Nurse Temple – Sam's mother – she realised with a pang. Nurse Temple. This had been her workplace. Of course like everything at Coates it had been trashed – medicine cabinet emptied, glass doors smashed, sheets on the cot soiled, reference books tossed around for no apparent reason.

Someone had made a little fire of medical records. The ashes were scattered near the window.

A bird had built a nest on a high shelf and then abandoned the nest. There were pin feathers wafting around on the floor, mixing with the ashes.

That's how she'd found the thermometer, by noticing the feathers. There was no way it would be sterile, of course, but nothing had been clean in the FAYZ for a long time.

Little Pete registered 103.1. And his cough was worsening.

'What are you going to do, Petey? Are you going to let yourself die?'

Did he even know he might be dying? Little Pete knew nothing about viruses. How would he cope with an enemy he didn't even know existed? He didn't understand germs, but he knew he was hot. A breeze had started blowing. How long until he blew this roof off?

Astrid heard Orc bellowing out a song downstairs. She couldn't watch him any more. If he wanted to drink himself to death, why stop him? For the sake of his immortal soul?

Orc drunk was Orc dangerous. She had seen him looking at her with a strange, intense gleam in his eyes.

She realised she was crying. Let him kill himself. Wouldn't she want to die if she were Orc? Didn't she want to die herself?

It was all a macabre joke. The FAYZ: full of sound and fury and signifying nothing but death and despair. Why cling to this life?

She tried to imagine being out in the real world. She tried to call up pictures of her parents and her old house. Of course that house was burned to the ground. And her parents would hardly even recognise her, let alone their son.

No, that wasn't true. They would recognise her and him and think they were still the kids they'd loved. Only gradually would they come to understand what monsters they were: grown as ugly inside as Orc was outside.

Maybe if the FAYZ ended, Orc might be restored to his normal form. But how would she ever be restored to hers? How would the girl who loved maths and science, who could read all through the night, the girl of sweet romantic daydreams and big plans to save the world, how was that girl ever going to exist again?

'It ends with all of us dead, doesn't it?' she asked Little Pete. 'It ends when evil wins and we all surrender.'

The sad thing was, they were already lost, all of them.

She could see her own breath. The room was getting colder by the minute.

She stuck the thermometer in Little Pete's mouth again. He coughed it out.

'Yeah, OK,' Astrid said. 'Petey, I . . . I think if you can't stop this. . . . All of this . . . Petey, it has to end. There are kids dying of this cough. And it's all because of this place you made, this FAYZ. You changed the rules and that has consequences.'

Little Pete did not answer.

She had not expected he would. There was a pillow. Press it down over his face. He wouldn't even know, probably. He wouldn't be afraid. He wouldn't suffer. He would cross painlessly from life to death and down would come the barrier and in would rush the police and the ambulances and food and medicine. And no one else would die.

Mom. Dad. I'm alive. I made it. But Petey didn't. I'm so sorry, but . . .

Astrid jerked back. She was trembling. She could do it unless Petey himself stopped her. She could. And she would never be caught. No one would ever reproach her.

'No,' she whispered in a shaky, uncertain voice. Then, stronger, 'No.'

It should have made her feel good. Maybe in the past it would have. Maybe she would have congratulated herself for making the high and mighty moral choice. But she knew deep down inside that her choice would condemn many to death. No police and ambulances rushing in through the open barrier. Just more of the plague, more of the monsters, more suffering and death.

Astrid put her hands together, meaning to pray for guidance. But the words would not come.

From the recesses of her extraordinary memory she dredged up an old, old text. A fragment from a lecture she'd attended. From one of the ancient Greeks. Aristotle? No, Epicurus.

Is God willing to prevent evil, but not able?
Then he is not omnipotent.
Is he able, but not willing?
Then he is malevolent.

Is he both able and willing?
Then whence cometh evil?
Is he neither able nor willing?
Then why call him God?

There was only one god in the FAYZ. God was a sick, disturbed, unaware child on a filthy cot in an abandoned school.

'I can't stay, Petey,' Astrid said. 'If I stay here . . . I'm sorry, Petey. I'm done.'

Astrid shivered, rubbed her hands together for warmth – the breeze had grown downright chilly – and walked out of the room.

Down the hall.

Down the stairs.

Out through the front door.

'Done,' Astrid said, standing for a moment atop the stone steps. 'Done.'

She walked off into the falling night.

THIRTY FOUR

'**YOU'RE** GOING?' DIANA asked.

'Of course,' Caine said. 'We're going. We're even going to bring Penny. She'll come in handy. Maybe Lana can fix her legs. And then she'll be very useful at controlling people.'

Caine started whistling happily as he stuffed clothing into a Dolce & Gabbana bag.

'You should grab some clothes,' Caine said. 'It might be a while before we get back here.'

'I'm not going,' Diana said.

Caine stopped. He smiled at her. Then his eyes went dead and she felt herself pushed by an invisible hand, shoved toward the closet.

'I said pack,' Caine said.

'No.'

'Don't make me do something we'll both regret,' he warned. Then in a more reasonable tone, 'I thought you loved me. What's all this about?'

393

'You're a despicable person, Caine.'

Caine laughed. 'And now you're shocked. Right.'

'I hoped –'

'What?' he snapped. 'Hoped what, Diana? Hoped you'd keep me happy? Hoped you'd tame me?'

'I thought maybe you were finally growing up a little,' Diana said.

Caine made a negligent, come here gesture with his hand. Diana was propelled toward him. She tripped but did not fall. He held her immobile with powers she could not resist and kissed her.

'I have what I wanted from you, Diana. And it's great. I mean that. I got you to give it up willingly. I could have forced you whenever I wanted, but I didn't, did I?'

She did not answer.

'But if you think,' he went on, 'that you've gotten some kind of control over me, well, guess again. See, I'm Caine. I'm the four bar. I'm the one running things. And I'm happy to have you be a part of that. You can go on teasing me and making fun of me: I'm not sensitive. I like having one person who can stand up to me and tell me what she thinks. A good leader needs that.' He leaned so close she could feel his breath on her ear as he whispered. 'Just remember: I'm Caine. And people who fight me regret it. Now pack up. Make sure you bring that little lacy black thing. I like you in that. Bug. Go tell Penny we're leaving.'

Bug faded into view. He'd seen and heard it all. From behind Caine's back he gave Diana the finger.

'We're going to figure something out, Dekka,' Sam said.

She sat perfectly still in the back of the boat. Sam sat beside her. Toto had been banished to the bow – Sam didn't want him pointing out every soothing lie.

'I'm not scared,' Dekka said. 'I mean, look, I don't know if any of us are ever getting out of the FAYZ alive.'

Sam didn't know what to say, so he just nodded.

'I mean, you think about all the kids,' Dekka said. 'Bette. The twins. Duck, poor old Duck. Harry. E.Z. Hunter.' After a pause, 'Mary.'

'Lots of others,' Sam said.

'Yeah. We should remember all their names, shouldn't we?'

'I try to. So if this ever does end, and I ever get out, I can talk to all their parents and say, "This is how it happened. This is how your kid died."'

'I know you worry about that.' Dekka put a comforting hand on his. He took her hand and held it in both of his.

'A little bit, yeah. I see, like, a trial, kind of. Old dudes and old ladies all looking harsh and asking me to justify . . . You know: what did you do to save E.Z., Mr Temple?' He shook his head. 'In my imagination they always call me Mr Temple.'

'What did you do, Mr Temple, to save Dekka Talent?' she said.

'That's your last name? I didn't think you had a last name. I thought you were like Iman or Madonna or Beyoncé. You just needed the one name.'

'Yeah, me and Beyoncé,' Dekka said with a wry laugh.

They sat silent together for a while.

'Sam, we don't know how well those things see in the dark.'

He nodded. 'I've been wondering. I have a plan. It's fairly crazy.'

'Wouldn't be any fun if it wasn't crazy.'

'You can swim, right?'

'No, because black folk can't swim,' Dekka said, sounding like the old Dekka. 'Of course I can swim.'

He called to Jack and Toto, asking them to join him. 'Can both of you swim?'

They both nodded apprehensively. 'But it's dark,' Jack said.

'The water doesn't get any deeper at night,' Sam said.

'Who knows what's in the water?' Jack argued.

'Trout and bass,' Sam said. 'They don't eat people.'

'Yeah, and snakes don't fly and coyotes don't talk,' Jack shot back.

'Fair enough,' Sam said. 'But I think we'd better take our chances. Here's what I'm thinking: you all go quietly into the water. I'll get the boat started, then I'll lash the wheel down and jump. If it works, Drake and his buggy friends will hear the boat and chase it. We'll go ashore and run like crazy.'

'They'll follow us,' Jack objected.

'They'll try,' Sam admitted. 'But they're insects, not bloodhounds. I doubt they can see tracks at night.'

'He's not sure,' Toto said.

'No, he's not,' Sam admitted.

'True,' Toto said. Then, to his imaginary friend, 'He's confusing.'

'Which way do we run?' Dekka asked.

'Drake will expect us to head straight for town. We don't want to fight him out in the open. So, towards the train.' He nudged Jack. 'You want another laptop, right?'

Jack squirmed. 'Well, at least some more of the batteries.'

'OK, then. Into the water. Swim for the marina. If they don't chase me, I'll come back before you can reach the dock and we'll think of some other plan.'

'Could we think of that other plan before this one?' Jack asked.

Caine stood in the bow of Quinn's boat as it ploughed through the very light chop towards Perdido Beach.

Quinn had warned him to sit down, but Caine wasn't worried about falling in the water: he would not fall. He used his power to support most of his weight so that his feet barely touched the deck.

He was not going to arrive hunched over. He was going to Perdido Beach like George Washington crossing the Delaware: standing tall.

He was floating. Almost flying. Physically, yes, but mentally as well. He was filled with a warm sense of perfect well-being.

They needed him. They had sent for him. They had found they could not survive without him. Him, not Sam. Him.

Penny lay crumpled in blankets in the back of the boat. Diana sat staring at empty space. Bug kept starting to whistle and then stopped himself, only to start all over again.

Quinn was at the tiller, looking at Caine's back. Caine could feel his eyes boring into him. Quinn's doubt and worry were written all over his open face.

Diana had been completely silent. Caine figured it was dawning on her that he was still in charge, that she still depended on him. That she still needed him as much as the kids in Perdido Beach needed him.

Well, she would get over it. Diana was a survivor. She would get past her disappointment. And together they would be the first couple of Perdido Beach, like king and queen.

The thought made him smile.

'It's a pity we don't have a camera,' Caine said. 'I'd love to capture the moment of my return.'

'I'm cold,' Penny moaned.

'You're just not getting enough exercise,' Caine said, then

laughed at his own cruel joke. Penny's sourness wasn't going to ruin this for him. Not her sourness or Diana's sullenness or Quinn's guilt.

This was Caine's moment.

Quinn manoeuvred the boat expertly alongside the dock. He tied it off and then stood waiting to help them up. Caine refused Quinn's hand. But looked at him hard. Eye to eye until Quinn had to look away.

'What is it you want, Quinn?' Caine asked.

'What do you mean?'

'What would make you happy, Quinn? What do you want above all else?'

Quinn blinked. Caine thought he might even be blushing. Quinn said, 'Me and my crews? We just want to fish.'

Caine put his hand on Quinn's shoulder. Caine looked him in the eye with that simulation of openness and honesty Caine could still manage when the occasion demanded. 'Then, Quinn, here's my first decree: you are free to fish. Keep doing what you're doing, and nothing else will ever be asked of you.'

Quinn started to say something but stopped in confusion.

Caine spread his arms wide, palms down, and levitated out of the boat and on to the dock. The grandiosity of it made Caine laugh out loud, laugh at his own sheer arrogance.

Behind him, Diana and Bug climbed wearily to the dock. Caine lifted Penny and set her, helpless, on the wooden planks.

'Things will be different this time,' Caine said. 'There was too much contention, too much violence the last time. I tried to be a peaceful leader. But things went badly.'

'I wonder why,' Diana muttered.

'These people,' Caine said grandly, sweeping his arm towards the town, 'need more than a leader. They need . . . a king.'

It had come to Caine in a flash of insight. Until just a minute earlier the thought had never entered his mind. But with all Diana's teasing about him being Napoleon, he'd found a screenplay about Napoleon in the mansion's library and he'd skimmed it.

Napoleon had taken over after the French people had grown disillusioned with a brutal, ineffectual republic. They had accepted Napoleon's rise to absolute power because they were just tired, burned out. They had wanted and needed someone with a crown on his head. It was only natural, really. It had been that way for most of human history.

Napoleon had named himself emperor. Like Michael Jackson had named himself the King of Pop and Howard Stern called himself the King of All Media. Weird thing was: that's how you got to be king, by calling yourself one. And getting others to agree.

King.

Caine saw Quinn's mouth drop open.

Out of the corner of his eye, he saw a disbelieving smile

form on Diana's face. She shook her head slowly, ruefully, as though finally understanding something that had puzzled her.

'From now on, Quinn, you'll refer to me as your king. And you and your people will be left alone.'

Caine felt all eyes on him. Penny savagely ready to enforce his will, however much she hated him in her heart. Bug smirking, ever the useful tool. And Diana amazed, and amazed by her own amazement.

'OK,' Quinn said doubtfully.

'OK?' Caine echoed, and raised one eyebrow expectantly. He smiled to show he wasn't angry. Not yet, anyway.

'Just . . . okay?' Caine prompted.

'OK . . .' Quinn glanced around, desperate, not knowing the answer. Then it dawned on him. Caine could almost see the wheels turning in his head. 'OK, Your Highness?'

Caine looked down modestly, and to hide the triumphant smirk that would ruin the moment.

'Go now, Quinn. Go back to work.'

And Quinn went.

Caine met Diana's disbelieving gaze and laughed aloud. 'Why so gloomy? Doesn't every little girl want to grow up to be a queen?'

'Princess,' Diana said.

'So, you got a promotion,' Caine said. 'Bug: find Taylor.'

Taylor was the biggest gossip in Perdido Beach. He needed information and he needed it fast. It was the middle of the night and he didn't know who was where or what they were doing. All Quinn had said was that Sam was out of town, Albert had been murdered, and Edilio was sick and might die.

Albert being dead was a pity. Albert was a born organiser and Caine was sure he could have used him. On the other hand, a dead Edilio would be excellent news. Edilio had been Sam's right hand from the start.

He didn't even know when these supposedly giant insects or whatever they were would reach Perdido Beach. It could be at any moment.

He would need to defeat the invasion. That was clearly the most important thing. But obviously kids were exaggerating. Giant insects? They were probably six inches long. Although the idea of them hatching inside your body was enough to make him sick.

Caine stood on the seawall that ran along the beach. Stood on the brink, he thought, the dividing line between past and future. Not just his, but everyone's.

The town was quiet and dark. Here and there the pale, eerie glow of Sammy suns could be glimpsed through windows. The moon was behind the strange cloud that hung too low over the western part of town.

On the brink, with so many possibilities. He felt as if he

might explode from the giddy joy of it. He was back. Back as their saviour.

Quinn had inadvertently shown him the way forward. Quinn had wanted exactly what most people want: to be left alone. To not be afraid. To not have to struggle. To not have to ask hard questions or make hard decisions.

We just want to fish.

Caine turned slightly to stare thoughtfully at Diana. He had given her hope, and taken hope away, and now she stood still, almost as if in a trance, counting up her losses, realising the totality of her defeat.

Resignation. Acceptance.

She could see now that he was in charge. When everyone saw that, and when everyone simply accepted that this was life now, that this was the only possible life, then he would have complete control.

He could feel the fear in Perdido Beach. They were leaderless. They were sick, weak, hungry, lonely. They cowered because of a microscopic flu bug and a very different, much larger bug.

When it was over, when he had won, he would say: *I have saved you. I alone had the power to save you. Sam failed. But I succeeded. And now settle down and do your work and pay no attention to your betters. Shhh: go to sleep, the king will make the hard decisions.*

Bug was back surprisingly soon, with Taylor.

'Where did you find her?' Caine asked.

Bug shrugged. 'Where she lives. I remember it from the old days when I used to sneak into town.'

'He means back when he used to sneak in and watch you get undressed,' Diana said to Taylor.

'He's a little kid,' Taylor said with a shrug. She looked Caine up and down, sceptical and appraising. Caine knew she did not fear him – not with her powers. She couldn't be intimidated. So he would have to reach her some other way.

'Have a seat with me,' Caine said, hopping down from the wall. 'How have you been, Taylor?'

'Life's one big party,' she said.

He laughed appreciatively at her joke. 'Things must be pretty bad for Edilio to send for me, huh?'

'Things are always pretty bad,' she said. 'We're at a new level of bad. I saw those bugs.'

Caine mustered all his sincerity. 'I have to go and fight these creatures. But I don't know much about them.'

Taylor told him what she knew. Caine felt some of his confidence drain away as she laid out the facts in gruesome detail and with complete conviction.

'Well, this should be fun,' Diana said dryly. 'I'm so glad we came back.'

Caine gritted his teeth but ignored her. 'Who can I count on to help me?' he asked Taylor.

404

Taylor laughed. 'Not me, dude. I've already gotten as close as I'm going to get.'

'What about Brianna?' Caine asked.

Taylor made a face. 'You mean the Breeze? She zooms in and starts yelling to Edilio about how the bugs are coming towards us and they're as big as SUVs. And since then, I don't know where she's been. Probably looking for Jack. Or Dekka,' she added with a leer.

Caine nodded and kept his face down so as not to betray his pleasure. Brianna was a problem: her speed was almost as effective as Taylor's power when it came to evading Caine. And she was absolutely loyal to Sam.

'What about Sam and Astrid?'

'Oh, no, there is no Sam and Astrid, not any more.' Taylor leaned closer and began to unload everything she knew. In ten minutes Caine had a very complete picture, far more detailed than what Quinn had grudgingly revealed.

Sam was definitely off on a harebrained search for water. Dekka and Jack, too. Astrid had left with Little Pete.

And Quinn had evidently not known the shocking but not unwelcome news: that Albert wasn't dead but recovering under Lana's care.

'So are the two guys who tried to kill him,' Taylor said. 'That'll be trouble.'

'What two guys?'

'Human Crew losers: Turk and Lance. Maybe Orc, too. No one knows what happened with him except that he's on a bender.'

Better and better. There was no one in town right now who could fight Caine. It was incredible. It was miraculous. It was fate.

Kings were supposedly chosen by God. Well, if there was a God in the FAYZ, it seemed like He'd made His choice.

But it wouldn't last. He would have to act quickly.

'Taylor, I need you for something very important,' Caine said.

'I don't work for you,' Taylor said huffily.

Caine nodded. 'That's true, Taylor. You have amazing powers. And you're a smart girl. But no one ever seems to respect you for it. I didn't mean to sound bossy.'

She shrugged, mollified. 'No problem.'

'I just think you're a very valuable, useful girl. I think you should have a place with me. I respect you.'

'You're just trying to get me to help you,' Taylor said.

Caine smiled broadly. 'True, true. But I can pay much better than Sam and Albert. For example, you know about the island, right? And you can bounce to any place you've seen, right? Any place you know?'

She nodded, cautious. But Caine could see she was intrigued.

'If I arranged to have you rowed out to the island, you'd be able to get back and forth anytime. Easy as pie.'

She nodded slowly.

'What would you say to a hot bubble bath?'

'I'd say, "Hello, long time no soak." That's what I'd say.'

'All kinds of food. Peanut butter. Chicken soup. Crackers. All kinds of movies in the system there. Popcorn to go with the movie.'

'You're trying to bribe me.'

'I'm promising to pay you.'

She didn't need to say it. He could see it in her eyes.

'I need to know where these creatures are, these bugs. How fast they're moving. Which way they're coming.'

'That's all?'

'That's all,' Caine said.

And suddenly Taylor was gone.

THIRTY FIVE

1 HOUR 55 MINUTES

SAM WATCHED HIS friends until they disappeared from view. Toto wasn't much of a swimmer, so they'd given him a seat cushion to float on and Jack hauled him along with one hand.

Jack wasn't much of a swimmer, either, but you didn't have to be elegant when you had ten times normal strength.

Sam fired up the engine. It roared as he gunned it loudly. Drake would have to be deaf not to hear it.

Then he threw it into gear and went tearing parallel to the shore.

The moonlight was faint, but it was enough to reveal the sudden rush of movement by the creatures on shore. They were falling for it.

Sam quickly lashed the wheel. He dived off the starboard side, jumping clear of the screws that blew past, churning water into foam.

He looked again to see that the bugs were in motion. They were a silvery swarm heading away. He did not see Drake.

Sam swam after the others. He'd stayed with the boat a bit longer than he'd planned and now he was a half mile from the dock. He had a long swim ahead of him.

But water was Sam's natural element. He'd surfed since he was a toddler, and powering through placid lake water was nothing compared to fighting the surf.

The cold water felt good. Clean. He switched from freestyle to backstroke for a while, gazing up at the night sky, but powering along as fast as he could all the while. If he were back in the world, he'd be looking to join the high school swim team. His butterfly stroke was weak, but his freestyle was as good as anyone's, and his backstroke even better.

What would it be like to be worrying about improving his butterfly or breaststroke instead of worrying that his friend was being eaten alive from the inside?

What was he going to do next? They trusted him, Dekka and Jack. They expected him to always have a plan. But beyond getting away from Drake and his bug army, he didn't have a plan.

Drake would go after Perdido Beach next. He would send those creatures rampaging through town killing everyone.

Then he would take Astrid and . . .

Don't get emotional, Sam warned himself. Just figure out how to win.

He heard clumsy splashing ahead. He rolled over smoothly into a crawl and powered hard and fast.

'Shhh,' he hissed as soon as he was up with them. 'You people make more noise than a bunch of littles in the kiddie pool.'

The four of them closed the distance to the dock. Sam motioned for Jack, Dekka, and Toto to slip silently beneath it. Toto had lost his grip on his cushion and it floated away. Jack banged his head on the bottom of the dock and cursed under his breath.

Sam palmed the dock and hoisted himself up, drenched.

'Hi, Sam.'

Brittney stood not twenty feet away.

He spotted three of the creatures over by the marina parking lot. They were waiting. Like a well-trained pack of attack dogs.

He'd been outwitted. Outplayed.

'Hi, Brittney,' Sam said, standing there, dripping.

'I asked you so many times to release me, Sam,' she said. Her voice was cold and far away. Not angry, not scared. Just maybe a little sad.

'I know, Brittney. But I'm not a cold-blooded killer,' Sam said.

Brittney nodded. 'No, you're a good person.' She said it without sarcasm.

'I try to be. Like you, Brittney. I know you're a good person.'

He glanced at the creatures. They hadn't moved, but they were alert. They could be on him in ten seconds.

'He hates you,' Brittney said.

'Drake?' Sam laughed. 'He hates everyone. Hate is all he's got.'

'Not Drake. Him. God.'

Sam blinked. What was he supposed to say to that? 'I thought God loved everyone.'

'I used to believe that, too,' Brittney said. 'But then I met Him.'

'Did you?' She had lost whatever grip on reality she'd had. He couldn't blame her. What Brittney had endured would leave anyone mental.

'He's not in the sky, you know,' Brittney said in a normal, conversational tone. 'He's not up in Heaven somewhere.'

'I didn't realise that.'

'He's in the earth, Sam. He lives in a dark, dark place.'

Sam's heart missed a beat. He felt cold. 'You met God in a dark place?'

She showed her twisted, damaged braces in a surprising, rapturous smile. 'He explained His great plan.'

'Yeah?'

'His time is coming. All of this . . .' She swept her arm wide. 'It's all like, like . . . like an egg, Sam. He has to be born from this egg.'

'He's a chicken?'

'Don't mock, Sam,' Brittney chided. 'He waits to be born. But He needs Nemesis to join Him, Sam, and you . . . you won't let that happen.'

'Nemesis? What's a nemesis?'

Brittney had a crafty look as she said, 'Oh, Sam. You know who Nemesis is. He has the power to complete God's plan.' She laced her fingers together, almost awestruck by the act, like it was sacrament. 'They must be joined, the Darkness and Nemesis. Together they will have all power, and then, Sam, it all ends, you know. Then the eggshell cracks and He is born.'

'That sounds . . .' He resisted the urge to say 'crazy'. 'It sounds interesting. But I don't think the gaiaphage is God. I think he's evil.'

'Of course he's evil,' Brittney enthused. 'Of course! Evil, good, there's no difference, don't you see that? They're the same thing. Like me and Drake. Yin and yang, Sam. Two in one, a duality, a . . .'

She faltered a little, like a child trying to explain something she didn't quite understand. She frowned.

'He lied to you, Brittney. The gaiaphage is not God. He reaches into people's minds and makes them do terrible things.'

'He warned me you would say that,' Brittney said. 'My Lord and Nemesis must be joined. And all of you have to die. You're all like a disease. Like a virus. A plague that must be wiped out so that He can unite with Nemesis and be born.'

Sam was getting tired of the talk. He'd never cared much for religion one way or the other, and some fantasy religion made up by a dead girl to justify the gaiaphage's lies was even less interesting than Astrid's religious excuses for not having sex. He was impatient to find out what Brittney meant to do. If there was to be a fight, then let there be a fight.

'And then what, Brittney? Did the gaiaphage explain that to you?'

'Then all the world will be remade. That's His purpose, you know.'

'No, I didn't know. I guess I missed that part. I was still back at the part where he has to kill everyone.'

'He was forged by a race of gods in the far reaches of space to remake the world, to create it anew.'

'Yeah, well, that sounds just a tiny bit insane, Brittney.'

She smiled. 'It's all insane, Sam. All of it. But He will make it all over again. Once He is born anew.'

Sam felt tired. He wished Astrid were here, maybe she could find out more. Maybe she could talk Brittney out of her lunatic delusion. But he wasn't Astrid.

'I'll tell you what,' Sam said. 'If your friend in the mineshaft wants me, he can bring it on. Because he's tried. And I'm still here.'

'Not for long,' Brittney said. 'Do you think these creatures just happened on their own? The Lord has molded them, created them to be indestructible, so that you could not stop them, Sam.'

'I'm sorry for what's happened to you, Brittney,' Sam said.

'You've been abused about as much as any person ever has been. But I'm still going to have to stop you.' He raised his hands, palms out. 'Sorry.'

Twin beams of green fire hit Brittney in the chest. They burned a hole through her.

The bugs leaped, raced to cover the few feet between them and the dock.

'Jack! Dekka!' Sam yelled.

Jack punched straight up through the planks of the deck, but he'd picked a bad spot. He erupted between Brittney and Sam, blocking Sam's fire.

Brittney screamed, 'Kill them!'

Jack tripped, which moved him out of the line of fire. Sam aimed and hit Brittney again but now she was running away. Her back melted, her spine exposed then burned through, and still she ran.

Sam swung his beams at the nearest of the onrushing bugs. Light beams hit the huge creature and bounced away to slice a sailboat's mast neatly in half. The stump was a torch.

Jack hauled Dekka up from the water and she struck even before she could stand. Gravity beneath the nearest creature ceased. The bug went airborne and its momentum carried it just over Sam's ducked head. It shot through Dekka's field and landed half in the water, with its rear portion on the dock.

'Push it!'

Jack slammed into the bug's rear end and it splashed into the water.

Jack spun, ran at the second giant roach. He ripped a plank from the dock and rammed it with superhuman strength into the gnashing mouthparts.

The board splintered. The creature didn't miss a step.

Jack fell on his back and the monster was on him in a flash.

'Jack!' Dekka cried.

Jack, flat on his back, kicked up with such force that the wood beneath him snapped.

The third creature swarmed over the first. Its mandibles swept Dekka, missed cutting her in half, but knocked her twenty feet away into the water.

Sam saw in a split second of clarity what he would have to do. He didn't like it.

The bug rushed at Sam.

The mouth blades sliced.

Sam timed his leap, shouted a desperate curse, and dived straight into the bug's gaping mouth.

'The days of uncertainty are over!'

Caine stood at the top of the steps to town hall. Below him the sick lay coughing and shivering. Edilio, helpless, as weak as a newborn kitten, shivering so hard he looked like he was having a seizure.

Beyond the sick were dozens of kids, many wet from having come through the rain in the west. Many still wiping the sleep from their eyes. Some of the youngest were carrying their blankies.

Diana stood apart, blank, downcast. Penny had been given a chair. Lana leaned against a tree in the plaza, her hand resting on her pistol, with Sanjit nervous beside her.

Caine saw it all. Every upturned, moonlit face. He saw the fear and the anticipation. He revelled in it. Gloried in it.

'First, I say this,' Caine said. 'Taylor, who has joined me, reports that the creatures are almost here. They are nearing the highway and will reach town in minutes. When they do they will hunt down, kill, and eat . . . every living person.'

'We can fight!' someone yelled. 'We beat the coyotes. And we beat you, too, Caine!'

'How will you fight without Sam?' Caine demanded. 'Is he here? No! Sam can't stop these creatures. He tried, and he failed, and now he has run away!'

He waited for someone to speak up in defence of Sam. But not a word.

Gutless, faithless weaklings, Caine thought. He was almost sorry for Sam. How many times had Sam put himself in harm's way for these ingrates?

'He saved himself,' Caine went on, 'for a while, at least, by running away with Astrid and Dekka. He saved his friends, but abandoned poor, sick Edilio there. And all of you.'

Stony silence.

'That's why Quinn – Quinn, who works night and day to feed you all – came to get me, to beg me to help.'

'What are you going to do?' someone shouted.

'What am I going to do?' Caine asked, relishing the moment. 'I'm not going to run away, that's the first thing.' He stabbed a finger in the air and shouted, 'When the ultimate danger came, Sam ran. And I came back. I was safe and warm and well-fed on my island. I had my beautiful queen, Diana. I had my friends, Penny and Bug. It was a very good life.'

He moved to Diana and gave her a little kiss. She let him, no more.

'A very good life. But when I heard what was happening here, what terrible dangers threatened to destroy you, I could not sit there eating delicious food and watching movies while swathed in clean sheets.'

He watched those words take effect. Food? Movies? Clean anything? They were magical concepts to these desperate, starved, and, until recently, parched kids.

And the subtle implication that he had been sleeping with Diana worked in a way, too, making older boys jealous, and some girls as well.

Caine smiled inwardly. It was working. He had them. The sheep.

'I will save you,' he said humbly, eyes down. 'But not just from this terrible threat. No. Isn't it time we all had a better life? Haven't we suffered enough?'

A murmur of agreement.

'You've suffered from hunger, from thirst, from violence. Well . . .' He waited, waited for the moment to build. He was deliberately stretching time, knowing they were picturing the insect horde advancing on the town. At last he said, 'Well, that's enough suffering.'

'What about Drake?' someone shouted.

'He's your friend,' another voice accused.

'No,' Caine snapped. 'I was the one who destroyed him. Or had. Until Sam and his followers allowed Drake to return.'

He paused, watching the reaction, hearing the murmurs of agreement. He sent Diana a secret droll look. Nothing worked better than a really big lie.

'Listen to me. You need a true leader. But this thing where they force you to elect someone, like it's some popularity contest, like we're picking a prom queen or whatever, that has to stop. Edilio is a good kid. But he's just a kid, just Sam's loyal dog. No offence.' He raised a hand indicating that he may have chosen his words carelessly. But kids were already nodding. Yes, Edilio was just like Sam's dog. Brave, yes, and decent, yes. But he hadn't saved them.

'And Sam?' Caine said, raising his voice. 'Sam was a brave

leader once, but he's burned out and you all know it. His heart was never in it. Now at last he's run away. Sam is not what the FAYZ needs. He's not a king.'

He turned away while that word sank in. He could hear a voice asking, 'Did he say a king?' And he distinctly heard a sardonic laugh from Lana.

Caine raised his hands high. 'We need a true leader, not someone who has to answer to a town council. Come on, folks, Howard is a member of the council!'

That earned a knowing laugh.

'So Sam's faithful dog Edilio reports to a known crook like Howard.' He allowed his smile to fade. It was time to finish it. 'You need a leader who will actually lead. A leader to save your lives today and give you better lives from now on.'

Caine spotted Turk and Lance waiting, smirking.

Caine had sent Taylor for them. He had told them he could use a couple of tough kids like them. He'd promised them a trip to the island.

'Turk. Lance. Come on up here,' Caine said.

They climbed up the stairs to stand beside him, pale and shaken, but sure they were about to be handed new and important positions.

'These two admitted to me that they shot Albert while robbing him.'

That started the crowd muttering angrily, and even some of

the sicker kids looked up bleakly. Albert might not have been popular, but he was necessary.

Lance and Turk exchanged a nervous, uncertain look.

'You'll be relieved to know that Lana has been able to save Albert's life,' Caine said. 'But what are we to do with two would-be murderers like these?'

Turk was looking even more pale. This wasn't going the way they had expected. Lance was edging away, getting ready to run.

Barely moving, and with a slight smile, Caine raised a hand and Lance found himself pushing weakly against an invisible barrier.

'Shall we convene a council meeting? Hold a trial? Waste everyone's time while minute by minute the threat gets nearer and nearer? We know what should be done. Justice! Quick and sure and without a lot of meaningless delay.'

'Hey!' Lance cried. 'That's not what you –'

'He says a lot of things,' Diana muttered.

With a broad, dramatic sweep of his hand Caine sent Lance hurtling through the air. Lance flew like he'd been launched from a catapult. Up into the night sky with every eye following. A thin scream floated down.

There was something comical about it and Caine could not keep from smiling.

The scream changed in pitch as Lance tumbled down and smashed into the ground at the far end of the plaza.

'Justice!' Caine cried. 'Not later, right now. Justice and protection and a better life for everyone!'

Turk lost control of himself. 'No, no, no, Caine, no, no.'

'But not justice without mercy,' Caine said. 'Lance paid the price in his way. Now Turk will pay by serving me. Isn't that right, Turk?'

He looked at Turk and in a low voice said, 'Bow down.'

Turk fell to his knees without any further urging.

'It's a sign of respect,' Caine said. 'Not for me. It's not about me. It's about you, all of you. You're the ones who need a ruler. Isn't that true? After so much suffering, don't you need one person to take charge? Well,' Caine said, 'that's what I'm doing. And when you bow down you're just showing respect. Like Turk here.'

In the mob of kids maybe half a dozen knelt. A few more executed awkward head bobs, unsure of themselves. Most did nothing.

Good enough, Caine thought. *For now.*

'The creatures are coming,' Caine said in a low voice. 'In all the FAYZ, who can defeat these creatures?'

He waited, as if he really was expecting an answer.

'Who can defeat them?' he repeated. 'Me. Only me.'

He shook his head as if marvelling at something awesome. 'It is as if God himself chose me. And if I win, if I save your lives, God's will shall be very clear.'

THIRTY SIX

1 HOUR 45 MINUTES

SAM LEAPED INTO the open mouth of the creature.

Head and shoulders made it in. The bug's throat spasmed, like wet rubber, crushing the air from his lungs.

His eyes were tightly closed, but he could not close his nostrils and nearly vomited from a wave of stench like rotten meat, seaweed, and ammonia.

He grabbed with his hands, trying to get something to grip, to pull his legs in before the mouthparts sliced, right now, quick!

Something sharp against his calves. But the bug was just reacting, choking, not yet trying to chop him apart.

He yanked his legs in. All the way inside the wet, stinking, pulsating throat.

Not fast enough: the mouthparts clipped his right heel. He didn't notice the pain, too awful, stifling, squashed, skin burning, blackness, no air.

He pushed his hands out and fired.

He couldn't see the light, his eyes were shut tight. But he could feel the shudder that passed through the bug's body.

He fired and moved his hands against the slimy insides, firing and firing, feeling his skin burn from whatever ammonia chemical was inside the creature, but then, far worse from the heat of his own killing light.

He had to stop or else he would cook himself.

He could feel the bug moving, like being in a car with square wheels, a violent shaking. The bug raced in mad panic as its insides bled and burned.

But no good, not enough, and in seconds he would die from lack of oxygen.

Ignore the pain: fire!

He laced his fingers together blindly, turning the twin beams into one. He pushed against the seizing guts of the creature and inscribed what felt like a circle.

Then silently screaming from the heat, the starvation of his lungs, the violent spasms of his own body rebelling, he kicked and kicked, pulled himself into a tight ball and kicked where he had burned, with all his fading strength.

Air!

He breathed and vomited almost at the same time. He pried open one eye. Jack stood above him.

'Gaaahh!' Jack said, disgusted by the sight of Sam cocooned in a steaming mess of bug guts.

Jack grabbed his hand and yanked him up and out with such force that Sam flew through the air. Sam plunged gratefully into the water.

He surfaced, sucked in air, and dived under again. He washed the reek from his body and quieted the burns. But it had broken the skin. The creature had cut him. His heel hurt, but far worse was the terrible fear that he was destined for Hunter's fate.

When he came up again he could see that the bug that had gone into the water was struggling, not far away, trying to get back to shore.

The dead one – the one Sam had killed from the inside – lay completely still. It almost seemed to Sam that it had a surprised look on its face. Or what passed for a face. Its creepy blue eyes glazed over.

One bug dead, one trying to get ashore, and the third still very dangerous.

'Jack!' Sam shouted. 'The mast! On that boat!'

Jack frowned in confusion, then he nodded. He leaped on to a nearby sailboat, grabbed the aluminum mast, planted his feet, and, with a Herculean effort and a sound like a slow-motion chainsaw, ripped the mast out.

Dekka raised her hands and the rushing bug motored its legs helplessly in the air. It would only hold for a few seconds, but that's all Jack needed.

'OK, Dekka, drop him!' Jack cried.

Dekka dropped the creature.

Jack lifted the mast – a thirty-foot-long spear – over his head and stabbed it straight at the bug's mouth.

The first thrust missed but gouged out one of the bug's blue eyes.

Jack backed up to the end of the dock and ran at the creature. 'Yaaaahhhh!'

He slammed the mast into its mouth and pushed madly, frantically, feet snapping deck planks, until the top of the mast suddenly burst through the creature's side in a squishy explosion of guts and goo.

Sam started to push himself back up on to the dock but his hands were blistered. Jack had to heft him up by his armpits.

'Where's Brittney?' Sam demanded.

Dekka shook her head.

'She ran away,' Toto said. 'But she seemed to be changing. One arm was . . .' He didn't seem to have words for it.

'Like a snake. A whip hand,' Dekka supplied.

'Yes,' Toto said. Then, 'I'm ready to go back home now.'

'I can barely walk,' Sam said. He had to grit his teeth to keep from crying out in pain. The skin of his heel was gone, a chunk sliced out of it. He was bleeding all over the dock.

Sam slipped off his wet shirt and wrapped it awkwardly around his foot, making a very poor bandage.

'Let's get out of here while we can. Drake will be back, with the rest of his army, and then we're bug food for sure.'

Sam started hobbling but Jack grabbed him and hefted him up on to his shoulders. It was ludicrous: Sam was a head taller and quite a bit broader than Jack. But for Jack it was as easy as carrying a baby.

'You rocked, Jack,' Sam said.

Dekka slapped Jack on the back. 'Got that right.'

Jack beamed although he tried not to show it. Then his face went green and he set Sam down and vomited on to a bush.

'Sorry,' he said. 'I guess it made me sick.'

'Nerves, dude,' Sam said. 'Been there. Let's get out of here. Back the way we came. Drake will expect us to take the most direct route back to town and if he catches us out in the open we're done for.'

'What happens when he gets to town with those creatures?' Dekka asked.

'Edilio's got Orc – I hope. Plus Brianna. Taylor. He's got his soldiers, although I doubt guns will work too well unless they can shoot through the mouths.' Sam shook his head.

His imagination went to Astrid. Too many awful pictures of what could happen to her crowded his head.

Could they reach town quickly enough to help in the fight? Maybe with him and Jack and Dekka joining the others they could stop Drake. Maybe.

Did Edilio even guess what was coming his way? Was he preparing? Had he found a way? Sam had not. Again and again he tried to find the way to win. Tried to imagine the scenario that would defeat this enemy.

Again and again he came back to the realisation that there were only two people with the power to stop the creatures.

One: Caine. And Caine was far off on the island.

The other: Little Pete. He was far off on a different sort of island inside his own damaged mind.

Caine and Little Pete.

'Listen, guys,' Sam said, 'I don't see a winning move here. Not from me, anyway. It's going to be on Edilio and the people back in town. I don't even know if they know what's coming. So we have to warn them.'

'How?' Dekka asked.

'Jack.'

Jack had been leaning forward. He stood back suddenly.

'Jack can move faster without us. With his strength comes a certain amount of speed. And he won't tire as fast as we will. Hills don't bother him, so he can go right over the hills, a straight line.'

'Yeah,' Dekka admitted. 'That makes sense. And don't get me wrong, Jack's become a hero and all. But is that enough? I've done the maths, same as you have. Orc and Jack and Brianna?'

'There are two who could do it,' Sam said. 'Caine. He might be able to do it.'

Dekka snarled. 'Caine?'

'Either him or Little Pete,' Sam said.

'Little Pete?' Jack looked puzzled.

Sam sighed. 'Little Pete. He's not exactly just Astrid's autistic brother.' He explained briefly while Toto added a chorus of 'Sam believes that's true' remarks.

'How do we get Little Pete to do anything?' Dekka asked.

'The last time Little Pete felt mortal danger he made the FAYZ,' Sam said. 'He needs to be in mortal danger again.'

Jack and Dekka exchanged a wary look, each wondering what the other had known or guessed about Little Pete.

'Little Pete?' Jack asked. 'That little kid has that kind of power?'

'Yes,' Sam said simply. 'Next to Pete, me, Caine, all of us, we're like . . . like popguns compared to a cannon. We don't even know what the limits of his powers are,' Sam said. 'What we do know is we can't communicate with him very well. We can't even guess what he's thinking.'

'Little Pete,' Dekka muttered and shook her head. 'I knew he was important, I got that a long time ago. But he can do that? He has that kind of power?' She pondered for a moment, nodded, and said, 'I see why you kept it secret. It's like having a nuclear weapon in the hands of, well, a little autistic kid.'

Sam stood up, winced as he rested his weight on his hurt heel. He put his hand on Jack's shoulder. 'Tell Edilio to get Caine, if they can do it in time. If not, Jack, you go and get Little Pete.'

'And do what with Little Pete?' Jack asked, obviously horrified at the entire idea and still getting his head around the fact that the little boy was the most powerful being in their universe.

Sam knew the answer. He knew what might be the only winning move. He had told Brittney he wasn't a cold-blooded killer. He wasn't. And this wasn't even his job any more, was it?

And yet . . . And yet he could see a possible solution.

'You pick him up, Jack. Carry him to the closest one of those bugs you can find.'

'Yeah?' Jack asked in a quavering voice.

'Toss him to the bug,' Sam said.

Drake's whip was curled around the mandible of the largest of the creatures, now racing towards the south, away from the lake. He had to lean almost flat forward to stay on, legs spread behind him.

Bring me Nemesis.

The voice in Drake's head was louder, more insistent than it had ever been.

With his free hand he pounded the side of his head, trying to knock it away, trying to silence that insistent demand.

Bring him to me.

In his mind's eye he saw Coates, his old school, his former home. The grim, Gothic main building, the gloomy vale around it, the iron gate. The picture was his own memory but it was the Darkness demanding he look at it, see it, and understand.

Nemesis was there. There!

Bring him!

But Drake had other needs. His overlord might need this Nemesis, whatever that was, but he, Drake, had an equally powerful need: to kill Sam Temple. If he couldn't catch Sam out here, then he would lure him to Perdido Beach. He would be waiting when Sam got there. Waiting with whip wrapped around Astrid.

Sam Temple had cost him his arm. He had destroyed his old life, left him trapped in this disgusting union with Brittney Pig.

Sam, who had kept him caged like an animal.

And now Sam had escaped death again. Beaten Drake again. And he was nowhere in sight, gone!

'Sam!' Drake howled in frustration. 'Sam!'

The bug moved quickly and the wind snatched Drake's cry

away, but he howled at the night again. 'Sam! I'm going to kill you!'

Bring me Nemesis!

No. Nemesis could wait. Drake served the Darkness but he was not just some errand boy. He had his own needs.

His mind flooded with pictures, lovely pictures of Sam helpless under his whip. And yet he would not kill Sam Temple, no, not until Sam had watched him reduce Astrid to a hideous skinless monster.

The vision was so clear in his head, so wonderful, it filled him with light and joy and a pleasure he could not even describe.

Nemesis!

'I'll get your Nemesis,' Drake muttered. 'But first . . .'

Drake's army rushed at breakneck speed away from the lake, scampering up the long slope that led from the lake to the dry lands beyond.

He felt a wave of fury directed at him. A wave of rage that shook him to his core. The dark tendril was wrapped around his brain, filling his thoughts, demanding, threatening. *Nemesis!*

'No!' Drake shouted.

The reaction was immediate. The swarm stopped dead in its tracks.

'They're my army. My army!' Drake bellowed. His own

hatreds were too strong to be denied. And he might even have defied the gaiaphage. But as Drake stood agonising, hatred contending with fear, he lost the ability to make the decision.

The choice of whether to pursue Nemesis or terrorise Perdido Beach would be Brittney's to make.

SAM HOBBLED ALONG more quickly than he had hoped. He leaned on Toto and benefitted as well from Dekka walking behind him and lessening gravity beneath them.

He felt low. All the lower because he'd actually managed just a little bit of hope earlier. He'd actually allowed himself to believe that things might be better now that they'd found the lake and the train.

But this was the FAYZ. And just because they were due for some good news didn't mean any was coming. In the space of a very few hours he had gone from the heights of optimism to utter despair.

Over and over again in his mind he played out the likely scenarios. Edilio would have his guys, plus Brianna, Taylor, hopefully Orc. If Jack reached town in time he would fight as well; Jack had really stepped up.

But it wasn't enough. Even if he and Dekka were there, it might not be enough. So instead of saving the town and showing them salvation in the form of water, noodles and Nutella, Sam knew he would arrive back at a town devastated.

Some were sure to survive. Surely, some.

Maybe Little Pete would save Astrid. He had the power. But was he aware? Did any of this penetrate to wherever his mind was?

'Do you think he'll do it?' Dekka asked. 'Jack, I mean.'

'No,' Sam said.

'No,' Dekka agreed.

'True,' Toto said, although whether he was agreeing with them or just automatically certifying that they believed what they were saying, Sam could not say.

'He's not that guy,' Sam said. 'He's not ruthless. Anyway, what are the odds he could even get to town and find Little Pete? And then, who knows if even that would shock Pete into doing anything.'

'You would do it, Sam.'

'Yeah. I would do it,' Sam said.

'He would,' Toto agreed.

'It's your gift, Sam,' Dekka said. 'It has been right from the start.'

'Ruthlessness?'

'I guess that doesn't sound so good,' Dekka said wearily. 'But someone has to do it. We each contribute what we have.'

Sam winced as his heel brushed a stone. 'Probably wouldn't work anyway. The Pete thing, I mean.'

'The train,' Dekka said. 'Those missiles.'

'I thought about that,' Sam said. 'But how would we get them to town? How would we even figure out how to use them?'

Sam stopped limping.

Dekka stopped, too, after a few steps. Toto kept walking, oblivious.

'Dekka?'

'Yeah?'

'How high does your power go? I mean, you cancel gravity, right? So things float upward.'

'Yeah. So?'

'I've seen you levitate yourself. I mean, you cancel gravity right beneath you and you float upward, right? Well, how high can you go?'

'I don't know,' she admitted. 'If I'm projecting it, you know, like I want to make it happen somewhere else, I can only reach maybe fifty feet or so. Maybe a little more.'

'OK, but that's you hitting it at kind of an angle, right? I mean, you're sort of shooting across gravity because gravity goes straight down.'

Dekka looked at him strangely. She spread her hands by her side. Immediately she began to rise, along with dirt and rock, a pillar of it.

Sam watched as she rose, staying well back from the swirl of debris.

In the dark he quickly lost sight of her.

'Dekka!' He tilted his head back, trying to make her out against the background of black velvet and pinpoint lights.

'Where is Dekka?' Toto asked.

'Up there.'

'That is true,' Toto said.

'Yeah. Watch where you step, unless you want to go floating, too.'

It seemed like a long time before Dekka finally appeared amid falling gravel. She floated easily down, regained her footing, and said, 'OK, more than fifty feet, that's for sure. I don't know how far I went, but a long way. Maybe you're right. Maybe it works better when I'm cancelling gravity straight down. But I can only fly straight up. So if you're thinking I can go all airborne and fly to town, that's not happening.'

'I'm thinking,' Sam said, 'that the FAYZ is a big bubble. Like a . . . what are those things with water inside and you shake them up with snow and –'

'A snow globe,' Toto supplied.

'Like a snow globe. And if you have a bubble inside that snow globe, what does it do? It rises to the top, right?'

'The top of this bubble is probably directly over the power plant,' Dekka said. 'I mean, if the FAYZ is a perfect sphere.'

'OK, tell me if this makes sense.' Sam frowned, trying to work it through as he talked. 'The train is near the northern wall of the FAYZ. So if you were standing there and you cancelled gravity . . .'

'You'd go scraping along the wall – very painfully – until you reached the top. Like a bubble rising to the top of a snow globe.'

'There are cars at the power plant. I mean, ones that have been used more recently, within the last month, cars Edilio drove there. So the batteries should still work. A lot have had their gas drained, but we wouldn't need much.' He was thinking out loud. Not even paying attention to Toto's repeated 'He believes it, it's true, Spidey' remarks.

'I can't beat the bugs,' Sam said. 'My power doesn't work on them. Not well enough, anyway. But they can be crushed. And I think maybe they can be blown up.'

'Are you talking about those missile launchers in the train?' Dekka asked.

'I'm talking about exactly that,' Sam said. 'You raise that container of missiles. You fly it to the top of the dome. You bring it down by the power plant. We find a vehicle with a gallon of gas and we go tearing for Perdido Beach.' He shrugged. 'Then we see how these bugs like the M3-MAAWS, Multi-role Anti-Armor Anti-Personnel Weapons System.'

Caine walked the few blocks from the town hall to the highway alone. A gunslinger out of some old cowboy movie.

Kids followed him, but at a safe distance. A dozen of them

crowded just inside the busted-out plate glass window of an insurance company. A couple more found seats in parked cars.

Good, let them watch as I save their butts, Caine thought.

But now, alone, standing in the middle of the highway astride the old divider line, he was far from confident. How many of the creatures would come? How large were they? How powerful?

Were they already watching him, out there in the dark?

And what about Drake? Would there be a chance for him to win Drake over? Drake could still be a very useful number two guy. Unless he was determined to be number one.

Fighting these superbugs plus Drake? Suddenly the island seemed very, very inviting.

He could walk away right now. Diana and him, just the two of them, alone on the island. Stick the townies with Penny and Bug. Just him and Diana. Food, luxury, sex. Wasn't that infinitely better than this battle?

An old suspicion shadowed his thoughts: was he being played? The Darkness had used him before. Was this the gaiaphage's will reaching into his mind again?

He didn't feel it. He hadn't felt the Darkness at all while on the island. Even before that, from the point where Caine had defied the Darkness, the gaiaphage had left him alone.

No. This was his own decision. But why? Why give up the island? For what? To be torn apart by monsters hatched in human bodies? Even if he survived, what would he face? Artichokes and fish, resentment, probably a fight with Sam, and Diana's sullen withdrawal.

'King Caine! Yeah!'

He rounded quickly, angry, assuming it was a taunt. A boy in the insurance company raised a fist and yelled, 'Wooooh!'

Caine nodded in his direction.

Sheep. So long as they had a shepherd to ward off the wolves, they were happy. Spineless, indifferent, weak, stupid: it was hard not to have complete contempt for them.

Of course, if he failed, they'd turn on him in a heartbeat.

Then again, if he failed, they'd be busy running for their lives.

A sudden flash of silver down the highway.

Caine peered into the dark. No light, of course, not even a Sammy sun up here by the main road. Just a little moonlight and a little starlight and a whole lot of dark.

But yes, something. Something moving.

And a sound. *Clickety-clackety,* very fast on concrete.

He saw flashing steel mouthparts, like moonlit machetes.

He couldn't tell how many of the massive creatures there were. Just that there were at least half a dozen, each the size of a city bus and close enough now that he could see red eyes glaring malignantly.

He pointed at the spectators lounging in a parked car. 'Get out of that car!'

The two boys shrugged as if they couldn't see why they should obey. Then, with a popping of slackening springs and the groan of metal, the car just beside them floated up off the ground.

They got the idea. They bailed out fast.

Caine raised the car up and up. It was hard to see colour in this light but it looked like it might be blue. A small, blue SUV.

'Let's hope this works,' Caine breathed.

He drew back his hand and hurled the car through the air. It whooshed over his head. It tumbled through the air towards the closest of the creatures.

It fell short, smashed into the pavement with a crunch of metal and shattering glass, then tumbled into the bug's mandibles.

Caine had no time to see what effect it had because a second bug scampered without pause up and over the SUV. One of the bug's pointed legs pierced the moonroof.

'I got plenty of cars,' Caine said.

He raised the station wagon the boys had been sitting in and hurled it in a quick, sidearm throw. The car turned once in the air and hit the leading bug at almost ground level.

'Yeah, suck on that!' Caine yelled. Not exactly a kingly thing to say, but battle first, propaganda later.

Caine couldn't see the creature's face, but he could see that its legs were kicking randomly, out of any rhythm.

'Scratch one.' This was going to be easier than he'd expected.

But just as he was congratulating himself a solid wall of creatures pushed itself up and over the first two. And worse, there were half a dozen of the creatures rushing up the highway from behind him.

They had circled around!

He had picked the wrong place for this fight. It was suddenly blindingly clear. The last thing he should do is fight on open ground where they could come at him from every direction like this.

Caine's heart thudded, his jaw clenched until his teeth cracked. He'd assumed the tales about the creatures were exaggerated. No. No. Not exaggerated.

Caine broke and ran. He raced at right angles to the two approaching forces. He leaped a ditch, landed hard, scrambled up and ran flat out across the service road, and flew past the shocked and confused crowd in the insurance company yelling, 'Run, you idiots!'

Two of the creatures were scampering to cut him off. He snatched up a delivery van as he passed it and hurled it quickly – so quickly it flew low and almost hit him in the head as it blew past.

The crowd in the insurance company panicked. They poured from the narrow door, jamming one another, cursing and screaming.

A boy slipped, caught himself, but the delay was fatal. A bug speared him with a leg and swept him into gnashing, slashing mouthparts.

'Oh, no, no, noooo!' the kid screamed. The sound died suddenly, replaced by a noise like a garbage disposal chewing up chicken bones.

Caine ran down San Pablo with the kids pelting behind him and the swarm was forced to funnel into this more narrow space.

Things had gone from bad to desperate far faster than Caine could have imagined.

A second kid was caught by what looked like a black frog tongue firing from a bug's mouth. She screamed as the bug reeled her in.

Caine stopped in the middle of the street. Shaking all over. Jaw clenched. He couldn't outrun them and this was as good as any place: middle of the block so he couldn't be attacked from the sides, at least.

The insurance company crowd splintered, kids rushing in every direction, all of them screaming, some beating helplessly against locked doors and crying to be let in. Others scrambled over fences into backyards.

Caine raised a parked car and hurled it, then another, another, three cars in rapid succession. It was like a pile up on a freeway, crashing, smashing, glass spraying, side mirrors popping off, rims rolling down the sidewalk.

His furious counterattack may have stopped or even killed some of the bugs – he couldn't be sure in the darkness – but the swarm never hesitated. Up and over they rolled, like a wave.

Shaking, he stood his ground and raised trembling hands. If he couldn't smash them maybe he could just hold them back.

The nearest bug slammed into an invisible wall of telekinetic power. Its legs motored madly, tearing gouges in the blacktop, kicking the smashed cars, but unable to advance.

'Yeah, try that!' Caine yelled.

A second, a third, a fourth creature, all pressed against the barrier, all relentlessly scrambling, pushing, determined. And all the while, Caine stood alone in the middle of the street.

But for how long? he wondered. The bugs didn't seem to be tiring. In fact they were scrabbling over one another in a mad tangle of legs and massive silvery carapaces and scythe-mandibles and always the gnashing mouths and glowing ruby eyes.

He faltered, seeing those eyes, and suddenly the wall of bugs surged a foot closer.

He redoubled his focus. But he was feeling something he'd never felt before when using his power: a physical push back, as if he was holding them back with his muscles as well as his telekinetic ability.

Without thinking, he had set his feet in a strong stance, and he could feel the weight on his calves and thighs, even more on his arms. He wasn't just projecting power as he always had, he was pushing back, at the limit of his powers, being pressed by thousands of pounds of thrust from dozens and dozens of stabbing legs.

They were just twenty feet away. Piling high against the invisible barrier. With a terrible shock he realised they were climbing over one another in a deliberate effort to get over the top of the invisible wall of energy.

Then, a far worse shock: some of the creatures had come around Golding Street and were rushing him from behind.

He switched his pose, one hand for the mass of bugs, one for the onrushing attack. But it would not do. He couldn't hold them.

'Should have stayed on the island,' he told himself. He had gambled and lost.

The two invisible walls were closing in. He was holding back tons of pushing, questing monsters and he couldn't do it, could not. He just did not have the power. And once he broke, they would be on him before he could blink.

'Hey! Jerkwad!'

He glanced towards the sound. Standing, arms akimbo, atop the flat roof of a two-story apartment building, was Brianna.

'Come to gloat?' he managed.

'See the front door of that house?'

'What?'

'That's where we're going.'

'No time!'

'No time,' Brianna mocked. 'Please. Just go limp.'

'Go limp?'

'Yeah: limp. And oh, by the way: it's going to hurt.'

He never saw her move but he felt the linebacker impact as she hit him at blazing speed.

Caine went flying. His shirt was ripped from his back. He spun crazily and fell hard on to the lawn. The bug armies crashed together like two waves behind him. Like the Red Sea closing behind Moses.

Caine tried to stand, but already there were hands on his back pushing him, propelling him forwards at insane speed. He hit the doorjamb on his way through. The bugs swarmed towards the door but it had already been slammed, locked, and barricaded with a chair.

Brianna stood in the middle of the room, examining her fingernails with theatrical calm.

'The whole superspeed thing comes in helpful at times,' she said.

'I think you broke my back,' Caine said. He felt sharp pain in his ribs. But it was very much better than the alternative.

The door exploded inward and a tangle of bug legs appeared.

'I can hold them, but I can't kill them all,' Caine shouted.

'Yeah. They're hard to kill. You got a plan?'

Caine bit savagely at his thumb, worrying the cuticle. They

were surrounded. The very walls were being battered. The windows were all smashed. They couldn't fit through the door but they would soon make it wide enough.

They stood, Caine and Brianna, in the kitchen, the centre of the house, as far as possible from the windows, but now the bugs had their mandibles shoved in through the doors and windows, questing, slicing the air, their rope like tongues lashing madly.

The entire house was like a drum pounded by dozens of drumsticks.

'You know, I'm kind of disappointed,' Brianna said. 'Situation like this? Sam would come up with a plan.'

THIRTY EIGHT

59 MINUTES

SAM HAD COME up with a plan.

Three, actually. One involved the very faint hope that Jack would reach Little Pete and do something awful.

The second involved something purely insane. Flying a huge container of missiles through the air, dropping them in just the right place, finding a vehicle with gas and a functioning battery, then figuring out how to fire the missiles in time to save the town.

That was insane.

The third plan involved Dekka. He wasn't even going to tell her about that. Because it wasn't just insane, it was monstrous.

None of the plans had a chance of working. Sam knew that.

Sam's foot was beyond pain. It was agony. Dekka was doing all she could for him by lessening gravity somewhat but he still had to move forwards, and he had to move as fast as he could.

'How are you doing, Dekka?' he gasped as he hobble-trotted.

'Stop asking, Sam,' she said.

'You have to – ,' he began.

'What? What do I have to do, Sam? They're eating me from the inside, what do you want me to say?'

'She's telling the truth –'

'Shut your stupid mouth, you freak!' Dekka snapped at Toto.

They were close, Sam could feel it. They had to be. They had to reach the train before the bugs finally burst from Dekka and ate her alive.

He needed her to live a while longer. To the bitter, bitter end, he needed her and she was spending her last minutes running and trying to help him and he was helpless, could do nothing but keep hoping she would stay alive, suffer some more, conquer her fear, all for a stupid, pointless, doomed plan.

'There!' Toto said. 'I see the train.'

The light was faint, grey, watery, and inadequate. But yes, Sam could see the train.

He gritted his teeth and ran now, full out, every step like a knife plunged into his foot with the pain radiating all the way up his leg.

'I can't even see which container it was, Spidey.'

Sam cupped his hands and grew a ball of sickly greenish-tinged light. It swelled until he could see the two faces of his companions. To his horror the light showed a bug had eaten its way through the front of Dekka's blouse. She was trembling.

'Dekka,' he said. 'You don't have to . . . I can . . .'

She grabbed his arm with a painfully hard grip. 'I'm with you, Sam. I guess I don't get to take the easy way out.'

'This is the container with the weapons,' Toto called. Then, as an afterthought he added, 'That's true.'

'Sam,' Dekka said. 'If I die . . .'

'Then we fall,' Sam said. 'You and me, Dekka. If I have to go, it'll be an honour to be with you.'

Sam slammed the container shut and the three of them climbed to the top. The container was not perfectly flat on top, it was ribbed for strength. But the steel ribs were no more than six inches high. They flattened themselves down on their backs, facing up.

'Here we go,' Dekka said. She spread her hands flat against the container, palms downward.

The container rose.

Sam lay staring up at the sky, which was no real sky. The stars were paling. The moon had set.

How fast were they rising? The barrier was quite near, just a few dozen yards away from the train. For the first time in his life, he wished he'd paid more attention in geometry. There was no doubt a formula for how long it would be before they scraped against the barrier.

If Astrid were here, she would be able to –

Scrreeech!

The door end of the container was scraping and the entire container tilted wildly.

'Hold on!' Sam yelled.

He gripped the ribs even tighter. But he realised with a pleasant surprise that he was weightless against the container. He was holding on to keep from floating up.

Chunk! Chunk! Screeee!

The container banged a couple of times, tilted even more sharply, and yet rose. Rose!

Suddenly Sam's knuckles, chest, and face were against the barrier. It was like grabbing a power line. Pain that obliterated every other thought. It was not his first time touching the barrier, but it was the first time he'd had his face pressed against it.

'Dekka!' Sam cried.

'Doing my best!' she yelled.

The container became more nearly level and Sam could at least loosen his grip on the steel ribs, which allowed him to press his hands down by his side and keep them from being crushed.

The barrier moved away from his face, blessed relief, but all the while the screeching sound of steel being dragged along the barrier continued.

Screeeeee.

Still rising. Faster. The air rushed past as their speed increased.

How high? They would either stall or fall or, if somehow Dekka could keep it up, they would rise and follow the curve of the dome. As they reached the top of the arc, their faces would be crushed against the barrier again. Sam wasn't looking forward to that.

Sam rolled on to his stomach and wormed his way to the edge of the container. There wasn't much to see below. No lights. No way to know exactly where they were. He wished he had Albert's map, maybe he could make some sense out of the patterns of shadow and dimly perceived, starlit heights.

Looking up, he could not see the barrier at this height; it was not the smooth, pearly translucence he was used to. It was more as if he was pressed against glass, seeing stars beyond it. He'd halfway expected to find the stars were something painted on, but of course that was crazy. The barrier maintained the illusion even up here. He felt himself flying, staring out into the near-void of space.

'How are you doing, Dekka?'

'I can't believe it's working. But Sam . . .'

'What?'

'I'm numb, I can't feel it, it doesn't hurt, but I can hear them, Sam. I can hear mouths chewing, Sam.'

What did he say to that? 'Hang in there, Dekka.'

'It's like we're floating through the stars,' Dekka said. 'I'm pretending we're floating up to heaven.'

'Kind of hope we're not,' Sam said.

The screeching sound had changed pitch as speed built. And there was a very stiff breeze now, pressing down on him as the container, unbound from gravity, flew and screeched.

'I wish you had not found me,' Toto said. 'I was happier alone.'

'Yeah. Sorry about that,' Sam said.

Sam tried to guess how fast they were going by judging the wind. He tried to visualise being in a car with the window down. How hard did that wind blow when the car was going thirty or sixty or eighty miles an hour?

Was it blowing that hard now?

'Oh God, oh God, no, no, I see it, I see it!' Dekka cried and the container lurched hard and sank like a dropping elevator.

It stabilised quickly and rose to once again scrape along the dome.

In an unnatural voice Dekka said, 'Sorry. I looked. It's eating my . . .' She couldn't finish. 'I don't think I have long, Sam.'

'Glide path,' Sam whispered. If they were moving as quickly as he hoped, wouldn't they keep some of that forward momentum even if Dekka dropped them?

Yes. And they'd hit the ground at terminal velocity and that would be that.

It felt as if the speed might actually be dropping now and when Sam stuck his hand up he got a shocking jolt. They were nearing the top of the dome and it was flattening out. Soon it would be full body contact and how long could they stand that?

Not long.

As the slope lessened their speed would drop and they'd be more and more pressed against the barrier.

'It's enough, Dekka,' Sam said. 'Start lowering us. But not slowly.'

'What?'

'Move your gravity field so it's stronger at the back end and weaker at the front.'

'That's what I've been doing so that we'd stay tilted away from the barrier.'

'Yeah. Just do it more. Weaken it all, but more at the front end, right? It should be like sliding down a slope, right?'

To his amazement Dekka laughed aloud. 'If I gotta die, this is the way to go. Wouldn't have missed this craziness for anything.'

Suddenly the constant screech stopped.

The container lurched so wildly that Toto lost his grip and came tumbling downhill toward Sam. He tumbled slowly – they were in reduced gravity – and Sam grabbed him.

'The people back at the facility would have liked to meet Dekka,' Toto said, with his face inches from Sam's.

'I'm sure they would.'

Another wild lurch and suddenly the container was sliding, dropping away forward. It was like a sled running down well-packed snow on a long slope.

'I can't see the ground,' Dekka said. 'I don't want to move. You have to tell me when we're close.'

Sam peered into the dark below, trying to pick out anything that might tell him where they were, where they were heading. But it was hills and scrubland and he'd never seen any of it from miles up in the air.

They were moving fast, sliding down an invisible slope, letting gravity pull them forwards as much as downwards.

'My –' Dekka cried out.

Like an elevator with the cable cut, the bottom dropped. The container spun sideways. Sam, Toto, and Dekka spilled off.

Sam windmilled through the air, flashing on sky and ground and sea and sky again, falling and spinning, and he was sure of one thing: they were too high up and the fall would kill them.

The creatures beat on the house like bulls slamming into a wall. The windows and doors had already been bashed in and now the walls themselves were splintering. The din was shocking. The living room wall splintered, showing broken two-by-fours and twisted conduit.

Caine and Brianna cowered in the kitchen. It only had walls

on two sides, with one side open to the breakfast nook and a counter separating the family room.

Caine looked around frantically for something to throw. Some furniture, some kitchen equipment, but nothing big enough to do any damage to motivated, armoured beasts able to bash through walls.

'This isn't right,' Caine said.

'You think?' Brianna yelled.

'They're animals. They shouldn't be this focused. They're intelligent!'

'I don't care if they speak Latin and can do trigonometry,' Brianna yelled. 'How do we kill them?'

'They should have gotten frustrated and moved off to look for someone else to eat,' Caine said.

'Maybe we're extra tasty.'

'There's an intelligence behind this. A plan.'

'Yeah, the plan is kill the two of us and no one will be left to stop them,' Brianna said.

'Exactly,' Caine agreed. 'Bugs don't think that way.'

'Shhh!' Brianna held up a hand. Caine heard it, too: the sound of gunfire. At least three or four guns blazing away.

'Edilio's guys,' Caine muttered. He was furious and relieved at the same time. He didn't want Edilio or his cops sharing in the glory of saving the town. On the other hand: so far there wasn't any glory.

'Upstairs!' Caine said. He ran for the steps but it meant passing close to the front door. One of the monsters had its mandibles all the way inside and was swinging them left and right, widening the shattered doorway.

Caine jumped clear of the scythes and Brianna, who was already past him and up the stairs, dashed back to grab his hand and pull him up.

'Watch out they have –' Brianna started to say.

Something barbed and painful slapped Caine in mid-back. He reached over his shoulder and grabbed a sticky wet rope.

'– tongues,' Brianna finished.

She drew a knife, slashed the tongue, and yanked Caine away.

Caine tore for the bedroom window. The house was entirely surrounded. At least a dozen of the behemoths ploughed the lawn with their pointy legs and drove their mandibles again and again, like battering rams, against the house.

Down the street, a block away, Ellen and two other kids fired at the backs of the creatures. The bugs ignored them.

'Yep, they are definitely focused on us,' Brianna said.

'I can't even reach a car from here,' Caine said. 'I have nothing to hit them with.'

And then it came to him: he did have something to throw.

Caine raised his hands. The bugs below spotted him and rose up on their hind four legs to come slamming themselves against the window where he stood.

Caine focused on the closest creature. And suddenly six sharp-tipped insect legs were motoring in mid-air. He lifted the creature as high as he could, then dropped it. The bug landed hard, but shook itself and was instantly back on the attack without so much as a broken leg.

'Turn them over!' Brianna yelled.

Caine reached for the same aggressive bug, lifted him, and this time gave the creature a spin before dropping him.

It landed on its back. All six legs kicked madly in the air. Exactly like a beetle turned over on its back.

'The washing machine,' Caine said. 'Is it upstairs –'

'Right down the hall,' Brianna said.

Caine ran, lurching into a wall as the bugs outside hit the house with concerted force. Found the washing machine and lifted it away from the wall, ripping power cord and hoses in the process, and levitated it down the hall to the bedroom.

He threw it through the window. It landed harmlessly on a bug's back. The one he had turned over had righted itself, so Caine flipped a different bug.

Then, while the creature was kicking madly trying to turn itself upright, Caine raised the washing machine high in the air and slammed it down on the creature's exposed abdomen. It hit like a cartoon anvil.

Whumpf!

Goo spurted from the bug's sides. The kicking legs slowed.

'Oh yeah: that works,' Caine said.

He flipped a second bug over, lifted the battered Maytag and smashed it down. This time the bug did not spray its guts immediately so he hit it again.

A huge crash and a sound of rending, twisting, ripping wood. The entire house jerked. Shuddered. And to Caine's horror the wall before him started to fall away.

The entire house was collapsing.

Brianna blurred and was gone. Caine tried to run but the floor was tilted crazily as it fell beneath his feet. The ceiling came crashing down and Caine landed on his back as the house collapsed atop him in a wild tornado of destruction.

Something crushed his stomach. Plasterboard pressed down on his face. His hands were pinned. He gasped for air and breathed dust. He could see nothing in his immediate field of vision but wallboard and part of a framed Weezer poster.

But he could feel his legs and arms. Nothing broken. Nothing punctured.

He had the power to lift the debris off himself. But if he did, then the creatures would be on him in a heartbeat.

Whereas if he stayed under the wreckage, he might be safe.

The creatures would finally give up on him and go in search of easier victims. Then, when they were gone, he could emerge and take them by surprise.

Caine took a shaky, dusty breath.

Playing dead meant letting some kids die so that he could live. Caine decided he was probably fine with that.

THIRTY NINE

38 MINUTES

EDILIO LAY ON the steps of town hall feeling as weak as a kitten. He had barely heard Caine's big speech. He couldn't have cared less. There was nothing he could do, not with delirium spinning his head.

He coughed hard, too hard. It wracked his body each time he did it so that he dreaded the next cough. His stomach was clenched in knots. Every muscle in his body ached.

He was vaguely aware that he was saying something in between coughs.

'*Mamá. Mamá. Sálvame.*'

Save me, mother.

'*Santa María, sálvame,*' he begged, and coughed so hard he smashed his head against the steps.

Death was near, he felt it. Death reached through his swimming, disordered mind and he felt its cold hand clutching his heart.

Santa María, Madre de Dios, ruega por nosotros pecadores,

ahora y en la hora de nuestra muerte.

And then in the swirling darkness he saw her. A figure dressed in a flowing white and blue dress. She had sad, dark eyes, and a golden glow came from her head.

She held up one hand as if blessing him.

He heard her voice. He was surprised that she spoke in English. He'd always thought of Jesus's mother as speaking Spanish.

'Run, Edilio,' she said.

He started to repeat the prayer. *Santa María, Madre de Dios...*

But she grabbed him by his outstretched arm and said, 'I know you're sick but run. RUN! I can't save you!'

For some reason the Virgin Mary had Brianna's voice.

Edilio stood up. The sudden movement sent jagged bolts of pain into his head. For a moment he couldn't even see, but he ploughed ahead on leaden feet. Fell and rolled and got back up, blind, staggering. He ran and ran and coughed until he doubled up on the ground.

He sat there for a while. Waiting to find the strength to follow Brianna's orders, to run.

He looked up and saw that he was across the plaza. He saw the desperate sick and the peaceful dead on the steps.

And he saw demons, huge monsters, armoured cockroaches with impossible red devil eyes.

They swarmed on to the steps.

* * *

Brianna saw Lana come charging out of the so-called hospital with Sanjit. The bugs were swarming.

Edilio had run, thankfully, now here was Lana. Brianna cursed and yelled, 'Lana, run! Run. Out the back of the building!'

Lana drew her pistol. 'No way,' she said. She took aim at the first bug she saw and fired three times. One of the ruby eyes drooled white and red pus, but the bug never stopped eating a girl who, Brianna could only pray, had already died.

'Don't be an idiot. We need you alive. Get out! Get out! You' – she grabbed Sanjit by the neck – 'get her out of here; we need her alive!'

Brianna had seen the most effective way to kill the bugs, but she wasn't Caine. She didn't have his powers.

But she had her own.

Brianna stuck out her chin. Caine had been crushed beneath the collapsing house. It was on her now.

The knife flashed in her hand. She was not going to win this fight, but she wasn't going to run, either.

Dekka had seen the beasts within her.

Death. *Oh God, let me die.*

Too much to bear. Death. She had to die, to end it, to kill them and herself and never see what they were doing to her.

The container had slipped from her. In blind panic, in sheer terror, she had lost control.

She tried to regain it now, but she was falling, wind-whipped, twirling like a top. She couldn't even tell which way was up or down.

She spread her hands and focused but focus on what? Where was the ground? Stars and pale mountains and black sea all spun wildly. The container flashed by again and again, as if it was an hour marker on a fast-running clock. And two twisting shapes, arms windmilling.

She had to save Sam. That much, at least.

Her breathing came in gulps. Her eyes were streaming tears, blurred to uselessness. How could she stop the spinning?

Dekka pulled her arms in tight and entwined her legs. Less wind resistance. She made some sense of it now: she was falling headfirst. She was still spinning, but slower, and she was definitely falling headfirst like an arrow falling to earth. Suddenly, far too clear, she could see a line of surf directly below.

She had to get lower than Sam. Sam and Toto were below her, still spinning crazily. But Dekka, with less wind resistance, fell just a little faster.

Suddenly, though, the ground was coming clear. Rushing up to smash her to jelly.

She was below Sam. Now!

She spread her fingers, focused, and cancelled gravity below.

And continued to fall. She had cancelled gravity. She had not cancelled momentum.

In seconds they would hit the water or the ground. Either would smash them to jelly.

Caine raised the debris off himself.

The bugs were all gone. He saw the tail of one as it raced away.

If he went after them, he'd probably get killed.

But stay here and do what? Be safe? He'd have been safe on the island. He hadn't come back to be safe.

Two possible outcomes: the bugs killed everyone and then who would Caine rule over? Or the bugs were defeated by someone else. And then how would he ever get control? Power would go to whoever won this fight.

Still Caine hesitated. A big, warm bed. A beautiful girl to share it with. Food. Water. Everything he needed, just a few miles away on the island. The logical, rational answer was obvious.

'Which is why the world stays messed up,' Caine said under his breath. 'People aren't rational.'

He took a few deep, steadying breaths, and prepared to die for power.

* * *

Orc had not managed to kill himself. Again.

He wept a bit when he realised that he was going to live. He was doing his best, but throwing up and passing out were getting in the way of death-by-drink.

He stood up, needing to pee, but he was already peeing as he stood. So no need.

Something moved. He swung his head ponderously to look. A monster. In a cracked fragment of mirror just barely clinging to the wall.

Orc stared at his reflection. Six feet, maybe more, of grey, wet gravel. He threw back his head, arms wide, and howled.

'Why? Why?'

He burst into tears and pounded his fists against his face. Then with stone fingers he ripped the last of the living flesh from his face. Blood ran red.

And now he howled at his own reflection. 'Why?'

He lurched away. He ran in bounding, wild leaps towards the stairs.

Astrid.

He had no clear thought for what he would do when he found her. She was just the only one who had ever helped him. She was the only one who had ever seen him as Charles Merriman and not just Orc.

She should feel his pain. She should feel it.

Someone had to feel the pain.

He reached the top of the stairs. He knocked the door of Little Pete's room open. He stared blankly, confused. A wind whipped through the room. Little Pete hovered in the air several feet above the cot. He glowed.

Astrid was not there.

'Astrid!' Orc bellowed.

From outside, clear and distinct through the open window, an answer.

'Is that you, Orc?'

Orc bounded to the window. It had been opened and in any case the panes of glass were shattered.

Orc's vision took a moment to stabilise enough for him to make out what he was seeing. And then he couldn't believe it.

Down below, in the first faint glow of morning, stood Drake.

Behind him and all around the school were things that looked like gigantic cockroaches.

It all had to be a hallucination.

'Drake?' Orc said, blinking hard to test the reality of this apparition.

'I thought that sounded like you, Orc.' Drake smirked. 'And you have Astrid up there with you? Excellent. Couldn't be better.'

'Are you real?' Orc asked.

Drake laughed delightedly. 'Oh, I'm real, Orc.'

'Go away.' It was all Orc could think of to say.

'Nah, I don't think I will,' Drake said. He ran lightly to the door downstairs and disappeared from view.

Orc was completely baffled. Drake? Here?

In seconds Drake appeared at the door of the room. His cold eyes looked past Orc and focused on Little Pete.

'Well, well,' Drake said. 'Nemesis.'

PETE

THIS WAS NOT his room.

That was not the ceiling above his bed.

He felt the burning lava build up in his chest and with a spasm he shot it out of his mouth.

When he coughed, it sent waves of pain crashing through his body.

He was all body now. No distant visions. No whispering voices. Only his pain-wracked body.

A breeze blew around him but the heat filled him still and he did not know how to come at it, what to call it. How could he wish it away if he didn't know what it was?

Where was his sister? Her eyes were gone. He was alone. Alone and trapped inside a body that lay helpless, beset by fire inside, and cold outside, and a whipping wind and always the scrape scrape of sounds, the rasp of saws, the assault of mad, shrieking colour.

A voice so big it made him want to run and hide said, 'Where's Ashtruh?'

Wet gravel was speaking, swaying, leaning perilously as though it might fall over.

'Ashtruh!' the monster bellowed. 'Ashtruuuuuh!'

Pete's mind recoiled, sank deep down, fled before the noise, but could not escape. Once more his body kept him tethered to the real world that had never been real to him.

The monster stomped away, still shouting.

Pete coughed a volcano.

He had to do something. His body had hold of him and his body was pain.

Panic was building inside him.

He had to do . . . something.

FORTY

25 MINUTES

SAM FELT SOMETHING wet. It was everywhere, a cloud rising from below. It was like falling through a tornado of mud. Salt water and sand, liberated by weightlessness, flew upward.

'Spread your arms and legs!' Sam shouted.

Friction. The painful slap of water, the grinding of sand, like flying into a tornado.

Sam felt like his skin was being flayed. He shut his eyes, turned his head to keep his nose and mouth from filling with wet sand, and smacked hard into a surface as solid and unyielding as concrete.

The air exploded from his lungs. It was like being kicked by a mule.

His back arched too far, tendons stretched, his head snapped back, every inch of him stung and water closed over his head.

Instinctively he kicked his way to the surface. The sand washed away and he could force one eye open. He was no more than a dozen yards from shore, in water not even five feet deep.

Then all the water and sand that had floated up to meet them came pouring down.

He looked around frantically for Dekka and Toto. He splashed his way towards the beach through a blinding downpour that lasted a full minute.

Toto was just down the beach, lying on his back and moaning in pain. Sam knelt by him.

'Are you hurt?'

'My legs,' Toto said, and started to cry. 'I want to go home.'

'Listen to me, Toto, your legs are broken, but we can fix them.'

Toto looked at him wonderingly, wiped sand from his face, and said, 'You are telling the truth.'

'I'll get Lana. Soon as I can. You just stay put.'

He stood up and yelled, 'Dekka! Dekka!'

She did not call back to him, but he saw her swimming towards shore. He ran out and helped her to get to dry ground.

'I'm so sorry, Sam,' she gasped.

'I'm OK. So's Toto. Just broke his legs is all.' He glanced left and right and spotted the container smashed into a low bluff. Oblong crates and their deadly contents had spilled.

'I don't know where we are,' Sam said. 'I think we're south of the power plant.' He looked around, frantic. His plan had always been reckless and hopeless, but he'd hoped, somehow, to come down near the power plant. There might be a car still in usable condition at the plant. But here? He wasn't even sure where here was.

And the container was wrecked. Many of the missiles would be, too.

'Sam!' A voice was calling to him from the direction of the sea. A boat. He saw four people in it, and oars splashing and pulling hard towards them.

'Quinn!'

The boat ran in and beached. Quinn jumped out. 'Where did you come from?'

'You wouldn't believe me if I told you,' Sam said. 'Quinn: tell me quick. What's happening in town?'

Quinn appeared overwhelmed by the question.

Sam grabbed him. 'Whatever it is, tell me. Dekka may not have another half hour. Quick!'

'Edilio's sick. Lots of people sick. It's bad, kids dropping all over the place. Edilio sent me to bring Caine back. To fight the bugs.'

Sam breathed a shaky sigh of relief. 'Thank God he did, Quinn. I probably can't beat the bugs, maybe he can.'

'But . . .' Quinn began, but Sam interrupted.

Plan Two might be dead. But Sam had one last trick up his sleeve, one last wild effort – not to save the town, but maybe to save his friend.

'Dekka, she's infested. They're hatching out of her.

I promised to . . . to make it easier for her. You understand?'

Quinn nodded solemnly.

'But I have an idea. How fast can you get us to town?'

'Fifteen minutes,' Quinn said.

They rowed like they were rowing for their lives. And in some ways they were, Sam knew. If the bugs emerged from Dekka while they were in this small boat, none of them would survive.

Toto groaned, lying on the bottom of the boat in two inches of fish-smelling water. Dekka lay against Sam in the stern. His arms were around her. He whispered in her ear not to give up.

He could feel them through her clothes. He was careful to avoid the emergent mouths, but he could not avoid feeling the surging horror of insect bodies moving within Dekka's body.

'Sam, you promised me,' Dekka moaned.

'I will, Dekka. I promise I will. But not yet, not yet.' To Quinn he said, 'As soon as we reach the dock, go for Lana.'

'Lana can't help,' Quinn grunted, never slackening his pace. 'She can't kill them.'

'She doesn't have to,' Sam said.

'I'll take the kid, Orc,' Drake said. 'Where's Astrid?'

Orc stared at Drake. So many emotions in his tired, drink-addled brain.

Drake was the cause of all his problems. If he hadn't escaped . . .

But hadn't he himself just stormed up here to take it all out on Astrid? And yet, Drake's sadistic, cocky grin made something like steam rise up inside of him.

'Whaddyou wan' with the kid?' Orc slurred.

'Drunk much?' Drake taunted. 'Friend of mine wants the 'tard. So, where's the sister?'

'Leave her alone.'

Drake laughed. 'Rock boy, I'm not leaving anyone alone. I have an army outside. I'll do whatever I want with Astrid the Genius.'

'She didn't hurt you.'

'Don't play the hero, Orc, it doesn't work for you. You're a filthy, drunken degenerate. Have you smelled yourself? What do you think you are, her knight in shining armour? You think she'll give you a big, wet kiss on your gravel face?' He peered closer at Orc as if looking inside him. 'Nah, Orc, the only way you ever get Astrid is the same way I get her. And that's what you were thinking, isn't it?'

'Shut up.'

Drake laughed delightedly. 'Oh, you sad, sick disaster. I can see it in your bloodshot eyes. Well, I'll tell you what: you can have whatever's left over after I –'

Orc swung hard, with surprising speed. The rock fist caught

Drake a little high, nailing the side of his head but only a glancing blow.

Still, a glancing blow from Orc was like a sledgehammer.

Drake stumbled sideways, slammed into the wall, but kept his feet.

Orc went after Drake, swung again, and this time missed completely. His fist punched a hole in the wall where Drake's head had been.

Drake was behind him, dancing away. 'You big, stupid idiot, I can't be killed. Didn't you know that? Bring it, Orc. Come on you lumbering, stinking pile of crap.'

Drake lashed him then. It didn't hurt Orc much. But he felt it.

Orc lurched towards him, but Drake was quick and nimble. He danced away, slashed at Orc again, and this time wrapped his tentacle around Orc's neck.

It wasn't easy to choke Orc, but it wasn't impossible. Drake was behind him, pulling as hard as he could, tightening his whip hand like a python, inch by inch, trying to squeeze the pebble skin.

Orc dug his fingers into the whip hand and pulled at it, tried to tear it free. But it wasn't working because somehow Orc's grip was weakening. He tried to breathe but couldn't.

Suddenly the whip hand released him.

The whip hand was withdrawing, shrivelling. Orc twisted to

face Drake as bright metal bands crossed his teeth. Drake's zero-percent-body-fat body became pudgy thighs and face.

'What?' Orc asked, blinking hard. Then he understood. He'd never watched Brittney emerge before but he knew it happened, had heard it happen as one voice gave way to the other.

'Hi, Orc,' Brittney said.

'Brittney.'

She looked around her, confused. Then her eyes fell on Little Pete.

'So, he is Nemesis.'

'He's Little Pete,' Orc said.

'We have to take him,' Brittney said. 'It's the only way. The Lord wills it.'

'No,' a voice said.

'Astrid!' Orc said. 'I was . . . looking for you.'

Astrid barely looked at him. 'I ran away. But I'm back.'

'Astrid, God has said He needs Little Pete,' Brittney said complacently. 'It's the only way.'

'I know you think you talk to God –'

'No, Astrid, He talked to me. I saw Him. I touched Him. He's a dark God, a God of deep places.'

'If He's a God, why does He need Little Pete? I thought God didn't need anything.'

Brittney got a crafty look. 'Jesus needed John the Baptist to announce His coming. He needed Judas to betray Him, and Pilate and the Pharisees to crucify Him so that He might redeem us. And the Father needed the Son to pay the price of sin.'

Astrid felt weary. There was a time in her life when Astrid would have welcomed an opportunity for a theological discussion. It wasn't as if Sam had sat around with her, debating. He was completely indifferent to religion.

But this was not the time. The sad creature that was Brittney was just a tool of the malevolent creature she had confused with God.

In any case, why was Astrid defending Little Pete? She'd been ready to see him die if it meant an end to the suffering.

'God doesn't ask for human sacrifices,' Astrid said.

'Doesn't He?' Brittney smirked. 'What am I, Astrid? What are any of us? And what was Jesus? A sacrifice to appease a vengeful God, Astrid.'

Astrid had nothing to say. She knew all the right answers. But the will was gone. Did she herself even believe in God any more? Why argue over a phantom? They were two fools arguing over lies.

But Astrid still had her pride. And she could not remain silent and let Brittney have the final word.

'Brittney, do you really want to kill a little boy? No matter what your so-called God tells you, isn't it wrong? When your beliefs tell you to murder, doesn't a voice inside you tell you it is wrong?'

Brittney frowned. 'God's will . . .'

'Even if it is, Brittney, even if that mutant monster in a cave really is God, and even if you've understood Him perfectly, and you're doing His will, and He wants you to kill, to deliver a little boy to Him so that He can kill, isn't it wrong? Isn't it just plain wrong?'

'God decides right and wrong.'

'No,' Astrid said. And now, despite everything, despite her own exhaustion, despite her fear, despite her self-loathing and contempt, she realised she was going to say something she had never accepted before. 'Brittney, it was wrong to murder even before Moses brought down the commandments. Right and wrong doesn't come from God. It's inside us. And we know it. And even if God appears right in front of us, and tells us to our faces to murder, it's still wrong.'

It was that simple in the end, Astrid realised. That simple. She didn't need the voice of God to tell her not to kill Little Pete. Just her own voice.

'Anyway, Brittney,' Astrid said. 'If you want to get to Petey, you have to go through me.'

She smiled then for what felt like the first time in a long time.

Brittney, too, smiled, but sadly. 'I won't, Astrid. But Drake will. You know he will. The bugs are all around this building, waiting. And when Drake comes, he will take Little Pete and kill you.'

The two girls had almost forgotten the swaying, bleary-eyed Orc.

He moved now with surprising speed. He grabbed Brittney by the neck and waist and threw her from the window.

'I don't like her,' he said.

Astrid ran to the window and saw Brittney lying flat on the ground.

The bugs turned their blue eyes upwards.

Indifferent to Brittney – who was already picking herself up, unharmed – they surged towards the ruined front door of Coates Academy.

'About time.' Orc laughed. 'Let's get this over with.'

'Orc, don't let them kill you,' Astrid said, putting her hand on his arm.

'You was always nice to me, Astrid. Sorry I . . .' Then he shrugged. 'Don't matter now. Better get out if you can. Most likely this won't take long.'

He ran into the hallway. Astrid last saw him as he laughed at the bugs below him, vaulted the landing rail and launched himself through the main doors into the swarm.

'You want Orc?' he bellowed. 'Come and get me!'

* * *

The boy, whose name was Buster, tried to get away, tried to stand up and run, but he was far too slow, far too sick. He coughed and stumbled and fell on his knees.

The bug's tongue attached to his neck and yanked him headfirst into flashing mouthparts.

A girl named Zoey coughed, doubled over with the pain of it, and a second later was caught and eaten.

It was a massacre.

Brianna flew like a madwoman, her knife flashed, her sawed-off shotgun barked, but the bugs were up the stairs and pushing inside, smelling the fresh meat in the hospital.

One of the bugs had grown so big it became jammed and blocked the doorway, but at least one of the creatures had made it inside already, and Brianna could hear muffled screams of terror from down below.

She darted, bypassed a flashing tongue, leaped over scythe mandibles, and stabbed a bug in both red eyes. Then she stuck her shotgun into the gnashing mouth and pulled the trigger.

The massive creature shuddered, but did not die.

Brianna barely leaped aside in time to avoid being caught. And then, out of the corner of her eye, she saw one of the massive creatures rise, turn in mid-air, and land hard on its back.

'Caine!' she yelled.

She threaded her way through the swarm, leaped easily

through the wildly waving legs of the overturned bug, and stabbed her knife into its guts.

Then, into the largest of the gashes she thrust the shotgun and pulled the trigger.

BLAM!

Bug guts and bits of shell blew back and covered her. But the legs were jerking wildly now, slower, slower . . .

Caine had overturned another bug and this one he hammered with a car, lifting and slamming, lifting and slamming, until the creature was a giant mess of stick-legs and goo.

The creatures turned away from feasting on the sick. There were only a dozen of the bugs left now, not counting the one that was down in the so-called hospital or the one stuck in the doorway.

'I'll flip them!' Caine yelled.

Brianna picked a piece of bug guts off her cheek and nodded. She quickly reloaded her shotgun and zoomed to mount the latest overturned creature. She was learning as she went along. The creatures had weak spots, one of them was the underside of what would be their chin. She stabbed with her knife, twisted to make an opening, pushed the shotgun into the gaping wound, and pulled the trigger.

The bug's head blew apart.

'Oh, yeah! Oh, definitely!' Brianna cried.

But Caine had been a bit too slow and now three of

the creatures were pursuing him. All three had latched on to him with their tongues and he was yelling his head off for help.

Brianna dashed down the steps, now slick with blood – human and insect.

She cut the first tongue and the other two reeled back defensively.

'Flip 'em!'

'Trying,' Caine said through gritted teeth. He turned one over but the bugs were learning fast. A second bug charged the first, slid beneath it, and heaved its brother back over on to his legs.

'Oh, no, we don't do that,' Brianna said.

Caine had to back away again as the creatures charged. If they caught Caine, then the battle was over.

Brianna raced, grabbed Caine's arm, and yanked him to temporary safety behind a tree.

Cuh-runch!

A bug mandible sliced the tree straight through.

Caine lifted and flipped the creature, but now the swarm was converging.

'They'll follow us,' Caine yelled to Brianna.

'I noticed.'

'Gas station,' Caine gasped. He was already running, flat out, arms pumping. Brianna caught up easily. The bugs surged after them, crowding the street.

'You understand?' Caine gasped.

'Not much gas left there,' Brianna said.

'Go!' Caine yelled, and Brianna zoomed away. She reached the gas station. There was a heavy padlock on the pump and, to her utter amazement, one of Albert's people sitting there guarding it.

'Unlock it!' she yelled.

'I can't unless Albert . . .' the kid started to say until Brianna laid her knife against his throat and said, 'Really no time for chit-chat.'

He unlocked the pump. Brianna grabbed the handle – the hand pump was the only way – and worked it as fast as she could. Unfortunately it wasn't the kind of thing that worked better at superspeed.

She grabbed the guard and yelled, 'You – pump! Pump unless you want to die.'

'I don't have a tank to put it in!'

'On the ground,' Brianna said. 'On the ground. All over the place. Pump it!'

Gas gushed in irregular spurts from the pump and splashed on to the concrete.

Brianna zoomed back to find Caine labouring hard and barely staying ahead as he reached the highway. Out in the open the bugs would be able to use all their speed and catch him long before he reached the station.

'Keep running!' she yelled.

She dashed straight at the foremost of the creatures. It snapped at her with its tongue. She grabbed the tongue in mid-air and, holding on to it as hard as she could, she dived beneath the creature's legs.

The bug stumbled and came to a halt, confused. Brianna released the tongue, scooted madly beneath the creature, and came out through its hind legs. She had bought Caine maybe three seconds. No more.

She took aim at the demonic ruby eyes of the next bug, fired at point-blank range, and blew back to the gas station.

She zipped past the panicky guard, who was still busily pouring precious gasoline out on the ground.

Inside what had once been the gas station's mini-mart, Brianna searched frantically through trash and debris before coming up, triumphant, with a blue Bic lighter.

Outside she saw Caine, still barely ahead of his pursuers.

'Get outta here, kid!' she yelled to the guard. 'Ruuun!'

The smell of gasoline was overpowering. It flowed in dark little streams across the parking area, filling seams in the concrete, forming shallow pools in low spots.

Caine raced past, feet splashing through the gasoline.

Brianna smiled.

The leading wave of the creatures hit the gas station,

needle-sharp legs stabbing at tiny rivers of unleaded gas.

The fumes filled the air.

Brianna knew something about speed. She knew that the Hollywood thing where people outrun explosions was nonsense. Not even the Breeze could outrun a fireball.

But there was standing around in the middle of a fire, and then there was blowing through it at the speed of sound. There wouldn't be an explosion, not right away.

It should work. Especially with a little cover.

She hid behind a pump and let the first creature draw level. She wheeled, flicked the lighter, and dodged in front of the bug as it ran by.

Whooooosh!

It wasn't a dynamite explosion. But it was definitely a fireball.

A wave of heat singed her hair and eyebrows. A blast wave of pressure that popped Brianna's ears. But the bug's bulk had shielded her from the worst of it.

The leading creature reached Caine, but he had thrown himself into the air and the fireball, the creature, and Brianna all rocketed past beneath him.

As he fell he flipped the bug over.

Three of the creatures were caught in the fireball. Fire curled their antennae and cracked their brittle shells.

The others were far enough back to dodge around the fire

but the heat and the smoke had confused them. They moved away but not fast enough.

The fire crept down the pump hose, down to meet the heavy gas vapour in the massive underground tank.

Ka-BOOOM!

Pumps, concrete, shelter, mini-mart, and the creatures exploded in a fireball that made the first blast look like a damp firecracker.

Insect parts, twisted metal, and chunks of concrete rained down.

Only the lead bug was still alive. It lay on its back, kicking in the air.

Brianna sank her knife into its chin, inserted her shotgun, and said, 'When you get to hell tell the gaiaphage the Breeze says, "Hi!"' She pumped two rounds into the creature and its head blew apart like a smashed watermelon.

FORTY ONE

13 MINUTES

ORC SMASHED HIS bottle against the blue-eyed bug's head. It did nothing. He hadn't thought it would.

The creature swung its mandibles in a wide sweep and caught Orc in the chest. Orc went flying, facedown on the gravel.

He was winded. Not dead, though.

He got slowly to his feet. Why hurry?

'You want me, come get me,' Orc said.

Three of the monsters motored straight for him. Orc threw a wild punch, caught nothing but air, and was facedown again. This time three rope-like tongues had attached to him and he could no longer stand.

Astrid screamed.

'Whatever,' he said, as flashing mouthparts closed in on him.

Jack had run and bounded along through the night. His goal

was Perdido Beach. But his mission, while clear, was not sitting well with him.

How could Sam have told him to throw Little Pete to the creatures? It was crazy, wasn't it? Crazy? Anyway, it had to be wrong, right?

He raced up hills and down. He was not quite tireless, but he was very strong and revelled in that strength now for the first time. Jack felt as if he'd been living behind a curtain, not really seeing what was happening around him.

That had started to change when he found the laptops on the train. Touching live keys again, seeing a monitor glow . . . Even though he hadn't had time to do much about it, it was like magic, like the magic touch.

And then, a very different feeling when he had fought. He had used his enormous strength and he had saved Sam's life and Dekka's and Toto's. Him! Of all people: Computer Jack.

He was a hero.

He still didn't look like one – he was no taller or more muscular than before, he had not turned into some muscle-bound wrestler type. He was still doughy, nearsighted Jack. But the strength no longer seemed completely irrelevant to him.

He could be Computer Jack. But he could be more, too.

And yet, what Sam wanted him to do was to kill Little Pete? Could that possibly be right?

He had run towards town or what he thought was toward town. From the top of a hill he had sighted the sparkly water in the distance and figured that town had to be, oh, around there somewhere.

But he finally realised he had become hopelessly lost. He was deep in forest now, and he figured it might be the hills where Hunter lived, but it might just as easily be the Stefano Rey.

Then he heard a cry. A human voice. A girl, he thought, screaming.

Jack froze. He was breathing hard. He strained to hear. But there was no second cry. Not that he heard, anyway.

What was he supposed to do? Sam had told him what to do. He had to warn Edilio. And he had to . . . He could barely even form the thought in his head of what he was supposed to do.

But he couldn't just ignore a scream, could he?

'Go find out,' Jack whispered to himself. 'Whoever she is maybe she needs help. And maybe she knows where we are.'

He did not say but thought: And maybe I won't have to go to town after all.

Jack ran towards the sound, across a deep ravine choked with bushes and up the other side. He found himself on a narrow road cut between tall trees.

'Coates!' he said.

He did not hear another scream, but he did hear sounds like a fistfight.

Suddenly the hero role was seeming less and less attractive.

He moved on at a wary trot. Through the iron gate of the school. And there, a scene out of a horror movie. A stone-fleshed monster buried by a swarm of impossibly huge insects.

Looking down at the scene from a window, Astrid.

And then, his tentacle arm just reaching its full length, Drake.

Yes, Jack decided, the hero thing had some real downsides.

Drake emerged to a world that could hardly be more wonderful.

Orc was going down beneath a crush of bugs.

Astrid was looking down in terror.

And for some reason Drake could not fathom: Computer Jack was standing there, gaping at it all.

Drake grinned up at Astrid. 'Don't go anywhere, beautiful, I'll be up in a minute to play. I just have to go say hi to my old friend Jack.'

'Jack!' Astrid shouted. 'Help Orc!'

Two of the creatures turned eerie blue eyes on Jack.

'What shall we do with you, Computer Jack?' Drake asked.

'I'm not looking for trouble,' Jack said.

Drake made a *tsk-tsk* sound and shook his head. 'I kind of think trouble is all around you, Jack. Trouble, trouble everywhere.' Then he had a thought. He peered closely at Jack. 'Where's Sam? Did he send you off on your own? Like a big boy?'

All the while Drake was moving closer, waiting, waiting until he could reach Jack with his whip hand. Jack backed slowly away.

Orc bellowed in pain. The creatures in Drake's army were banging into one another like cars in a demolition derby, all striving to get at the boy-monster.

'You were all bold and dangerous up at the lake, Jack,' Drake taunted. Another few feet and he would be within range.

'I just . . .' Then Jack gasped at something he'd seen behind Drake's back.

Drake turned to see and in that split second Jack leaped. Drake whipped around, quick as a snake, but all that did was bring his face into direct contact with a blow of staggering power.

When he picked himself up, Drake saw he'd flown a good twenty feet through the air.

He stood up and rubbed his chin. 'That was a pretty good trick, Jack. I didn't think cheap shots would be your thing. Wow. That would have killed me. You know, if I could be killed.'

Jack tried to dodge past him, rushing for the door, no doubt rushing to rescue the damsel in distress.

Drake laughed and swung his whip arm. He wrapped around Jack's leg and should have tripped him, but he hadn't counted on Jack's strength. Instead of tripping Jack, it was Drake who went flying face-first into the ground.

He released, rolled, and stood up in one swift, fluid move, but it was humiliating.

Drake's whip hand snapped, hit Jack's back, and drew a gasp of pain. But Jack didn't stop; he ploughed straight on into the melee of bugs. He grabbed the nearest leg and yanked it hard.

The leg came away. It didn't stop the creature or even seem to affect it, but it gave Jack a weapon.

'Better save Orc fast, there, Jack,' Drake taunted. 'He looks like he's going down.'

Orc's roaring voice was hoarse and fading. The clash of carapace against carapace was louder and more frenzied.

They would kill Orc soon. And then Drake's army would deal with Jack. All he had to do now was keep Jack distracted.

Jack broke the leg into two pieces, one thick and stubby, the other pointed.

Drake snapped his whip and drew blood through Jack's shirt.

'Come on, Jack, you know you can't win,' Drake said. 'You can't kill me. And you can't stop my army. Only way out is for you to join me.'

'No,' Jack said.

'My side is the only side now, Jack. There's a whole other bug army eating its way through Perdido Beach right now. Who do you think you're even fighting for? Whatever the red-eyes don't finish, we will when we get there.'

'You don't know what's going on in Perdido Beach,' Jack said.

'The Darkness tells me,' Drake lied. 'He gave me power over them. We're cleaning everyone out, Jack. By the end of the day all of them will be dead and gone. Join me and he may let you live.'

He snapped his whip with lightning speed and caught Jack unprepared. His whip curled around Jack's throat. Jack hauled on the whip but all that did was to yank Drake straight into Jack. Face-to-face Drake laughed and coiled ever tighter around Jack's throat and squeezed, squeezed, seeing Jack's pale face redden.

Jack punched him in the chest so hard his fist went all the way through. But Drake's grip never loosened and Jack's eyes bulged and Drake laughed and Orc's voice was no longer heard over the sound of mouthparts gnashing.

'Sam, Sam, you swore you wouldn't let them!'

The boat touched the dock and Quinn sent his rowers racing, all shouting Lana's name.

'I have a plan, Dekka,' Sam said.

Her body was no longer like anything human. Beneath her clothing it pulsated. The creatures were tearing through in places, mouthparts flashing, mandibles questing. One burst all the way out. It froze for a second, staring at Sam with eyes the colour of jade.

He grabbed for it, caught it, and dropped it. But Quinn was quicker. He threw a fishing net over the creature, stepped on the edges of the net, and held it pinned in the bottom of the boat.

'Now!' Dekka begged. 'Now, Sam! Now! Oh, God, now!'

A second bug could be clearly seen moving beneath the skin of her thigh, nothing but a thin membrane of flesh covering it.

'I have a plan, Dekka, I have a plan, hang on, hang on,' Sam begged.

'Noooo!' It was a pitiful wail of despair.

Sam shot a hopeless glance at the shore. Nothing. No Lana. The crew had all disappeared.

Quinn had grabbed an oar and was smashing it down on the trapped bug like a pile driver, again and again, smashing away, and yet the creature lived.

Suddenly a rush of wind and Brianna stood at the end of the dock, vibrating, covered with gore. 'About time you showed up . . .' She fell silent as she realised what was happening to Dekka. 'What the –'

'Breeze: Lana. Now! NOW!' Sam cried but the second 'now' was said to the air.

'I got to . . . I got to see her again . . .' Dekka chattered.

'Don't give up on me, Dekka. Don't give up on me.'

But Dekka's eyes were rolling wildly, her entire body was in spasm.

'Quinn. What I'm going to do . . . Just hold her down. Hold her down no matter what.'

Quinn smashed the bug one last time and if it wasn't dead it was at least not going anywhere. He dropped to his knees and held Dekka's shoulders.

'What are you doing?' Quinn asked.

'Surgery,' Sam said dully.

He held up his right hand. The green light, as focused as a laser, sliced through Dekka's clothing and skin.

Brianna found Lana retreating with Sanjit towards the eastern edge of town.

'Lana!'

'You're alive!' Lana said. 'The kids?'

'A lot dead,' Brianna gasped. 'A lot more hurt, but the bugs are done for.'

'I'm coming,' Lana said and started to trot back toward the plaza.

'Yeah. Wrong way and too slow,' Brianna said. 'Give me your hand. You can heal yourself later.'

Brianna took off, dragging Lana, who instantly tripped. She dragged the Healer the rest of the way down the street, then down the length of the beach.

Dragging her, Brianna couldn't do anything like full speed, but she could move faster than any human runner.

The Healer's legs were scraped raw by the time Brianna yanked her to her feet at the end of the dock.

'Got her!' Brianna announced. Then, 'What are you doing?'

Sam's face was a mask of horror. He had sliced Dekka open from neck to pelvis. Dekka's organs – a slaughterhouse mess – crawled with a dozen bugs, all swarming out of her.

Quinn snatched at the bugs and tossed them from the boat into the water. He was elbow-deep in blood.

'Lana, keep her alive,' Sam said.

Lana jumped down into the boat, which rocked madly back and forth.

Dekka was beyond speech, past even crying out.

Lana laid her hands on Dekka's contorted face.

Brianna followed her into the boat, landed lightly, and pushed both Quinn and Sam aside. 'I got this,' she said.

One by one she snatched the emerging creatures – some of which raced to attack Sam, others of which just ran like panicked cockroaches around the bottom of the boat – turned them on their backs, and blew them clear through the bottom of the boat with shotgun blasts.

Quinn tossed a rope over the dock cleat and pulled the sinking boat in. Sam and Quinn shoved and hoisted Dekka on to the dock where she lay split open like a burst orange.

Lana held Dekka's head on her lap.

Sam, Quinn, and some strange-looking guy Brianna thought

497

looked vaguely familiar stood watching, a circle of horrified fascination.

The boat sank. The blasted bodies of the insects floated.

Dekka's mouth was moving but no sound came out. Her eyes were like marbles, rolling, searching without seeing.

'She's trying to say something,' Quinn said.

'She should shut up and let me keep her alive,' Lana snapped. The Healer shot a malignant look at Brianna. 'You owe me a pair of shoes.'

Again Dekka tried to speak.

'It's you, Breeze,' Sam said. 'She wants you.'

Brianna frowned, not sure Sam was right. But she knelt beside Dekka and put her ear close.

Brianna listened, closed her eyes for a moment, then stood up without saying anything.

'What did she say?' Quinn asked.

'Just thanks,' Brianna said. 'She just said thanks.'

She turned and took off but not so quickly that she missed the strange new boy saying, 'That's not the truth.'

FORTY TWO

3 MINUTES

ASTRID WATCHED, HELPLESS.

She could no longer see Orc. He might already be dead down there.

Jack seemed unable to free himself from Drake's choking grasp. And Drake knew it. He looked up at Astrid and winked.

She had reached the decision not to harm Little Pete, to let him live even if it meant others would die.

The right and moral decision.

But in a minute or less Jack would asphyxiate. And Drake would catch her. She had no illusions about what that psychopath intended.

Drake and his army would kill and go on killing. And what could stop them? Who could stop them?

She found she could hardly breathe.

Her whole body seemed to buzz with some strange energy. Was it fear? Was this what panic felt like?

Jack's face was turning dark. His struggles were less focused.

499

His fingers clawed impotently. His eyes bulged like they might pop out of his head.

Drake was going to kill her. But not quickly.

And he would go on to kill many, many more, for as long as the FAYZ existed.

Enough. It had to end. All of it had to end.

Astrid stepped to Little Pete. She gathered the floating boy in her arms. She moved to the window and stood there, hesitating, with his limp, sweating body cradled.

Drake saw her. The colour drained from his face.

His tentacle lessened its grip on Jack's throat.

'No!' Drake cried. He unwound his python arm and began to run towards the main doors, yelling, 'No! No!'

'Sorry,' Astrid whispered. 'I'm so very sorry, Petey.'

Drake was now at the door to the room. 'No!' he cried again as she heaved her brother towards the sea of insects.

'Get him!' Drake cried.

He pushed past Astrid to the window as Little Pete fell.

'Don't hurt –' Drake shouted. His words were cut off by a weak but well-aimed punch from Astrid.

Little Pete almost hit the ground. He stopped inches from impact.

His eyes opened wide. He stared into a dozen eerie blue eyes.

'Don't hurt him!' Drake cried. 'The Darkness needs him!'

But it was too late. The bugs surged towards Little Pete.

Their tongues snapped. Their mouthparts gnashed.

There was no explosion.

No flash of light.

The bugs simply disappeared.

There. Then gone.

Little Pete sank to the ground. He coughed once, with incredible violence. And then he, too, simply disappeared.

Astrid and Drake stood side by side, both staring down in horror.

Astrid closed her eyes. Was it over? Was it all finally over?

'I'll kill you,' Drake said, but his voice was faint.

Astrid opened her eyes and saw his face already changing, melting from the hard-edged shark features to a softer, rounder countenance.

Jack came pounding up the stairs.

Lying on his back with one leg gone, Orc groaned in pain.

'Where is he?' Brittney asked. 'Where is Nemesis?'

Astrid barely heard her.

She had done it. She had killed him. She had sacrificed Little Pete.

'Let's get out of here before Drake comes back,' Jack said. He took Astrid's arm. But she would not go with him. Not yet.

'You killed him,' Brittney said. She spoke more in wonder than in accusation.

Astrid heaved a shuddering sigh. Tears ran down her face. She had no words.

Brittney was becoming angry. 'He'll get you for this, Astrid. His rage will find you. Sooner or later.'

'Drake or the gaiaphage?' Jack asked.

Brittney bared her braces in a feral grin. 'We are the arm of the Darkness. He will send us to take you. Both of you.'

'Let's go, Astrid,' Jack said, without taking his eyes off Brittney. Astrid felt the strength of his grip on her arm. She yielded.

She was almost blinded by her tears, her mind a confusion of emotions: self-loathing, disgust, anger.

And worst of all: relief.

He was gone. Little Pete was dead. And now it would end at last. The FAYZ wall would be gone. The madness would be over.

Relief. And the sickening realisation that she was glad she had done it.

Jack led her down the stairs. He lifted a terribly injured, mangled Orc effortlessly. Orc was moaning in pain and crying that they should leave him to die.

'No one is dying,' Jack said harshly. 'We've had enough of that.'

Astrid walked obediently behind Jack as he carried Orc down the hill towards town.

And she wondered as she walked, how it could be that the FAYZ was ended and yet Jack was still so strong.

* * *

Dahra Baidoo emerged from the so-called hospital for the first time in what felt like days.

Virtue held her up, although he was shaking so badly he could barely walk himself.

Both of them were covered in gore. The hospital was a slaughterhouse. The single bug that had made it inside had simply massacred kids too sick to stand, let alone run.

Virtue told himself that most of those kids were too sick to survive anyway. But that knowledge would never wipe the horror from his memory.

He had been wedged into a corner behind a cot, cowering and praying, and begging to be spared. He had thrown things at the bug, but bedpans and bottles were nothing to the monster.

And then, in an instant, the creature was gone.

Its bloody mandibles had been scraping the wall, trying to dislodge Virtue. Inches and milliseconds from gruesome death.

And then . . . nothing.

Gone.

Virtue had heard nothing but the sound of his own sobbing.

And then the sounds of others crying.

And an insistent, mad howl of despair.

Dahra was screaming as he drew her gently from beneath a body.

'It's gone,' he'd said.

She couldn't stop shaking. Couldn't stop howling. And Virtue was suddenly back in that refugee camp in the Congo, remembering things he'd witnessed when he was still too young to understand.

A terrible fury boiled up inside him. An uncontrollable rage against everyone and everything that made the world a hell of fear and pain and loss.

He wanted to smash things. He wanted to bellow like a wild animal.

But Dahra had ceased howling, and now just stared up at him, needing someone, someone to finally take care of her.

Virtue took her hand and put his arm around her shoulder. 'We're getting you out of here,' he said gently.

There were kids crying out in pain. But Virtue knew that Dahra could no longer respond. So he led her out into the cool, fresh air.

The bodies of the bugs were all gone. The bodies of those they had killed were not.

Virtue didn't know where to take Dahra. After all, she was the one kids took other kids to. He didn't know anyone to help her. Maybe no one could help her.

He led Dahra to the ruined church. It was quiet inside, although it, too, had been a scene of battle. He cleared a space for her in a pew. He sat her down, sat beside her, so weary, and closed his eyes and prayed.

'God in your heaven, look down and take pity on this girl. She has done enough.' He sighed and added a doubtful, 'Amen.'

Virtue did not stay long. There were still kids needing help.

He ran into his brother heading towards the hospital. Sanjit hugged him tight and said, 'They're gone, Choo. They're all gone.'

Virtue nodded and patted Sanjit's back reassuringly.

Sanjit held him out and looked at his face. 'Are you OK, brother?'

'I've had better days,' Virtue said.

'So, I guess the island's looking even better now, huh?' Sanjit asked. 'You were right, it's one big open-air asylum.'

Virtue nodded solemnly and glanced back at the church. 'Yeah, but there's a couple of saints mixed in with the crazies.'

Caine walked stiffly back to town. He was burned, scraped, punctured, bruised, and might, he thought, have broken a couple of ribs.

But he had won.

The only downside – aside from the various pains that made him wince with every step – was that he hadn't done it alone. Brianna had scored an assist. He couldn't stand her, but man, was she good in a fight.

And some unseen, unknowable force had caused the bugs the two of them had just killed to disappear. Even their broken-off legs, their fluids and guts had disappeared. Like they'd been wiped entirely out of existence.

Brianna had zoomed off to leave him limping all alone. No doubt she was bragging and claiming all the credit.

But it wouldn't work. No, everyone had seen him walking towards the threat. And now the threat was gone, just as he had promised. He had delivered. He had earned his rightful place.

Just as he crossed the highway into town, the first kids came rushing up to him, grateful, giddy, wanting to slap palms.

'You did it, man! You did it!'

He refused their high fives and stood very still, looking at them, and just waited.

They seemed uncertain, a little worried. And then it dawned on them.

The first one bowed his head. It was a jerky, awkward gesture, but that was OK with Caine: they'd learn.

The second kid, then a third and a fourth, rushing up to join in, bowed their heads to Caine. He nodded in solemn acknowledgment and walked on, no longer feeling nearly so much pain.

THE MORNING AFTER

SAM COULD NOT face the town and the kids there. If he went into town now, there might be a fight with Caine. He couldn't face a fight. Later. Not now. Not yet.

He had seen the sudden and complete disappearance of the bugs. One minute the creatures that had hatched inside Dekka had been floating in the water and the next second they were gone.

He thought he knew what had happened. Only one power was great enough to cause them to cease to exist.

Against all odds, Jack must have succeeded in throwing Little Pete to the bugs. Only Petey could have done it. Sam's desperate, lunatic plan had worked, had actually worked.

But once Astrid knew that he was the one who had ordered Jack to do it, she would never speak to him again.

The town was saved. But Sam was lost.

You ordered the death of a five-year-old autistic boy, Mr Temple?
The accusing tribunal was back.

That's right, he told them in his imagination. *That's what I did.*

He walked until he found himself at the cliff. The last time he'd been there . . . Well, groping Taylor seemed like a fairly small sin, now.

That's right. And because I did the bugs were destroyed. And lives were saved.

You don't get to make those decisions, Mr Temple. God decides life or death.

'Yeah?' Sam said aloud. 'Well, I don't think much of His decisions.'

He stared out at the sea. He was standing just where Mary had stood when she jumped. But he was not tempted to follow her. Mary had been driven to insanity.

'That's right,' Sam said to no one. 'I did it. And it worked.'

'Sam.'

He spun on his heel. Astrid stood there. Jack was a hundred feet back and showing no desire to come any closer.

'Astrid.'

Her eyes were red and swollen. She was looking past him, staring at the barrier with an expression he couldn't read.

'It's still there,' she said.

He glanced at the impervious wall. 'Yeah.'

'But . . . but Petey's dead,' she said. 'It should have stopped. It shouldn't be there. It should all be over.'

'I'm sorry about Little Pete.'

'It's still there.'

'I guess –' he began.

'For nothing! I killed him for nothing!' Astrid cried. 'Oh, God, no! I did it for nothing!'

'You? You didn't . . .' But then he saw the look in Jack's eyes. Jack nodded, then looked down at the ground.

Instinctively he moved to Astrid, to put his arms around her. But something stopped him. He knew she wouldn't welcome it.

It struck him then with the force of a revelation that she could not be with him while she felt weak or out of control. Astrid needed to be strong. She needed to be . . . Astrid.

And right now? She wasn't. He had never seen her look so lost. He would have so happily taken her in his arms. But she wouldn't have him. Not like this.

'Astrid . . .'

'For nothing,' she whispered.

He stepped back. 'Astrid, listen: I had told Jack to do it. It was the only way. If you hadn't . . .'

But she wasn't listening. A look of pure hatred, a look he'd never have thought she was capable of, transformed her face. Was it for him? For the barrier?

For herself?

'I left, you know. I left town with Orc. And then I left Petey. I just walked out the door at Coates. I abandoned him. Him and Orc. Both of them needed me. But I walked away because I thought, "If I stay, I'll be tempted." A simple act of murder. You know how a phrase will get stuck in your head and go around and around?'

He didn't answer. She didn't want him to answer. But yes, he knew.

'I knew if I killed Petey, it would all end,' she said. 'And then, you know what? I walked around out there in the dark, just around in a big circle. And I talked myself out of it. See, I made sense of it all in my mind. Because I'm very, very smart.'

She laughed bitterly at that.

'Who is smarter than me? Astrid the Genius. I worked it all out and I made all the right arguments. And I prayed. And I came to a good and moral decision. And then? When I was there, and Drake . . . and I thought about Drake . . . when I thought . . .' She couldn't go on.

'Astrid, we've all had to do –'

'Don't,' she said. 'No. Don't.'

'Look, come with me,' he said. He reached for her, but he could feel a cold and impenetrable wall around her. She was somewhere else now. She was someone else. His hands dropped back to his side.

'How you must laugh at me with all my arrogance and superiority,' Astrid said quietly. 'I wonder how you could stand me. Don't you want to say, "I told you so," Sam? How can you not? If I were you, I'd say, "See? See, you silly, sanctimonious idiot? Welcome to Sam's world. This is what I do, these are the decisions I make."'

Yes. A part of him wanted to say that. A part of him wanted to say those very words. *Welcome to my world. It's not so easy being Sam, is it?* He tried not to let that emotion show on his face, but it must have because Astrid nodded slightly as if he'd spoken.

He said all he could think of to say. 'I love you, Astrid. No matter what, I love you.'

But if she heard him, she gave no sign. Astrid turned and walked away.

FIVE DAYS LATER

IT HAD BEEN a long time since so many kids filled the plaza. Not everyone had come, but most had. Looking down from the town hall steps, Sam saw faces that were fearful, others that were happy, and of course, as with any group of kids, some were just playing.

It was a good thing, he told himself, this ability to find some little piece of joy to hold on to.

The graveyard had swollen terribly. But the flu had burned itself out at last. There had been no new cases for forty-eight hours. No one was celebrating, no one was relaxing, but the deadly flu seemed to have run its course at last.

He stole a glance at his brother. Caine looked confident, certainly more confident than Sam felt. Caine wore the look of a self-appointed king well, Sam thought gloomily. He was perfectly dressed in grey slacks and a navy blazer over a pale blue collared shirt. How had he managed it?

The rest of his 'court' were nowhere near as well turned-out, but were nevertheless better looking than Sam or his crew.

Diana, Penny, Turk and Taylor all stood behind Caine.

Sam was with Dekka, but no longer the seemingly fearless, intimidating Dekka he had always known. She was weak in body, still recovering, and weaker still in spirit.

Brianna wasn't standing so much as vibrating in place, unable to keep entirely still. She looked distracted and angry and was definitely refusing to make eye contact with Dekka.

Jack was the surprise to Sam, that he would bother to dress neatly and remember to show up. Jack was growing, had grown, as a person.

Edilio sat in a lawn chair. He looked like he was still close to death's door, but the cough was gone, his fever was down and he was determined.

The most notable absence was Astrid. She should have been there. He scanned the crowd for any sign of her. But no one had seen her. The gossips said she'd moved into a small apartment at the edge of town. Others said they'd seen her walking down the highway towards the Stefano Rey.

Sam had hoped she would appear today for the Big Break-Up, as Howard had dubbed this strange ceremony. But she was nowhere to be seen. And Sam's friends now carefully avoided mentioning her name.

Toto stood awkwardly, self-conscious, twitchy, between the two separate camps.

'I think everyone is here,' Caine announced.

'He doesn't believe that,' Toto said.

Caine smiled indulgently. 'I think everyone is here that is likely to come,' Caine corrected.

'True,' Toto said.

'Yeah,' Sam said. His mouth was dry. He was nervous. He shouldn't care. This shouldn't matter. It wasn't as if he'd ever wanted to be a leader, let alone a popular one.

Caine held up his hand, signalling it was time for everyone to quiet down.

'You all know why we're here,' Caine said in his fine, strong voice. 'Sam and I both want peace –'

'Not true,' Toto said.

Caine's eyes flashed angrily. But he forced a smile. 'Toto, for those of you who don't know, is a freak with the power to tell truth from lie.'

'True,' Toto said.

'So. OK. Let me start over,' Caine said. 'Sam and I don't like each other. My people don't like his people, and his people feel the same way about us.' He paused to look at Toto.

Toto nodded and said, 'He believes this.'

'Yes, I do,' Caine said dryly. 'We have different visions for the future. Sam here wants to move everyone to this lake of his. I want to stay here in Perdido Beach.'

The crowd was very quiet. Sam was both irritated and relieved that Caine was doing all the talking.

'Sam and I also have different ideas about leadership. Sam thinks it's a burden. Me? I think it's an opportunity.'

'He . . . he believes that,' Toto said. But he was frowning, perhaps sensing something about Caine that was neither true nor false.

'Today, each of you will make a decision,' Caine said. 'To go with Sam, or to stay here. I won't try to stop anyone, and I won't hold it against anyone.' He placed his hand over his heart. 'For those who choose to stay, let me be very clear: I will be in charge. Not as a mayor, but as a king. My word will be law. My decisions will be final.'

That caused some murmuring, most of it unhappy.

'But I'll also do everything I can to leave each of you alone. Quinn, if he chooses to stay, can still fish. Albert, if he chooses to stay, will still run his business. Freaks and normals will be treated equally.'

He seemed about to add something else but caught himself after a sidelong look at Toto.

The silence lengthened and Sam knew it was time for him to speak. In the past he'd always had Astrid at his side for things like this. He was not much of a speaker. And in any case, he didn't have much to say.

'Anyone who goes with me has a vote in how we do stuff.

I guess I'll be more or less in charge, but we'll probably choose some other people, create a council like . . . Well, hopefully better than we had before. And, um . . .' He was tempted to laugh at his own pitiful performance. 'Look, people, if you want someone, some . . . king to tell you what to do, stay here. If you want to make more of your own decisions, well, come with me.'

He hadn't said enough to even cause Toto to comment.

'You know which side I'm on, people,' Brianna yelled. 'Sam's been carrying the load since day one.'

'It was Caine that saved us,' a voice cried out. 'Where was Sam?'

The crowd seemed undecided. Caine was beaming confidence, but Sam noticed that his jaw clenched, his smile was forced, and he was worried.

'What's Albert going to do?' a boy named Jim demanded. 'Where's Albert?'

Albert stepped from an inconspicuous position off to one side. He mounted the steps, moving carefully still, not entirely well even now.

He carefully chose a position equidistant between Caine and Sam.

'What should we do, Albert?' a voice asked plaintively.

Albert didn't look out at the crowd except for a quick glance up, like he was just making sure he was pointed in the right direction. He spoke in a quiet, reasonable monotone. Kids edged closer to hear.

'I'm a businessman.'

'True.' Toto.

'My job is organising kids to work, taking the things they harvest or catch, and redistributing them through a market.'

'And getting the best stuff for yourself,' someone yelled to general laughter.

'Yes,' Albert acknowledged. 'I reward myself for the work I do.'

This blunt admission left the crowd nonplussed.

'Caine has promised that if I stay here he won't interfere. But I don't trust Caine.'

'No, he doesn't,' Toto agreed.

'I do trust Sam. But . . .'

And now you could hear a pin drop.

'But . . . Sam is a weak leader.' He kept his eyes down. 'Sam is the best fighter ever. He's defended us many times. And he's the best at figuring out how to survive. But Sam' – Albert now turned to him – 'You are too humble. Too willing to step aside. When Astrid and the council sidelined you, you put up with it. I was part of that myself. But you let us push you aside and the council turned out to be useless.'

Sam stood stock-still, stone-faced.

'Let's face it, you're not really the reason things are better here, I am,' Albert said. 'You're way, way braver than me, Sam. And if it's a battle, you rule. But you can't organise or plan ahead and you won't just put your foot down and make things happen.'

Sam nodded slightly. It was hard to hear. But far harder was seeing the way the crowd was nodding, agreeing. It was the truth. The fact was he'd let the council run things, stepped aside, and then sat around feeling sorry for himself. He'd jumped at the chance to go off on an adventure and he hadn't been here to save the town when they needed it.

'So,' Albert concluded, 'I'm keeping my things here, in Perdido Beach. But there will be free trading of stuff between Perdido Beach and the lake. And Lana has to be allowed to move freely.'

Caine bristled at that. He didn't like Albert laying down conditions.

Albert wasn't intimidated. 'I feed these kids,' he said to Caine. 'I do it my way.'

Caine hesitated, then made a tight little bow of the head.

'I want you to say it,' Albert said with a nod toward Toto.

Sam saw panic in Caine's eyes. If he lied now the jig would be up for him. Toto would call him out, Albert would support Sam, and the kids would follow Albert's lead.

Sam wondered if Caine was just starting to realise what Sam had known for some time: if anyone was king, it was neither Sam nor Caine, it was Albert.

It took Caine a long time to answer. His smile faded as understanding dawned on him. He could only tell the truth. Which meant believing it.

Accepting it.

In a deflated voice very unlike his lordly swagger earlier, Caine said, 'Yeah. Albert decides anything about money or work or trade back and forth between Perdido Beach and the lake. And the Healer goes wherever the Healer wants to go.'

Sam had to resist an urge to laugh out loud. After all that had happened between him and Caine, after all Caine's posturing today, it wasn't big, charming, handsome, and very powerful Caine, or Sam either, who ran the FAYZ. It was a reserved, skinny black kid whose only power was the ability to work hard and stay focused.

Caine's big moment, his great triumphant return, had been tarnished.

'OK,' Sam said. 'I'm going to Ralph's. Anyone coming with me, head over there. I'll wait two hours. Bring bottled water and whatever food you have. It's a long walk to the lake.'

He walked down the steps, turned away without looking back, and walked towards the highway. He had the strangest feeling that he was walking alone.

At the highway he paused. Brianna was there, of course. Dekka, too, and Jack. Jack carried Edilio like a baby – a very large baby.

In addition there were forty or fifty others who had picked up and left their homes to follow him.

Quinn came forwards and Sam pulled him aside. His old friend looked tortured and sad.

'What's up, brah?' Sam asked.

Quinn couldn't speak. He was choked with emotion. 'Dude . . .'

'You want to stay in town.'

'My crews . . . my boats and all . . .'

Sam put a hand on his shoulder. 'Quinn, I'm glad you found something so important to do. Something you really like.'

'Yeah, but . . .'

Sam pulled him into a brief hug. 'You and me, we're still friends, man. But you have responsibilities.'

Quinn nodded miserably.

Sam scanned the crowd again, searching for Astrid. She was not there.

It wasn't far to Ralph's parking lot. Sam sagged against a parked car. Some of the kids came up to offer statements of support or encouragement. But most came up to say things like, 'You really have Nutella?' Or 'Can I live on a boat? That would be so cool.'

They were coming for Nutella and noodles, not for him.

He felt numb. Like everything that was happening was happening to someone else. He pictured himself at the lake, on a houseboat. Dekka would be there, and Brianna and Jack. He would have friends. He wouldn't be alone.

But he couldn't stop himself from looking for her.

She no longer had Little Pete to worry about. They could be together without all of that. But of course he knew Astrid, and knew that right now, wherever she was, she was eaten up inside with guilt.

'She's not coming, is she?' Sam said to Dekka.

But Dekka didn't answer. She was somewhere else in her head. Sam saw her glance and look away as Brianna laid a light hand on Jack's shoulder.

Dahra was staying in the hospital, but a few more kids came. Groups of three or four at a time. The Siren and the kids she lived with came. John Terrafino came. Ellen. He waited. He would wait the full two hours. Not for her, he told himself, just to keep his word.

Then Orc, with Howard.

Sam groaned inwardly.

'You gotta be kidding me,' Brianna said.

'The deal was kids make a choice,' Sam said. 'I think Howard just realised how dangerous life can be for a criminal living in a place where the "king" can decide life or death.'

To Sam's relief, Howard did not come over to talk to him. Orc and he sat in the back of a pickup truck. Other kids gave them a wide berth.

'It's time,' Jack said.

'Breeze? Count the kids,' Sam said.

Brianna was back in twenty seconds. 'Eighty-two, boss.'

'About a third,' Jack observed. 'A third of what's left.'

'Wait. Make that eighty-eight,' Brianna said. 'And a dog.'

Lana, looking deeply irritated – a fairly usual expression for her – and Sanjit, looking happy – a fairly usual expression for him – and Sanjit's siblings were trotting along to catch up.

'I don't know if we're staying up there or not,' Lana said without preamble. 'I want to check it out. And my room smells like crap.'

Just before the time was up, Sam heard a stir. Kids were making a lane for someone, murmuring. His heart leaped.

'Hey, Sam.'

He swallowed the lump in his throat. 'Diana?'

'Not expecting me, huh?' She made a wry face. 'Where's blondie? I didn't see her at the big pep rally.'

'Are you coming with us?' Brianna demanded, obviously not happy about it.

'Is Caine OK with this?' Sam asked Diana. 'It's your choice, but I need to know if he's going to come after us to take you back.'

'Caine has what he wants,' Diana said.

'Maybe I should call Toto over,' Sam said. The truth teller was having a conversation with Spidey. 'I could ask you whether you're coming along to spy for Caine, and see what Toto has to say.'

Diana sighed. 'Sam, I have bigger problems than Caine. And so do you, I guess. Because the FAYZ is going to do something it's never done before: grow by one.'

'What's that mean?'

'You are going to be an uncle.'

Sam stared blankly. Brianna said a very rude word. And even Dekka looked up.

'You're having a baby?' Dekka asked.

'Let's hope so,' Diana said bleakly. 'Let's hope that's all it is.'

PETE

HE WALKED ON the edge of a sheet of glass a million miles high.

On one side, far, far below him, the jangly noises and eye-searing colours were dimmed. He saw his sister's yellow hair and piercing blue eyes, but now he was too far away for them to hurt him.

He saw the echoes of the lurid, bright-eyed monsters who had tried to eat him. They were ghosts sinking lazily down towards the greenish glow far, far below.

They had reached for him with stinging tongues and slicing mouths. So he had made them disappear.

The pain in his body was gone. He was cool and light and amazingly limber. He turned a cartwheel along the edge of the glass and laughed.

His body, full of heat and aching and coughs like volcanoes, had gone away, too. Just like the bugs.

No body, no pain.

Little Pete smiled down at the Darkness. It did not try to touch him now. It shrank away.

It was afraid.

Afraid of him.

Little Pete felt as if a giant weight had been lifted off his shoulders. All of it, the too-bright colours and the too-penetrating eyes, and the misty tendrils that reached for his mind, all of it was so very far off.

Now Little Pete floated up and away from the sheet of glass. He no longer needed to teeter precariously there. He could go anywhere. He was free of the sister and free of the Darkness. He was free at last from the disease-wracked body. And he was free, too, from the tortured, twisted, stunted brain that had made the world so painful to him.

For the first time Little Pete saw the world without cringing or needing to run away. It was as if he'd been watching the world through a veil, through milky glass, and now saw it all clearly for the first time in his brief existence.

His whole life he had needed to hide. And now he gasped at the thrill of seeing and hearing and feeling.

His sick body was gone. His distorting, terrifying brain was gone.

But Pete Ellison had never been more alive.

WWW.EGMONT.CO.UK/GONE

WWW.THEFAYZ.CO.UK

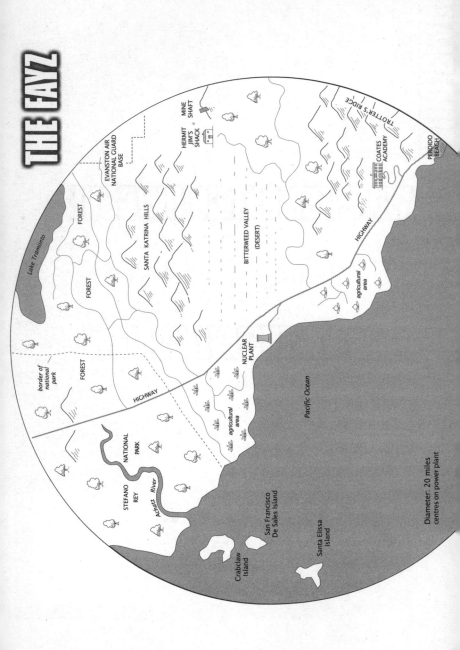

THE FAYZ

FOREST

Lake Tramonto

Evanston Air
National Guard
Base

HERMIT
JIM'S
SHACK

MINE
SHAFT

FOREST

SANTA KATRINA HILLS

TROTTER'S RIDGE

FOREST

BITTERWEED VALLEY

(DESERT)

COATES
ACADEMY

border of
national
park

FOREST

HIGHWAY

HIGHWAY

PERDIDO
BEACH

STEFANO
REY

NATIONAL
PARK

Achatz River

NUCLEAR
PLANT

agricultural
area

agricultural
area

Crabclaw
Island

San Francisco
De Sales Island

Santa Elissa
Island

Pacific Ocean

Diameter: 20 miles
centres on power plant

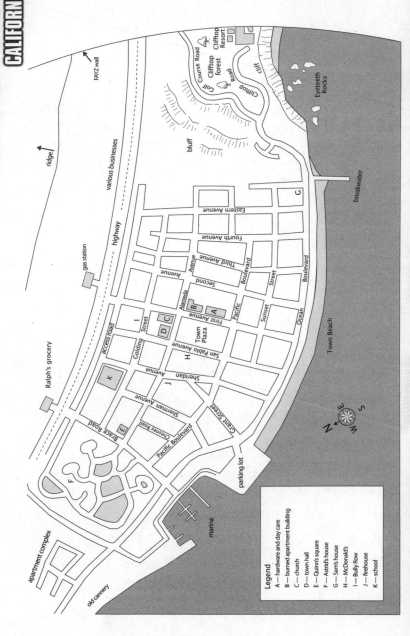

PERDIDO BEACH
CALIFORNIA

FAYZ wall

ridge

various businesses

highway

gas station

Ralph's grocery

access road

Black Road

apartment complex

old cannery

marina

Pacific Boulevard

Chesney Road

Sherman Avenue

Grant Street

parking lot

Sheridan Avenue

Colding Street

San Pablo Avenue

First Avenue

Town Plaza

Alameda Avenue

Second Avenue

Pacific Boulevard

Sunset Street

Ocean Boulevard

Third Avenue

Fourth Avenue

Eastern Avenue

Town Beach

breakwater

Eyeteeth Rocks

cliff

Clifftop Road

Clifftop forest

Golf Course Road

Clifftop Resort

bluff

Legend
A — hardware and day care
B — burned apartment building
C — church
D — town hall
E — Quinn's square
F — Astrid's house
G — Sam's house
H — McDonald's
I — Bully Row
J — firehouse
K — school

THE STORY CONTINUES IN

'PATRICK, YOUR GENIUS is showing!' Terry cried in a high falsetto voice.

'It iiiiis?' Philip asked in a low, very dumb voice. He covered himself with his hands and a wave of laughter rose from the assembled audience.

It was Friday Fun Fest at Lake Tramonto. Every Friday the kids rewarded themselves with an evening of entertainment. In this case, Terry and Philip were doing a re-creation of a *SpongeBob* episode. Terry had a yellow T-shirt painted with spongelike holes, and Phil wore an arguably pink T-shirt for the role of Patrick Star.

The 'stage' was the top deck of a big houseboat that had been shoved out into the water so that it wallowed a few dozen feet off the dock. Becca, who played Sandy Cheeks, and Darryl, who did a very good Squidward, were in the cabin below waiting for their cues.

Sam Temple watched from the marina office, a narrow,

two-storey, grey-sided tower that afforded him a clear view over the heads of the crowd below. Normally the houseboat was his, but not when there was a show to put on.

The crowd in question was 103 kids, ranging from one year old to fifteen. But, he thought ruefully, no audience of kids had ever looked quite like this.

No one over the age of five went unarmed. There were knives, machetes, baseball bats, sticks with big spikes driven through them, chains, and guns.

No one was fashionably dressed. At least, not by any of the normal standards. Kids wore disintegrating shirts and jeans in sizes way too large. Some wore ponchos made of blankets. Many went barefoot. Some had decorated themselves with feathers stuck in their hair, big diamond rings made to fit with tape, painted faces, plastic flowers, all manner of bandannas, ties, and criss-cross belts.

But they were clean, at least. Much cleaner than they'd been back in Perdido Beach. The move to Lake Tramonto had given them a seemingly endless supply of fresh water. Soap was long gone, as was detergent, but fresh water did wonders all by itself. It was possible to be in a group of kids now without gagging on the stink.

Here and there, as the sun sank and the shadows grew, Sam could make out the flare of cigarette butts. And despite all they'd tried to do there were still bottles of booze – either original or moonshine – being passed around the small gaggles of kids. And probably, if he'd bothered, he could have caught a whiff of marijuana.

But mostly things were better. Between the food they grew and the fish they caught in the lake, and the food they traded for from Perdido Beach, no one was starving. This was an accomplishment of epic proportions.

And then there was the Sinder project, which had amazing potential.

So why did he have this itchy feeling that something was wrong? And more than just a feeling. It was like something half-seen. Less than that. Like a feeling that there was something he should have seen, would have seen if he just turned around quickly enough.

It was like that. Like something that stood just outside the range of his peripheral vision. When he turned to look it was still in his peripheral vision.

It was looking at him.

It was doing it right now.

'Paranoia,' Sam muttered. 'You're going slowly nuts, dude. Or maybe not so slowly, since you're talking to yourself.'

He sighed and shook his head and formed a grin he hoped would spread from without to within. He just wasn't used to so much . . . peace. Four months of it. Sam heard footsteps on the rickety stairs. The door opened. He glanced back.

'Diana,' he said. He stood up and offered her his chair.

'Really not necessary,' Diana said. 'I'm pregnant, not crippled.' But she took the chair anyway.

'How are you doing?'

'My boobs are swollen and they hurt,' she said. She cocked her head sideways and looked at him with a degree of affection. 'Really? That makes you blush?'

'I'm not blushing. It's . . .' He couldn't really think of what else it might be.

'Well, then, I'll spare you some of the more disturbing things going on with my body right now. On the good side, I no longer throw up every morning.'

'Yes. That is good,' Sam said.

'On the downside, I have to pee more or less all the time.'

'Ah.' This conversation was definitely making him uncomfortable. In fact, even looking at Diana made him uncomfortable. She had a definite, noticeable bulge beneath her T-shirt. And yet she was no less beautiful than she'd ever been and still had the same knowing, challenging smirk.

'Shall we discuss the darkening of areolae?' she teased.

'Please, I'm begging you: no.'

'The thing is, it's early for some of this,' Diana said. She tried to make it sound casual. But she failed.

'Uh-huh.'

'I shouldn't be this big. I have all the books on pregnancy, and they all say I shouldn't be this big. Not at four months.'

'You look OK,' Sam said with a certain desperate edge in his voice. 'I mean good. You look good. Better than good. I mean, you know, beautiful.'

'Seriously? You're hitting on me?'

'No!' Sam cried. 'No. No, no, no. No. Not that . . .' He let that trail off and bit his lip.

Diana laughed delightedly. 'You are so easy to mess with.' Then she grew serious. 'Have you ever heard of the quickening?'

'Like for taxes?'

'No. No, Sam, that would be "quicken". The quickening is when the fetus starts to move.'

'Oh. Yeah. That.'

'Give me your hand,' Diana said.

He was absolutely sure he did not want to give her his hand. He had a terrible premonition what she would do with his hand. But he could not think of a way to refuse.

Diana looked at him with an innocent expression. 'Come on, Sam, you're the one who can always find a way out of a life-or-death crisis. Can't you think of a way to refuse?'

That forced a smile from him. 'I was trying. Brain freeze.'

'OK, then, give me your hand.'

He did and she placed his palm against her belly.

'Yep, that's a, um, a definite belly,' he said.

'Yeah, I was hoping you'd agree that that is a belly. I needed a second opinion. Just wait . . . There!'

He had felt it. A small movement in her tight-stretched bulge.

He made a sickly smile and withdrew his hand. 'So, quickening, huh?'

'Yes,' Diana said, no longer kidding. 'But here's the thing, Sam: human babies all grow at basically the same rate. It's clockwork. And human babies do not start kicking at thirteen weeks.'

Sam hesitated, not sure if he should acknowledge the use of that word, 'human'. Whatever Diana feared or suspected or even was just imagining, he didn't want it to be his problem.

He had plenty of problems already. Distant problems: down on a deserted stretch of beach there was a container-load of shoulder-fired missiles. As far as he knew his brother, Caine, had not found them. If Sam tried to move them and Caine found out, it would likely start a war with Perdido Beach.

And Sam had problems nearer to his heart: Brianna had discovered Astrid's haunt in the Stefano Rey. Sam had known Astrid was still alive. He'd had reports of her staying near the power plant for a few days after the great bug battle and the Big Split that had separated the kids of the FAYZ into Perdido Beach and Lake Tramonto groups.

He'd also learned that she had slept for a while in an overturned Winnebago on a back road in the farm country. He had waited patiently for her to come back. But she never had, and he'd heard nothing about her for the last three months.

Now, just yesterday morning, Brianna had located her. Brianna's super-speed made her an effective searcher on roads, but it had taken her longer to thread her way through the forest; it was not a good idea to trip over a tree root at seventy miles an hour.

Of course, searching for Astrid was not Brianna's main mission. Her main mission was to find the Drake-Brittney creature. Nothing had been seen or heard of Drake, but no one believed he was dead. Not truly dead.

Sam came reluctantly back to the problem of Diana. 'What's your reading on the baby?'

'The baby is a three bar,' Diana said. 'The first time I read? Two bar. So, still growing.'

Sam was shocked. 'Three bar?'

'Yes, Sam. He, she or it, is a mutant. A powerful one. Growing more powerful.'

'Have you told anyone else?'

Diana shook her head. 'I'm not stupid, Sam. Caine would come after it if he knew. He would kill us both if he had to.'

'His own child?' Sam had a hard time believing that even Caine would be that depraved.

'Maybe not,' Diana said. 'He made it very clear when I told him that he wanted nothing to do with it. I would say the idea sickened him. But a powerful mutant? Very different story. He might just take us. Caine might want to control the baby, or he might want to kill it, but for him there's no third choice. Anything else would be . . .' She searched his face as if the right word might be written there. '. . . Humiliating.'

Sam felt his stomach churning. They'd had four months of peace. In that time Sam, Edilio, and Dekka had taken on the job of setting up a sort of half-aquatic town. Well, mostly Edilio. They had parcelled out the houseboats, sailboats, motorboats, campers, and tents. They'd arranged for a septic tank to be dug, well away from the lake to avoid disease. Just to be safe they had set up a system of hauling water from halfway down the shore to the east in what they called the lowlands, and forbidden anyone to drink the water where they bathed and swam.

It had been amazing to watch the quiet authority Edilio brought to the job. Sam was nominally in charge, but it never would have occurred to Sam to worry so much about sanitation.

Fishing boats, with crews trained by Quinn down in Perdido Beach, brought in a decent haul every day. They had planted carrots, tomatoes, and squash in the low patch up by the barrier, and under Sinder's care they were growing very nicely.

They had locked up their precious stash of Nutella, Cup-a-Noodles, and Pepsi, using those as currency to buy additional fish, clams, and mussels from the ocean, where Quinn's crews still fished.

They also had negotiated control over some of the farm-lands, so artichokes, cabbage, and the occasional melon could still be had.

In truth Albert managed all the trade between the lake and PB, as they called it, but the day-to-day management of the lake was up to Sam. Which meant Edilio.

Almost from the beginning of the FAYZ, Sam had lived with fantasies of a sort of personal judgment day. He pictured himself standing before judges who would peer down at him and demand he justify every single thing he had done.

Justify every failure.

Justify every mistake.

Justify every body buried in the town plaza in Perdido Beach.

These last few months he had begun to have those imaginary conversations less frequently. He'd started thinking maybe, on balance, they would see that he had done some things right.

'Don't tell anyone,' Sam cautioned Diana. Then he said, 'Have you thought about . . . Well, I guess we don't know what the baby's powers might be.'

Diana showed her ironic smirk. 'You mean have I thought about what might happen if the baby can burn things like you can, Sam? Or has his father's telekinetic power? Or any number of other abilities? No, Sam, no, I haven't even thought about what happens when he, she, or it has a bad day and burns a hole in me from the inside out.'

Sam sighed. 'He or she, Diana. Not it.'

He expected a wisecrack answer. Instead Diana's carefully controlled expression collapsed. 'Its father is evil. So is its mother,' she whispered. She twisted her fingers together, too hard, so hard it must be painful. 'How can it not be the same?'

'Before I pass judgment,' Caine said, 'does anyone have anything to say for Cigar?'

Caine did not refer to his chair as a throne. That would have been too laughable, even though he styled himself 'King Caine'.

It was a heavy wooden chair of dark wood grabbed from an empty house. He believed the style was called Moorish. It sat a few feet back from the top stair of stone steps that led up to the ruined church.

Not a throne in name, but a throne in fact. He sat upright. Not stiff, but regal. He wore a purple polo shirt, jeans, and square-toed black cowboy boots. One boot rested on a low, upholstered footstool.

On Caine's left stood Penny. Lana, the Healer, had fixed her shattered legs. Penny wore a sundress that hung limply from her narrow shoulders. She was barefoot. For some reason she refused to ever wear shoes since regaining use of her legs.

On his left stood Turk, supposedly Caine's security, though it was impossible to imagine a situation Caine couldn't deal with on his own. The truth was that Caine could levitate Turk and use him as a club if he chose. But it was important for a king to have people who served him. It made one look more kingly.

Turk was a sullen, stupid punk with a sawed-off double-barrelled shotgun over his shoulder and a big pipe wrench hanging from a loop on his straining belt.

Turk was guarding Cigar, a sweet-faced thirteen-year-old with the hard hands, strong back, and tanned face of a fisherman.

About twenty-five kids stood at the foot of the stairs. In theory everyone was supposed to show up for court, but Albert had suggested – a suggestion that had the force of a decree – that those who had work to do could blow it off. Work came first in Albert's world, and Caine knew that he was king only so long as Albert kept everyone fed and watered.

At some time in the night a fight had broken out between a boy named Jaden and the boy everyone called Cigar because he had once smoked a cigar and got spectacularly sick.

Both Jaden and Cigar had been drinking some of Howard's illegal booze, and no one was exactly clear what the fight had been about. But what was clear – witnessed by three kids – was that the fight had gone from angry words to fists to weapons in a heartbeat.

Jaden had swung a lead pipe at Cigar and missed. Cigar had swung a heavy oak table leg studded with big nails and he had not missed.

No one believed Cigar – who was a good kid, one of Quinn's hardworking fishermen – had meant to kill Jaden. But Jaden's brains had ended up on the sidewalk just the same.

There were four punishments in King Caine's Perdido Beach: fine, lock-up, Penny, or death.

A small infraction – for example, failing to show proper respect to the king, or blowing off work, or cheating someone in a deal – merited a fine. It could be a day's food, two days' unpaid labour, or the surrender of some valuable object.

Lock-up was a room in town hall that had last imprisoned a boy named Roscoe until the bugs had eaten him from the inside out. Lock-up meant two or more days with just water in that room. Fighting or vandalism would get you lock-up.

Caine had handed out many fines and several lock-ups.

Only once had he imposed a sentence of Penny.

Penny was a mutant with the power to create illusions so real it was impossible not to believe them. She had a sick, disturbed imagination. The girl who had earned thirty minutes of Penny had lost control of her bodily functions and ended up screaming and beating at her own flesh. Two days later she had still not been able to work.

The ultimate penalty was death. And Caine had never yet had to face imposing that.

'I'll speak for Cigar.'

Quinn, of course. Once upon a time Quinn had been Sam's

closest friend, his surfer-dude buddy. He'd been a weak, vacillating, insecure boy, one of those who had not handled the FAYZ very well.

But Quinn had come into his own as the head of the fishing crews. Muscles bunched in his neck and shoulders and back from pulling at the oars for long hours. He was the colour of mahogany now.

'Cigar has never been any kind of trouble,' Quinn said. 'He shows up for work on time and he never shirks. He's a good guy and he's a very good fisherman. When Alice fell in and was knocked out from hitting an oar, he was the one who jumped in and pulled her out.'

Caine nodded thoughtfully. He was going for a look of stern wisdom. But he was deeply agitated beneath the surface. On the one hand, Cigar had killed Jaden. That wasn't some random act of vandalism or small-bore theft. If Caine didn't impose the death penalty in this case, when was he ever going to?

He sort of wanted to . . . In fact, yes, he definitely wanted to impose the death penalty. Maybe not on Cigar, but on someone. It would be a test of his power. It would send a message.

On the other hand, Quinn was not someone to pick a fight with. Quinn could decide to go on strike and people would get hungry in a hurry.

And then there was Albert. Quinn worked for Albert.

It was fine to call yourself king, Caine thought. But not when the real power was held by some skinny, owlish black kid with a ledger book.

'It's murder,' Caine said, stalling.

'No one's saying Cigar shouldn't be punished,' Quinn said. 'He screwed up. Shouldn't have been drinking. He knows better.'

Cigar hung his head.

'Jaden was a good guy, too,' a girl with the improbable name of Alpha Wong said. She sobbed. 'He didn't deserve to be killed.'

Caine gritted his teeth. Great. A girlfriend.

No point stalling any longer. He had to decide. It was far worse to piss off Quinn and possibly Albert than Alpha.

Caine raised his hand. 'I promised as your king to deliver justice,' he said. 'If this had been deliberate murder I'd have no choice but the death penalty. But Cigar has been a good worker. And he didn't set out to kill poor Jaden. The next penalty is Penny time. Usually it's a half hour. But that's just not enough for something this serious. So here is my royal verdict.'

He turned to Penny, who was already quivering with anticipation.

'Penny will have Cigar from sunrise to sunset. Tomorrow when the sun rises clear of the hills it begins. And when the sun touches the horizon over the ocean, it ends.'

Caine saw reluctant acceptance in Quinn's eyes. The crowd murmured approvingly. Caine breathed a silent sigh. Even Cigar looked relieved. But then, Caine thought, neither Quinn nor Cigar had any idea just how far down into madness Penny had sunk since her long, pain-racked ordeal. The girl had always been a cruel creature. But pain and power had made her a monster.

His monster.

For now.

Turk hauled Cigar off to the lock-up. The crowd began to disperse.

'You can do this, Cigar,' Quinn called out.

'Yeah,' Cigar said. 'No problem.'

Penny laughed.

Michael Grant has always been fast paced. He's lived in almost 50 different homes in 14 US states, and moved in with his wife, Katherine Applegate, after knowing her for less than 24 hours. His long list of previous occupations includes cartoonist, waiter, law librarian, bowling alley mechanic, restaurant reviewer, documentary film producer and political media consultant.

Michael and Katherine have co-authored more than 150 books, including the massive hit series Animorphs, which has sold more than 35 million copies. Working solo, Michael is the author of the internationally bestselling series GONE and the groundbreaking transmedia trilogy BZRK.

Michael, Katherine and their two children live in the San Francisco Bay Area, not far from Silicon Valley. Michael can be contacted on Twitter (@thefayz), Facebook (authormichaelgrant), and via good, old-fashioned email (Michael@themichaelgrant.com).

EGMONT PRESS: ETHICAL PUBLISHING

Egmont Press is about turning writers into successful authors and children into passionate readers – producing books that enrich and entertain. As a responsible children's publisher, we go even further, considering the world in which our consumers are growing up.

Safety First
Naturally, all of our books meet legal safety requirements. But we go further than this; every book with play value is tested to the highest standards – if it fails, it's back to the drawing-board.

Made Fairly
We are working to ensure that the workers involved in our supply chain – the people that make our books – are treated with fairness and respect.

Responsible Forestry
We are committed to ensuring all our papers come from environmentally and socially responsible forest sources.

**For more information, please visit our website at
www.egmont.co.uk/ethical**